PATRIDA

PATRIDA

Peter Katsionis

David Matthew Publishing
Burnaby, British Columbia

Patrida. Copyright © 1994.2005 by Peter Katsionis. Printed in Canada. All rights reserved. No part of this book may be reproduced without written permission from the author. This includes all electronic or mechanical means.

Published by: David Matthew Publishing.

Canadian Cataloguing in Publication Data

Katsionis, Peter, 1957-
Patrida.

1ˢᵗ Edition

ISBN 0-9680543-2-3

1. The story of Piros. 2. The story of Dioxippus. 3. The ascension of Alexander the Great.

For additional copies of this CD-ROM, e-book and covered book, please contact the publisher.

David Matthew Publishing
5450 Braelawn Drive
Burnaby, British Columbia
Canada
V5B 4R7
e-mail: pkatsionis@yahoo.com

Acknowledgements

*Writing is a solitary activity. Yet it never is really done alone.
Without the encouragement, support and occasional criticism of
family and friends a book like this cannot come to fruition. So to my
wife, Maria, the superwoman who works hard to maintain a career
and family so that I can have the time to indulge myself in writing,
words cannot express my feelings but you know what they are. To my
sons, Matthew and David, it is your youthful vigor that inspires me
to leave you a legacy of love that just happens to reflect a part of
your history.*

*I have been encouraged by the early "reviews" from a few others.
My cousin Alex or in his words, "...like brothers without the
complications" has steadfastedly supported this and other writing
endeavors so to you I extend my sincerest appreciation. To my friend
George, a true supporter of this novel, I thank you for your
enthusiasm. It's contagious. To my friends Mike and Jim your input
and advice has been welcomed.*

*When writing an historical novel you are indebted to the historians
and researchers who dedicate their lives to keeping alive the days of
yesteryear. To me, history is the most important subject taught in
schools and those professors, lecturers and teachers around the
world are to be commended for what they bring to society. You
should all be applauded.*

*In writing this novel I rediscovered my "Greekness". I encourage
everyone, regardless of ethnicity to rediscover your roots. Every
culture contains unimaginable wealth. Don't let yours pass you by.*

Peter Katsionis

A Guide to the Characters

PIROS *freeborn son of slaves; raised and trained in Thebes in the pankration*

DIOXIPPUS *born a slave but trained to be a pankratiatist; an innovator in the martial arts*

FOTIS *formerly a Helot slave for the Spartans, freed by and now serving Piros*

DELIA *Hebrew princess captured and sold into slavery, mother of Piros*

TSAKA *African medicine man of royal descent, captured and sold into slavery, father of Piros*

KRUTZIOS *master of Tsaka and later Delia*

PHYLIA/IYEA *twin sisters who were enslaved by Dionys*

DIONYS *master of Phylia, Iyea and Dioxippus*

DEMOSTHENES *Greek orator*

ISOCRATES *Greek orator*

TYSOS/ HAGLIOS/HELEN *athletes and friends of Piros*

YEMESTOS/ XADROS *Theban regulars who were part of Piros' scouting party*

PAUSANIAS *high-ranked officer in the King's Companions, friend to Piros*

PHILIP *Macedonian king*

CLEOPATRA *one of Philip's several wives, neice of the general Attalus*

OLYMPIAS *Philip's first wife, mother to Alexander*

PATROCLUS *a eunuch slave owned by Cleopatra*

ALEXANDER *son of Philip and Olympias, heir to the Macedonian throne*

KATHOS *a paid assassin used by many royal families*

PETROS *opponent of Dioxippus in the Olympiad*

PANTHEA *daughter of Helot slaves*

CLYTEMNESTRA *mother of Cleopatra*

MISTOPHANES *one of the ten Hellanodikai, and the one responsible for the draw in the pankration*

YIORGAKAS *opponent of Dioxippus in the ring*

LYNCESTIANS *brothers from one of the royal Macedonian families*

KINOVAS *personal guard to Olympias, former Sacred Band member*

Athens, 338 B.C.

Piros

The dust.

It swirled in fine circles, filtering the harsh brightness of the sun. To the spectators, the dust appeared to almost caress the contestants as it gently enveloped them.

Entangled within this ephemeral cloud, two men, strong, fierce warriors, struck, grabbed, twisted and kicked with a bestial fury. Yet as clenched fists exploded on the battered heads and naked bodies of the combatants, the dust, ever present, tenderly settled on the oil and sweat streaked torsos of the pankratiatists.

The surreal calm presented to the spectators contrasted sharply with the accelerating action within the dancing dust cloud. Slashing with a kick to his opponent's thigh, the taller man grimaced with pain as the other man dropped to one knee bringing his elbow axe like on the extended shin of the kicker. Then in a sweeping motion the shorter man swung his own leg and kicked out the other combatant's supporting leg, bringing him crashing to the ground. For the taller one, desperation raised the bile to his mouth as the growing panic struggled to gain control over the screaming muscles of his body. Relentless, the compact man seized the wounded leg of his opponent, twisting the ankle and forcing the taller man to slam, chest first onto the dry, hardened earth. The dust, to the spectators still a billowy, benign entity now seared the lungs and nasal cavities of the fallen pankratiatist. Unable to breathe, his vision a blurry morass of dust, tears and blood, Dioxippus thumped the ground with his right hand. At the sign of surrender, the compact man released his hold.

As both men slowly rose, the twenty or so spectators broke into laughter and good-natured banter. A few exchanged some coins as bets were settled. Slowly turning to leave, one old man looked over his shoulder at the pankratiatists, by now on their feet, and yelled out a disparaging epithet to the defeated Dioxippus. Despite being covered in bruises and welts with tendons and muscles stretched to the point of snapping, Dioxippus felt the harsh sting of the insult far worse than the assault on his body. Embarrassed he turned to Piros.

To those who knew him, Piros exemplified the Greek ideal of mental and physical aptitude. Known for his understanding of the mechanics of the body, as well as the medicinal herbs that provided relief to all sorts of ailments, he was widely construed as a man gifted by Olympus. However, his extremely muscular physique, welded onto a broad, compact frame created an aura of raw, uncontrolled power around which even campaigned warriors trod warily. While known for his fanatical devotion to the Macedonian king, Philip, demonstrated in battle after battle, his skills as a soldier paled in comparison to his prowess in the pankration ring. Winner of two Olympiads and countless regional games, Piros was revered as the foremost athlete in the most important, most dangerous contest in Hellas. But reverence was tainted with fear, for Piros, son of slaves, had suffered torturing denigration at the hands of the Thebans. The furies from his tormented youth would rush forth whenever he felt angered or betrayed and to those who dared to challenge Piros these eruptions of violence were as unstoppable as a force of nature. For this reason, no man would risk suffering the wrath of a creature whose soul was said to be as black as his skin.

In sharp contrast stood Dioxippus. Younger by ten years but taller by six inches, the light skinned, blue-eyed teenager with the long, straw-coloured hair, was anything but fearsome at this moment. Slightly stooping, more out of shame than pain, his lanky frame appeared almost shriveled while his disheveled hair, matted with dust and oil stuck to his scalp in clumps. He resembled a whipped cur who had been tied to the back of a chariot and dragged through the dirty, overcrowded alleys of the slave districts. Yet, even in this state of discomfiture, he looked searchingly at Piros. To Dioxippus, the dark-hued soldier did not inspire the bowel-quaking paranoia of the other pankration trainees. Piros had taken a paternal interest in Dioxippus that in spite of the beatings he administered to the youth in the training ring, was truly born of love. And to Dioxippus, a boy trapped within a man's body, the knowledge, the dreams, the ambitions, even the violence, shared by the unlikely coupling with the freeborn son of slaves, was to him the embodiment of caring, guiding love.

Piros raised his coal-black orbs until they met with Dioxippus' sea-blue eyes. Staring, his face as expressionless as a slab of weathered granite, he let no emotion escape from the confines of his body. Dioxippus, by now desperate for a reaction, any reaction, parted his cracked lips as he struggled to maintain a deferential appearance. But Piros remained motionless. No words issued forth from his lips. No encouragement. No disparagement. Just a gaze.

2

Then slowly, so slowly that Dioxippus did not at first notice any movement, the corners of Piros' mouth began to move, millimeter by miniscule millimeter upwards. Piros tried to fight the growing smile as a rush of emotions surged against the barriers erected by his disciplined mind. But enough of his good will had escaped to catapult Dioxippus across the training ring to Piros. Relieved, happy, proud, sad, frightened, Dioxippus would have found it impossible to catalogue his sentiments at that moment. Jabbering incessantly, the teenager assaulted the ears of his mentor. Piros, forcing himself to retain control of his demeanor was swept along, a leaf in a torrent of adolescent garrulity. His teeth flashed white; his head rolled back as he began to laugh, slowly at first but rising into a crescendo of guffawing. To Dioxippus, Piros' laughter was something almost spiritual as his affection was manifested so obviously.

"Master Piros. Master Piros! Have I done well today? Or are you moved to mirth by my ineptitude? Please answer me." Dioxippus' entreaties appeared to fall on deaf ears. "Master!"

Piros, who could be so violent, so angry, so feared, looked at his training charge. Why did he feel such a paternal instinct to a lad who was tall enough to look down on him? Why did he feel protective of this blonde slave? Why did he want to guide the body and soul of the person whom ten minutes earlier he could have crippled? These and other thoughts careened around in his mind.

"Calm, Dioxippus. You did well today. Come, let us bathe and I will review your efforts of today". And with that, Piros beckoned Dioxippus to the low retaining wall, where a balding, aged man stood beside a terra-cotta, oval-shaped pot. In his right hand, the old man held two square-edged instruments.

"Barba Fotis!" The old man grinned or grimaced (depending upon one's affection for teeth or in this case, lack of them) upon hearing Piros' call. Although his personal slave, Fotis was treated like a respected uncle, obvious by how Piros addressed him and it never failed to elicit a smile. Smiling was something that had been alien to him ten years earlier. As a Helot in Sparta, he had worked for the warrior elite of this military city-state. With no rights, subject to the predation of the Spartan youths, his life was a constant struggle for survival. But when the Macedonian king, Philip, started "negotiating" with the Greek city-states, the Helot slaves of Sparta, instead of

3

banding together with their Spartan masters to repel this scourge from the north, aided the enemy by supplying foodstuffs, water and other supplies to the occupying armies. Although many remained in Sparta after the "assimilation", others such as Fotis were taken as slaves by the Macedonian army. Piros, who single-handedly savaged three Spartan soldiers who had discovered Fotis' complicity with the Macedonians and who were exacting revenge for it, took Fotis with him when the occupying forces left Sparta. To go from a life scratching ground as hard as the marble of the Acropolis merely to have his crops ravaged by Spartan youths eager to demonstrate their survival skills to their elders, to the life of a trainer with one of the finest pankratiatists of history was the fulfillment of a fantasy he was not even capable of having before Piros effected his rescue.

"Barba Fotis!" called out a now frustrated Piros.

Fotis snapped out of his reverie and sheepishly moved toward the two men. He handed Dioxippus one of the strigils, the sharp-edged instrument he would use to scrape off the oil and dirt from his skin.

The naked Piros sat down on the edge of the retaining wall with his back towards Fotis. Slowly, with the care of a barber performing a shave, Fotis scraped off the layers of the by now caking grime, from Piros' skin. After a sectioned area had been cleaned, Piros would lift the terra-cotta pot and with extreme care, further cleanse the now sensitive skin with cooling water.

As Fotis executed his duty, Dioxippus performed his own ablutions. Although a relaxing, serene activity, the young pankratiatist was so tired from his earlier exertions that he had trouble controlling the path of the strigil. His fingers numbed, his lower back and legs rapidly stiffening from sitting, and his bruises, blackening as the blood rushed to the battered areas further precluded the smooth operation of the edged tool. Consequently, he nicked himself, drawing blood and eliciting a yelp.

"Well, well, well, young warrior. You suffer the pain of the ring in silence but the slip of a piece of metal makes you cry out!" laughed the watching Piros. "What will your master say if I return you to him not only blemished but tattooed?"

4

"My master seeks only to win the youth tournament at Marathon. I have been promised freedom with a victory at the next Olympiad but I feel there has been little progress. Today I failed to press my advantage," replied an obviously dispirited Dioxippus.

"Rather than dwell on your failings, focus on that which has proven successful. Your boxing skills are formidable. Your left hand in particular, is confounding, and my swollen cheeks will attest to that. As for your kicking, from where did you learn to raise your kicks above the waist. I have not seen or felt a kick such as the one you caressed my thankfully hard head with," continued the suddenly jocular Piros. "You are forcing me to study these aberrations of combat techniques with the soles of your feet."

"Yes, Master Piros, I did manage a successful blow or two but that last time..." Dioxippus grimaced at just the thought of the agonizing block on his shin. In fact, the throbbing started anew on that portion of his shin that was now covered by the blue-black of the burgeoning bruise. Reflexively, his hand moved to rub the sore spot. Looking up, he saw Piros swaying, ever so gently, the movement barely discernable. Piros had his eyes closed and was humming a chant. Leaning a shade forward, trying to hear the almost inaubible tune, Dioxippus momentarily forgot his pain as he stared at this man; this enigma whose fearsome reputation he had never been witness to but of which he was assured was true.

Fotis had now moved down to the legs of his master. The dark skin, glistening like slate as the water droplets caught the last rays of the afternoon sun, could not conceal the muscles or tendons. In fact, the internal forces driving Piros appeared to manifest themselves in the physical part of his being and these parts were ready to explode through the thin barrier of his *derma*. Fotis, for all his age and experience could not help but marvel at the statue-like form of his master.

Piros, oblivious of the awe his student and slave had succumbed to, stood up as Fotis rinsed the last traces of the day's dirt from his body. Stooping, he picked up a rectangular cloth and a black, leather-braided belt and with a few quick motions, had created an ankle-length tunic. The chiton, a resplendent royal blue, dignified the fighter and in fact lent him the air of a scholar. And as befitting an athlete, he walked barefoot.

Dioxippus, not yet a man, and still a slave, dressed himself in an oft-washed basic white chiton that came down no further than the knees. He also walked barefoot as he turned to follow the leaving Piros and Fotis.

The late afternoon sun cast long shadows on the three men as they made their way up toward the city. The chaotic rush of humanity that crowded the narrow streets and alleys was conspicuously absent. Ensconced in quiet, the city of Athens resembled more a glorious tomb than the vibrant, almost living thing it normally was. But as the three men negotiated the complex system of paths, lanes and thoroughfares, the muffled scratching of their bare feet on the dried-out, hardened earth was the only significant sound cracking the mantle of silence.

"The heat. It has driven everyone off the street," commented Fotis, to no one in particular.

"What? Oh, yes, you are right. The city sleeps," replied Dioxippus, he too to no one in particular.

Walking slightly ahead, to Piros, immersed in his own thoughts, the conversation between his charges was as the drone of insects, insignificant and inconsequential. He barely noticed that the Athenians had en masse decided to seek shelter from the sweltering heat. He barely noticed the way the receding sun coloured and reshaped the marble forms of the city's larger structures. In fact, he did not even notice how the Acropolis, high above the city, glowed in colours of gold, azure, ivory and scarlet, or how the Parthenon, the magnificent temple crowning the Acropolis, unmatched in the beauty and intricacy of its design, was even more glorious wearing a cloak stolen from the exploding lights of a prism. Piros was oblivious to all of this.

"Is he bewitched?" asked a concerned Dioxippus.

"No, young lion," answered Fotis. "He thinks of revenge." The old man looked concernedly at Piros then turned to Dioxippus. "I advise silence. His soul is possessed by a force from Hades. Come, we approach the road to your master's. He will be angered if we delay any longer. Leave Master Piros, he will walk until he can walk no longer then he will return to his villa." And with that, the old man and

6

the young slave, turned from the main road. Glancing over their shoulders, they watched the dark shadows cast by the buildings wrap themselves around the black form of the fighter until he too was no more than a shadow.

Piros remembers...

Hard, calloused and so big they could cradle a melon in the palm. These were his father's hands. After so many years, his father's face had become an agonizing blur that drove him to tears as he, with tightly shut eyes, attempted to reconstruct in his mind's eye, the visage of the man he loved, even worshipped. But the hands, so unique in size and shape, he could never forget.

Piros had tried to erect obstacles to his past but his memory, like a lichen attaching itself to the rock it will eventually crack, refused to be subjugated. He had long ago realized that his parents' faces would never again be revealed to him. At times he had forced himself to forget. At other times he offered sacrifices to not only the gods of the Greeks but to the God of his parents, as he begged for one more last look at those faces he so cherished. Yet, only those hands, massive, powerful could he see. And it was not the dirt, or the fine, silvery dust that would line the cracks in his father's hands like fine sown seams that he would recall. To Piros, his father's hands were as soft as a newborn lamb's fleece. Those hands that could with a single downward blow of the bronze pick, reduce a rock the size of a man's head, to rubble, were remembered for the way they would caress his cheek, tousle his hair.

Other tantalizing flashes careened through his aching head at the memory of his father. Smells, colours, sounds united into a cacophony of faces, voices and images. Piros raised his hands to his temples as the struggle to remember shot bolts of pain into his brain. His eyes teared, and suddenly angered, his teeth bit down hard, catching the edge of his tongue and drawing the salty taste of his own blood. Hardly noticing he spit it out.

Now he could see what earlier had been a kaleidoscope of colour. Over there, by the far wall, he could see his mother Delia, a tiny, delicate woman with an almost coppery complexion. Her black hair, luxuriously long, was braided and arranged on her head in a circular pattern. Clothed in a long, flowing chiton, her arms bare and devoid of any jewelry, Piros' mother still presented an aura of confident pride.

Captured by Egyptians during an inter-tribal war, Delia had entered slavery as a young adult. Coming to Memphis in chains had been the ultimate humiliation for this daughter of a rabbi or holy man. Her diminutive stature had sparked a great deal of interest amongst the Greek, Persian and Phoenician traders and a life in a harem or brothel appeared imminent. Thus, it was with fear and trepidation that she observed the auction from her holding pen. Admittedly, she had been treated fairly well by her captors but that was almost to be expected in a world where anyone at anytime could be on the losing side of a war and have to serve the rest of their lives owned by another.

As Delia was led up to the auction block, the crowd shifted forward. Among the jostling, shoving mass of traders, soldiers and curious observers, stood two men: one, a wizened little man of obviously great age; the other, a black giant, proud and unyielding. Together they formed an odd duo. Even from the dais Delia spotted the two men. The black man stared right at her, implacable in his expression. She in turn lowered her eyes and turned her head to one side although she demurely observed him out of her peripheral vision.

"Come now! What do I hear for this lovely desert flower? She is of a size and delicateness rarely seen in this world of cows and other beasts. You, yes you, the Greek with the robes of red. What do you bid for this delicacy?" barked the round-bellied, shaven-headed Egyptian in perfect Greek.

The target of his jibe, a Greek trader from the island of Mykonos, gave Delia a long, searching stare. Then with his hand raised he flashed his first two fingers.

Responding immediately, the gnome-like man with the black behemoth for a companion thrust three fingers into the air. The big man beside him stood immobile, his face frozen. However, if one had looked a little closer at him, he would have noticed a barely perceptible arching of the right brow.

Suddenly excited by the competitive bidding the Egyptian trader's voice rose an octave as he continued his hyperbole.

"Gentlemen, gentlemen. Why bid so low? This gem will bring you pleasures unimagined in your native lands. Come now sir, are you willing to let this young thing fall into the hands of another," barked the trader to the scarlet-clad Greek. "You look like a man of

9

good breeding and exotic tastes. Surely you can better the paltry sums offered thus far."

The Greek, succumbing to the entreaties of the Egyptian, uncurled four fingers and held them in front of his face. A murmur rose from the crowd.

Again, without hesitation, the little man flashed five fingers. The crowd's murmur dissolved into gasps, cries and protests.

The Egyptian, almost bursting with orgasmic delight, started sweating profusely. The drops on his head made a slow descent downwards leaving a silvery trail of moisture on the skin of the head and neck. Yet it went unnoticed as he again urged on the bidders.

"Now we have somebody who shows serious intent. Five hundred dinari is a price that is beginning to approximate the true value of this fine creature. You, friend Greek. Have I told you that this lovely girl is untouched by any man. Have I told you that she comes from a holy family where chastity and good manners are stressed above all else. Look at her. Yes, look at her closely. See how finely she is formed," described the Egyptian. He then reached over, grabbed the upper portion of her garment and attempted to tear away the bodice. The girl, diminutive, raised to obey men, nevertheless reared back then jerked forward to bite the grabbing hand. Almost instantaneously she kicked the shin of the trader.

The crowd exploded in laughter. The Egyptian snapped his wounded hand back and took a couple of hops on his unhurt leg. His first reaction was to beat the now thoroughly frightened girl senseless. But his mind raced ahead of his emotions and his sales instincts rendered a potentially harmful situation to his benefit.

"Yes, yes laugh my friends. It seems my princess of the desert intends to keep her treasures intact. Quality control such as this is impossible to find. I add another hundred dinari to the price from my own pocket!" yelled out the Egyptian.

The gathering had by now swelled to triple the proportions of the opening trades. But with the Egyptian's last comments the crowd was silenced.

Completely dumbfounded, Delia stood with her hands crossed over her breasts, staring out of the corner of her eye, at the man trying to sell her. She was completely confused as to his intent. Was he going to keep her? Was he asking an impossible price for a purpose? Who would get her? Both bidders were aged and appeared Greek. A harem seemed unlikely but a brothel...

Silence permeated the auction ring. Nobody seemed to know what to do, say or think. The Egyptian had raised the price to an unheard of level for a female slave. The Greek clad in red shook his head and abruptly turning his back on the podium, left.

The Egyptian was now sweating even more profusely. Little rivulets of perspiration streaked the oak coloured skin of the trader. He had taken a chance raising the price so abruptly. He wondered if the mass watching knew he was bluffing. Another trader may have been worried about losing a sale of this magnitude. But the Egyptian began to feel a heightening of his senses and he could feel the blood coursing through him as even his skin began to tingle with the adrenalin rush precipitated by the dealmakers' ultimate pleasure. Not the sale, not the girl, not the loss of the money made incursions into his mind-state. He wanted that crowd to know that he was controlling the situation; that he was the person responsible for bringing some life to this dreary port. At this instant, he felt omnipotent.

"Six hundred and fifty," a low voice spoke.

The people massed together looked around them, unsure of the identity of the speaker.

Dioxippus

As the troubled Piros ruminated on days long passed, Dioxippus and Fotis stood on the stoop of the whitewashed building.

"I had better go. My master's generosity stops when his meal awaits," said a now thoroughly tired Dioxippus.

"Here. Take this," said Fotis, handing the teenager a palm-sized leather sack. "Master Piros told me to tell you to crush the leaves and herbs and to add a small amount of water. Make a poultice and apply it to the bruise on your shin. You will be thankful tomorrow." And with that the old man turned and left.

Opening the heavy oak door, Dioxippus entered the building. Immediately, the rush of cool air to the door fanned his sweating body providing a cool relief from the fiery oven outside. He walked down the narrow hallway, approximately 15 paces long, and entered an expansive courtyard. The glimmering sunlight cast intricate patterns on the tiled floor as it negotiated its way through the leafy barriers of the olive and fruit trees ringing the courtyard. The pollen-thickened air lent a perfumed-heaviness to the open space but combined with the shade and the breeze circulating throughout the villa, it proved calming, peaceful, begging to embrace the weary body and soul.

Moving about the courtyard, slow but purposeful, were two young girls of approximately 10 years of age. The fair-skinned one was dressed in an ankle-length tunic of dyed-yellow cotton. Her darker counterpart wore a similarly styled but off-red tunic. Both were cleaning the yard by sweeping away fallen leaves with straw brooms. The boredom of the work, combined with the heat and time of day, made their movements appear slowed although the preciseness of the methodical motions lent an air of gracefulness to the whole procedure.

Dioxippus, warrior-trained, had made no sound upon entering and his presence went unnoticed by the young girls. Even though he had witnessed this or similar scenes many times, he could not but marvel at the aesthetic beauty of this life tapestry. And even more surprising was the fact that Dioxippus knew that his master intentionally bought things (including slaves) that would satisfy his craving for the beautiful, the handsome and the different. The two girls, matched in size and build but contrasting in colour, fit the courtyard as well as custom-ordered statues.

"Dios, Dios!" The excited squeals of the little girls upon spotting Dioxippus echoed joyously as the voices bounced of the walls of the courtyard bringing a smile to Dioxippus. Their hugs and kisses as they leaped into his arms brought him further joy. Such an exhibition of unadulterated love and affection may have shamed some of his peers but to Dioxippus, these innocent children provided a beacon to his emotions ...and he liked what he saw.

"Dios. Listen, listen...we went to the market today and we saw a camel and an animal that was so big and and..." gasped Iyea as she tried to squeeze a dayful of excitement into one breath.

"And we saw a man with a robe on his head and a big beard who was selling carpets and..." interrupted Phylia.

"A woman from far away in the ocean who had made these pretty dolls and she would let us buy two for the price of one but we had..." countered Iyea.

"No money!" and with that Phylia ended the see-sawing narrative that she and her lighter sister Iyea were trying to convey to Dioxippus.

Laughing, Dioxippus asked, "Is Master Dionys here?"

At the name of their owner, the girls' joy vanished. "No," they replied in unison. "He is on his way to the square for the debates tonight."

"Then let us eat together for a change. Bring bread, fruit and meat. Bring wine and water too," gently ordered Dioxippus. The rare treat of supping with their beloved Dios lit fires under the girls' feet as they ran to get the late meal ready. Dioxippus could hear their giggling and smiling arranged himself lengthwise on the small couch. Propped on his left elbow, legs extended along the seat, he rested comfortably while awaiting his meal.

The Philippics

Filing slowly into the agora or city center, the procession of distinguished, older men walked with an authority obvious to even the most ignorant of observers. The quiet talking amongst the men seated upon the rising marble tiers of the small amphitheatre tapered off into silence as the procession was sighted. Everybody watched as the council sat themselves in a semi-circle.

"Friends!" a voice boomed out. "Why are we gathered here? Are we so afraid of our benefactors that we must meet to discuss how best to usurp them? Have we succumbed to that dreaded disease, cowardice? Hear me. Listen to me. Obey me! This gathering is within your rights as free men in a democracy. But to let ourselves be worked to a frenzy of desperate, irrational action is not acceptable to the reasoning mind. The Macedonians, led by their King, Philip, have not made threatening overtures to Athens. Philip has not marched on us even though we are closer to Macedonia than many of the other Greek city-states that he has seized. He respects us. He respects the Athenian way of life. This is no secret. Philip has even retained Aristotle, surely one of Athens's greatest thinkers and most reasonable and aware men of our generation in his court to instruct young, Prince Alexander. The court of Philip follows not Greek custom but Athenian. It is our knowledge, our way of life, our philosophical beliefs that he seeks to make a part of his empire. I have been assured that Philip does not seek to conquer but to become a part of Athens." With that, the eminent head of the council, Isocrates, sat down.

Murmurs of agreement rose into a cacophany of yells and shouts as hundreds of the observing Assembly roared their approval. And slowly but building up to a crescendo of unified voices was the call for Isocrates to speak again. The robed patriarchs of the Council urged him forward. Looking around him, immeasurably pleased by the reaction to his speech, Isocrates could not suppress the pride within as he broke into a triumphant grin.

"My friends. You do me honour with your calls," said the rising Isocrates. Amidst shouts of order and requests for silence the old philosopher's voice was barely heard. Miraculously, within seconds of the old man's statement, complete silence enveloped the massive throng of the Assembly.

"Too long have we Athenians adopted a policy of isolation. We are first and foremost Greek. By continuing to exist as an entity unto ourselves, we risk the antagonism and ill-will of our brethren..." Isocrates' voice, always weak, was now hoarse from the inflamed oratory he had given. His shoulders, noticeably slumping, indicated to the observing Assembly how the ravages of time had affected Isocrates. Yet he continued. "I am old. I am tired. I have outlived too many good friends, too many loved members of my family. I have been witness to too many wars amongst people of our own blood. When will this fraticide end? When will we come together as a nation, as opposed to a pack of scavenging hyenas fighting for a single piece of meat? Yes, we are Athenians. But the Gods made us Greek first. Let Philip provide the leadership for a Panhellenic confederation. His vision should be ours. Let us welcome him. Let us strive for peace."

The applause was deafening. Many rose to their feet. Isocrates, by now sitting, bowed his head in acknowledgement. The euphoria of the Assembly was almost palatable. Nothing could diminish this moment. It seemed.

Nobody noticed him at first. After speaking against Philip at the last two meetings of the Assembly, he had decided to stay out of the public eye. So harangued had he been for expressing his opinions on the Macedonian king that many thought that the shame and derision heaped on him would drive him out of the city. Nobody expected him here. When he was finally noticed making his way to the center of the amphitheatre, the surprise shocked the Assembly into a grudging silence.

Inwardly, Demosthenes smiled at the discomfiture of the audience. Belittled, his reputation for sane, well-thought out presentations shattered, he nevertheless knew that his gift of oratory would transfix even those who criticized him. Looking at the Council, at the center of which sat his nemesis, Isocrates, Demosthenes noted the tension lining their faces. He also noted the nervous twitching of some of the others. Demosthenes knew, with the knowledge gained from many oratories that an audience uncomfortable with a speaker was an audience that would sit rapt with attention.

"Many speeches, men of Athens, are made in almost every assembly about the hostilities of Philip, hostilities which ever since the treaty of peace he has been committing as well against you as against the rest of the Greeks; and all (I am sure) are ready to avow, though they forbear to do so, that our counsels and our measures should be directed to his humiliation and chastisement: nevertheless, so low have our affairs been brought by inattention and negligence, I fear it is a harsh truth to say, that if all the orators had sought to suggest, and you to pass resolutions for the utter ruining of the commonwealth, we could not methinks be worse off than we are..." so came forth the harsh indictment of the Assembly from Demosthenes. So many were aghast at this attack that they could issue no comment. As Demosthenes' continued his oratory he noted with a sharp appraiser's eye that many were shaking their heads yet not a soul sat disinterested.

"...If now we were all agreed that Philip is at war with Athens and infringing the peace, nothing would a speaker need to urge or advise but the safest and easiest way of resisting him," continued Demosthenes. His voice, so carefully modulated, made his last statement sound like a reprimand. The sarcastic bite of the comment stung his listeners. But Demosthenes did not let the wound fester. With scarcely a break to draw a breath, he forged on but this time in a more conciliatory tone.

"...there are men so unreasonable as to listen to repeated declarations in the assembly that some of us are kindling war, one must be cautious and set this matter right: for whoever moves or advises a measure of defense is in danger of being accused afterward as author of the war."

As Demosthenes explained the process which Phillip had used to gain control over most of the Greek city-states, Pliogras, an old friend and advisor to Isocrates, leaned over and whispered to his compatriot. "His words flow, his voice enchants. A truly blessed orator and a master of rhetoric. It is unfortunate that he is incapable of foreseeing the good an alliance with Phillip would be for the Athenians."

Isocrates gave no indication he heard or was even aware of Pliogras' comments. Although a gifted orator himself, he knew that he was experiencing an event that had historical significance. Never had he listened to such beautiful language, such compelling arguments. He looked around him at the Assembly. All were leaning forward, eagerly awaiting every word, like sheep awaiting access to a lush field. Isocrates feared Demosthenes as he feared no other.

"People who would never have harmed him, though they might have adopted measures of defense, he chose to deceive rather than warn them of his attack; and think ye he would declare war against you before he began it, and that while you are willing to be deceived? Impossible." The obviousness of Demosthenes last statement caused a ripple of murmuring in the Assembly. Some took the opportunity to nod knowingly and seek approval with their friends.

"Defend yourselves instantly, and I say you will be wise: delay it, and you may wish in vain to do so hereafter. So much do I dissent from your other counselors, men of Athens, that I deem any discussion about Chersonesus or Byzantium out of place." And with that Demosthenes outlined his plan to combat the Macedonian king.

As Demosthenes spoke, Piros, sitting in the lower rows with the most honoured Athenians, began to tense with anger. Snapped out of his earlier melancholy, he was now struggling to control his temper. As a loyal subject and valued soldier to the Macedonian king, Piros could not accept what he interpreted to be blind stupidity in Demosthenes. The speech, melodius, nevertheless preached half-truths. If an orator less-gifted than Demosthenes had been delivering it, he would have been removed from the Assembly. Piros however, had no intention of sitting idly while Demosthenes roused the Athenians to an ill-conceived, poorly organized and morally wrong military action.

"...Many rights did the people surrender at last not from any such motive of indulgence or ignorance, but submitting in the belief that all was lost. Which, by Jupiter and Apollo, I fear will be your case when on calculation you see that nothing can be done. I pray, men of Athens, it may never come to this! Better die a thousand deaths than render homage to Philip..."

The Assembly erupted into a chaotic orgy of nationalism. All were on their feet, waving their arms or raising their fists in military salutations. Nobody could hear another talk. Demosthenes stood watching. He gave the appearance of disinterest but his mind marveled at the effectiveness of his speech thus far. But he could not stop yet. He raised his arms outwards, imploring through this action for silence. Within moments, the Assembly returned to its former attentive state.

Again Demosthenes outlined a plan that would unite the disparate Greek states into one political and military body. The systematic aligning of the Greeks was laid out in a logical, orderly fashion and the Assembly paid very close attention.

"...Prepare yourselves and make every effort first, then summon, gather, instruct the rest of the Greeks. That is the duty of a state possessing a dignity such as yours." continued Demosthenes. But by now, the Assembly was in such a state of agitation that even Demosthenes could not keep them controlled. Sensing this he concluded, "Such are the measures which I advise, which I propose: adopt them, and even yet, I believe, our prosperity may be re-established. If any man has better advice to offer, let him communicate it openly. Whatever you determine, I pray to all the gods for a happy result."

And with that Demosthenes sat down.

The Assembly again exploded in applause. Their patriotic fervor was as intense as the blast furnaces of the Lythian smelters. Everyone was on their feet. Except Isocrates. Silently as a ghost, he left the cheering mob and made his way back to his villa.

Piros meanwhile had stood and was trying desperately to speak. The cheering mob however took no notice. Having no recourse to other methods, Piros shouldered his way into the center of the amphitheatre. Royal in his dress, with a physique emanating strength and purpose, Piros' instantly attracted attention. Most of the Assembly of course recognized the Olympic hero, and many others had heard him speak before. Out of deference to his accomplishments and knowledge, the members of the Assembly stopped their raucous behaviour and waited attentively for Piros to address them.

"Fellow Athenians. Today you have heard truly gifted orators. I will not assume to match their eloquence. However, it is my duty to expose to you the failings of Demosthenes' arguments. He has continually warned us of Philip. In fact, I have even heard his speeches referred to as Philipics. Why is Demosthenes so vehemently opposed to the Macedonians? Why does he wish to plunge us into yet another war? Why should we trust the other Greeks who not 20 years ago were our sworn enemies? Macedonians are our brothers and have always been so. Now they seek to reunite the family of Hellenes into one cohesive nation. How is this bad? How will Greece not benefit? Why must we fight yet another war amongst ourselves when the enemies in Asia are ready to devour us as lions would cattle? These are questions that Demosthenes has not answered." Piros' voice rang out through the Assembly.

But his pleas were ignored. Demosthenes had succeeded in his mission. The Athenians were going to war.

Dioxippus

Oblivious to the resurrected martial spirit of the Assembly, Dioxippus lay resting. The dinner he had just had with the girls had been wolfed down as his fuel-starved body replenished itself. Watching this ravenous youth, Iyea and Phylia had unabashedly giggled as Dioxippus gulped huge chunks of bread and lamb, scarcely taking a breath. Yet in spite of the meager, if any, conversation between the young people, the silence only broken by Dioxippus' odd grunt or the girls' muffled laughter, the mood was buoyant as they revelled in each other's company. Now satiated, Dioxippus craved only sleep and quick digestion.

"Why are you closing your eyes?" asked Iyea and Phylia, almost in unison. "Tell us about the games. Are you going to win. Yes, you will win. But. Maybe...no, you will win," commented the indecisive Iyea.

"Oh, you are so silly. No teenager is going to beat our Dios. He is stronger, and better, and..."

"Meaner, and tougher and about to tell you to go to your cots so that you may sleep," a grinning Dioxippus interspersed.

With hugs that almost crushed their Dios, the two girls said their goodnights and ran off to their room. Looking after them, Dioxippus felt a tinge of loneliness but that was quickly dispelled as he re-oriented his thoughts to the subject that had haunted the back of his mind all day.

His mind kept returning to the pankration ring. Earlier today he had almost had his leg broken. Most would consider this enough justification for retirement or at least a temporary reprieve from the ring. Dioxippus however had no intention of retiring or suspending training. He could not: pride, ambition and most of all freedom, depended upon his success in the dusty circle.

While he supped with the girls, Piros' earlier comment pounded in his brain. He had stunned, albeit very, very briefly, the almost immortal Piros with a kick to the face. Dioxippus, in the heat of battle, had introduced a technique that even Piros had never seen. Unfortunately, Dioxippus was not really sure how he had done it.

True, kicking was an accepted weapon in the pankratiatists' arsenal, but it was never executed above the waist and in most cases was used to immobilize the opponent's legs just before the grappling began. To use one's foot as a striking instrument in the same way one would use one's hand or fist was a concept too abstract for the brutally simple sport of pankration. Dioxippus knew that without exception, all contests were decided on the ground. Consequently, the roll call of champions was dominated by shorter, stockier men with great strength. Piros was the embodiment of a pankratiatist. Dioxippus was not.

As of late, despite Piros' encouragement and unflagging support, Dioxippus had begun to feel that the disadvantages of his above average height, coupled with an admittedly weaker upper body, were working in unison against the success he so craved. He knew that the other youths were good wrestlers who would salivate at the ease with which they would bring down a gawky lad with so much leg to trip up, so much arm to twist. And in spite of the fact that his hand speed was formidable and he would probably succeed in the boxing ring, Dioxippus was determined to win at pankration, the hand to hand combat that passed for sport.

Which returned him to his original thought; using the kick to his advantage. Getting up from his couch, Dioxippus moved to the sandy area near the wall that bordered the tiled courtyard. Most of the area was cloaked by shadow as the sun gradually set. Out of the searing heat, fed, refreshed and rested, Dioxippus felt fit and able. Not worrying about his fatigued muscles he prepared to first stretch to be then followed by the more strenuous exercise. Dioxippus bent at the waist, started to rotate his trunk in a clockwise direction, stopped and began to rotate it the other way. The day's earlier stiffness eased itself out as he slowly limbered up. The bruises, with the onslaught of circulating blood, started to throb but the pain was minimal.

Positioning himself with his back to the waning light, Dioxippus was able to use the long shadow cast by his body as a guide to his movements.

Assuming the wrestler's open stance, trunk facing forward, legs braced shoulder-width apart and arms bent at the elbows with the open hands extended, Dioxippus thrust his right leg out in a kicking motion. The leg rose quickly but reached its apex at approximately chest height. At that moment, Dioxippus felt a sharp, painful pull in the back of his thigh as his hamstrings screamed in protest. Immediately he dropped his leg and in one motion he was curved over it, massaging the muscles deeply. Dioxippus, trained to appreciate the mechanics of the body, knew without hesitation that he had not hurt himself but he had been warned. What was he doing wrong? Dioxippus let the pain subside and decided to shift his attention to another of his extremities.

He looked carefully at his foot. He started to run his hands over it, feeling, pulling, massaging the toes, the arch, the ball and the ankle. Dioxippus studied his foot as if a surgeon about to perform surgery. If he was going to use his feet as weapons he had to know what parts would be most effective. He knew that the small bones in the foot were prone to breakage and he was well aware of the risk to the tendons of both the foot and ankle from the grappling holds Piros had taught him. Dioxippus continued his ruminations. Now cradling the foot in his hands, he felt the ball and the edge of the foot. These were very hard with few bones in the immediate vicinity. This decided Dioxippus would have to be the impact points of his feet. Now to design a kick or kicks that would utilize these point effectively.

Standing up he prepared himself for another kick. From the wrestlers' position his foot could only come straight up the front. Only the ball of his foot could follow the trajectory of his leg and hit the target with any force. Gingerly extending his leg, with the toes curled back, Dioxippus rested the kicking foot on the wall of the compound. The gritty surface barely made an indentation on the calloused ball of his right foot. He retracted the leg about a foot length and then sharply extended it again. The ball of the foot smacked against the wall. A little of the mortar grit was loosened upon impact but that was the only damage that occurred. Dioxippus was very pleased. This kick, with a little practice, was capable of transmitting real force to a target area.

His spirits buoyed, albeit by a small success, Dioxippus tried a few more kicks from the facing position. Each time he was able to exert more snap into his kick. The immediate results indicated that the greater the speed, the greater the impacting force. He made a mental note.

By now Dioxippus was snapping out the kicks at a pace faster than the beating of a heart. The area on the wall absorbing the kicks was beginning to wear smooth as the hard pads of Dioxippus' feet attacked the mortar like an abrasive polishing brush.

Continuously alternating legs but still focusing on the one spot on the wall, Dioxippus was ensconced in a cocoon of concentration. He failed to notice that the rhythmic thumping of foot against structure gave the garden an eerie vitality, almost as if it were alive. The long shadows, the muffled sounds of scurrying animals, the trees creaking and groaning with age; all contributed to the almost mystical atmosphere that permeated the space that Dioxippus chose to create an artform in. He was of course oblivious to it all.

Now huffing like a marathon runner at the end of the course, his sweat no longer a moist glow but a rash of salt-laden streams, Dioxippus' exhausted body at last rebelled. The legs refused to rise with any sort of determination. The knees were quivering so much that Dioxippus was forced to kneel in the dirt to prevent himself from falling. Even the soles of his feet, normally as tough as Phoenician ship leather, were bruised and sore. He was finished for the day.

As he lay resting, the sound of voices intruded into the serenity of the garden. Although Dioxippus could not decipher the conversation, he could tell that the speakers were very agitated about something. Thinking it better that he not be caught prone in the dirt, he got up, shook himself off and made his way to the main building. Behind one of the outlying wings was the lavatory. Taking a large, unadorned urn, Dioxippus relieved himself into an opening at the top of a clay pipe and then rinsed his body with the water from the container he was carrying. Now he was ready to retire to his sleeping quarters. Even though the need for sleep tore at his eyelids he could not help but feel guiltily smug over his new discovery. One day they would all see.

Piros questions the Athenians

"I tell you, we've all gone insane. Who in Hades' controls the minds of the assembly? I cannot believe that enlightened, intelligent men, veterans of who knows how many wars and skirmishes let themselves be sucked into a morass of yet more conflict, more fighting..." The obviously angry Piros was ready to explode. His audience, four assemblymen loyal to Isocrates, shrunk away from Piros' vehement tirade. "And if that was not enough, we are expected to take up arms to fight what is now a non-existent enemy. When Philip hears about tonight, which he will, he will systematically destroy this city. Ignore his army, (unmatched believe me). Ignore his leadership qualities, (none of which are matched in Athens). Ignore the skill of the Macedonians in combat, (battle-tested for years). Ignore all of this. We are still the most self-centered, untrusting, disloyal race on earth. Greek will most assuredly turn against Greek for whatever reasons. Alliances built upon mistrust never ever succeed. This city I fear is doomed. I see little recourse but to leave."

Piros' companions stood aghast. This talk was treasonous, even from an avowed Macedonian loyalist.

"Wait, friend Piros," called out one of the men walking with the angered pankratiatist. "Surely there must be an alternative to anything so rash as to leave Athens. Let us discuss this. Possibly the threat is not what we perceive. I ask, no I implore you to reconsider."

Half-turning to face the speaker, his eyes only partially open, Piros fixed a searing glare on his companion. His anger was compounded by the inability of these Athenians to see what a decision to go to war meant. The last generation to go to war had by now been decimated by long-forgotten battles, punishing diseases and worst of all, debilitating old age. Few of Piros' peers had witnessed much less taken part in any conflicts. For them the old Spartan axiom, 'Come back with your shield, or on it' echoed romantic adventures full of the promise of wealth and glory. The realities of war were simply not part of the consciousness of these naive hanger-ons. To Piros, this was the ultimate tragedy about to befall Athens.

Piros remembers...

During the few seconds that Piros' fiery gaze castigated his young companion, thoughts and images raced through his mind. He remembered, with surprising distaste his first "kill" (as the Captain of his unit had referred to it). It happened while he was on patrol with the Theban scouts, long before he had even heard of Philip, much less served under him. The scouts, numbering eight, were searching for a raiding party of Spartans. What they were doing so far from their homeland was a mystery but there was no doubt that the men killed outside of the city's gates were Spartans. The Theban regulars had lost the trail of the escaping raiders, consequently, the scouts had been sent after them. They were to locate the Spartans, hold them if possible and/or contact the battalion for help. Piros, on his first foray into the countryside was excited and eager to right the wrong the Spartans had perpetrated on the Thebans. Visions of besting a warrior in battle dominated his thinking. He almost salivated at the thought of testing his knowledge of hand-to-hand combat in a real situation. The pankration had readied him and he wanted a taste of the enemy. With the adrenalin pumping, his skin felt incapable of containing his flesh. And, coming upon a fresh spoor, Piros was ready to explode with the anticipation of meeting his enemy face to face.

Thinking his silence was a signal to be left alone, Piros' companions spoke no more. They did however continue to walk beside him. Piros meanwhile was unable to shake those images from his head.

Focusing again on that day long ago, Piros was on the trail of the raiding Spartans. Treading carefully, lest any sound give away their position, the Thebans, now the hunters, could sense the proximity of their quarry. Working their way through the olive grove, the faint yet tantalizing smell of a newly lit fire wafted towards them. Using a discreet hand signal to halt the party, the captain and leader of the group stood immobile. It was not discernible at first. The rustling of cloaks and skirts almost disguised the sounds. But it was unmistakable. Human voices.

The captain ordered his men to remove their cloaks and to place their pikes, short spears, on the ground beside them. Using hand signals again, the eight men passed through the grove with nary *a sound. Even the night animals were part of this conspiracy as absolute silence enveloped the Thebans. Their unsuspecting quarry was as a deer struck dumb before the wolves tear it apart.*

Piros could hardly breathe. His pectoral muscles were so constricted his lungs could barely function. And how could he keep quiet when his heart beat with the force and power of his ancestors' war drums. The earlier bravado, where was it? Piros was genuinely frightened now. What if his body refused to cooperate with his mind? What if he was killed? Or even worse, what if his inability to fight caused the death of somebody in his group? Oh, Gods of Olympus, how he wanted to relieve himself!

By now the avenging Thebans could see the Spartan encampment. But it was not what they expected. This was not a group of highly trained warriors on the hunt for glory. These people were nothing more than escaped Spartan slaves or Helots. There were only three adult males visible. The rest of this miserable party consisted of four adult women and some young children. The goods they had stolen from the Thebans had been placed at the edge of the clearing and were really nothing more than a couple of terra-cotta urns and a few horsehair blankets. In fact, thought Piros, this whole situation was quite pathetic and he turned to leave. There would be no battles fought tonight.

Suddenly a shriek shattered the night. Whipping his head around Piros caught the briefest of glimpses at the Theban charging into the small encampment. Dismayed, Piros turned to his fellow soldiers but they too had leaped up and were running like hunting dogs to a treed quarry. He could not believe what he saw. He rubbed his eyes fiercely; to no avail as the Thebans crashed into the camp scattering its inhabitants in four directions. Piros had never seen such savagery. Within seconds, the poorly armed Helot men lay butchered. The efficiency of the Thebans was starkly brutal, Piros lost control of his stomach and began to vomit. Within seconds he was dry-retching as his body tried to punish the mind that was accepting this abomination being perpetrated by the Thebans. Shivering uncontrollably, even though the sweat poured off him, Piros stood watching the rest of this tragedy.

The Thebans had by now captured the women and children. Placing them in the middle of the camp they gathered around them in a rough circle. One of the soldiers, Yemestos, sported a carnivorous grin as his gaze focused on the youngest of the female prisoners. Piros noted, with considerable consternation that the girl was still a child, probably no more than ten years old. And although no words were spoken, there was absolutely no doubt that all the captives including the girl knew what Yemestos' intentions were. As if by telepathy, they huddled closer together, never lifting their eyes to meet those of their captors. Their terror was tangible. Piros felt a bitter taste in his mouth. He did not know if he was imagining it or not.

Piros causes concern

"I wonder if he has the sickness...he is mumbling again and I do not even think he knows we are here," commented one of Piros' companions to the man walking beside him.

"He frightens me when he enters this trance. I think that our good friend is marching beyond the boundaries of sanity. He constantly talks to himself and appears immersed in these fantasies. Piros no longer appears to know what is real and what is not. This alone makes him most dangerous. Look at him now, walking not more than ten paces from us and he is completely unaware of our presence...and he invited us to walk with him! Look, his head jerks once again. It is as if his brain is waging war on his soul. Gods protect us from that man's past." With that, the two companions dropped further back until a side street intersected the main thoroughfare and they were able to leave this temporary fellowship forged by the brooding, self-removed Piros.

The two remaining associates were slightly askance to their leader so they were well aware of Piros' self-absorption. They however had known the pankratiatist since he had first come to Athens five years earlier. Their analysis of Piros focused on his strengths, of which there were plenty. The apparently random ponderings that Piros' mind often engaged in did not bother these two. In fact, they stayed even closer to him, both to protect him from others who would take advantage of this mind-state and from himself, who during this time was incapable of observing even the most basic cautions.

"It appears I have been deserted."

Tysos and Haglios turned immediately at the sound of Piros' voice.

"My apologies good friends. At times I feel compelled to examine the life I have come from and compare it to the life I now enjoy. Again, your forgiveness," spoke the now calm Piros. "Our other compatriots have obviously decided it not prudent to walk with not only a Macedonian loyalist but a possible lunatic. I venture that their analysis is probably correct. You, however, have chosen to remain. I trust that your decision is not fatal for you or your families."

Piros' resigned tones somewhat alarmed Tysos and Haglios. They were expecting a vehement attack on the foolishness of the Athenians and they were receiving a self-pitying introspection. This was not the Piros they knew. Where was the athletic demi-god of the games? Where was the orator with the voice that boomed across the amphitheatre? Where was the warrior whose feats as a soldier were almost legendary? Tysos and Haglios were not prepared to risk their lives for a man whose leadership was suspect. They wanted the warrior. Piros was giving them the peace-monger.

"Piros, when you speak like this you alarm us," stated Tysos. "Why this depression...why this self-deprecation? Whom are you trying to convince of your perceived failings? Not us surely. Haglios and I have stood by you through all arenas. We need not be convinced of your aptitudes. We do need however to formulate a course of action that will serve our people best. If they refuse to see the obvious, then we must make plans that will benefit those loyal to the greater good. You Piros are the only one amongst us who has traveled and served throughout Hellas. You are the only one who knows what Philip truly wants. And you Piros are the only one who has an idea what might best serve Athens in the future. So break this melancholy and have supper with two loyal friends and their families."

Succinct, honest and eloquent, Tysos' few words snapped the cord binding Piros' spirit. "Come my friends. I am starved from the ravages of the ring and the assault of the assembly. Tysos I hope your wife has made enough food for three hungry men...oh, and what will you eat?"

With the reference to Piros' prodigious appetite, all three men broke into laughter. As they walked away, the now animated conversation, interspersed with bawdy jokes, reverberated down the narrow street.

Dioxippus fears for the twins

Lying on his cot, straining mightily to pick up the faint pieces of conversation wafting in with the evening breeze, Dioxippus' futile effort at eavesdropping proved frustrating to the young man. From the odd word he did catch and from the tone of the speakers, Dioxippus knew something momentous had occurred. Still young, the excitement was a tangible entity that sent the adrenalin coursing through his body. Realizing that sleep was probably not forthcoming tonight, he sat up on his cot and stared at the intricate pattern formed by the countless hairline cracks on the wall. But before the patterns burned onto his retina, the hex was broken...the master was home.

The tap tap tapping of the cane against the courtyard tile sounded like a stonemason chipping away with his iron tools on the stillness of the night. Dioxippus' breathing began to grow shallower with the apprehension of what might next happen. And as a slave, he knew he would remain rooted to the cot, no matter what he heard transpiring.

The tapping assumed the rhythm of a heartbeat or so it seemed to Dioxippus. Now the sound moved off in a direction tangent to where he was sitting. He knew too where the sound, like some insidious creature, would end up. And he also knew what he would do when the tapping stopped. Nothing.

For a few stolen moments, silence enveloped the compound. But before Dioxippus could even exhale in relief he heard a door squeak with such force that for a split second he thought it a small animal twisting in its death throes. The analogy made him morose. Any instant he would hear...

The first scream scalded him. His body was rigid. His breathing was labored. The pounding of blood in his eardrum shocked and disoriented him. He felt dizzy and the nausea threatened to spill his internal pollutants all over himself and his sleeping quarters. The second scream, now accompanied by hysterical sobbing, invaded his very soul. But Dioxippus refused to beg for help or to seek relief. He wanted the pain. He needed to feel wretched agony. He wanted to die. For the rape and sodomizing of his beloved Iyea and Phylia would go on uninterrupted by him.

But the Gods were not finished. The brutality of Dionys' attack on the slave girls was of such savagery and hatred that any man or woman with even the flicker of a soul would have found a way to intercede. But Dioxippus was young, frightened even stupid. He equated his master with freedom. For this and this alone, he would let the beast finish his monstrous lusts. And he would remain in his room.

Time is a relative entity. When pleasure runs rampant, time is never long enough. But when the spirit is being desecrated by miscreant logic, time never ceases. The comparatively brief time that Dionys subjected the innocent children to his bestial lechery was to Dioxippus an eternity. Every second dragged, exhausting his body, his spirit and his morality. By the time the wailing subsided, to be replaced by bone-racking sobs, Dioxippus was numbed.

He heard the door open again. This time there was only a barely perceptible creak, as if the door itself was ashamed of what it had let into the room of innocents. The tapping of the cane resonated across the courtyard, the triumphant pulsation of a child molester reveling in his abusive behaviour. No other sound cracked the mantle of shame enveloping the courtyard. Even the night creatures had turned their heads while the moon, glorious this time of year, had pulled a veil of clouds over her face. Only the darkness tried to throw a shroud over this repeating tragedy. But the silence and the dark failed to hide the smirk on the now satiated Dionys' face. His countenance suggested a perverse pride, not a justifiable guilt. And as he opened the door to his sleeping chamber, he knew sleep would come easily.

With the closing of his master's door, Dioxippus forced himself off the cot. It was then that the shivering started. Dioxippus had sweated so profusely that he had soaked his sheets and his body had cooled itself so much that the mere brush of air against his skin chilled him. He reached over to his chair, grabbed the chiton and threw it over himself with such violence that one of his fingernails left a welt across his chest and ribcage. The superficial wound angered him. And with that anger his sense of justice returned. Unlike the other nights, this time he was going to go over to the girls' quarters and offer what meager support, care and love he possessed.

There was no danger of Dionys' hearing Dioxippus. His desires met, his sleep would be deep. Nevertheless, the barefoot Dioxippus walked as Piros had taught him, as furtive as the jungle cat. When he reached the girls' room, he stood outside the door, listening for the voices of Iyea and Phylia. Initially, he heard nothing. As panic began to manifest its ignorant self, Dioxippus heard something. It was not conversation but rather the pitiable moaning of a wounded creature. Interspersed with the whimpers was the soothing voice of one of the girls although Dioxippus could not recognize its owner.

His mouth almost touching the door, Dioxippus tapped gently and whispered forcefully, "Iyea, it is me, Dios. Please, open the door." No response. "Phylia, it is Dios. Come, open the door. Let me help you. Please."

A faint shuffling. A voice choked with tears. "Dios...Iyea is hurt. I do not know what to do. Please help her. She will not talk to me. There is blood everywhere. Ohh, Dios." The sobbing started anew and Dioxippus did not hear the last few words. But the door opened.

A dinner for Piros

Piros was enjoying dinner. His friends and confidantes, Tysos and Haglios, were good company and had managed to finally relax him with their banter and humour. Tysos' wife had set a bountiful table and as Tysos possessed no slaves, his wife had dutifully served them the meal. Piros noticed that Helen (Tysos' wife) had not adopted the servile attitude of many of her peers. Her posture, straight, emanated confidence tempered by discipline. Her movements were graceful, like a dancer's. But her wit, as honed as a barber's razor, most impressed Piros. He noticed that Tysos did not exclude Helen from the conversation; in fact he encouraged her participation. This was so unlike the Greek custom that Piros was at first taken aback...from surprise rather than disapproval.

"I hope this mess with Philip is taken care of soon. The Theban Games will take place within 3 weeks and I am eager to add my name to the victors' list," said Tysos.

"I am sure you are," replied his wife Helen. "But tell me, will the winner's garland repair the damage to that face."

"What damage could possibly hurt that face any more," interupted Haglios, who barely finished his sentence before roaring with laughter.

"I would not be so quick to comment Haglios. Your head looks like the deflated pig's bladder the street urchins are even now kicking outside," retorted Helen. Scarcely taking a breath, all three men pounded the table good-naturedly and began their convulsions anew. "And why are you laughing like some hysterical child, Piros. You think that because you are in the pankration that you are any better than these so-called boxers. The only damage they do is to their heads and hands. I am not sure which should be deemed more valuable. But you, you roll around in the dirt, trying to tear off your opponents' limbs. That is sport? Look at you three. Why do you not concentrate on having families and leading productive lives?"

Helen's suddenly serious tone caught the men unawares. Their involvement in two of the most dangerous of the Olympiad events had never been questioned. The boxers were past champions and had never really suffered any serious injuries. Piros had been a loner for so long, any life outside the ring was strictly on the periphery of his existence. Consequently, the responsibilities of family and friends had never been considered. As the only wed one of the three, Tysos' duty to his wife had not manifested itself in his lifestyle. But it was now painfully obvious, that Helen's teasing sarcasm was couched in fear, for her husband and for his two friends. She had seen good, young men killed in the Games. And for what, a garland of olive leaves?

Trying to inject some levity into a conversation turned dour, Haglios, feigning sorrow, opined, "Helen. All you have said has been taken under advisement. But look at us. Piros over there is a parody of the human body. He has far too many muscles for one human being. And that head. If his brain was as small as its container, he'd be pulling a plow, not giving oratories at the assembly."

Tysos held up his forefinger to his thumb and pretended to measure the circumference of Piros' head. With that they all broke into laughter again, including the now-frustrated Helen. Piros responded to this latest attack on his person with a slap to the back of Tysos' head. He responded by jumping on top of the pankratiatist. Overturning his chair in his eagerness to partake in this childish romp, Haglios dove for Piros' legs. Within seconds all three were on the floor, rolling around and acting no better than a pack of dogs worrying a bone. The three friends wrestled good-naturedly, their grunts and groans punctuated with laughter. Helen just stood back, a look of resignation chiseled into her countenance. She realized that the man she called husband, still possessed that selfish characteristic that marks all men of achievement. By intruding in his world she was forcing him to reassess his priorities which if done incorrectly, could distract him enough to imperil his safety in the ring. Rolling around in mock combat, tittering between gasps of breath, Tysos was no more than a child. By assuming a simplistic outlook to life in general, Tysos was able to focus unwaveringly on the simplistic task he was considered one of the best at, beating another man senseless using only his hands. Grudgingly, Helen admitted that for her long-term interests, it was best to encourage rather than denigrate Tysos' involvement in the ring. At least with friends such as Piros and Haglios, a certain degree of safety was assured. So, forcing a smile, she scolded the three by now exhausted athletes, who like meek children got up from the dirt floor and sat again at the table. While

Helen went to bring some wine, they engaged in a discussion on ring strategy. And in this way they continued the evening.

Dioxippus confronts his worst fear

The stench assaulted his olfactory nerves. Blood, excrement, urine, combined in a pungent symphony, flowed like notes from a stringed instrument, entering through the mind and body's receptors but unlike the sweet sounds of gently played music, the acrid odor of the bedroom seized the throat and crushed the logical mind. Dioxippus' senses were numbed. His mental faculties refused to function. His limbs paralyzed. Man is a visually-oriented creature. Dioxippus was rendered immobile by the fear of his eyes confirming what his sense of smell had already told him.

Phylia, who had opened the door, was extremely calm. The violence perpetrated on her by the bestial Dionys had not been forgotten but the urgent necessity of tending to the wounded Iyea had precluded attending to her own injuries. Grabbing Dioxippus firmly by the wrist, she led him into the room.

At first, nothing was visible. For the span of less than a single heartbeat, Dioxippus felt the dreaded apprehension begin to alleviate. The bedroom, veiled by night, had only a small lantern in a far corner trespassing on its murky domain. The beatific glow it cast on the body in the unkempt cot, lent an almost holy cast on this surrealistic scene. And, incredibly the violence of what had transpired within this chamber appeared somewhat mitigated by the sheer serenity of the physical setting.

As Dioxippus' eyes adjusted to the low light, his other senses began to gather, assess and transmit their findings to his brain. His barefoot feet relayed the first of what would be a torrent of sensations; the soles of his feet were becoming encrusted with a mixture composed of sand and blood. He felt a cold shiver and he involuntarily shook his head from side to side, trying desperately to keep from disgorging what little was left in his stomach. Without realizing it he had continued to move closer to the cot. The child on the bed was curled up in a fetal position and had been covered by a ragged cloth of an indeterminate color. There was now no sound coming from Iyea. In the poor light, Dioxippus could not tell whether or not she was even breathing. One last step and he was by her bedside.

Dioxippus slowly reached out his hand to caress Iyea's temple. He expected her to cringe at the touch of a male hand. What he did not foresee was Iyea suddenly galvanized into action as she simultaneously grabbed his wrist with both hands and sat upright. The abrupt motion caused the sheet to fall away, exposing her upper torso. Even the modest light could not hide the carnage.

Dioxippus sat transfixed. Amidst the contusions littering her neck and chest were several broken bones. Iyea had not been the object of a deviate's perverted lust: she had been the victim of a brute's misdirected hatreds. Dionys had tried to kill the child in the most horrible manner possible. What had staved off the attack...no one could answer. But the shattered ribs marked the intensity of Dionys' criminal actions. And without even examining the genital or rectal areas, Dioxippus knew that Iyea was near death from this most severe of assaults. Slowly, he eased Iyea back down into her cot. He covered her again to prevent any chill complicating her condition even further. He turned to Phylia who had by now come up beside him.

"Go to my room. On the table you will find a bowl containing a paste. Bring it back here and make a poultice. Put it on Iyea's bruises and wash her gently with a dampened rag. I must get Piros. He will know what to do. Do not be frightened. I will be back shortly," and with that Dioxippus got up to leave. He turned once more to Iyea and whispered, "Iyea. Forgive me. I am a coward."

Dioxippus ran through the courtyard, his path unlit by the still shamed moon. Approaching the wall, he increased his speed and hitting the wall with first the right then left foot he vaulted to the top of the structure. Scarcely stopping, he jumped, landing noiselessly on the other side. He was now further hidden by the night of the city. Dioxippus, effectively blind because of the darkness, experienced the heightened senses of some nocturnal creature and he ran down the path unerringly to Piros' villa. Panic, fear, love, guilt created a complexity of emotions that pounded his brain but increased the speed of his feet.

Piros remembers....

Piros' night of revelry had come to an end and he had bid his friends a gracious farewell. As he walked, a little unsteady after the libations imbibed, he let his mind slide into the nether world of his subconcious. And into this realm of images, thoughts, dreams and desires he searched for he knew not what. He cast about, looking, as would a man with a lantern on the docks of Pireaus strangled by the mists of low-lying fog. And what would his mind permit him to see? Ghosts, shadows careening past in an orgy of frenzy? Smiling, happy faces twisted into leering ghouls? Love, joy, hope fused and transformed into despairing pain. And fear. An alien entity to a man disdainful of physical threats. Nothing more than asinine superstitions to a man hardly in awe of the supernatural. But madness...it was to be feared. And as reality slowly eroded into the unconscious Piros became more and more frightened.

He was back in the clearing now. He looked down. No he was still walking in the street. The scream snapped his body like a bullwhip. Piros looked around. He turned around. Nobody was there. He was aware of the fact that he was walking. He was alone. He was in the clearing again. Piros' eyes froze. A heaviness on his eyelids forced them down, making him blink repeatedly. He felt himself leaving. Somewhere, far away, he heard a voice calling him...but he could not answer. With agonizing slowness, he began to focus on the blurry image tantalizing his sanity. It was him.

By now, the Theban, Yemestos, had unbuckled the belt supporting his sword. His compatriots stood over the rest of the captives but their vigilance was lessened in anticipation of what was to transpire.

The captives were sobbing quietly. With their men dead, the women had resigned themselves to their fates. As slaves, they expected no mercy. After the men's lusts were satiated, they would be executed. They knew that and accepted it.

On the periphery of the unfolding tragedy stood the young Piros. This adventure had turned into a repugnant task. He wanted to return home to his friends, his relatives and his parents. He felt himself nothing more than a little boy.

In one swift motion, Yemestos seized the young girl kneeling at his feet by the hair and yanked her to her feet simultaneously letting his leather skirt fall away, revealing an erect monstrosity. The hair covered, blood-engorged creature shocked the onlookers and thoroughly cowed the female captives who immediately averted their eyes. The soldiers burst into laughter and shouted raucous encouragement to the half-naked, sneering Yemestos.

Suddenly, with an economy of violent motion usually the domain of trained fighters, the young girl pulled a blade of some sort from her undergarments. With one gliding motion she stabbed Yemestos in the groin. The blade ripped through the scrotum, severing skin, tissue and veins. With a slight turning of her wrist she continued the savage thrust up into the pelvic area, almost severing the now bloody pulp that mere moments ago was ready to split her asunder. The splattering body fluids covered her yet nonplussed she drove the blade up into the abdominal muscles now breaking ribs and puncturing internal organs. The almost disembowled Yemestos sunk to his knees gently, as if lowered by a spirit...in this case the spirit of death.

Within the few heartbeats it took for the young girl to thoroughly destroy her would-be attacker, the other captives broke and fled. Pandemonium erupted in the camp. The Thebans ran about in confusion, some deciding to avenge their fallen countryman; others giving chase to the escaping slave-women.

The young girl meanwhile, found herself trapped. Even though mortally wounded, Yemestos had not relinquished the hold on her hair. As his body sunk into the final paroxysms of death, his by now unconscious grip on her hair had become solidified into a cast claw. The young girl, so calm in her expert murder of the rapist, now began to cry as the other Theban soldiers rushed towards her.

But springing to the child's defense were two of the slavewomen. Galvanized by the death of Yemestos into defending themselves, the women seized still burning firebrands, and warily waving them in figure eights in front of them, kept the Thebans at bay long enough for the young girl to cut through some of her own tresses and free herself from the corpse. Released, she begged the women to run and they broke for the grove where Piros was standing.

39

Not realizing that he stood directly in the path of the escaping women, Piros made no effort to move. But as they charged upon him, the women began to scream out profanities. Not seeing Piros move, they assumed that he was preventing their flight to freedom. Within a space of a few running steps, the Spartan women raised their firebrands and as they approached Piros wielded them not unlike cudgels.

Attacked, Piros responded reflexively. As the first woman swung downward with the still flaming fagot, Piros moved, not in an evasive manner but forward. Crossing his wrists he was able to trap the offending arm before it could complete its downward journey. Using the attacker's own momentum, he turned his right wrist in a tight arc outwards and grabbed the woman's wrist. In an almost delicate movement, he brought her whole arm around and in less time that it took to blink, he locked it into a controlling hold. But the adrenalin that had been subjugated so long poured forth rebelliously. In one quick snap, Piros' left elbow crushed his prisoner's skull.

The second escapee, mere steps behind the first, saw her companion destroyed. But she was following so close and running so fast she could not stop. Piros, perceiving another threat, stepped slightly to his left and in one motion swung his right forearm up and out, rotating the clenched fist downward. The sudden crack sounded like nuts being crushed. The Spartan woman did not see or feel the impact of that club that passed for an arm. Nor did she know or care that her thorax had been crushed and her neck broken. She died still holding the smoldering piece of wood in her hand.

The young girl, mesmerized by the devastation had slowed to almost a walk. She said a quick prayer and prepared to die. Piros however, made no effort to prevent her escape. Sensing rather than knowing it, the young girl did not fear Piros and as she approached this black creature, more brute than man, she felt almost safe. In two steps she was by him and with that immediately bolted into the now dark woods. Piros did not even turn to look.

The pursuing Thebans had now surrounded Piros. They too had witnessed the shocking efficiency of the Spartan women's executions. In fact, they were in awe of this young warrior. No one said a word as they stared at the two bodies. The escaped girl and the other escaped women were temporarily forgotten. But not by all.

"What in Hades name do you think you have done? Are you an idiot? Speak to me, bastard slave!" The troop's captain was livid. He had seen a mere child castrate then kill one of his fiercest warriors with the ease of a battle-scarred veteran. He had seen what was going to be a night of lascivious revelry degenerate into a tragic comedy. And this strangely coloured child disguised as a pankratiatist let the murderous little bitch get away. "Woman-killer. Warrior. Are you proud of yourself? The soon-to-be-great Olympian. Slaughterer of defenceless females. They will sing great songs about you Piros," spit out the now thoroughly disgusted captain. "The one you should have stopped you let go. Are you happy, noble one? That shrew you let fly free killed one of our own. Your brother-in-arms. Your compatriot. And the man who would have sacrificed himself for you in battle," continued the captain, Xadros. "I should kill you myself," spit out Xadros in a spray full of venom.

Piros just stood. The invective from his superior did not shame him. He did not feel any loyalty to this pack of mad wolves. Xadros' accusations were so hypocritical they made no sense. Piros was glad he let the girl go. She truly was a warrior.

But Piros was far from satisfied with himself. He was deeply shamed by his murder of the women. All his life he wanted to be a warrior and his first kills were two Helot females. In this the captain was right...he really was nothing more than those he disdained. In fact, he was worse. He cold-bloodedly snuffed the spark of life from two innocent people: people who had lives, family...children. In light of this, he deserved the castigation from his superior.

"Piros, you will pay when we return to Thebes. Soldier...Huh! You are not part of this troop. You will always be an outsider. Understand...understand! Piros! Piros!

Dionys

"Piros. Piros. I have been calling you. Oh, gods of Olympus answer me. Piros!"

Piros looked up but he did not see Xadros. Standing there, flushed with excitement was Dioxippus.

"I have been searching for you. Come quickly...please. My master..." Dioxippus took a moment to discharge a large gob of saliva in the general direction of Dionys' villa before continuing. "He has hurt Iyea. He has hurt her badly and we need you. We need your medicines. Please hurry," cried the panicked Dioxippus simultaneously pulling on Piros' arm.

The urgency of the youth was obvious. Grabbing Dioxippus by the wrist he urged him to run beside him. Falling into a practiced rhythm almost immediately, the two men, different in age, size, race and upbringing trotted together in such unison that only one set of feet striking the ground could be heard in the dark, late night air.

Arriving at Dionys' villa, after a short stop to pick up Piros' bag of medicinal herbs, poultices and plants, the two men decided to forego entering through the main gate. They circumvented the wall until they found a place where they could not only climb over with the least amount of effort but where their arrival would be concealed if Dionys should wake. With a boost from Dioxippus, Piros gained the top of the wall where he quickly turned around, reached until a jumping Dioxippus could grab his outstretched hand, and pulling sharply brought the young man up beside him. Cat-like they crouched on the wall, their silhouettes barely visible to a roving eye. Ears attuned to the slightest sound alien to this nocturnal world, their eyes adjusting to the low light, Piros and Dioxippus looked at each other assuredly. The two men then shifted slightly and with apparently no perceivable movement alighted noiselessly on the tiled courtyard below.

Bent at the waist, their heads no higher than their chests, the two scampered across the courtyard to the girls' lodging. Cautiously rapping the door, Dioxippus called out to Iyea to open the door. The passing seconds seemed an eternity, but the battered old oak door finally yawned open...once again admitting intruders into its violated confines.

Positioned directly in front of them, what meager light there was at her back, was a forlorn Phylia. No utterance came from her. To Piros, she was dead. Only her body had not decided to finalize the decision of her spirit. Her twin had died. Piros was as sure of that as he was of the dawn. He had seen it before...this strange incorporeal bond that possessed no physicality but tied the thoughts and emotions of its owners stronger than the heaviest chain. The passing of one doomed the other twin to a life void of wholeness, of completeness of the right to live as an independent entity. Piros knew the shock would wear off. The girl however would always remain the shell of the unit destroyed.

Dioxippus of course did not possess his mentor's perception so he did not recognize the change that had transpired in this tragedy during his absence. He cast a cursory glance at Phylia as he hurriedly stepped past her through the antechamber into the sleeping room. Even with the now shrouded body directly in front of him Dioxippus did not or could not believe that the child he loved was dead. Kneeling by the cot, his hands, as gently as a fanning breeze, drew back the homespun cotton sheets to reveal not the soft, vital, pink-tinged kukla or doll he adored but a pummeled carcass. Shocked, he gasped for air, almost hyperventilating in his anxiety. No words. No tears. Just a rasping struggle to inhale as quickly and as often as possible.

Piros kneeled beside Dioxippus. He reached over the grieving youth and almost mechanically laid his middle finger over the carotid artery in Iyea's neck. He did not expect a pulse; he did not feel one. He squatted back on his haunches, the movement putting him slightly back from Dioxippus. The grieving youth was thus left alone. Glancing over his shoulder Piros noticed that Phylia had not moved from the narrow hallway. She too was grieving alone. Piros felt no anger but the sorrow was devouring him. He had once saved a young girl. This time he had not.

"Do slaves never sleep?" The booming voice reverabated in the tight confines of the sleeping room.

Startled, shocked, Piros almost fell back off his haunches. His fumbling to right himself lent an almost comic air to this dire progression of events. He did however see the two men.

Phylia was being held by a behemoth of a man. His great size, barely contained by his clothing belied a mass of musculature reminiscent more of a rock quarry than a human being. Buried under this avalanche of bone and sinew was the barely visible Phylia, her mouth covered by one saucer-sized hand.

"Well, the revered Piros worships a mound of flesh. Do you always pray thus?" drawled Dionys sarcastically. "And you boy...Dioxippus. Do you not have training tomorrow? Why are you here, beside the bed of a little harlot?"

Dioxippus' first reaction was to leap up and rip the head off of this evil. Piros must have sensed it also because he had grasped Dioxippus' calf with his right hand, preventing the teenager from rising. Feeling Piros' hand, and remembering the battle strategies of his mentor, Dioxippus narrowed his eyes into a glare but otherwise made no movement.

"Is there nothing to be said? No cries of indignation? No wailing? No laments?" asked Dionys, his sneer devoid of pity, of mercy. "Did you think that two little sluts could satisfy a man of my needs, my desires? What, one die? I'll replace her tomorrow. What are you looking at boy? Piros, tell the slave that I, and I alone control his fate and he had better accept that. Piros, tell him how it is to work in the mines...like your father. Or better yet, tell him how pleasurable it is to have your manhood chopped off with a pair of shears so you can be a guard for some rich noble's wife or mistress. Or tell him how fortunate he is that he can hide in the pankration ring while others his age are sticking their asses in the air in the hope of being poked by someone rich enough to satisfy their petty wants," proselytized Dionys. He turned to Dioxippus and said, "Get back to your quarters Dioxippus. I shall forgive this transgression. You will however say nothing. And as I promised you, win at Marathon and you walk free forever. Do not waste your future because of this. The girl probably had a weak heart...a defect I should have been warned about on purchase. Go now...go," a suddenly conciliatory Dionys said to Dioxippus.

"You have committed a crime." Although Piros' voice was low it carried as well as the boom from Dionys. "Slave or not, you have killed a child. The council will not be predisposed to believe that a ten year old brought this upon herself. You are a rapist and murderer. Even for you the punishment will be death."

"Piros, your black countrymen may be subject to your pathetic attempts to frighten or cajole me...but I am a Greek, by blood. I will be the one that will be innocent. It was you Piros that will pay for the death of that child. You killed her...after you subjected her to your bestial lusts. And in the process you attacked me. During the ensuing fight, Dioxippus and the other girl were killed. That is the story the council will hear," stated the extremely confident Dionys.

Embroiled in this verbal exchange, Piros had not noticed that Dionys had been slowly retreating into the antechamber. By the time he was aware of the shift in positions, Dionys and his bodyguard were almost outside. Vaulting forward, Piros and Dioxippus cleared the space separating them from their enemies in an instant but their quarry was even faster as the door leading outside was jolted open. Piros and Dioxippus charged through the door not an eye blink behind Dionys.

Piros had taken less than two steps before the cord stretched tautly across the front step of the room tripped up his feet and sent him flying into the hard marble tile of the courtyard. Immediately, a net was thrown over him and he lay trussed like a prize piece of meat. He nevertheless fought the lines binding him, grunting and growling with effort as he twisted back and forth in paroxysms of fury.

In the few seconds it took to trap and immobilize Piros, Dioxippus was able to sidestep the ambush. He spotted Dionys' other "friend" just as the net was released. Before Piros' attacker had even recovered from the throwing of the net Dioxippus was on him. The now startled man swung his right arm in a wide arc, his hammer-like fist whistling through the air toward the fragile temple of Dioxippus. The young pankratiatist dropped onto his right knee and with the now bent left leg pulling him forward was not only able to duck the punch but was able to slide his body toward his opponent and with that momentum slam the heel of his open palm into the floating ribs of his enemy. The force of the blow cracked the ribcage forcing the victim to bend over at the waist. With no hesitation, Dioxippus who had positioned himself behind the net-thrower reached over the now horizontal back and grabbed a handful of hair. Yanking upwards, the torso of Dionys' confederate was wrenched brutally, causing excruciating pain from the shattered ribcage. The resounding scream petrified all those witnessing the systematic slaughter. Dioxippus finished the attack by seizing his foe's chin with his left hand. Pulling with his left hand and pushing with his right, Dioxippus twisted his adversary's neck in a quick jerk, simultaneously breaking the neck and killing his enemy.

The blonde giant released Phylia. Sporting a salacious grin, he approached Dioxippus. Although he moved slowly, deliberately, he could not conceal the power locked in his limbs nor could he reduce the energy emanating from his being. If Dioxippus were not so overcharged with fury and vengeance he might have been fatally awed by this descendant of Herakles. As it was, his martial skills were heightened by a cautionary awareness.

As the distance between the two fighters lessened, Dioxippus moved both his feet forward simultaneously, almost gliding across the tiled floor. The loosely curled fingers of his left hand suddenly contracted as the arm shot out of its bent position like an arrow out of a bow. The impact of the fist over the right eye of Dionys' bodyguard split the skin. Blood, seeking escape from the confines of the body spurt forth in a fine crimson-coloured spray while the resulting flow started its cascade into the eye. Barely had the fist struck when it was retracted and released again. This time Dioxippus hit his antagonist on the bridge of his nose. As the bodyguard was moving his head from the first blow, the second jab had its force dissipated over a larger area. The nose stayed intact but the eyes welled up in tears further confounding the vision. Sensing rather than seeing his opponent stunned, Dioxippus planted his feet, pivoted his hip and swung his right fist in a tightly controlled, slightly curved trajectory. His whole body was concentrated in that one blow and he knew there was no escape for the blonde leviathan.

Absolutely no effort was made to avoid the blow. Dioxippus hit his adversary so hard that the force rattled the tendons and ligaments in the back of his hand and his wrist. Sharp pain stabbed into the sensitive areas of his forearm and for a flashing moment he feared he had broken his arm. The recipient of Dioxippus' thunderbolt staggered back, eyes rolling and breathing spasmodically. His massively muscled quadriceps trembled like leaves in the wind throwing his balance off so much he appeared ready to crumple. Dioxippus, a land-shark smelling blood, lunged in to tear his victim apart.

But the shark underestimated the victim. As Dioxippus pressed his assault, the pummeled enemy seized Dioxippus by the torso and effortlessly lifted him to his shoulder. Turning him in mid-air, he leaped up then downwards crashing on top of the now shocked and very frightened Dioxippus.

The worst had happened. Dioxippus was now forced to wrestle with someone who was much larger, much stronger and much more accomplished. All he could think of doing was twisting like a hooked fish in order to prevent his opponent from gaining a strong hold on him. The behemoth on top of Dioxippus was attempting to control him by using his weight until his head cleared from the vicious blow he had just received. Consequently, he did not press his advantage. Freeing his left hand, Dioxippus spiked his left thumb into his would-be executor's right eye. The thumb drove into the eye. Amid the blood, torn skin and fluids were flecked tiny hairs from the eyelashes. The burning pain forced a shriek that rattled the eardrums of the prone Dioxippus. But the momentary paralysis caused by the spear-like thrust allowed Dioxippus to roll free and to get to his feet shakily.

Dionys' bodyguard, on one knee, right hand trying to contain what was left of the eye structure, turned his head slowly toward Dioxippus. The rage and the hatred in that baleful stare whipped through Dioxippus like a damp, cold wind. He found himself shivering. His knees felt incapable of supporting his legs. And he could just feel a trickle as his bladder began to lose control.

Suddenly, his antagonist charged. Dioxippus stood immobile. The bloodied, severely wounded bull was almost upon him. From the doorway, Dionys finally smiled. Piros, almost free of the entangling net shouted a warning. Dioxippus still did not move.

Four steps, three, now two...a blur from the ground. Dionys' bodyguard stopped as if impacting a wall. The head snapped back as the vertebrae separated, the shutting jaw fragmented teeth forcing the shards into the bloodied tongue and gums and the big man staggered back, standing but already dead.

As the body crashed to the ground, an oak felled by a single cut of an axe, Piros threw off the last strands of the net and got to his feet. He was speechless. In less than the span of time it took for a stone to hit the ground after being dropped, Dioxippus had unleashed a technique so fast, so furious, that Piros thought it otherworldly. How could a foot move from the ground to the height of a tall man's chin so fast?

Dioxippus' master meanwhile had taken a step or two back. The bluster was gone. The braggart was humble. The master was now the slave and one soon to be sentenced to death. Dionys began to cry. Then he began to scream. Piros yelled at him to stop but Dionys bellowed even louder. Piros moved toward him and Dionys raised his cane in a poor mimicking of self-defense. Before the cane could even be moved, Piros slipped in and with one quick twist wrested it away from the now terrified and extremely agitated Dionys. Piros raised his left hand until it lay on Dionys' collarbone, approximately a finger length away from the throat. It was almost a lover's caress.

From the moment his hand touched the collarbone to the second it seized and crushed the larynx, less than the time it took for one breath to be inhaled passed. Dionys' face turned white, then red and finally blue as as all the air passages to his head were crushed together like eggshells. And so great was the strength of Piros, that Dionys' ability to resist was completely obliterated. Dangling like a broken doll, his beautiful robe soiled in much the same manner as the child that he had destroyed Dionys was now nothing more than a cadaver. But the screams had alerted neighbours. Voices could be heard outside the compound walls. Occasionally a beacon of light would slash through the darkness as one of the neighbours swung one of the fat-burning lamps being used in the search for whatever or whoever had screamed. As more and more light rays cut through the night it was apparent to the huddled group within the villa that the numbers outside the wall were increasing quickly.

Dioxippus and Phylia were mute. The shock of the night's events was just beginning to manifest itself in the adolescent boy and the prepubescent girl. Piros looked at them. He could see they were now next to useless and the first priority was to get them out of Athens. That thought upset him. He adored this city. It was the first place that had treated him as a human being not a slave, and he did not want to leave. Yet, he knew that regardless of what had just transpired in the courtyard his remaining days in Athens would have been few anyway as political allegiances changed. The tragedy tonight merely hastened the move. They had to gather their things quickly and flee Athens.

Pella, Macedonia, 336 B.C.

Piros remembers...

He could not sleep. He continually tossed, first to the right and then to the left. Finally, he just lay on his back and stared at the ceiling, mindlessly counting the tile pieces making up the mosaic decorating the room.

It was the first time since Chaeronea that he had had trouble sleeping. In that one climactic battle, Philip had destroyed the armies of Athens and Thebes. And Piros, who personally fought at Alexander's side had not only come away with many honours but felt that he had at last exorcised the Theban demons that had haunted his dreams and thoughts since he had been a teenager.

Then why could he not sleep? Piros tried to force himself to relax...to no avail. He shifted his thoughts to his parents, particularly to his mother who so often told him stories of her youth, her capture and her life with his father. Unconsciously he smiled, and the tension faded as his eyelids were slowly drawn down.

Six hundred and fifty dinari. For a slave. A female. The crowd watching the auction was hushed as efficiently as if a giant hand had clasped their collective mouths. The Egyptian trader started sweating anew with the adrenalin running riot in his veins. No woman had come near to giving him the orgiastic elation he now felt. Six hundred and fifty dinari. One sale had financed him for another 2 years. The Egyptian put a hand to his chest, the frantic beating frightened him. He could not die. It would not be fair to die of a heart attack at the moment of his greatest sale. He took a small rag, wiped his forehead and prayed to Issus.

Delia had not immediately understood what had happened. All she saw was a frenzied mass of people suddenly silenced by a very large black man waving his hands and fingers to the trader beside her. She could smell the acrid odor escaping from the Egyptian, its essence flavoured with spices, sweat and an almost animal-like odor redolent of the herd animals in heat. Although she could not understand the languages being spoken she could understand that something momentous had occurred and it had something to do with her. Delia knew she should be frightened but for some reason unfathomable to her conscious mind she was not.

Kruzios, the little man, so old he appeared as dried up as a sun-roasted fig, looked up at the man beside him. He was surprised, not at the bidding for the woman, after all he was going to buy her for him regardless, but rather for the fact that his companion had just made an outlandish bid with what Krutzios could guess was his own money. Krutzios knew that Tsaka had been saving what meager earnings he had from extra jobs to buy his freedom. To spend it all on a woman made no sense to the old man. Searchingly, he gazed at this veritable giant hoping to transmit the question through his eyes, why?

And Tsaka, the calm in the eye of the hurricane? After signaling his bid he stood as immobile as a slab of marble. The noise, the excitement, the jeers were all ignored. He saw something in that tiny little flower that mesmerized him and he had to have her, even at the cost of his own freedom.

In Africa, Tsaka had not only been a man of medicine but a spiritual counsel and oral historian. Regardless of size and demeanor, this black colossus based his life philosophy in living harmoniously with nature and man. Even his slavery had not changed his beliefs. Consequently, Tsaka stayed with the little man who had bought him many years ago even though there was really no deterrent to prevent escape. The only thing missing had been a mate and although it was not an uncommon custom for a man to wed a slave (for Delia was now his slave) Tsaka would have preferred a more honourable and civilized wooing of the woman he desired. But as his owner Krutzios had told him earlier, for a slave quite often the only method of securing a mate was through the auction block. Spending his life savings had not been part of the plan for Krutzios had been quite willing to finance the purchase for Tsaka, whom he had come to love as a son. The astronomical price Tsaka had finally paid for Delia had been fueled by a hunger, not a lustful one but one that could only be satiated by sharing his life with that petite woman barely visible on the dais. For a man who prided himself on logic and the suppression of outward emotions, this instantaneous love released a torrent of thoughts ranging from pleasure to fear to confusion. He began to wonder what he had done.

The Egyptian gently escorted Delia to the edge of the platform and called upon Tsaka to claim his purchase. Tsaka may have been somewhat shocked because Krutzios ended up taking him forward. The Egyptian, ecstatic from the sale (and overjoyed he had

not died from a heart-attack), started beating rhythmically on a drum located to the side of the platform. Others joined by clapping to the steps of Krutzios and Tsaka and soon all the specators joined in the revelry. The thumping got louder with every step taken until...

Pausanius

The thumping got louder and louder and Piros' eyes snapped open. His body immediately tensed, preparing itself for any danger.

"Hey Piros. Wake up. Come on. Open the door," called out an obviously inebriated voice. "It is me, Pausanias...your only true love, hawww," the words barely came out through the laughter.

Piros grinned. His friend and comrade was once again trying to outdo Dionysius, the God of Wine. Piros could only guess what party his friend had ended up at. He swung himself out of the cot and walked to the door.

As Piros raised the bolt, Pausanias, who had been leaning against the door, fell through the opening right on top of the surprised Piros. In the process of trying to right themselves they staggered around the room inadvertently imitating two elephants in a mating ritual.

Piros managed to steer Pausanias to a footstool and sat him down forcefully. "Your breath is enough to poison a room," said Piros, crinkling his nose in disgust.

"We are not all sweet flowers like you Piros. You should smell yourself, particularly downwind after a match. With your face and that pig's perfume you call sweat, I cannot understand why there is not a legion of love-starved women breaking your door down," sarcastically replied the drunk but surprisingly erudite Pausanias.

Realizing that exchanging insults with his intoxicated friend was futile, Piros sat on the edge of his cot and asked Pausanias, "Why are you here in the hours before the sun rises? Could you not go home and sleep? Why do you have to disturb me? Pausanias, are you listening?" Piros watched his friend slump over. Piros half got up and grabbed Pausanias by the tunic and shook him.

Pausanias muttered something incomprehensible as he sat up. His face broke into a smile.

"Piros, I did something very stupid tonight."

The carefree smile that had played on Piros' face from when he had let Pausanias in began to waver. He knew that Pausanias was utterly fearless in battle and as loyal as the Gods could make him but he also knew that Pausanias did not know when to keep his mouth shut and diplomacy was an unknown entity to him. Piros' stomach began to knot with burgeoning tension. His sixth sense told him that Pausanias was going to be in trouble.

Dioxippus

That was it. He had had enough. If his situation did not change soon, there would be violence. Just then, he spotted his nemesis, surreptitiously crawling in the shadows by the wall. Dioxippus noiselessly rolled out of the raised platform that served as a bed and alighted without a sound on all fours. His movement had not been noticed.

Nothing stirred.

Suddenly, it was as if everything detonated. Dioxippus leapt up, charging his adversary, screaming the warrior cry meant to paralyze the enemy. In amongst the shadows Dioxippus pursued the foul foe, always one half step behind.

But the room, small and with only one entry, barred escape. Dioxippus had him cornered. Turning with a ferocity reserved for a life-death struggle he took his position, determined to die fighting for his life.

Dioxippus concerned only with eradicating this menace did not hesitate for a moment as he seized his sword off the table and in one fluid motion threw the weapon at his tormentor. The sword whistled as it completed one cutting revolution through the air.

It was surprising how he felt no pain. The bronze tip, sharp as a razor cut into him as smoothly as his teeth bit through soft bread. It was odd how he could not move, not even to close his eyes.

Dioxippus took a cautious step toward his victim. He took this extra precaution because too many times had he seen even a remnant of a life force galvanize the near dead to action. But this time there was no worry. Death had claimed another.

Dioxippus looked up...at nothing in particular. Taking a deep breath as his heart began to slow after the effects of the earlier exertions he whispered harshly, "I hate rats." And with that he pulled out the sword embedded in the floor, shook off the vermin stuck on the end and unceremoniously kicked the remains of the vile creature out the door.

The laughter made him turn his head. Seated on a low, wooden bench, wrapped in a blanket was Barba Fotis.˙ Dioxippus could not talk. When he, Piros and Phylia had fled Athens they had not been able to go back for Fotis. Avenging Athenians had patrolled the streets for days while they hid in a grain shed until the furor had died down enough for them to escape to Macedonia. The ensuing war of course had terminated any opportunity to return for the faithful servant. In the aftermath of Chaeronea, so many had been dislocated that finding anyone had been impossible. Piros and Dioxippus had assumed that Fotis had passed on or been killed. Now Dioxippus was looking at what might be a ghost.

Philip

"She is beginning to frighten me," whispered Philip to his new young wife Cleopatra. He raised his head from her naked breast where he had been resting it and looked at the beautiful niece of Attalus with almost reverential awe. Cleopatra was so free of sin, avarice and duplicity that he did not quite know how to act in front of her. But here in the privacy of their bedchamber, relaxed after the rigors of their rather animated love-making, he, the conqueror of Hellas, would-be conqueror of the civilized world, was expressing fears and doubts to not much more than a child. Part of him questioned this exposure of weakness yet part of him needed a safe outlet for his insecurities. Cleopatra provided this haven.

"That witch is determined to destroy me. I find myself constantly on guard and am beginning to trust no one. Even my son Alexander sides with her. A son against his father. That more than anything else wounds me," continued Philip. "Did you hear how he insulted me on our wedding night? Was I to be faulted because one of my closest friends, your uncle, in the spirit of revelry, toasted to a pure Macedonian heir? No slight was made to Alexander intentionally. How could I be more proud of him? From a child he has been the embodiment of a warrior-king. My heart near bursts when I am told of his exploits, his bravery, his loyalty to his men. Why would your child mean more than he does? But that bitch-mother of his, Olympias, turns him against me. She claims Zeus-Ammon fathered him. I fathered him! And not by some divine blowing of spirits or other ghosts. She lay on her back and was penetrated like any common animal. My seed is in Alexander. He is a part of me. He is me," and the now sobbing Philip buried his head once more into the welcoming bosom of Cleopatra.

She caressed his temple, gently brushing back the curly hair. Her long, delicate fingers slid softly across his cheek, stopping before they could become entangled in his coarse beard. She knew that tonight had been one of too much drink, too much festivity and far too much self-examination. Now this one-eyed, lame old warrior was wallowing in self-pity. The excessive imbibing of Greek wine had caused that; his fear of Olympias on the other hand was based on observed fact.

Cleopatra, although but a recent addition to the court, already had her network of spies in operation. Olympias' favoring of Alexander was of course old news. Her worship of Dionysius was not. A eunuch slave attached to the Macedonian queen was enamored of one of the maidens belonging to Cleopatra. What he saw, heard and felt was almost immediately reported to Cleopatra. She had heard of the orgies, the elaborate rituals, the sacrifices of animals maybe of children too. She knew also of Olympias' cavorting with gigantic snakes imported from Africa. This growing fascination with the mystic religions of countries far away was beginning to manifest itself in court procedures and official policy-making. More and more of the Macedonian aristocracy was becoming involved with the Queen's macabre excuse for a religion making court life extremely unpredictable for everyone. Cleopatra knew that the queen hated her too, and was probably biding her time to either oust or assassinate her. To protect herself (and of course Philip) she had slaves test her food and always went about with a select group of bodyguards. Because of these and other real or perceived threats Cleopatra's existence resembled that of a city under siege. Philip, ruler of this growing empire, was himself living under the cloud of treachery. His usually light-hearted toughness had been stripped by the liquor tonight, exposing his true fears. Tomorrow, sobered, he would either not remember tonight or ignore it.

Cleopatra looked down at the now sleeping Philip. She shifted her weight slightly, pulled the coverlet a little higher and tried to sleep. An intuitive sense of foreboding chilled her, making her body involuntarily shudder. The still slumbering Philip did not wake although his body too quivered in response. Cleopatra held Philip a little tighter then forced her eyes to close.

Pausanius questions Philip's rule

"You said what! Are you insane? Do you know what he might do to you? He is the king's new brother-in-law. Where in Hades was your brain tonight?" Piros demanded of the now solemn Pausanias.

"I do not know," whimpered Pausanias. "I drank too much. You know what it is like when the wine flows. We all talk too much. It was just that when I saw the old man all the memories came back. Piros, I, I could not stand it any longer. Attalus telling us war-stories, how he killed fine men, destroyed cities and so on, and the whole time he is looking at me, mocking me... while he fondles the ass of some..." the exasperated Pausanias could not even spit out the words he wanted to say.

"Listen. It was years ago. You were stupid and you were made to suffer for it. But if I remember correctly, you were compensated rather handsomely for your moral indignation. Since then you have shown yourself to be a man and in the process you have risen to the rank of captain in the King's bodyguard--not bad for someone who a short time ago showed his asshole to every Greek noble with an itch to satisfy."

"Piros, you are my friend, my best friend, but do not dare to call what happened to me at the order of Philip a moral indignation. I was rejected, cast aside and I was barely more than a child. I did nothing to warrant such ostracization! As for my compensation, it was Philip's way of keeping our affair quiet. He knew my family would pursue this insult if they were told and he feared the vendetta. I took the money not for myself but because I was in love with him."

"Pausanias, you know, and have always known, that most of the Greeks that have boy lovers have many. The king used you to satisfy a temporary carnal need just like he used the other Pausanius, who need I remind you, has been dead for quite a while. Both of you were blinded by Philip's attentions and promises. It cost the other his life. Please my friend, don't let yourself be consumed by plots, real or imagined. That episode is over. Look to the future." said Piros.

Pausanius looked away.

"Pausanias, good friend. I sympathize with you for your pain. Yet I cannot help but feel that the memory of a past transgression no matter how bad, would elicit such a diatribe from you to a general. There is more to this than you are telling me. So, remove this facade of righteous fury and tell me why you really insulted Attalus." Piros' tone changed from a conciliatory to an insistent one as he probed deeper into Pausanias' reckless actions earlier this evening.

"Piros, what I tell you now, you keep secret. I want you to swear on the life you owe me. Piros, do you understand? I saved you at Chaeronea from that brute with the spear. You promised to honor me the rest of our days. Now you must honor me. What I tell you remains confidential. Promise me!"

Piros nodded his head twice. He said nothing.

Pausanias leaned forward but not before glancing around apprehensively. His voice was a harsh whisper and Piros had to lean forward to hear it.

"A fortnight ago, the Queen invited me to supp with her. Piros, if you see how beautiful and desirable she is, you will..."

Piros interrupted, "Pausanias, I know the Queen. Cease the platitudes and continue. At this rate it will be dawn soon."

Feeling chastened, Pausanias assumed a more straightforward manner and continued.

"The Queen expressed legitimate concerns about Philip. She fears that his excessive drinking coupled with the traitorous company he keeps will lead to a crumbling of the Macedonian empire. Piros, believe me, she loves the king. She was adamant on that point. But she loves our kingdom more. That is why she wants to excise the evil growths that poison the court. And for her to choose me, a lowly captain, to help her achieve eternal glory for Macedonia....aaaah...that is simply a dream to be savored."

Piros recoiled and then angrily said, "Is this the same Pausanias that single-handedly unseated three Theban horsemen with only a short spear? Is this the man who fought without a helmet or shield against too many to count so that King Philip could escape from the field? What have you become Pausanias, a plaything for that sex-starved perversion we call Queen? What did she do, stroke your manhood and tell you that yours was the biggest she had ever seen. Or did she let your dagger taste her sweet fruit? Think Pausanias, she is trying to use you to dethrone the king."

"And is that so wrong, Piros? This military genius you so faithfully follow like a starving dog is dragging us down. He talks of conquering Asia yet he cannot even walk straight. Ask Alexander."

Piros winced at the reference to that night when Philip had gotten into an argument with his son Alexander. Alexander's sarcastic assessment of his father was on everyone's lips. Obviously, the Queen had taken Alexander's disparagement of his father's inability to walk when inebriated much less conquer Asia and had twisted it until she was able to use it as a weapon against him. And in Pausanias she had found her missile; a missile whose lusts, for men or women, always seemed to bring disaster.

"Pausanias, sleep here tonight. We will discuss this further when you are sober. Hush now, your talk is treasonous and there may be others about. Here take this blanket and go to sleep," said Piros.

The wine that had earlier so agitated him now began to force Pausanius' eyelids to close. His vision began to blur and he felt himself flying like Icarus.

Piros sat staring at his recumbent friend. He sighed. The stupidity of men, particularly when a bit of tantalizing flesh tickled their manhood, never failed to amaze him. Looking at the unconscious Pausanias again, he shook his head, blew out the candle and tried to fall asleep.

Olympias

A tigress protecting her cub. She smiled at that reference. She could not remember where she had heard it: it did not matter. It was enough to know that it inspired fear in those who had said it.

She looked at herself in the burnished bronze plate that served as a mirror. She did not look fearsome. Her fair skin contrasted sharply with most of the court and her eyes could be said to be small but in comparison to her peers she was still stunningly beautiful. She turned her head sideways, checking the skin under her jaw. Still tight. She then checked her profile. Straight nose, petite jaw, pouty yet full lips. She turned to face the mirror once again. Letting her elegant robe, dyed the deep purple royalty favored, slip from her shoulders, she sat mesmerized as she stared at the reflection of her now exposed breasts. She lifted her right hand to heart. Then slowly, she drew her long fingers across her bosom, alternately squeezing and caressing her rapidly stiffening nipples. A smile began to form at the corners of her mouth. Any man capable of an erection would die to have her. Her breathing became more rapid as the movement of her hand increased in speed and force. That bastard Philip, why did he need a new wife when he had her. She had given him a son, one who would conquer the world for her. Now that pig Philip was thrusting his most valuable weapon into a teenage harlot. Her breathing became more shallow as the heart rate increased. Both her hands fluttered like butterflies over her heaving bosom. Small, barely discernible exhalations of sound came out of her mouth. She twisted in her seat. No man refused her, including the king. Her eyes began to narrow until only a slit remained. He would pay for the insult. She was more woman than he could ever hope to have. Shoving her aside for an inexperienced, moronic little tramp would cost him dearly. The tension, coupled with the almost violent stimulation of her breasts had caused her to perspire. The resulting glow captured what little light there was causing her body to radiate its life-force. She seized the mirror with both hands, her eyes fixated on her image. Standing up in her eagerness to join the image cast on the shiny metal, the rest of her robe fell away exposing long, graceful legs framing a soft, inviting treasure crowned with a delicate down of light-coloured hair. She raised the mirror and with the practiced ease of a dancer twirled once around. That bastard Philip was giving up this. He must be out of his mind. The things she knew that could give him pleasure were not limited by morals, customs or the imagination. But he, like all those rutting Macedonian pigs, was only concerned by thrusting himself to a quick, selfish ejaculation. Men like Philip were not interested in the different often dangerous techniques she had learnt from masters who came from all over the civilized world just to seek her out. She was a real woman. Powerful, lustful and feared. She did not notice although she was still staring at her image in the mirror that she resembled a feline creature of the night, much the same as the ones the Egyptians worshipped. Even if she had known, it would have been doubtful that Olympias, engrossed in her self-examination, would have been concerned. In fact, comparing her to a feline would have flattered her.

The knock on the door went unanswered. The second knock also failed to garner a response from the narcissistic Queen. Opening the door quietly, gently calling her name, the young man entered the Queen's bedchamber. Many would have been struck dumb, frightened or the very least been extremely uncomfortable with watching a demi-god cavort about unclad the whole time moaning with pleasure as she stared at herself in a mirror she grasped as tightly as life itself. Patroclus however was unimpressed.

Sensing another's presence, Olympias whirled around to face her servant. A cat-like sneer twisted that beautiful face into a macabre mask. And standing there naked, flushed with raw sexuality, she emanated omnipotence. She expected men, whom she always considered the weaker sex, to grovel in her presence. This miserable slave was no exception.

Patroclus was not privy to Olympias' thoughts. Consequently he did not feel obligated to play the subservient slave. He moved forward to deliver his message.

Olympias intuitively detected a certain haughtiness in this feeble excuse for a man. She too moved forward, making absolutely no attempt at modesty. When she was within arm's reach of Patroclus, she lunged, grabbing his hair with both hands and pulling his head into her chest. Jerking his head from breast to breast, muffling with tender flesh what sounds could escape him, she was determined to sexually ravage this stoic youth.

Patroclus tried to push her away but the combination of her lustful fury and her station precluded success in this venture. All he could hope for was getting enough air to breathe.

Olympias meanwhile forced his head lower and lower, leaving a trail of saliva and sweat down across her abdomen. He could already smell the odor of a lust run rampant. Just as his lips and tongue were about to make contact with her womanhood, she twisted her wrist, yanking his hair painfully forcing him to lift his head up.

"Do you want a taste slave? Beg, beg like the dog smelling the bitch in heat. Do you want me? Come closer..." and with that Olympias released Patroclus' hair and grabbing his buttocks with her left hand, lifted his knee-length chiton simultaneously leaning forward to take him into her mouth.

She reeled back. Both her hands came back to cover her face. Inadvertently, one hand slipped down and now covered her still naked breasts. Even her face, flushed with the pleasure she was giving herself, turned dark red with the humiliation. She, a queen, had tried to give herself to a eunuch.

Patroclus stood immobile. No expression graced his countenance--that would be too dangerous. Inwardly, he laughed at this whore who would be a god. And the message he was to deliver would make her even more unhappy. Keeping from breaking into a grin would be very, very difficult.

Fotis reappears

"Do you have nothing to say to the old man who helped train you?" asked Fotis.

Dioxippus was still dumbfounded. He simultaneously felt ecstatic and embarrassed. He loved the old man. Yet it was he who had ruined Fotis' idyllic existence. It was he who had forced Piros into abandoning the faithful servant. To run to Fotis now, to hug him, to tell him how happy he was to see him seemed trite and a mockery of the relationship they once had. He needed to have the old man forgive him, if that was possible.

"Well, it seems the intervening years have not only added an incredible amount of muscle to your body but also to your head. From the flowing rhetoric I hear from your mouth, it appears that the mass you have added to your chest and arms has cut off the circulation to your brain. This old man does not have many years to live, at least not enough to wait for a greeting from one he loves as a son." Fotis stood up, arms slightly outstretched in the direction of Dioxippus.

Suddenly, Dioxippus felt a tingling in his scalp, followed by an itch on his forehead and a rush of heat to his cheeks. Fotis had made the first move but his embarrassment or shame refused to subside.

Fotis urged him on. "Dios, are we no longer friends? Come before this night air permeates my bones even further."

Dioxippus took a couple of halting steps forward. The movement shook him out of his melancholic self-disparagement and within a body's length he was running toward the old man.

As they closed, Dioxippus seized Fotis with both arms and lifted him off the ground. Fotis was so small and light that his legs were swung around in almost a full circle. Dioxippus was so ecstatic that he did not notice the old man's tears staining the shoulder of his tunic.

"Come inside, tell me where you have been, what you have been doing, why you are back..."

"Calm my young friend," interrupted Fotis. "You have obviously not lost the ability to turn your mouth into a waterfall of words. Let me make myself comfortable and I will tell you my story. But it approaches dawn and maybe we should sleep."

"I have not seen you for two years and you want me to sleep!" countered Dioxippus. "No, tell me your story now...that is of course if you are up to it. I should consider your welfare."

"Hah, at my age sleep robs one of a few hours every day. I would rather talk." Fotis made himself comfortable on Dioxippus' bed and began.

"The first night was the worst. I had not retired to bed because I was waiting for my master. But age, the heat of the day and the lateness of the hour made me, I am ashamed to say, extremely tired. Well, all I know is that I fell asleep sitting by the main door. I was awakened by someone pounding the door like one of the lunatics they send to that island."

"That was me, Barba Fotis. I was looking for Piros," interjected Dioxippus.

"Aah, that explains one mystery. I am sorry lad that I did not answer. By the time I awoke, roused myself and limped to the door...you were gone. As I looked out the door however I saw masses of people milling about. To be honest, I had no idea why there would be so many about late into the night. Although I may be old, at times I have the curiosity of a child. So, I threw on a robe and went into the street and began to follow the crowd.

Dioxippus, I could not believe my ears. This rabble that passed for an assembly were calling Piros a traitor, a turncoat. Others were yelling for him to be exiled. And a few, the ferrets that turn on their own kind, wanted him executed. To say I was dismayed is like saying Mt. Olympus is a molehill. If I were not so old and worn, I would have taken those ungrateful morons and twisted their necks like chickens for a pot.

Well, we continued on, most of the mob carrying firebrands, and yelling at the population of Athens to unite against the evil hordes from Macedonia. (As if all those sleeping in their beds were going to get up, get dressed and march about the city in the late hours of the night). No matter, to continue.

We had been marching like this for a while when we heard screams or cries from what appeared to be your master's compound. They appeared to be appeals for help so a good part of the crowd moved towards the outside walls. None of us was prepared for what happened next..."

Dioxippus shifted uncomfortably on the low stone bench. He was sitting partially obscured by shadow so Fotis, engrossed in the telling of his story, did not notice how Dioxippus tensed with the memory of his last night in Athens.

"There you were, running along the top of the wall. Right behind you was a small figure, (at the time I did not know who) and behind both of you was Piros, recognizable only by his dark skin (and by the way he was running with his chiton pulled up around his waist like some woman urinating in a field--quite funny actually). At first the confusion kept anybody from venturing inside the gate. Eventually that little donkey's organ Yiovanis forced his way in. I may be old but I had to see".

Dioxippus let out a sigh. The flashes of the carnage left behind shot sharp pains into the area behind his eyes. He blinked several times. The pain began a slow throbbing that with every heartbeat put pressure on his eyes. This time he shifted noticeably and Fotis noticed.

"I apologize Dios," said the now subdued Fotis. He had been so engrossed with his tale that he had not even begun to consider the effects on Dioxippus. The loquacious Fotis had not had the opportunity in the last couple of years to speak so long, so uninterrupted to a captive and willing audience, consequently, the words spewed forth like torrents in a storm. Now he regretted that he had not pondered on Dioxippus' emotional state.

"Barba Fotis. Continue please. I am quite capable of hearing your story without wringing my hands in weak emotionalism," declared Dioxippus.

"Excuse me my prince," laughed Fotis. "I was not aware of the great progress you have made intellectually since last I saw you. Weak emotionalism...mmmm...that is quite the phrase, young Plato". The mocking sarcasm was tinged with affectionate humour and Dioxippus found himself laughing at his own snobbery. The tension lifted, Fotis continued his tale, albeit with more caution.

"I will not go into detail but that garden was a mess. And you know those Athenians. They may spout democracy but let a slave raise a hand against (much less destroy) one of their own...no fury exists in Hades as unconstrained as that of vengeance-seeking Athenians. Dios, it was if they had drunk of a potion created specifically to induce insanity. They ran about tearing out their hair, shouting obscenities, weeping tears of grief...it made me ill to my stomach. They hated your master. To them, Dionys was a poisonous snake; dangerous unless kept fed. And that bastard fed on children. They all knew it. And when they found the body of Iyea, battered and violated, they knew it was Dionys who had killed her and for a moment everyone hushed. But that little dung-eating parasite, Yiovanis, started wailing how good a civic leader Dionys was, and how his murderers should be brought to justice...I barely kept the vomit down. To not burden you any more with an old man's feeble attempt at rhetoric, I decided that it was time to leave so I slipped out of the city that night. I hid on my father's cousin's farm, approximately 2 leagues out of the city. I hoped that Piros might find me but it was not to be."

The last few words were spoken haltingly. It was obvious that even the garrulous Fotis had tired out. His eyes grew heavy and his speech started to slur. Dioxippus moved to the bed, lay a hand on the old man's chest and gently pushed him back until he was prone. He then took a tattered blanket and gently placed it over Fotis. Even though it was now approaching dawn, he decided to try and sleep himself. Dioxippus took his outdoor robe, rolled it into ball, placed it on the low-lying bench and rested his head on it as he lay down.

Olympias challenges Patroclus

"You saw nothing, slave," hissed the Queen. She got off her knees and slithered to the other side of the room. At least that was the way Patroclus perceived her.

"You are here for a reason. Speak quickly or I'll take what's left of your jewels and feed it to you personally," continued Olympias, her haughty manner returned.

"The king sends a message...O' esteemed Empress of Mollossis," stated the bowing Patroclus. The ostentatious display of servility was not lost on the Queen nor was the use of her former title appreciated. Her burgeoning anger at the insolence of this messenger had already discolored her pale, almost translucent skin into a mottled collage of reds as the blood rushed to the topmost layers of skin. She began to feel a pressure in her chest and she had to force herself to take several deep breaths. Her mind-state was further compounded by her growing inability to conceal her agitation. The sheer audacity of this slave did not bode well for her. He knew something.

"Well...are you planning on continuing your little speech or are you going to stand there, doing nothing, much like you would should a beautiful woman need a man," drawled the queen, making sure she emphasized the word man.

Patroclus smiled. He was playing a dangerous game with this witch.

"Philip, King of Macedonia, requests that you, Olympias, remove yourself and your belongings from this suite within the passing of three days. He further requests that all courtiers associated with your person be asked to leave the palace."

"Where am I to relocate myself...slave," spit out Olympias.

"The king suggested the east wing. He also stated that your personal slaves would be given the opportunity to serve someone else...in order to break up the monotony of serving but one lord. The king trusts this meets with your approval," concluded Patroclus. He braced himself for the expected attack.

The color drained from Olympias' face. Her teeth ground as she fought to control her fury. The tendons in her slender neck raged to tear themselves through the brittle skin. For the briefest of moments, she could not see. But her mind, brilliantly calculating, overrode her unbalanced emotional state enabling her to present an obviously angry yet controlled demeanor. For the first time since he had began this verbal sparring, Patroclus felt he was in danger.

During the course of the exchange, Olympias had dressed. Now she occupied herself with the clasping of the robe at her shoulders. As she purposely fumbled with the clasp, wasting time and not speaking to Patroclus, the tension from her body manifested itself like some wraith from Hades in the room.

Outwardly, Patroclus displayed no discomfort. He maintained the stolid deportment of his warrior kin despite the taut passions on the verge of rupturing. Yet, an insidious fear began to grow, feeding on itself. Already, Patroclus was experiencing difficulty containing his bladder and he could swear his knees were trembling.

Olympias had the heightened senses of a hunting carnivore. She smelt the fear in Patroclus. She attacked.

"What is your name, slave?" asked Olympias, her voice sweet, kindly...beckoning.

"Patroclus," replied Patroclus, chiding himself immediately for so easily giving away his identity.

"You appear to be an intelligent young man. I think the king's plan to provide me with a change of personal attendants is a good one. It is not proper for a slave to become too attached to his mistress or master. I am glad that you brought me the message. It has afforded me the opportunity to personally select what might be the first of my new entourage--you!"

Her comforting smile twisted into a leer while her eyes flashed cold. Patroclus struggled to maintain calm but he knew the king, after moving or more accurately throwing her out, would not risk offending Olympias further by refusing her a slave, particularly a court eunuch. Even Cleopatra would have a difficult time keeping him. With Patroclus part of her entourage she would have the right to do anything with him as she pleased.

Although Patroclus made no discernible move after her announcement his panic entered her body through all her pores. That terror was an elixir. She could now feel her heart start to race as the adrenalin charged through her veins. Her breasts screamed to be touched and she unconsciously started sliding her hand down across her lower abdomen. The power she now had over this, this thing provided her with almost ecstatic sexual gratification that was better than any of the erotica she was constantly importing. And it would get better when she dealt with the king.

Philip arises to Pella

The first light had barely begun to make its way across the shadows covering the Macedonian capital. The dew glistened as it caught the sun's rays and refracted them into sparkling stars. Occasionally, the droplets acted like minute prisms as they dispersed the rays into spectrums of color.

To most of the now rising tradesmen, farmers, servants and whoever else needed to begin work at dawn, the city's morning incandescence was not representative of nature's unsullied, pure beauty. To them the dew was an unwelcome dampness that cut through their lightweight chitons, chilling them. The moisture on the ground, shimmering like something alive did not amaze or awe the workmen trudging to their jobs: it wet their feet, ankles and shins and set their legs to trembling with the cold.

Not all of the citizens of Pella muttered curses at the hour, the duty or the morning condensation. While his fellow revelers would no doubt sleep until midday, Philip always made sure he was up with the dawn. To him, the splendors of Greece paled in comparison with his city, his home. Not that he could compare Pella's basically rustic layout and architecture with the glorious Athens but the simple straightforward lifestyle of his capital reflected his own outlook on the world around him.

Philip considered himself an uncomplicated man. He administered the bureaucracy that ran his government, he went to war when he felt the need to expand and he planned on making Hellas the world leader it should be; approached correctly, rather straightforward goals. He had an army, not large by international standards, yet so well-trained that they routinely defeated forces two to five times their size. He had subordinates who were not afraid to make decisions and were almost insanely loyal to him. And through strategic marriages and diplomatic ruthlessness he had annexed most of the Greek city-states to his empire. Now as he looked out from the palace over the city, he wondered why with all the factors in his favor, his hopes for an empire that would transcend time and history were about to vanish like the evaporating mist now steaming into nothingness as the rising sun's heat raised the temperature higher and higher.

Standing here alone, momentarily separated from the chaos his life was becoming Philip could ask himself the questions no one else would dare. Did he love Cleopatra? Had he ever loved Olympias? Had he ever loved anything? He felt, he could not describe it. It was an awareness that quite possibly everything he did was to gratify himself only. Wives or countries, both were the same. He wooed them, made love to them, conquered them. Some were happy, some were not. He did not particularly care as long as they acknowledged him as their supreme leader. If in the process, he developed a great affection for them it was a gift to thank the gods for. But to say he truly loved any one person, any one philosophy or any one culture--it could not be said. He questioned this lack of true, unmitigated passion. Everything he did was pre-calculated to measure the effects of the particular action. True spontaneity he could not muster. Blind, unflagging love he could not bring himself to develop. As far as he could tell he was emotionally bereft. And for some unknown reason, this made him feel less of a man, less a part of society. Philip would surpass almost all his contemporaries in his accomplishments of that he was sure. But no one would know or care about him as a living being, someone who breathed, who ate and drank, who fornicated with women. He was a man, nothing more, nothing less. Circumstance and ambition would not let him remain one.

Then he thought of Alexander. His son. He loved him so fiercely that he felt real physical pain when he was separated from him. In battle, his own effectiveness was compromised as he constantly kept his mind focused on Alexander's safety. Fortunately, Alexander seemed to be protected by the Gods as the extraordinary chances he took would have claimed the life of any ordinary man. And even though Philip feared for his son's well-being he nevertheless felt intense pride at Alexander's successes on and off the field. In Alexander, Philip saw the culmination of all he had done well.

What had happened? They were barely speaking to each other now. Alexander had seen fit to go to Asia without him, supposedly on a mission to check the viability of annexing even more territory. But he knew the truth. Alexander no longer respected him as a father. Philip felt a stabbing pain in his chest. Why Alexander, he asked himself. What could come between a son and his father? Philip knew the answer as he asked the question. That slut of a Queen, Olympias, wanted him removed or dead, whichever proved more convenient. And since he had married Cleopatra, well...he thought to himself, he had had to increase his bodyguard including the food tasters. Philip had survived almost crippling injuries from his enemies in conflicts too many to remember. Now this harlot from hell would probably succeed where legions had failed. And what made the thought unbearable was that Alexander would assume the throne not knowing how much his father truly loved him. If Olympias could only understand that his plans for Alexander were almost identical to hers there would be no need for this subterfuge and treachery. It was not to be. Alexander had fallen under the spell of his mother and in the process forsaken his father. Philip let out a sigh. This melancholic soliloquizing was serving no purpose. He turned to go back to his room.

The slowly escalating brightness of the rising sun momentarily blinded Philip as he entered the relatively dark confines of his bedroom. As his eyes readjusted to the changing light, Philip noticed that Cleopatra was sitting up in their bed. She had drawn up the coverlet so it covered her nakedness. Philip noticed how this made her even more alluring and he felt the first traces of a blood rush to his groin area. Even Olympias, with her almost unnatural beauty and ravishing sexual appetite did not excite him as much as this nubile teenager. His eyes caught her's as they refocused and he could not help but wonder how this innocent creature could survive the intrigues of the court without him to protect her. And as he moved closer to the bed her petiteness imparted a sense of fragility that begged to be handled with an extra modicum of care and love. The sheer helplessness of Cleopatra drove him mad with the need to offer himself as a shield to cover her. It also drove him mad with the need to grab her, hold her and penetrate her with abandon, always knowing that he and he alone would be the only man to own this flower.

As the naked Philip slid in beside his wife, delirious with desire, he failed to notice the faint but smug smile tantalizing the lips of Cleopatra. Burying his head into her firm young breasts, his mouth clamping over her erect and gloriously pink nipples, he twisted his hips back and forth desperately trying to insert his achingly hard penis into Cleopatra. Teasingly, she would let the short pubic hairs just touch Philip making him cry out with desperation as his testicles screamed to have the pressure within released. They tousled back and forth for what seemed to Philip an eternity before seizing her buttocks and pulling her hips forward as he thrust into her. His hands were holding her so tightly, that the areas surrounding his fingers turned white as the blood circulation was cut off. His invasion continued, the pace blistering as he plunged in and out oblivious to all but satisfying his lust. His groans and harsh breathing muffled the squealing, almost pain-filled chirps from Cleopatra but he heard enough to drive himself even harder, the violence of his love somehow cleansing, purifying him of the evils surrounding him. His mind a blank, his sweaty body streaked with fluids from the both of them he felt himself explode again and again. Cleopatra too let out a guttural cry as her husband's fluids spurted into, onto her. Philip's body spasmed.

Cleopatra held him in her arms, much like she would a child. She could feel his back rise then sink as her king tried to suck in air as rapidly as his body depleted it from his lungs. She could learn to love this man; his character fascinated her almost as much as his power. She stroked his forehead, relaxing him.

"My lord, the pleasure you give me is immeasurable. I love you like no other...I would die for you," whispered Cleopatra to the recumbent Philip. "Do you love me?"

"Only you," lied Philip. "I crave you night and day". This was not a lie.

"My only desire is to be your wife and mother of your children. I exist to satisfy you. To make you happy. You know this," said a plaintive Cleopatra. Philip nodded in agreement. "But...I am unsure how to tell you," said Cleopatra as she cast her eyes down submissively.

A wolf unaware of the trap, Philip replied, "Whatever the problem, I am here to solve it." He raised himself on one elbow and grinning, in a somewhat condescending manner, he said, "Now tell me what troubles you...you may reward me after I offer a solution."

Cleopatra bowed her head, blushing. Her peripheral vision indicated that this moronic game-play was having its effect on the old warrior. She marveled at how easily she could manipulate this man, someone renowned for assessing character instantly, no matter what the situation. Philip could form an accurate appraisal of a soldier within moments. This was probably why he was an exemplary commander of his troops. But when it came to women, all he could or would understand was that they needed him more than he needed them. Only Olympias had proven to be different--and he feared her.

Cleopatra took the gamble. "My lord, I request but one thing."

"Anything," replied Philip.

"I would like to have the Queen's chambers moved. She and her retinue of perverts frighten me. Please say the word and I will have the orders obeyed immediately. I assure you, I will not insult or belittle the Queen. I will give her reasons that will not reflect on you at all."

Philip pondered for a moment. Olympias was beginning to frighten him too. A permanent solution was still out of the question. And if Cleopatra was willing to talk the Queen into moving, what harm could come to him?

"If you can convince the Queen to move, I would not object."

Cleopatra threw herself on Philip, whispering thank you over and over. And as her hand searched for him, driving him again into a sexual frenzy, she smiled; for at that moment, the first of the porters were already moving Olympias' belongings out of her apartment.

Piros trains his charges

Piros watched the trainees intently. Occasionally one's technique would pique his interest: sometimes one's aggressiveness would draw a lingering look. Still, it was difficult to excite oneself with the pool of talent being so shallow. Admittedly, these Macedonians were tough, extremely tough. They refused to acknowledge pain, even in training, which of course made it simple to suffer debilitating injuries. If Piros could teach these farmboys the intricacies of the pankration he would have a team of fighters unstoppable in the Games. All he had now were man-boys with big muscles and thick skulls. Piros shook his head. What purpose was he serving instructing these novices? Piros was anything but a defeatist. This time however, he was prepared to throw his hands up. Not having a winner would be a great loss of face to both King Philip and the prince Alexander, especially now that the Greek city-states had been subjugated by the Macedonians. Piros did not know what to do. He called out some instructions to a pair of grappling students and made his way down to the training pit.

"Enough!" yelled Piros to the twelve pankratiatists. "Come over here...now!" There was a rush of shuffling and bodies bumping awkwardly into each other. "Sit down and listen," said Piros, crinkling his nose with disgust at the sheer ineptitude of this group.

"The pankration is not a sport. It is not an arena to show off beautiful bodies. It is not the sport that will win you great favors. Nor will it provide you with worshippers and admirers," Piros stated coolly. "The pankration is war. You against your opponent. If you do not try to maim or kill him, he will definitely maim or kill you. In order to do that, you must follow a system, a plan of attack that integrates all your techniques. For example, if I want to bring down this Titan, Panos, how would I do it?"

The group broke into cautious laughter. Panos was almost a foot taller than Piros with a musculature resembling a war elephant from India. The disparity in size looked comical but as Piros himself was neither laughing nor smiling, the pankratiatists quickly hushed. One raised his hand and spoke.

"The legs. You must start on the legs."

"Good. And from there where do we go?"

Another student answered. "Attack the body and the head will fall."

"Careful now. That would be a good answer--if you were a boxer with many rounds to go. But this is the pankration. As soon as you close to hit the body, your opponent will grab you and attempt to throw you to the ground. If he is quick enough or you are too slow, he may even grab your arm and snap it off like a twig on a branch."

"Follow a kick to the legs with a rapid punch to the head. Then grab him by the hair and twist his head off," answered one of the seated men, a smug smile the only thing differentiating him from the rest. One of the older pankratiatists, sitting on the periphery of the ring, turned his head away and covering his mouth with his hand, smiled...he had seen this before.

"Ahhh, a scholar of the martial arts. Come my friend. Demonstrate your attack on me. But be gentle, the Gods of Olympus have stolen my best years," said Piros to the man who had espoused on the ease of detaching heads.

The conscripted volunteer stood up. He was a youth of approximately nineteen. His Macedonian heritage was evident. He had short, curly hair, so red that when it caught the sun it shone like a beacon. In build, he was taut, with very little body fat concealing his muscles. Although not short, his height was misleading because his elongated trunk stole precious inches away from his legs. He had a thick neck but his youth still lent it an air of gracefulness and combined with the still unbroken facial features he was not unpleasant to look upon. Piros of course saw and remembered everything in his opponents. But in this case, he paid far more attention to how the pankratiatist approached him for that would tell him how the man moved, how he might attack and how much confidence propelled him.

The youth, Dimitris, strode into the middle of the ring. Of the Macedonians, he considered himself the best. Many had fallen victim to his speed, particularly in his hands. He also knew that his disproportioned torso lent him an incredible advantage in grappling and wrestling. Combined with his low center of gravity and legs as thick as Dorian pillars, he was almost unbeatable in the ring. And unlike the others, Dimitris had fought competitively albeit not successfully in the adults' divisions. Now however, he possessed skills he never imagined a year ago and he was hoping to win the olive wreath at the games.

Piros waited. Two years of relative inactivity had softened some of his chiseled edge. He had retired from the pankration ring a demi-god: he had reaped extensive financial and political rewards for his efforts. The hunger, the drive to not only win but to destroy had been compromised by the accompanying wealth and easy living. Even the baleful stare that would defeat his opponents before the match started had been replaced by an intelligent, analytical gaze...as befitting a scholar, hardly intimidating. To further compound his own effectiveness, his role as a teacher precluded his showing any great effort in the ring. As a champion he was expected to defeat all opponents. As a teacher, he was expected to only use enough force to instruct. Piros knew that Dimitris would fight with abandon because he had nothing to lose.

While these thoughts flashed through Piros' mind, Dimitris closed the gap between the two in the ring. His left leg was slightly ahead of his right and both hands were raised approximately chest level. Fingers were curled but unlike the boxer's were not closed into a fist.

Piros assumed a similar stance with only his hands a shade lower. He gave a curt nod to Dimitris.

A quick shuffle forward and the left hand, each of its fingers curling with its mate into a clenched fist even as it moved through the air, whistled toward Piros' head. Simultaneously, the right leg catapulted out of its supporting position toward Piros' left quadricep muscle.

Instinctively, Piros turned his head. He had half-expected Dimitris to surprise him with something other than the discussed drill. But the left jab had been faster than he had anticipated. Eluding the punch had left him open for the kick and as it impacted into his upper thigh he gritted his teeth in pain and anger as he chided himself for giving this youngster the opportunity to not only show off but to also hurt him.

Twenty years in the ring however had left him with enough knowledge and toughness to weather the most pugnacious of attackers. As his left leg buckled, Piros accelerated the motion by falling onto his left knee. With his bent right leg pulling him he slid under the wide-open legs of Dimitris, reached up under the crotch with his left arm and seized his opponents' left buttock. His right arm went the other direction, partially encircling Dimitris' trunk. Within the blink of an eye, Piros twisted upward turning Dimitris a full circle in the air. At the peak of the revolution, Piros released the Macedonian, whose body, now freed from the control of the retired champion, smashed into the ground, raising small puffs of dust.

Dimitris, the wind knocked out of him, lay where he had landed. The shock of the impact combined with the shock of how easily he had been manhandled left him immobile. The other students, who had held their collective breath, let out a gasp and then ran to their compatriot. Seeing he was relatively unhurt, like small children, their excited voices raced each other until only an unintelligible babble could be heard by someone outside the group.

Piros slowly raised himself. He surreptitiously rubbed his leg with the hardened palm of his hand. Inwardly, he smiled. The youngster had nerve.

"Well done old man."

Piros turned around. Standing not twenty paces from him was an incredibly handsome youth. With his long blond hair, blue eyes and clean-shaven (rare for the time) face the youth radiated beauty. But that beauty paled in comparison to the power emanating from him. Here stood a god. Here stood Alexander.

Dioxippus makes a discovery

He strained to hear the breathing. It was faint, barely discernible from the other morning noises. Dioxippus slowly pushed himself up from his reclining position until he could see the sleeping form of Barba Fotis. There was no doubt; the old man was still breathing although if one were to judge by the noise level only a miniscule amount of air was entering the lungs. Dioxippus stared at the aged trainer. He could not help but compare Fotis to a small, helpless child.

The sun's morning rays had already slashed through the shadows at the far end of the house dazzling the interior with bursting colors. Dioxippus blinked twice as the glare stung his sleep-laden eyes. The sting in his eyes made him aware of the late hour. He had to train. He would let the old man sleep.

Dioxippus slowly made his way out, after all he did not want to wake up Fotis. Outside, he allowed himself to relax and grabbing a square piece of cloth and a small clay pot of water, he went to the back of the small house where he emptied his bladder and then performed some perfunctory washing. Refreshed, he proceeded back to the front of his dwelling. Looking around, for no one in particular, and noting he was unobserved, he sat down cross-legged in the dirt.

He had only noticed it two days earlier. How could he have missed it? He looked down. Scattered among the grains of sand and multi-coloured pebbles was a stick, more a sliver really. Dioxippus picked it up. Holding the finger-length piece of wood between his thumb and forefinger he began to draw in the earth.

Dioxippus swore softly under his breath. The stick figures he was drawing began to take shape. Mumbling again, he drew what two days earlier he had witnessed--the bucking of the wild horse. There, now he could see it in his mind. The soldiers were trying to break the colt but the animal was so frightened it refused to yield to the rope being vainly thrown at it. At first the horse reared and galloped around the enclosure. That changed as soon as the first loop encircled its head and neck. Two strong Macedonians pulled down hard on the other end of the rope and even though the young horse was able to initially drag its captors about the pen, the strain on its neck finally exhausted the creature. A few spectators who had ambled over when they heard the shrill screams of the horse intermingled with the cursing and yelling of the soldiers, began to cheer the horse and yell derisive comments at its new masters. But the horse, now lathered from its exertions, slumped its head down and stood as immobile as if it had been carved from marble. One of the soldiers holding the rope released it and began to walk cautiously toward the defeated animal. An experienced horseman, he approached the beast, not from the front but from an oblique direction so when he got near he was on a right angle to the horse's potentially deadly hooves. Dioxippus, watching this little drama, admitted to himself that these Macedonians knew their animals. He turned to leave.

Suddenly, Dioxippus looked back. Galvanized by some inner spirit, the horse stood on its front legs and viciously kicked out with its rear ones. The thrusting movement of the hind legs combined with the twisting hips forced the front legs to pivot in the direction of the outthrust rear. In mid-stride, the approaching Macedonian soldier was struck down as the hooves simultaneously tore through skin, hair and bone to crush as effortlessly as an egg, the face and skull of the soldier. So quickly did this happen, that the other man still held on to the rope. Only stunned momentarily, he yanked the rope hard in the opposite direction. The arc of the circle was now too great for the horse to swing his legs in the original trajectory and have any chance of striking his second nemesis. Then the unforeseen. The horse, perhaps possessed of a greater intelligence than its brothers or perhaps imbued with a supernatural spirit, snapped its head hard away from its enemy. The soldier, still holding on to the rope was jerked forward abruptly. Instantaneously, the rear legs swung up and out forcing the front hooves to pivot but this time in the opposite direction. But he had been forewarned. The Macedonian threw his arms up to protect his head. Like the warclubs of the hill savages, the hooves tore the muscles, severed the sinews and broke the bones that constituted the arms of the Macedonian. He too fell, unconscious from the impact and shock but still alive.

All this transpired in the span of heartbeats yet many of the spectators were already leaping into the pen and running towards the untamed brute that crushed the life of one man and maimed the other. Seeing the oncoming humans, frightened by their yells and menacing actions, the horse trotted off to a corner of the pen, snorting its anger as it took steps first in one direction then the other. Unbeknownst to it, Alexander had issued forth a decree banning the destruction of good horses so the expletives hurled its way by the frantic humans was the only harm that would come its way.

Dioxippus had sat mesmerized. Why, he had not known? He neither knew the horsemen nor cared about them. Death and injury were part of life. The tableau before him barely interested him now that the play was finished. Why then was his brain screaming for his eyes to open? He had returned to his training later that day completely disoriented. He felt himself tantalized by a secret he could not learn.

But today, sitting in the dirt, Dioxippus had a revelation. The horse. The kick. That was what it was. In watching the horse fight its captors, Dioxippus had seen a devastating weapon unleashed. And he could have it.

Taking the tiny stick he drew a horse's rear leg in the ground in front of him. He studied it. Then he drew a human leg. He compared them. Where the knee bent on a human and where the hock joined the fetlock on a horse there was a similarity of structure that could not be overlooked. There was of course the obvious difference that the bend in the horse's leg was reverse of the bend in the human leg. Still, the motion of the horse's leg could be imitated by a man. If so, a kick could also be designed to simulate the one he saw two days earlier.

Dioxippus thought back to the day he first learned that a kick could be effective above the waist. Since then he had refined what he referred to as the front kick until it could be used from a variety of positions at a variety of targets. It had proven to be the equalizer in the pankration rings when he fought bigger, tougher or more experienced opponents. Now he was sitting here in the dirt yet again, designing a weapon best used by a dumb animal. Dioxippus smiled. He knew others were critical of his unorthodox style of fighting and if they saw him now they would also be critical of his sanity. Dioxippus was not overly concerned by others' opinions of his skills or mental state. He only cared to win.

Dioxippus stood up. He glanced around. This time there was no wall to experiment his new kick on. He considered the house. No, he would wake up Barba Fotis. There was a small fig tree near the back of the compound. It was rather narrow but it would provide a target that could be impacted. And as the tree was fairly slender it would give with the blow minimizing the jar on his foot and leg.

Dioxippus walked over to the tree. He focused on a spot where the trunk was approximately the circumference of two large hands touching thumb to thumb, middle finger to middle finger. Immediately, there was a difficulty with the physics of the kick. The horse kicked in basically a rearward direction; Dioxippus knew that duplicating the motion of the horse would necessitate turning his back on his opponent which at best would prove suicidal. Nevertheless he thought it best to at least attempt the kick the way he had seen it.

Dioxippus focused on the spot he would kick. It was approximately halfway up the trunk and relatively smooth of protruding bumps, knots or bark. With scarcely a thought, Dioxippus kicked back with his right leg at his chosen target.

The results were disastrous. The thrust from the kicking leg pulled his body toward the sapling. This forced his supporting leg and foot to slide in underneath his body, altering the center of balance, resulting in a face-first dive into the dirt. Pain compounded the embarrassment when his kicking foot missed the trunk but his first toe did not. The glancing blow on the extremity sent shards of agony up his leg. So there Dioxippus lay, in the dirt, curled in a fetal position, holding his foot and definitely not feeling the almost holy elation he had had bathe him when he had created the front kick two years earlier.

"Is that a new love dance or do you plan on plowing the ground with your teeth?" laughed a mocking voice.

Philip and Olympias

"You requested an audience," asked Philip in the most royal of tones.

The kneeling figure did not look up at the Macedonian king. Hunched over, the forehead touching the ground, the shapeless form was the personification of humility and servitude. The veils covering the face bespoke an Asian custom not a Greek one. Philip was intrigued.

"Will you speak?" queried Philip.

"Yes my lord."

That voice. It cut through him as effectively as a sheepherder's castration of a ram.

Olympias turned her face upwards, letting the fine gossamer of the veils slide gently aside, exposing the dark almond-shaped eyes and full, blood-filled lips. Her posture may have been servile but her face was that of a queen--powerful, fearless and angry.

Inadvertently, Philip gasped. His wife, one of several, was merely a woman, married to solidify alliances. Yet he feared her.

"My lord, have I incurred your displeasure? You no longer grace our chambers with your presence," pined Olympias, the wail in her voice scarcely concealing the venom. "Might my lord share even a crumb of his affection with the woman who bore him Alexander."

Philip winced at the reference to his son. This harpy used her control over Alexander to browbeat and humiliate him every chance afforded her. If his son was not so attached to his mother and the fawning courtiers she surrounded herself and Alexander with, Philip would have found the means to surreptitiously rid himself of her--permanently. For now he had to engage in these ridiculous games of intrigue.

"My dearest Olympias. Stand, come beside me. You know that you, my first wife, are the only one I consider myself truly married to. If I have neglected my conjugal duties of late, it is only because the political situation demands that I seal alliances by taking other spouses. None of them compares to you in beauty. None spark the desire in me that you do." Philip reached forward with his arms, seized Olympias around the waist and drew her to him. In one motion, he grasped the back of her head, pulled it towards his face and kissed her ravenously. She returned his passion, biting and sucking on his lips, tongue and throat. The bodyguards standing less than ten paces away modestly cast their eyes down although neither one relaxed the grip on his short sword nor looked away from the twisting heads on the dais above them.

Philip was surprised, not unpleasantly, by the fury of his wife's ardor. His own state of arousal was beginning to physically hurt him, especially after Olympias, clad in mere puffs of fabric climbed into his lap and sat straddled across his groin. Not once, even for the briefest of moments did Olympias cease or even slow her amorous attack on Philip. Philip could barely catch a breath. He wanted her. He would have her; right on the throne. Frantically, he started pulling and tearing on the costume concealing her treasures. His sexual frenzy knew no bounds.

But somewhere, buried in the recesses of his logical mind, a voice screamed at him to stop. The dangers of starting a sexual relationship with this madwoman possessed by the goddess Aphrodite were so great that even in the turmoil of touching, grabbing, squeezing, they began to penetrate the mind of the lust-crazed Philip. Fear, growing slowly at first but rapidly gathering momentum, assumed the form of a pit in his lower abdomen. Philip, regaining his sanity, pushed Olympias back, trying vainly to avoid her probing tongue and biting teeth. She in turn had not yet realized that he was rejecting her so she forced herself even harder on the king. Philip was startled by the strength of Olympias, who was probably half his weight. Nevertheless, he managed to break the seal binding them together.

Olympias was furious. To be twice rejected in two days was an alien concept.

"Bastard!" shrieked the panting Olympias. Before Philip could even stop her, she dove onto him. Her left hand grabbed the leather and cloth warrior skirt (which Philip favored wearing over a chiton) and with her right hand driving under it almost skewered his testicles. Philip's reflexes, slowed by both his mind-state and his body's desperate need for sexual release, were not able to prevent Olympias from assaulting him.

Instantaneously, the two bodyguards, members of Philip's elite King's Companions, seized Olympias and dragged her off the pain-grimaced Philip. They held her with as little force as possible; loyal to the King but respectful of the Queen. Philip leaned back in the throne, grinding his teeth as the jaw muscles tensed under the control he was exerting over the rest of his body. A tinge of nausea and a pain centering itself behind the eyes were the only lasting results from the groin injury. Taking a few deep breaths through his nostrils, as to not show to Olympias the effect of her spear-like thrust, Philip tried to be composed.

"Why is it necessary that all our meetings end up so violently? I was not rejecting you, my love. But you would have us fornicating in the throne room in front of witnesses. Your carnal lusts must be controlled. Remember, you are a queen, not a whore," said Philip, his tone considerate, almost tender. "I still love you. Why do you treat me in such a brutish manner? Is not the son we produced a glorious testament to our bonding? Why is it necessary that your jealous tirades cost us so much peace and happiness? I only want you to be happy." Philip was quite smug upon concluding this conciliatory plea. So enamored was he with his words and so relaxed did Olympias now appear, that he actually believed that Olympias would accept this hypocritical hyperbole.

Olympias, still being held by the King's Companions, relaxed, the tension in her body dissipated. She turned and looked up at the men locked onto her arms, gave them a wan little smile then turned to face Philip.

"You are my husband. I am your wife. Yet you treat me worse than a concubine. At least they get some gratification. Am I so ugly? Have I offered harm to you or your entourage? Why have you chosen to leave me out of your life? I only live to serve you and my son. I came here to warn you, not make love to you. Is it my fault that I desire you; you desire me. I was overwhelmed by my lord's and husband's masculinity. Yet it is I who is cast aside, failing in my matrimonial duty and ridiculed in front of these...guards. I only want to be your wife, to look out for you, to make sure you live to see your grandchildren. Am I asking too much?"

The pathetic attempts being made by both the king and queen to ingratiate themselves to each other were so ridiculously insincere that it took an enormous amount of self-control to keep the king's bodyguards from reaching over and slapping both royal powers to their senses. It was particularly dismaying seeing Philip, the most charismatic, accomplished leader in the world at that time, effectively grovel in front of this trollop. Both soldiers caught each other's eye out of their peripheral vision. Disgust and anger were reflected in both.

"You said you were here to warn me," said Philip, trying desperately to change the subject.

"What...yes, yes I am here to warn you," replied Olympias. "It has come to my attention that some plot against you."

"That is nothing new. I have had many try to usurp me. All have failed. All will fail," interjected Philip.

"Yes, my lord but how many of these traitors come from the ranks of your own King's Companions?"

The two bodyguards, who by now had released Olympias, started. Immediately they turned to Philip, mouthing protests at the accusation. Philip caught their eye, and in a code perceptible only to a King's Companion, warned them to silence. His curiosity was however piqued. "Continue," he urged on Olympias, his face impassive.

"One of your closest friends speaks against you. He has been heard bragging in the brothels that when you are 'disposed' of, he will be given the rank of general by the new rulers. But he does not plan against you directly. He is far too intelligent to openly revolt. No, he instead plots against your new in-law, Attalus. The rumor has it that he will provide the means for another to assassinate the old warrior. Once this is accomplished, the alliance between Pellas and Epros will be weakened, possibly causing a domestic war, and leaving the opportunity for those critical of your policies to assassinate you without having to worry about extensive repercussions from the military. The plan also calls for the execution of the royal family, including Alexander, whom they would probably poison, as no one is brave enough to face him and his own Companion guard openly."

Philip stared at Olympias. He watched her mouth, her movements, her eyes, during the whole narration of the story. His first reaction was to simply ignore what she said. His own network of spies had not reported anything out of the ordinary. A plot so insidious it involved the best of the best would or should have been ferreted out---if it existed. Knowing the Queen, little credence could be given her tale. Philip had dealt with traitors before and he knew that to catch them he had to pretend that he believed them. This would cause them to make the critical mistake that would implicate them on a charge of treason. In order to flush out these criminals he would have to play the ignorant all-trusting leader. And even though he suspected Olympias of the worst duplicity it would be imprudent to accuse her of treason while she maintained such a strong power base with Alexander and his followers. He did not believe that one of his own elite would turn against him. He went out of his way to insure that the King's Companions were loyal to him and him alone. They were the most pampered, well-treated and honored soldiers in the empire. They were also the fiercest, best-trained and most effectively deployed troops under his command. And they always fought beside him. As he went so did they. To have one accused by this incarnation of evil was almost laughable. However, he did find himself interested in who she would accuse.

"Well, who is it?" asked Philip.

Olympias, for the first time, felt a twinge of nervousness. Some said she was as fearless as any man. Those who knew her stated that no man was as fearless as her...save her son. But now she was trying to play the king for a fool. Nothing could be more dangerous. The gamble excited her.

"The traitor is...Pausanias!"

Alexander

For one of the few times in his adult life, Piros could not think of anything to say. His famed eloquence had been replaced by a child's dumbfounded stare. He could feel the blood rushing to his cheeks and without being aware of it his embarrassment forced his eyes to look at the ground.

"It is good to see that you have not let a life of leisure soften you to any extent. In fact, I think you enjoy spanking these 'children'," continued a smiling Alexander. "Would I be showing disrespect to the honorable teacher if I were to ask him to join me in a private conversation?"

Piros had by now recovered his composure. Of course he would speak to Alexander. Piros knew that Alexander was not being facetious in his manner or his words. Many said that Alexander's thirst for knowledge was a greater driving force than his ambition, which in itself was considered limitless. Consequently, Alexander surrounded himself with the brightest, most erudite scholars in the empire. On every campaign, large contingents of botanists, archeologists, geographers and other scientists accompanied the troops. New lands, new flora and fauna, new people, new customs, all these were studied and all findings documented. Alexander himself read as many of these reports as humanly possible and on many occasions made his own comments and contributions. Anything of particular interest was sent hastily back to Pella or Athens so his mentor, Aristotle, could see what he was seeing. Piros knew all this, and for that reason he knew that to Alexander, a teacher was the most respected member of his society. Alexander, with aspirations even at this young age to conquer the world, still felt it proper to ask a teacher permission to interrupt his class. This humanness in a man rumored to be part god, endeared him to his people.

"I would be pleased to speak with you Alexander. Allow me to assign a set of exercises to the students and I will join you immediately thereafter," said Piros. Then turning to the now rising Dimitris, he said, "You will lead your fellow pankratiatists through the grappling drills. Make sure they all do at least fifteen repetitions of each movement from both sides of the facing stance." Piros turned to the prince, "Alexander, let us sit by the far bench so we may speak with as little interruption as possible."

Alexander smiled and nodded. He was pleased that Piros did not acquiesce easily to his request. He was also impressed by the way that Piros handled Dimitris. By allowing the young man to assume the leader's position so soon after being taught a lesson in such a painful manner, Piros proved that he was less concerned with his own ego than with building up the confidence of his pupils. Alexander felt that initiative and bravery should always be rewarded. Yes, he had to admit, in Piros the best of the Greeks was apparent. It was unfortunate that Piros was loyal first to Philip then to Alexander. The prince would have been ecstatic to have made him a commander in his own corps of elite warriors, the Companions.

Piros and Alexander made themselves comfortable on the low, stone-carved bench.

"I will not waste your valuable time. I have heard rumors of a fighter named Dioxippus. It has been told to me that he has added a new dimension to the pankration--something no one has done successfully before. Is this true?" asked Alexander.

"Yes Alexander. I am not quite sure how he does it, but I have seen him kick an upright man in the face. With an incredible amount of power I should add. Now he trains fanatically, doing calisthenics until noon, and pankration drills and sparring in the afternoon. He has also gained weight and filled out his muscles. He has become quite an intimidating force in the youth games. In fact, just two moons ago, he placed third in the adult division at the Nemean games."

Alexander nodded, looked up behind Piros and signaled someone with his eyes. Piros caught the look. It was wiser to ignore it.

"Tell me Piros, has this Dioxippus had any battlefield experience? Can he use weapons? Will he follow orders? Is he the type who will remain loyal to his commander? unit? partner?"

Piros knew where this was going. Alexander wanted Dioxippus to join his personal bodyguard, the Companions. Normally he would have been thrilled to have one of his students join what some argued was the best fighting force in the world. Even the King's Companions, Philip's elite, were said to be a half-step slower than the younger, hungrier troops of Alexander. The Companions were a reflection of Alexander. They had adopted the Spartan lifestyle, eating little, training hard and shunning luxury of any sort. Each one was insanely loyal to Alexander and would die willingly rather than risk a loss of face to his leader. They were further buoyed by the daring, fearless attitude of the prince. Alexander, even though a brilliant tactician for one so young, did not sit back and plan strategy with his other generals once a battle had started. He relished combat. He never felt so alive than when near death. Money, sex, power all inevitably failed to provide Alexander with the blood rush, the euphoria of hand to hand combat. And the Companions were the same. This intensity made them the best warriors on the planet. It also made them the most unpredictable and the most dangerous even to their allies. Piros was not sure that Dioxippus would be able to or want to assimilate himself into a group walking the edge of disaster. There were other things about the Companions rumored also. And these concerned Piros.

Alexander was extremely perceptive. Within moments he noticed that Piros was stalling. He made a mental note.

"To answer your question Alexander, Dioxippus has had no actual battlefield experience in the context you refer to. He has had to defend himself and others, often in life-threatening situations and has always emerged the victor. In the pankration he could possibly be the best ever, he knows so much. His ability to adapt and improvise are phenomenal. He understands the mechanics of the body so well that there is almost no hold he cannot break," said Piros, his voice rising slightly. Then he realized what he was doing. He was making Dioxippus sound like the mythical Herakles. Alexander's eyes were ablaze with excitement. Piros inhaled and tried to downplay the damage as much as possible.

"But on the battlefield, surrounded by the chaos, the confusion...I cannot predict his actions. He has never had to take orders in a group situation. And remember, he was a slave and it is quite well-documented how slaves converted to soldiers never show the loyalty or dedication of regular troops. To expect him to commit himself to the Companions might be too much. I am his friend, his trainer, his liberator. I cannot in good conscience recommend him to you."

Alexander's face did not change. A smile still played on his lips and his demeanor was relaxed. But the gleam in those sea-blue eyes had transformed into a glare. He knew that Piros, for reasons of his own, was deliberately refraining from saying what he really felt. Alexander was as good a judge of character as his father. He also had a memory that never forgot names, faces or places. He had seen Dioxippus at the youth games last year and had been impressed by the high level of skill and unorthodox fighting style. Alexander thought him perfect for his bodyguard. Now Piros, known throughout Hellas as one of its most honorable citizens, was telling him, Alexander, that his assessment of Dioxippus was incorrect. He did not make mistakes when it came to soldiers. Something about this whole conversation bespoke deceit. He looked hard at Piros.

"Of course your opinion is noted and appreciated," said Alexander. "However, I still would like to meet with the both of you in two day's time. Perhaps Dioxippus himself could express his concerns or desires at that time and between the three of us a solution may be formulated."

"Dioxippus will be training for the Olympics in two moons' time. I know I may speak for him when I say that we would be honored greatly to have Alexander meet with us," replied Piros.

Alexander nodded curtly and turned to go. Stepping out of the far wall's shadow was another gloriously handsome youth. Approximately the same height as Alexander, he was olive-skinned with black, curly hair growing down to his shoulders. He was as fine-featured as Alexander and had a well-proportioned body with long legs tapering to rather small feet. He was dressed in a standard military-type short skirt with a matching tunic. The similarity to a standard issue dress ended there. The cloth had been died deep blue with such subtle variations in the tone as to make it appear to shimmer. As the light from the sun caught the youth emerging from the dark, Piros was almost convinced that the tunic was a living thing. There was no need to convince himself of the extraordinary allurement of the young man. And even though Piros was not in the least interested in pursuing the Athenian custom of maintaining male lovers, he had to admit that someone like Hephaestion could make you at least understand some of the reasons why. Nobody knew, or would dare venture to guess what Hephaestion's relationship was with Alexander. Friends, intimates or lovers, all that anyone needed to know was that they were inextricably bound to each other, and one would die for the other without a thought. Hephaestion was the ultimate bodyguard; he would not hesitate to stop an assassin with his own flesh.

Alexander rose, nodded to Piros, and with Hephaestion walking beside him, made his way back to the palace. As Alexander grew smaller and smaller the further he went, Piros marveled at how this prince, this general, this god could walk down the streets unescorted (other than by Hephaestion), greeting shopkeepers, soldiers and other citizens, most often by name. An exceptional man thought Piros. He turned to his students.

"Excellent, Dimitris. If you please, I will now instruct. Everyone now, two laps around the palace. The run will increase your endurance and the rocks will toughen your feet!" said a jocular Piros as he led the students on the first of today's runs.

Dioxippus learns a lesson

It hurt. And with every pulse, it hurt more. Dioxippus clutched his foot even tighter trying vainly to cut off the circulation to his toe. But the throbbing pain continued.

Fotis sauntered over to the prone Dioxippus. The youth still lay in a semi-curled position, gripping that foot like life itself. Fotis smiled. It never failed to amaze him how much punishment the human body could take and continue to function. He had seen pankratiatists, with limbs broken, often near death, recover enough to defeat their opponents. He had even seen the mighty Piros once beaten into unconciousness whilst maintaining a leg lock around the torso of his adversary. Yet Piros had managed to not only crush the lungs but break the ribs of his attacker. So as Piros lay comatose, his opponent surrendered and lost the match. Such was the toughness of the pankratiatist.

Watching Dioxippus squirm like an injured child also reminded Fotis how sensitive certain parts of the body were. How often had he seen a match end in the first few moments after one pankratiatist had gained a finger lock? an ankle hold? a face grab? Some parts of the body focused energy to such a degree that the slightest injury immobilized the rest. So as Fotis gently teased the now sitting Dioxippus, he really could sympathize with the youth.

"I think I know what you did wrong. First rise, then I will show you how I think that kick should work. I have brought something that may be kinder to your foot than that tree," Piros said. With that he tossed Dioxippus an inflated pig's bladder.

Dioxippus caught the ball. He noticed how light it was, and how the skin itself had a certain elasticity. Dioxippus turned it in his hands, feeling the texture of the oblong shape. A strip of leather had been sown into the bladder to serve as a handle. He shot Fotis a querulous look.

"Dios, that pad will serve as a target. I will hold it by the handle and you will kick it. Simple. Good."

"I do not know, Barba Fotis," sighed the rising Dioxippus as he stepped gingerly on his injured foot. "It seems there are things not meant for a human being to do. Kicking like a mule is one of them. Even if I kick successfully, my back is turned to my opponent. I tried twisting my head and I ended up in the dirt. How is any technique effective if you are blind during its execution?"

"I am not the expert, Dios. I am an old man, a farmer by trade. You know better than I what will work and what will not. It is presumptuous of me to assume to tell you what to do."

The plaintive tone of Fotis' voice was not lost on Dioxippus. It was obvious that the old man only wanted to help. But Dioxippus had heard far too many opinions, criticisms and recommendations to take anyone else's comments seriously. Growing up without parents, nothing more than a marketable commodity, had bred within him a strong aversion to outside biases. He realized that Fotis meant only the best for him but the ridiculous suggestion that he had just heard only served to reinforce the conviction to be independent of others. Only Piros, his guide and mentor, could plot strategy, suggest techniques and design training programs for him. All others were intruders. Even Barba Fotis.

However, he felt remorseful dismissing the aged trainer's offer. In his most placating voice, Dioxippus said to Fotis, "I will think about your suggestions. But for now, how would it be if you assisted me with some stretching exercises. The front kicks demand loose hamstrings." He finished his statement with a tooth-filled smile, a shade condescending yet genuine in its affection. Dioxippus tossed the pig's bladder back to Fotis.

Fotis snatched the ball out of the air. He then bent his head forward, mumbled something, and shuffled toward Dioxippus. So shamed was he that he could not look up at the face of his young charge.

Dioxippus felt terrible. He had not meant to insult his friend. It was true, he guessed, old people were as sensitive as children. Dioxippus took a step forward, stretching his right arm out to embrace Fotis by the shoulders. The old man looked so pathetic.

Instantaneously, something hit Dioxippus in the eye. The tears welled reflexively. Then he felt, he knew not what, an object bouncing off his head, his shoulders then his head again. None of it hurt but he still had to cover himself with his arms.

"Here. Take this, and this and..." huffed Fotis, scarcely slowing down the swings he was taking at Dioxippus with the inflated bladder. His grip on the handle was so fierce that it began to tear with the impact. "Smart man. Huh! You are nothing more than a precocious stooge. Wake up! Do you flex your brain as much as your arms? Maybe you should!" continued Fotis, still battering the young man with the animal skin. The aged Fotis, so small that any healthy child could manhandle him, was furious at being politely dismissed. He had watched Dios kick. He had seen him fall. He had seen him stub his big toe. Fotis could show Dioxippus how to make that kick an effective part of his arsenal. The inflated bag was to minimize injury.

Now this conceited, over-grown man-child was too good to listen to his suggestion. If he had to beat it into Dios he would. Fotis felt another rush of anger-driven adrenalin. He started swinging harder and yelling curses in a local dialect that no person in all of Macedonia could understand.

Dioxippus started to laugh. And with every hit, he laughed harder. Soon he was rocking from the effort. Fotis did not stop hitting the youth but there was an appreciable slowdown. Dioxippus clutched his sides and tears started anew with the convulsions. Fotis, breathing hard with the exertion, stopped swinging, bent at the waist and gave a few coughs to clear the fluids and phlegm from his throat and lungs. Dioxippus looked at him, maybe for the first time.

"Enough...enough! I apologize. I will listen. Stop, old man...you have won," said Dioxippus, puffing from the laughter.

Fotis had no more strength to swing even the air-filled bag again. He just looked at Dioxippus, his face chiseled into grim resolve. So determined did he look that even the still chuckling Dioxippus ceased ridiculing the old man.

"I told you, I apologize. Come now Barba Fotis, are you planning on hitting me again? I would much rather have you teach me something."

"Why do you take that superior attitude with me? You were born a slave just as I was. And am I so stupid that after close to ten years with Piros, I have failed to gain any knowledge of the pankration? Why do you find it impossible to listen to what may be a good suggestion? Do you think Piros would have ever spoken to me in such a manner?" queried Fotis. "No! Respect is more than having money or property. It is more than having simpletons kiss your ass as they fawn all over you. What have you done to merit respect? Beating another senseless while simultaneously trying to dismember him is not an honorable vocation. It is sport. One in which the spectators, bored morons, watch others overexert themselves in an exercise that they only recognize at its basest physicality. Those are the ones that worship you. Those are the ones you should ignore. Not me!"

Dioxippus was taken aback. He did not know that the aged trainer could speak so eloquently, so forcefully. Obviously, the ten years with Piros had enlightened him in more subjects than just the pankration. Dioxippus withstood the tirade it was the only respectful thing to do. When Fotis appeared finished, Dioxippus spoke, "Why do I always find myself apologizing to you? Come show me this weapon that I am to master. But bring a rag to clean the dirt off of my face. I suspect that I will be kissing the ground many times today."

"Your apology and your eagerness both overwhelm me." The sarcastic bite of the comment was not lost on Dioxippus. Fotis took a step toward Dioxippus, pointed at the ground and continued, "The first problem I see is in the position of your feet. When you kicked back, you dragged the supporting foot in the direction of the kick. Now, look here in the dirt. You see how your toes point in a perpendicular angle to your kicking leg's trajectory. You do not have enough foot on the ground to support you when you move in that direction."

Dioxippus was stunned. He never expected such a technical description from the old man. He looked at the track he had made. Fotis was right. The sliding feet had created what looked very much like the letter Gamma "Γ". It was obvious that when the kick was executed, his supporting foot had not moved from its locked position much less pivoted. Now Dioxippus remembered the horse. Its supporting hooves had turned in the direction of the kick, the back of each one, equating the human heel, facing the enemy. The horse had slid into the thrust too, but its legs did not have to undergo the extreme torque in the knees that he did. Maintaining balance had been easier for the equine warrior than for the human one.

"See, if this foot turns in the direction of your kick, you will have more balance over the center of your body. Done correctly, you should not fall down," explained Fotis.

Dioxippus could not help but observe that the old man was completely engrossed with his subject. Fotis had now knelt, his right hand just touching the ground to keep him from falling over. He traced Dioxippus' footmark and then drew another where he thought the foot should be positioned. Unconsciously, Dioxippus shifted his own feet. Maybe the old man was right.

"Now let us try the kick again," ordered Fotis confidently. He held out the inflated bladder. "Hit this if you can."

Dioxippus aligned himself with the target. This time he did not turn his back on it: he took a more sideways position so he would be able to see the target. Taking one, two, three breaths he suddenly jerked his leg out at the bag. The bag, hit sharply, spun around the point where the handle held it. When it reached its apex, it swung back down again.

Fotis whooped in excitement. He pointed at Dioxippus' tracks as if gold lined his very steps.

Philip is angered

"Pausanias!" thundered Philip. His bodyguards reflexively seized Olympias by the arms. Their grip was so sudden and hard that bruises erupted almost immediately. They looked to Philip for further instructions. Philip did not notice them. He was so angry at what had to be the vilest, most baseless accusation against his most trusted confederate that he was oblivious to all. Slowly he rose from his throne, a king, a conqueror, a warrior to fear like no other. The pure savagery in his demeanor bespoke a violent death for Olympias.

Olympias, in the vise-like grip of the King's Companions, was immobilized. She instinctively shrank back when Philip raised himself to his full height. At this moment he was an apparition from hell, ready to tear her apart. She was so frightened she bit her inside lip to keep from crying, or fainting. It had come to this; all her machinations to usurp Philip would be in vain. Her son would always be his lackey. And she, the rightful ruler of Hellas, was about to be destroyed by this crippled, warrior-king. And although her mind told her she was smarter, better bred and more deserving than the one-eyed demon descending on her, her body separated itself from her brain and began trembling violently with fright. As Philip came down the steps toward her, she became nauseous. Her stomach felt knotted and she desperately wanted to throw up.

Philip stood in front of his wife. His one eye tore through Olympias, searing her with its ferocity. He leaned forward, so close that his breath, like the blast from an oven, scorched the tender white skin of her face. He whispered, so quietly that the bodyguards holding Olympias could not hear, "Prepare to die, traitor!" Barely had the hiss come out of his mouth before he grabbed Olympias by the throat, squeezing it slowly, stealing the breaths, one at a time, making the strangulation agonizingly prolonged. A smile, growing proportionately to the gasping sounds now emanating from Olympias, cracked the beast-like veneer of Philip. The hand crushing the life out of Olympias did not waver.

The bodyguards, still holding the Queen, noticed that she had closed her eyes, and her lips, turning blue with the lack of oxygen, were moving in some sort of rhythm. Even this bitch prays to someone they thought.

Praying was the last thing Olympias thought of doing. She was trying desperately to remember a technique for breaking a chokehold one of her Asian lovers had taught her. At the time it had been a game, something to add a little danger to their lovemaking. But now she was fighting for survival, not an orgasm. And she could feel her consciousness leaving her.

Suddenly, she snapped her head around, forcing it in the direction of Philip's thumb. The torquing action, focused on the weak part of the grip, broke the hold. She pulled her head back with such force that the bodyguard on her right lost his footing and stumbled back. The grip on her arm relaxed and she twisted free. She gasped for air. In between breaths, she hoarsely cried, "I have proof."

Philip did not retreat. All his anger, his frustration, his fear was embodied in this cowering little woman. With scarcely any effort he could beat her to death. And no one would question it. Save Alexander. This made him hold back.

Seizing the momentary lapse in the attack, Olympias spoke, her voice gruff yet effective, "The traitor even now brags to his friends. He endeavors to win others to his cause. Quickly, send one of these goons to your beloved Piros. Ask him yourself. You know he can be trusted above all others. Pausanius slept at his villa last night. Ask Piros, I beg of you. Ask him what Pausanius said. I bore you a son. I deserve some consideration."

At the mention of Piros' name, Philip stopped. Piros was as a brother to him. If there was any substance to Olympias' tale, the retired pankratiatist would verify it. Still, he refused to believe that Pausanius, a King's Companion, would conspire against him. But these were strange times, and if Olympias, so close to dying was willing to risk an even more violent end to her life by bringing in Piros to substantiate her claims, he should allow it. One more thing nagged at Philip. If he killed this banshee, his son would go insane. Then he would have no choice but to also kill Alexander.

Piros ventures to the agora

The last of the stragglers was just coming in. Piros watched with amusement. These young, supposedly vital men had experienced a tremendous loss of face after Piros, laughingly referred to as the old man by his charges, came back from the run around the amphitheatre far ahead of even the most fit of the trainees. The limping, staggering youths coming in now ran with their heads drooped, their tongues flopping like dogs'. Shame and exhaustion clouded their faces. The catcalls from their peers only added to the agony of the run. And to face Piros, so soon after they bragged about leaving him lying in the dirt, was the ultimate humiliation.

Piros grinned. There was no use in pursuing an attack on the confidence of his trainees. His ego did not need to be caressed. He turned and yelled out, "That is enough for today. Go to your homes. Rest. Tomorrow we spar."

The students turned and looked at each other; then they looked at Piros. A couple looked around nervously. Piros nodded and they all started to shamble off in different directions.

Piros sighed. He shook his head once. What a morning! He rubbed the sore spot on his leg. That had been an interesting conversation with Alexander. What was he up to? That sparked another series of thoughts. Where was Dioxippus? He almost never missed a workout. Piros walked over to the bench. Underneath it, hidden by the cooling shade was a clay water container. Piros took a draught. The overflow ran down his chin and onto his naked body. The fluid made trails through the dust on his torso. Although not much fell on him, the liquid cooled the still-sweating skin. He would go look for Dioxippus. It was not like him to miss a workout. He slipped on his chiton, a much plainer shade than he usually wore. Piros had eschewed wearing a belt this morning so the garment just hung down straight. Once he had checked for comfort, he turned in the direction of the street and started walking.

The main thoroughfare was packed with people walking, animals pulling and troops pushing through. Shopkeepers barked prices and deals incessantly, while customers, gesticulating wildly, fiercely bargained for the best price. All kinds of wares, ranging from fruit to vegetables to dried meats overflowed from baskets piled high, one on top of another. Other vendors, hawking more exotic items competed for space amongst the foodstuffs and in more than one instance, raucous arguments broke out between merchants. Occasionally, some shoving would start which inevitably would attract more people to a particular area. Even more confusion would then result.

Piros wound his way through this maze of merchandise, foodstuffs and humanity as if he had been born amid the chaos. The frantic pace of the market had its own heart, its own soul.

Piros respected the ebb and flow of street life. And with his dark skin, his prideful walk and esteemed reputation, he stood out amongst the human ants rushing about their nests. Piros was called out to, greeted, sometimes hugged as he negotiated a pathway through the turmoil. In every instance, he would return a greeting, smiling amiably, wishing the best to a particular person or family. Beautiful fabrics were thrust out to him, to touch, to comment on. Anything more than a cursory glance would elicit whoops of joy from the merchants who would take the opportunity to call out anew to their customers, claiming a testimonial from Piros was almost as good as god-blessed. Piros enjoyed the people. He liked calling out to friends or neighbors. He really was interested in their lives and would take the time to catch up on all the events in a particular person's life. Today it seemed that every street vendor in Hellas knew him. From one to the other, he was bumped or jostled. Hugs from the men, kisses from the women, laughing cries from the children, the celebrity that was Piros received them all. To Piros, this outpouring of affection, two years after he had retired, was something physically tangible, a feeling to be savored, much like a good wine. And to a man separated from his roots, his heritage, this involvement with the Macedonian community, limited as it was, sustained him when he was lonely or suffering from the melancholy of being different in an adopted society.

Piros continued making his way through the throngs. He found himself alternately shifting sideways or forward, depending upon the amount of space opening up at any one moment. Occasionally someone would step on his foot, or drag on his robe. Piros barely noticed these intrusions on his person. No angry word ever escaped his lips. He had to admit to himself though that he would be glad to escape his sea of admirers. And if his vision was still good, he could see the end of the swarm coming up soon.

A few more well chosen, forceful steps and Piros found himself free. The air, now allowed to circulate freely, cooled him as it began the long process of drying his sweat-streaked clothing. The open space also afforded him the luxury of walking unimpeded. Within a few lengths of a human body, Piros was striding. At this pace he would reach the cottage Dioxippus lived at in the time it took for a normal man to eat a small meal. Outwardly he was not worried about the young man. Dioxippus had proven himself in too many dangerous situations to warrant any worry. However, Piros could not let himself relax. The blond youth was as a son to him with all the requisite worries and concerns. His father had been a worrier. Piros knew with all his heart that his father never relaxed when Piros was out of his sight. This sort of paternal concern was rare for the time and even rarer for a slave. Piros had to admit his father had been quite the man. If he closed his eyes, just for a moment, he would see his father again.

Slowly Piros felt his eyes drawn downward. The rhythmic slapping of the bare feet against the hard earth further assuaged his restless spirit. His eyes, locked into a non-seeing stare, glazed over. Piros felt himself entering an alternate plane or so he thought. The fear of madness jerked his head up, but his vision remained bolted. He could not see. He did not want to see. Yet.

Piros remembers...

At first, Delia was full of trepidation. The black man was a monster in size. He also spoke a language she could not understand. He wanted her. That had been obvious from the podium. But why?

The crowd's cadence was as well orchestrated as if it had been rehearsed. Delia barely noticed it though. As had been taught to her, she kept her head bowed, in the manner of all well-bred Hebrew women.

As the noise died down, Krutzios began to speak to Delia. His speech was halting and he often stopped to search for a word. Communicating in a difficult tongue he had not used for years was a painstaking process. Nevertheless, Krutzios' command of Hebrew was good enough to convey his and Tsaka's thoughts to Delia.

Delia listened to the wrinkled little man. Occasionally, she would sneak a look at the dark-skinned colossus. She heard Krutzios but did not believe him or her interpretation thereof. This African wanted her for a mate. Not a slave. She would be his wife, the mother to his children. And if what Krutzios was trying so hard to say was true she would be treated with honor and respect. This was too much for her to absorb. Reflexively she put her hands to her temples. The gesture caused a slight panic in the two men facing her. Both spoke at the same time, their native tongue bouncing from Delia uselessly. Yet the timbre in their voices, fragile with care, was not lost on the rabbi's daughter. They, for reasons not known to her, really cared about her welfare. Not since her capture in the desert had any human beings been more than perfunctory in their concern for her well being. There was no question in Delia's mind. The thought of being married to this man frightened her. Yet, something about this man intrigued her, attracted her. Immediately, her face blushed and she begged her god's forgiveness for her less than pure thoughts. She wished her father were here.

Krutzios was trying his best to placate the desert maiden. Again he reassured her of Tsaka's good intentions. To emphasize his point, he told Tsaka (in Greek) to bow to Delia and in the kindest tone possible, ask her to marry him.

In a motion so smooth that a professional dancer would have been shamed, Tsaka stepped directly in front of Delia. With no flourish, Tsaka bent his head forward. As his head moved downwards, his right hand gently grasped Delia's and raised it to approximately her chest height. Still bowed, Tsaka looked into the maiden's eyes, and in a voice so soft, so gentle yet so full of power and pride, he asked her to share his life with him.

Delia was overwhelmed. The black man standing in front of her dwarfed her. When he picked up her hand, his first three fingers all but obliterated it from her sight. She started trembling again and she berated herself for not controlling her fear. And then she looked at him. His eyes, as black as obsidian made even blacker by the contrasting white surrounding the irises, were not fierce, not angry. Delia was mesmerized by the emotion, the passion she could see in Tsaka. She was not being confronted by some base savage nor she was being threatened with the dehumanizing fate promised her by the slave trader. In Tsaka, Delia could see faith, hope and even love. Her trembling stopped. She nodded her assent.

The communication barrier still existed. It made no difference. Tsaka had understood. He broke into a smile. He took Delia by both hands and with Krutzios in tow, started walking away from the pier and toward the town. Far ahead of them they could see children running and playing. Their squeals of joy could be heard at even this great distance.

Piros reunites with Fotis

The joyous laughter seemed particularly loud. Piros looked up. There were no children. Delia, Tsaka and Krutzios had vanished. The pier was gone. The town had changed. Piros was confused.

"Piros! Come, come quickly. I have a gift for you. Hurry!" yelled out the excited Dioxippus upon sighting his mentor coming up the alleyway.

Piros now realized where he was. He could see Dioxippus waving his arms and crying something out. There was another person standing with his back toward him. Something about the posture looked tantalizingly familiar. Whoever it was, was small, bent and probably old. He also seemed to be holding something in his hands but Piros was too far away to see what it was. A mystery he thought to himself.

As Piros got closer his heart increased its beat. Piros hurried his steps. He did not know why but he felt elated. He got closer and closer. Dioxippus was still calling out. Piros' attention was focused on that little body. He could not hear a thing. Inexplicably a rush, more of happiness than adrenalin, coursed through his body. A few more steps and he would...

Fotis turned around just before Piros was upon him. He did not have a chance to take a breath much less voice a greeting. Piros swept the old man up, crushing him with love. Around and around Piros swung the old man, oblivious to all. Only when he heard the dizzy whimpering of Fotis did he release his embrace. Fotis put his feet down, standing a little unsteadily after the spinning. His grin, punctuated with spaces made by missing teeth, was reflective of so much joy, that Piros felt compelled to again seize the old slave. Only Fotis' and Dioxippus' restraining gestures kept Piros from crushing the little man to death with happiness.

"Where have you been? What have you been doing? Are you healthy? fit? Why are you here? Why did you not come to me immediately?" Piros asked these questions so fast that he scarcely caught a breath.

Fotis sighed. He looked about. He saw the stone-carved bench and signaling to the still-talking Piros, he walked over and sat on it. Piros and Dioxippus followed. Piros sat beside the old man. Dioxippus sat on the ground cross-legged. When everyone was relatively comfortable, Fotis retold his story to Piros. An occasional nod was the only sign that Piros was listening although both Dioxippus and Fotis noted that the smile was now gone.

After an elapsed time, Fotis finished. Piros stood up slowly. In a low voice he said, "Old man, you are now free. No longer will you have to live the life of a slave. You may choose to do what you want."

Fotis looked stunned. He could not believe it. After spending virtually his whole life in slavery he had been set free. A free man. What a concept. Until he thought about it a little more.

"Are you insane? Have I wronged you so badly that you would cast me out to be a beggar? Freedom. Huh! What is that? I cannot eat it. It will not keep me warm. This is your gratitude. I thought you were glad to see me. Obviously, you have had far too many punches to the head!" The old man's voice rose louder and louder.

Piros was flabbergasted. To his father, freedom had been the ultimate gift. To Fotis it had been the ultimate insult. Piros considered being insulted but thought it better to be amused. So he started to laugh. And laugh. And laugh.

Pausanius faces Philip

He would have to have one of the court philosophers, maybe even Aristotle explain it to him. How could a man enter battle knowing that death was imminent and not be afraid? How many times had he been cut, slashed, wounded? He still did not cower from the battleground. How often had he whispered a prayer to any god he thought might listen to him, not asking for salvation but for glory, even in death? He had never been afraid. Not of injury. Not of his life becoming extinct. Was he then fearless? No. Because if he were, he would not now be standing here so scared that his teeth could barely be kept from rattling. He surreptitiously glanced down at his knees. They appeared still although to him they felt as if they were shaking uncontrollably. This dichotomy of emotion kept his logical mind occupied while his illogical mind ran rampant with the controls to his body.

"Have you nothing to say, Pausanius?" asked Philip. He looked steadfastedly at the countenance of his subordinate. Philip could instantly appraise the strengths and weaknesses of a soldier. He could see Pausanius was scared. Why? Was he really the traitor his wife Olympias had charged? Or was he afraid because he knew no one was called to meet the king privately unless something was drastically wrong? Philip was well aware of the types of fears that could manifest themselves in a loyal subject who was trying to outguess his superior. Paranoia was a weapon to people in power, and Philip knew how to use it. Still, this time he was hoping that Olympias was wrong and that he could stop torturing his friend with innuendo and veiled threats.

"Well...are you going to answer?" asked Philip.

Pausanius opened his mouth. Nothing came out. He swallowed once, twice. Words finally began to come out slowly. "I do not know what warrants the king calling me out at this hour. Why must I be escorted like a common criminal? And why must I be brought to you by these boy lovers of Alexander? Do I not at least deserve to be escorted by real soldiers? My compatriots. Who are these shaven pretty boys?" Pausanius' tone was getting almost belligerent as he began to recover his composure.

Inwardly, Philip was glad at Pausanius' response. His friend should be angry. Pride was a very carefully cultivated characteristic in all of the King's Companions. If Pausanius was any less forceful in his reply, Philip might begin to suspect that one of his most loyal bodyguards did indeed have something to hide. Philip relaxed his shoulders. His gaze remained firm however. Even the most faithful dog could turn rabid.

"The 'boys' you refer to are Alexander's own elite. I thought it best to summon you here with men who are not your friends...or rivals. Nobody has accused you of anything so I do not understand your discomfiture. Can we not just talk, like old friends?" queried Philip. His voice was low, evenly modulated.

Pausanius did not detect any menace in Philip. But he had also served far too long with the warrior-king to know that if Philip had wanted to talk to him as an "old friend", he would have invited him to an all night sortie at one of the local drinking establishments. He had been called here for a purpose. And Pausanius was not drunk or stupid. Somehow, Philip had learned of his liaison with the queen. It then followed that Philip had an inkling of the traitorous talk he had engaged in. Pausanius racked his brain trying to figure out who could have betrayed him. And what of the Queen. If Philip suspected him, he would definitely charge his wife with treason. Philip's hatred for his first wife was well known. He would seize the opportunity to execute her. Pausanius could not let that happen! He had to protect Olympias. The nobility of purpose coupled with fear and anger gave Pausanius a much-needed rush of adrenalin. Suddenly, he felt himself invincible. He looked Philip right in the eye.

"If we are truly old friends, I may speak to you as an equal," said Pausanius. Philip nodded affirmatively. "You bring me here under armed escort. Do you fear me? Have I ever given you reason to doubt my loyalty? At Charonea I stood shoulder to shoulder with you. If I wanted you dead, one moment of inattention would have been enough to suffice. I am a King's Companion. I am not a traitor."

The forcefulness of the words was not lost on Philip. He could kick himself for listening to that woman. Now he had lost face in front of one of his most loyal men. He would have to apologize.

"You say you look for traitors. Why not consider your new in-laws? Many have questioned whether their interests are the same as Macedonia's" continued Pausanius.

"Well...the warrior remembers how to bite," replied Philip. His one eye tracked Pausanius' movements. Now this was unexpected. What did Pausanius mean by casting doubt on the loyalty of Attalus? Why was he so concerned with the interests of Macedonia rather than Philip? And why did those few words sound like something Olympias would have said? The space where Philip's eye had once been began to throb with pain. Philip was not as assured of Pausanius' loyalty as he had been only moments before. He could not be sure but there was treachery afoot. The rapidly accelerating pain of the headache made this convoluted thinking impossible. Philip looked at Pausanius. The bodyguard's chest was inflated with self-righteousness, while his demeanor bespoke defiance. There was something wrong here. Philip took one last look at Pausanius, waved his hand and dismissed the bodyguard.

As the now relieved Pausanius left, Philip signaled one of Alexander's Companions. The youth, delicately featured and finely muscled, jumped up to the podium and stood at attention. Philip could not help but notice how handsome the soldier was. But he also marked the hard lines of the war-veteran that were barely concealed by the still elastic skin of the young man. This soldier was a warrior. Philip did not doubt that. He would be perfect for the job.

"Follow him. Night and day", ordered Philip.

The Companion, his face expressionless, turned and walked through the throne room and out the far door. So silently did he move that Philip was not really aware of his departure until he felt the momentary draft from the opening and closing door.

Philip leaned back in his throne. He stroked his forehead with his right hand. The pain was still there.

"I do not think I will live to see my grandchildren," sighed Philip.

"You said something my King."

Philip was taken aback at the immediate response. Alexander had trained his men to razor sharpness. He looked over at the guard and shook his head in a negative reply. Immersed in thought he sat there as immobile as a slab of marble.

Olympias plots with Kathos

"Bring me Kathos," snapped the queen to her servant. The boy, barely a teenager, did not move. Olympias could not tell if he was scared, confused or just stupid. "Now, not tomorrow!" roared the queen, her powerful voice sounding odd coming from such a small body. The boy wheeled and ran headlong from her bedchamber.

Olympias grunted, her frustration too great to be articulated with any civility. She was sick of dealing with the morons who passed for slaves now attached to her person. This little joke of Philip's was designed to purposely drive her insane. Olympias would not stand for it much longer.

Glancing around, Olympias assessed her new situation. This suite was smaller than her last one and although tastefully appointed, did not reflect her character. Laying out her robes for cleaning and pressing were two girls, the first probably fourteen or fifteen years old, the second was probably a pre-teen. The older one had been born with a split lip, which when combined with her rotund shape and low intelligence, made her extremely unattractive. Whoever had assigned the slave to her had done it intentionally so Olympias could not include her personal attendants in her perverted sexual liaisons. Olympias hated to admit it, but it had worked. She was repulsed by the girl's ugliness. The second girl, little more than a child, was different. She was slim, with long dark hair, more auburn than brown. The child was finely featured and would one day probably be a beautiful woman. Yet in her own way she was as odd as her co-worker. Olympias had rarely seen such an emotionally destitute person. The girl never talked, and refused, even after repeated cajoling, to look her in the face. She was dutiful, listened well and was able to anticipate Olympias' needs in advance of the actual order. Obviously, the girl possessed a great intelligence but she chose to not demonstrate it. So aloof was this slave that even Olympias chose not to challenge her. It was not because Olympias felt any sympathy for the child: it was simply that to mentally terrorize someone, one needed for the victim to be afraid. This slave girl feared nothing--not even death. Consequently she was left alone by all including Olympias.

The tapping on the door was barely audible. Olympias, her senses honed to animal-like keenness, not only heard the faint knocking but also identified it as that of the slave boy she had sent to fetch Kathos. She gathered her robes about her, called out for the slave to let himself and Kathos in, and in her most imperious manner strode to the middle of the room and awaited her 'guest'.

Olympias had not seen Kathos for years. When he walked into the room her nose crinkled in disgust. He had not changed.

The queen assessed the man standing in front of her. Kathos was evil embodied. From his youth, when he had, through perfidy and slander, managed to destroy the unity of one of the oldest aristocratic houses in Pella to his later days as a bodyguard and confidant to Philip's father, his influence was felt throughout the kingdom. Kathos and the nefariaous muleskinners he would employ were indispensable to the fratricidal coalitions fighting to establish power bases within the rapidly expanding empire. There was no assignment too immoral, no deed too nefarious for the diabolic Kathos. He sought no honor. His reward was drawn from the act itself. The malevolent genius that was Kathos savored the debauchery of his most heinous actions as if they were fine wine. And what Olympias had planned for him would utilize his unique talents to their full potential.

Pella, Delphi, 336 B.C.

Dioxippus overcomes a challenge

He rubbed the back of his knuckles. The strong massaging action helped relieve the cramping. He took a deep breath, vainly trying to control the accelerated beating of his heart. People were talking to him but all he could hear was an annoying buzz. He shook his head once. The sounds did not become any clearer. Slowly, he raised his right hand so that it rested on his chest. His heart pounded, the force so great that he was sure the organ would rend his chest like some escaping beast. He turned his head and looked down. Fotis was feverishly applying a medicinal paste to his shin. Did the little man not hear it? The noise of his beating heart deafened him. Fotis, engrossed in his job acted as if he was oblivious to it all. Dioxippus jerked his leg angrily. The diminutive gnome snarled as he reeled backwards. Yet as soon as he regained his balance, Fotis went right back to massaging the leg, trying to make up the time lost with his uncooperative host. The object of his ministrations was still engrossed with the very perceptible rhythm emanating from his 'stithos'. Dioxippus could not help but think that maybe his body would surrender before his mind did.

"Dios...Dios!"

From somewhere far away, he could hear a muffled cry. He could not quite make it out. It did sound strangely familiar.

"Fotis, look at his eyes. They are open but he cannot see," yelled Piros to Barba Fotis. "Bring me that urn, no, not that one, the other one" instructed Piros, pointing at a jar still sealed. "Hurry!"

Fotis scampered to the container Piros was pointing at, picked it up and brought it to the now agitated trainer.

With scarcely any effort Piros peeled back the wax and papyrus seal off the clay urn. Immediately an acrid scent polluted the air. Holding his breath, Piros shoved the jar right under the nose of Dioxippus. The biting odor tore through the nostrils and sinuses of the near unconscious pankratiatist. His head snapped away reflexively but there was no escape from the demons fleeing the confines of Piros' urn. Dioxippus wheeled his head away again, this time in the opposite direction, vainly trying to avoid the fumes. Tears welled up in his eyes and he started to cough. The extreme discomfort coupled with a growing fear jerked his body up until he was halfway off the bench he had been sitting on. He was stopped before he could fully rise by one of Piros' thickly muscled arms. So, immobilized, suffering intolerable pain, Dioxippus readied himself for surrender.

"Dios, can you hear me now? The referee returns. Get up man Your opponent awaits and I think he has recovered. Dios!"

The fog clouding his brain, impermeable to his efforts had been dissipated by the concoction from Piros' urn. He could now hear his mentor and he sensed the extreme urgency in his voice.

The match was beginning again. Now he knew where he was and what he was doing. This was a qualifying fight for the games. The Olympics. And that man, sitting across the ring, glowering at him like some rabid dog was trying to prevent him from competing later by systematically destroying him. The thoughts now rushed back to Dioxippus. That brute had used every dirty and illegal technique to disrupt his attack. He had gouged, poked and bitten until even the referee had been forced to whip him with the stick that all officials used for enforcement. When that had failed the referee had called for a break. At that moment of disengagement, Dioxippus' adversary had blindsided him with a stiff right arm. The referee had been quick to smack and then chastise the perpetrator for his unsportsmanlike conduct. Unfortunately, the haranguing from the official did not alleviate the damage to Dioxippus. He remained standing but there was no vigor left in the young man. The referee, breaking with the normal sequence of events, called time so Dioxippus could recover his composure. For a few panic-stricken moments it appeared he would not. Piros' witches' brew had cleared his head just in time. Dioxippus would continue.

"Kick low, punch high and come up under his right side and take him down with a leg trip. Make sure you come down on top of him. Straddle his lower back with your legs positioned wide so he cannot roll you," said Piros, his instructions spoken so rapidly that to Dioxippus they were one breathless slur of words.

Dioxippus stepped into the ring. He glanced around him. Few spectators attended qualifying matches. The stillness of the setting was not representative of the ferocious activity about to resume in the ring. Dioxippus heard his opponent snort. He looked at him, analytically. Petros was built along the lines of Piros, not tall, not short. His shoulders sloped rapidly, giving the impression of slimness although in actuality he outweighed Dioxippus by twenty pounds. Petros had short, bowlegs with quadriceps the size of Dioxippus' waist. Low kicks would not have an effect quick enough for Dioxippus to capitalize on. He decided to continue with the long-range jabbing attack that he had used. This time he would be prepared for the unexpected and the illegal.

The referee, a slight man, dressed in a three quarter length chiton, contrasted sharply with the two pankratiatists standing on either side of him. He looked and felt like a sapling between oaks. To a spectator it might have appeared ludicrous that such a puny man would be able to control the free-for all that passed for a competitive sport. Yet he was always called to officiate at the most important events. Never had his final judgment been overruled by the sanctioning heads of states. His confidence in himself eliminated the indecision of some of his colleagues. Knowing that, competitors invariably asked for him. No man, living or dead had ever accused him of impropriety. But this Bycean, Petros, had tried even his tremendous resolve. In a hundred matches, some even ending in death, he had not seen such a flagrant disregard for even the most basic of rules. He should disqualify Dioxippus' opponent. And he normally would have. This match however was different. To an athlete the caliber of Dioxippus a win by disqualification was tantamount to being labeled a coward. He would never allow it.

The three men had reached the center of the circle. Once again the referee explained the rules, few as they were. For emphasis he waved his official's stick, warning both fighters of the consequences of any illegalities during the bout.

As the referee spoke, Dioxippus stared into the eyes of his adversary. He could not have been more than six to eight inches away from him yet he could not see his reflection in the pupils of his enemy. Normally, his image would be clear. This time all that was visible was a dull gray film coating the most lifeless eyes he had ever seen. Petros' face was a blank but not like those unfortunates born devoid of intelligence. Petros' eyes showed no care, no humanness, no life. Dioxippus now knew that he was in real danger.

The referee gave a hand signal. The combatants stepped back from each other. A moment later, the referee made a popping sound with his tongue against his cheek. Instantly, the two pankratiatists charged forward.

Before Dioxippus could take two steps forward, he felt two rapid kicks, one to the back of his right calf and the other to the side of his left thigh. Neither was hard enough to cause any injury or real pain. He slid his feet forward and raised his own leg to respond in kind. Barely had his left foot left the ground when it was jammed tight by Petros' extended leg. Reflexively, Dioxippus started to move his other leg. Again his leg was jammed into its chambered position, effectively neutralizing his most feared weapons. Frustrated by Petros' strong defense, Dioxippus leaned his torso forward and released two quick, hard jabs at the face of his competitor.

Caught slightly off balance, Petros could not duck both punches. The first clipped his ear, cutting it across the lower lobe. The second punch missed completely. Petros countered with an uppercut to the exposed ribs of Dioxippus. He felt his knuckles contract sharply as they impacted on the thick mass of abdominal muscle and bone. He heard a short hiss of air as the diaphragm released itself. Barely had his fist made contact before his right knee, chambered tightly, rushed from the ground to meet the face of the now bent over Dioxippus.

Dioxippus, pained by the blow to the ribs, could not help himself from bending at the waist. Petros' knee, already in the air slammed into his shoulder. The pain was excruciating. Stabs from nerves consumed with fire seared into his neck. Involuntarily, he closed his eyes. His collarbone had been broken.

Sensing the injury, Petros brought his palm down hard on Dioxippus' fractured bone. But Dioxippus, overcome with nausea had fallen to his knees. Petros' onrushing strike ended beyond its planned point of contact, lessening the force of the impact. Nevertheless, Dioxippus felt new, even sharper pains tearing through his upper torso. Positioned on all fours, his good arm bearing the most weight, Dioxippus, broken, beaten, waited for the referee to stop the fight. It was over. The referee moved forward. No signal had come from Dioxippus signifying surrender. It was not possible for any human being to continue with such a serious injury against an opponent as fierce and determined as Petros.

Petros refused to wait for Dioxippus' surrender. As his hand slammed into the injured shoulder, he was already snapping his right leg forward into Dioxippus' kidneys. The force of the kick into such a vital organ crumpled Dioxippus into a rolling ball of agony. Petros leaped at him like a snarling leopard. A sense of survival being all that remained to Dioxippus, he added a revolution to his roll, momentarily putting some space between him and the diving Petros. His brain had cleared enough to recognize that Petros would kill him if he did not signal defeat. He glanced at the referee. In that briefest of contact, Dioxippus saw the sorrow and concern in the referee's eyes. This fight was over. He began to raise his hand.

Barely had the movement begun when a tremendous force knocked him back down. Petros, in one fluid motion had recovered from his fall and thrown his body at the rising Dioxippus. Unable to avoid the human projectile, Dioxippus had absorbed the heavy impact and in the process been smashed back into the hard ground. Pain so intense that it drove Dioxippus to tears coursed through his body like burning lava. But this time, through the torment, anger, white-hot, suppressed the anguish. Dioxippus, entangled in the arms and legs of the predatory Petros, decided that live or die he would not admit defeat.

Petros had somehow positioned himself across the upper body of Dioxippus so that his forehead was buried in the space between the shoulder and neck. His arms had seized the trunk and were trying to turn Dioxippus over. The dirt, mixed with the oil and sweat on both men precluded getting a good grip. Dioxippus however, knew that to continue wrestling was fruitless with one side of his body basically immobilized. Out of desperation as much as strategy, he freed his good arm and without hesitation grabbed a handful of Petros' curly black hair and with all the strength left in his battered form, yanked hard, twisting his wrist at the same time. Petros' head was lifted away from the protective confines of his opponent's body. Within the space of half a heartbeat, Dioxippus slammed his forehead into the nose of Petros. The reaction was instantaneous. Petros' nose, now a bloody pulp, caused his eyes to well with tears, momentarily blinding him. Dioxippus raised his good arm and like a blacksmith's hammer descending, struck Petros on the upper cheekbone, breaking more bone. Petros roared in pain. Dioxippus, renewed with a torrent of rushing adrenalin, twisted free of the clutching Petros, rolled once and rose to a standing position. Petros, blinded, could still make out the shape of the erect Dioxippus. Crazed by his injuries, furious at having a sure victory slip away from him, he lurched toward Dioxippus, bellowing fearsome obscenities. He had not taken two steps before Dioxippus himself stepped toward him, turned sideways and in one graceful motion pulled up his leg and with flashing speed thrust it out. Petros, warned by some remote part of his brain of the danger of this kicking phenomena's arsenal, raised his arms to protect his head and chest. But Dioxippus knowing that the high chambering of his leg gave the impression of a kick to the head aimed low. The heel, catapulted out of its tight position, tore into Petros' legs just above the kneecap. The force of the blow exploded on the fragile bones, cartilage and tendons comprising the joint. Shards of bone ripped through the skin, sending spurts of dark blood splattering over Petros and Dioxippus. Petros screamed, his pain knowing no limits. Dioxippus stepped back. His adversary, bawling incoherently rolled on the ground crying out for help, begging for anything, even death, to stop the pain.

Shocked by the action of the last few moments, the referee signaled Dioxippus the winner and immediately called for Petros' trainers to lend assistance to their pankratiatist. Piros and Fotis also responded immediately as they rushed to the barely vertical Dioxippus. With scarcely any effort, Piros picked up his young friend, and as tenderly as carrying a bird with a broken wing, brought him to the side of the ring where he gently laid him down. Although the air was hot, the shock of the injury had started Dioxippus shaking so Fotis laid a cloth over his naked body.

Piros examined the broken collarbone. The break had been clean and his practiced eye told him there were no fragments lodged anywhere. He turned to Fotis and said, "Hold him down firmly. Take that rag. Yes, that one. Roll it up and put it in his mouth. When I count to three, hold him tight."

Still in shock, barely aware of what was transpiring, Dioxippus felt something put in his mouth. He panicked when his breathing became restricted and he began to struggle. He looked up at Piros. All he could see were his trainer's eyes, full of tears. Dioxippus heard some sounds from his friend and then lightning struck his body. He shrieked. Then he fainted.

Phylia

"That bastard can rot in Hades as far as I am concerned. Who does he think he is giving me orders like some dimwitted slave? His time will come. And I will be there waiting!"

Phylia barely looked up. The Queen was ranting again. Best to ignore her when she was in this kind of mood. Surviving in Olympias' household was simple...see nothing, hear nothing, say nothing. Phylia looked down. Her hands were engaged in massaging and kneading the muscles and tendons in the Queen's feet. They were so small. The Queen was so small. Yet she had enough venom in her for ten women. And now, angry at some injustice, real or imagined, perpetrated by her husband Philip, she was letting loose the most spiteful, vitriolic harangue that Phylia had ever heard. She bowed her head even lower as if she could conceal herself by reducing the space her body occupied.

"One-eyed, crippled, uncouth dirt-farmer. That's all you are Philip. You may own Hellas but you will always be a Macedonian, one of a people barely removed from the caves they used to inhabit in the mountains. Conqueror, huh! Any moron with a bad temper can ram a sword into some unsuspecting victim. He thinks he is so special because of the, the...damn it, he makes me crazy!"

Phylia was beginning to have trouble holding on to Olympias' feet. Her tirade had so agitated her that she was squirming in her lounge making it impossible for Phylia to retain control of her oil-covered feet. Phylia pulled back, waiting patiently for the Queen to calm down. She did not raise her head

Olympias stopped to take a breath. Looking around her, suspecting even the walls, her gaze remained steadfast as it scanned the room, daring anyone foolish enough to spy on her to report to the king. Except for the elaborate folds of the hanging fabrics decorating the room, it was bare. It was also devoid of any life (except for Olympias and Phylia); plant, animal or human. Accentuated by the predominance of white, the sterility of the Queen's chambers was overwhelming. And in spite of the excessive sexual adventures still taking place within these walls, the room still lacked a basic humanity. Even Olympias, devoid of most emotions, save anger, could feel although not identify the tangent missing from this equation. Fortunately for Olympias, she was not subject to the wild paranoias of the other treasonous courtiers. Consequently, she dismissed quite quickly those thoughts of the paranormal. She stared at Phylia.

From that first day that Piros had mysteriously appeared at the gates of the capital with the young warrior and this girl, Olympias had been fascinated with Phylia. Never had she seen a child so beautiful yet so dead. The vacant eyes, the monosyllabic speech pattern, the refusal to be cowed by a superior all these made Phylia irresistible to the snake worshipping, sex-crazed fanatic that was Olympias. She immediately interceded with the King to have her placed under her care. Philip, not wanting to challenge his wife while he was secretly courting Cleopatra spoke to Piros. The pankratiatist, wanted for murder by the Athenians, and suddenly encumbered by two children felt it best to leave Phylia with the Queen. At least with her he felt that the young girl would be taken care of. Olympias had been ecstatic. But her joy was short-lived. She found that she could not frighten or intimidate this slave. And although her beauty made her wanted by the many lovers, male and female, that Olympias entertained, her apparent removal from the human race made her so cold, so spiritually unattainable, that Olympias did not include her in her sexual sorties.

Phylia started massaging the feet again. Olympias, her eyes narrowed to mere slits, continued to stare at the girl. In some ways, Phylia reminded the queen of herself, beautiful yet not of this world. In Phylia, Olympias saw the absence of emotion that so dominated her own personality. To be ruthless, truly ruthless, love, loyalty and trust had to be eschewed for treachery, ambition and pleasure. Only Alexander was deserving of anything more.

Olympias was so engrossed with Phylia and her own musings that she did not notice the faint knocking at her door. Phylia ceased her ministrations and looked up at the queen. The movement startled Olympias out of her trance and with a motion that would have been missed by most, bade Phylia to open the door.

The young slave girl glided to the door. Putting her head sideways against the aged, oak timbers, she called out to the person on the other side. Olympias, sitting not five human lengths from the entrance herself, heard not a thing. Phylia's voice was as soft as the plaintive cry of a small bird. Nevertheless, the person on the other side of the door must have heard because a voice growled in reply. Phylia opened the door and let Pausanius in.

Even the queen was shocked. The proud warrior was no more. Instead there stood a decrepit, over-indulged sycophant whose purpose in life had gone from serving a king on a battlefield to begging for deviant sexual thrills from Olympias. Pausanius, by nature a driven man, had allowed the attributes which made him a great soldier propel him blindly into the world of the sexual and moral degenerate. To reduce the mental torture of conflicting needs, Pausanius drank, ate and whored to such excesses that his constitution was ravaged. And the more he saw himself slip, the more his self-loathing forced him to continue the punishing regimen. For the want of fleeting sexual gratification, Pausanius had reduced himself to a level lower than the scum who haunted the alleys and the piers.

"Pausanius, you do me honour with your presence. May I have the girl bring you something to eat, drink?" asked the queen in her most gracious tone.

Pausanius rubbed his chin with the back of his hand. The stubble from a three days' growth of beard scratched the soft skin. He licked his lips and turning towards Phylia grunted something the young girl interpreted to be a yes. She immediately went to a beautifully cast bronze urn and prepared a cup of wine for Pausanius.

"You have come for a reason my lord?" queried the queen with just a touch of sarcastic emphasis on the last two words.

Pausanius stopped watching Phylia and turned to Olympias. He took a deep breath, simultaneously straightening his shoulders and trying his best to present a military air. Coughing once, desperately trying to cover his nervousness, Pausanius said, "My queen, it is with humbleness that I make this request."

Olympias' interest was piqued. What could this shell of a man want from her--other than her pleasures?

"The king no longer considers me a Companion. I am ignored, and of late, belittled by those that were once my inferiors. I now know that I said stupid things many months ago. And even though I may have been critical of Philip, never did I speak treason. Furthermore, the lifestyle I have pursued for the last while I now find...not suitable to a soldier." Pausanius had to catch himself with his last few words. He had meant to say offensive but that would only prove to be critical of the queen and at this moment he needed her goodwill.

"You wish me to speak to Philip on your behalf. Consider it done", stated Olympias, almost obsequious in her manner.

Pausanius smiled. With a flourishing bow, a silent thank you, he turned and left the room, nodding to Phylia who was standing there with his undrunk wine.

Olympias watched the door close. She waved Phylia over to her. "Get the King. I want him here now," ordered Olympias brusquely.

Recognizing the tone, Phylia ran to the door, barely opened it before squeezing through and in a flash was gone from the room.

Finding herself alone, the queen began to think aloud. "I think it is time for Pausanius to pay back the favors I have so generously granted him the last few months." Olympias looked around, almost expecting someone to answer her. "Philip, I think the time has come for Alexander to sit on your throne. In fact my beloved," Olympias spat out the word *beloved*. "I foresee an imminent and probably permanent separation about to occur." The most radiant smile lit up the queen's face. For the first time in a long period she felt herself as young as a child. If things worked out, soon she would be the real queen of an empire limited only by her son's vision.

Olympias was moving about the room as she spoke to herself, gathering up shoes, veils and other items she would need to go out in. Dressing herself quickly, she took a look over her shoulder at the room and then exited.

Outside in the great hall, dozens of slaves, courtiers, politicians and soldiers milled about. All were scrambling, running errands, seeking favors, presenting petitions, doing whatever was necessary to further their own interests. And what proved to be the most fascinating to Olympias, now watching this ordered chaos, was that Philip handled almost all the daily administration himself. Give the bastard credit she thought, he knew how to run a government. This was one aspect of the kingdom Olympias had overlooked. She would have to educate Alexander in the more mundane responsibilities of leadership.

So engrossed were the people in the hall that Olympias stood unnoticed. This struck her as odd, as first there was not a single woman (other than herself) present, secondly, she was a queen and she expected to be noticed. Normally, this situation would have angered her. She smiled. Moving forward, her steps so light, her body so small that she was almost elfin-like, she walked amongst the teeming mass, waiting to savor their reaction.

At first no one noticed Olympias. Within moments that changed. First one, then two, then many slaves fell to the ground prostrating themselves, praying fervently that they had not inadvertently incurred the wrath of the notoriously unforgiving queen. So afraid were they of her that not one dared lift his head to look her in the face. The rest of the crowd, although not slaves, could not help but be impressed by the obvious sublimation.

Some nodded, most bowed and all, royal supplicants or not acknowledged the presence of Olympias. In fact, some went so far as to verbally grovel in front of her. None of this went unnoticed by the slyly smiling Olympias. These morons feared her. She liked that.

One man stood aside however. He ignored the tableau unfolding before him. He felt embarrassed by the actions of his compatriots. Even the behavior of the slaves for some unaccountable reason made him blush. Why did these strong, able men reduce themselves to such low levels because a woman, a puny, out of favor one at that, walked into their midst? What was Olympias after all? She bred like any other mare. Not even as well. She had only the one son. And he was what he was because of Philip. Not this bitch. So why should he, Attalus, bow to her? Philip, and now Attalus' niece, Cleopatra were the real rulers. Now that he was back from Asia, it would not be difficult to have someone slit Olympias' throat: they would blame a jilted lover, which would calm Alexander, and Philip and his court would be rid of her forever. Attalus smiled.

Olympias had noticed that all save Attalus had come to her. She knew that now that his niece was sleeping with Philip he thought himself safe from her. A foolish mistake. Olympias would make Attalus pay and pay dearly for his lack of respect. Even his re-assignment to Asia Minor might work in her favor. Olympias smiled in return, her almond shaped eyes lending her expression a distinctively feline appearance. She would have loved to stay and verbally spar with the general but she had more important things to attend to. Breaking herself free from the still floor-scraping slaves, she gathered her robe about her shoulder with just enough flourish to show her royalty and turning away from Attalus, left. That last, small rearranging of facial muscles had effectively transmitted the message she wanted Attalus to be left with. His time would come.

For now, she had to hurry. There was no telling how long Kathos would remain in Pella. A man like him was reviled by all those with even the tiniest shred of decency. Only evil followed him and his sorry band of cohorts. Consequently, their stay in any one place was usually limited. Only their 'clients' interceding for them with the authorities allowed them within twenty leagues of any city-state in Hellas. But when people such as Olympias sent a message, all pathways were immediately free of all obstacles--physical, legal or moral. Kathos was thus saved the inconvenience of trial and punishment. And in this case the queen had made him and his partners very comfortable for the last few months. However, constant harassment from local authorities coupled with extreme boredom had put the itch into him and he was ready to leave. That had necessitated sending a message to Olympias. She now realized that the time had come for a decision to be made concerning her son's future.

Olympias came to the door of Kathos' lodging. She rapped hard. Suddenly, a hairy arm, as thick as one of her boas encircled her throat and the point of a very sharp knife forced its way through her chiton until it rested forcibly on her rib cage. Breathing was next to impossible, and the metal being forced on her torso caused extreme pain. A tear forced itself out of her left eye, leaving a faint trail down across her cheek. Yet she refused to show fear to her potential murderer.

The door opened. Standing there naked, unabashed was Kathos. Behind him stood a young boy, just entering pubescence. He too was naked and horribly beaten. Even Olympias, inured to even the basest sexual perversions could not stomach the excessive, pointless violence that Kathos reveled in. But with a knife at her ribs and an arm choking the life out of her she was less concerned with Kathos' lover than with her own salvation.

Kathos smiled, his rotten teeth poisoning the air with their fetidity. He just looked at his bodyguard and that was enough for the queen to be released.

Olympias gasped once or twice and straightening her clothing (while surreptitiously rubbing the spot where the knife had been held) took a step forward. The difference in height between her and Kathos was over a head. To Olympias it did not matter. She angrily thrust her chin up and prepared to chide him.

This woman has nerve, thought Kathos. Neither his obvious nakedness nor her proximity to death appeared to fluster the queen. Kathos knew how dangerous he was. How dangerous was she?

"Well...is this simian going to stand behind me for the whole time I am here?" demanded Olympias of Kathos. "And is it necessary to remind you that I am a queen and expected to be treated like one? Do you understand?"

"Ohh...I would be most happy to treat you like a queen. Which one do you fancy? Lytheran? Argolian?" replied a still smiling Kathos.

Olympias shivered. Both those queens had been horribly tortured then killed. Officially, no one knew who the murderers were. Olympias did remember that both kings had remarried rather quickly. Perhaps it was best to get to the matter at hand. Threats were counterproductive. For now.

"The job is ready to be done," said Olympias.

"You know my terms," replied Kathos. He reached down, grasped his engorging penis and said, "My pleasure."

Dioxippus refuses to succumb

"You cannot continue to expect that all your opponents will observe the rules as carefully as you," said Piros. He finished tying the sling supporting Dioxippus' shoulder. "This should do until the bone heals. It may be wise to forego your next match even though Kefallas will not arrive for a few more days from Sparta."

Dioxippus grimaced as the tightening sling put painful pressure on his collarbone. Without looking up at his mentor he replied, "I will not pull out of the Olympics. I have waited my whole life for these games. Piros do not misinterpret what I am saying. I do not want to be a god or hero or anything else. But how can I give up when I am so close. You said the break was clean and would heal quickly. You are a magician when it comes to medicine. Find a cure for me. Please..." Dioxippus' voice trailed off into a choked sob. He could not control his emotions at this juncture of his life.

Piros took half a step back to survey what he had done. His Dios was no longer a gawky adolescent. Here was a young man, full of promise, desire and potential. Here also was a young man whose life was one of loss. And now, he had to see Dioxippus give everything up once again because of a vicious injury. The cruelty of the situation bothered him greatly. He did not know whether to offer sacrifices to the Greek gods or to pray to the Hebrew God of his parents. This was a quagmire with no escape. Piros thoughts were on what would his father have done? The ebony giant who had sired Piros would have told him to solve the problem and not expect outside help, physical or spiritual.

"Piros...tell me that I can heal enough to fight Kefallas," implored Dioxippus.

An idea struck Piros. He had heard of a compound used by the Persians to alleviate pain during surgery. From what he could remember, when this paste was applied to the wound it caused sharp, smarting pains but within a few heartbeats it deadened the skin and nerves surrounding the area. If Piros could apply a similar concoction to Dioxippus' shoulder before the fight began, it was possible to minimize the pain enough for Dioxippus to participate. And if Dioxippus defeated his adversary quickly, any further damage to the collarbone would be minimal. He would have to go to the market and seek out the Arab traders. Piros inadvertently smiled.

"You can do it," responded an elated Dioxippus.

"I will try. Rest now. I will be back as quickly as I can," said Piros. He strode over to the doors, looked back once and left.

Dioxippus sighed once then shifted his body repeatedly until he found a comfortable position for his wounded shoulder. The movement sparked a small, sharp pain. Reflexively, Dioxippus gritted his teeth. The pain subsided quickly and Dioxippus finally began to relax.

He began to analyze the contest he had just emerged victorious from. There was no question that Petros had been the toughest fighter he had ever come up against. The techniques he had used had all been chosen for their destructive powers. The pankration, when fought by people such as Petros, was transformed from a healthy, sporting event into a melee resembling more the dog pits than the Olympics. Dioxippus winced at the simile. The pankration, especially at this level, had undergone changes, some subtle, some not so subtle, since the glory days of Piros. No longer were the pankratiatists satisfied to wear the olive wreath. Now they wanted financial compensation, incentives and bonuses, depending on how well they did in the games. This crass commercialization of an athletic event as pure as the pankration jaded the honorable Piros even though he had to admit that the giving of monies to the winners had attracted many more people into the Olympiad. When Piros had competed, he would have had to fight no more than three times in two days to win the wreath. Dioxippus on the other hand had already fought twice, the second a life threatening contest, just to qualify for the Olympics. To reach the finals he would have to fight three more times. With this sore shoulder, Dioxippus did not feel too self-assured at this time.

Dioxippus looked around. He had not noticed that he was alone. Fotis must have gone with Piros. Dioxippus swore softly. He was extremely thirsty with no one to fetch water for him. He smiled ashamedly. Who was he to expect to be waited on? Piros would have had a fit if he knew that Dioxippus would sit there until somebody served him. The young pankratiatist swung himself slowly off the couch. He planted his feet firmly and stood erect. All his muscles had stiffened and for a few steps he had difficulty maintaining his balance. He shuffled over to the terra cotta pot that contained the water and with his good arm and hand lifted it to his mouth. As the pot was raised, Dioxippus noticed two things: first, the container was extremely light; second, there was no sloshing of fluids. Dioxippus shook the urn once, noticed that there was only a negligible amount of water in it. So muttering, he dropped his arm to his side, leaving the urn resting against his hip and outer thigh and proceeded to the door. Dioxippus would have to go to the well himself if he was to drink water that day.

Although Pella was the capital of Macedonia, it was still relatively backward in comparison to Thebes and Athens. The water supply was still drawn from wells, most of which were located somewhat outside the city gates. In Pella itself, there were a few wells that were considered communal, and it was to one of these that Dioxippus made his way. He did not mind the chore because these communal wells were also great places to catch up on the news of the community, city and empire. They were also great places to hear the latest gossip, rumors and innuendos. To Dioxippus, this contact with the bawdy, robust people of the Macedonian empire was worth all the pain and discomfort that this walk exerted on his shoulder.

As Dioxippus neared the well he usually used, he noticed a large number of people milling about in a loosely constructed circle. They appeared to have their attention focused on something occurring within that circle. From their laughter and catcalls, Dioxippus guessed that "the event" was at the center of that group of people.

Suddenly, a scream pierced the air and then a yell, angry, defiant and pained. Almost simultaneously, the circle of people opened up and a man, his chiton torn or cut into several barely united sections came running out. Blood was also spattered on his garment although where it had come from could not be ascertained in the few, brief seconds that Dioxippus glimpsed him.

Dioxippus stood there unsure of what to think or do. He looked back at the open circle and saw that standing there, by herself, was a girl so beautiful that the gods must be jealous. Dioxippus was transfixed. The girl had long blonde hair that shimmered when the sun caught the naturally curled tresses. Her face was extremely fine-featured, almost royal in its bearing. The girl was not tall but neither was she short. Her posture, her demeanor both suggested better breeding. Yet the clothing the girl wore was more reminiscent of a slave rather than an aristocrat.

The mass of people started to disperse. Dioxippus collared one man and asked, "What happened down there by the well?"

The farmer took one look at what appeared to him a giant and said, ever so quietly, "That girl, a slave really, just carved up that sorry excuse for a man like he was a pig, ready to be served. Never have I seen such skill in the use of a knife. It flew through her fingers as if it had a life of its own. Incredible." And with that the farmer hurried away.

Dioxippus was perplexed. What happened did not make any sense. Had the girl been attacked? Why were the other people so lackadaisical in their attitude? For answers, he would have to go look himself. Admittedly, he was very keen to meet the girl that had sent such a big man running.

Dioxippus weaved his way through the talking, yelling, laughing crowd. He alternately twisted this way and that, trying desperately to keep his shoulder from being bumped. So focused was he on protecting his wound, he did not see the girl until he was almost on top of her. She turned just as Dioxippus was about to bump into her. The collision, although not hard, jarred Dioxippus' shoulder, forcing a painful grunt out of him. The girl, realizing that somehow she had managed to hurt this man, apologized profusely.

Dioxippus did not hear a word. He stood mesmerized by the vision in front of him. When her talking finally broke the trance he had fallen into, he blushed and managed to stammer some sort of reply. And for the life of him he did not know what he said.

The girl, or rather the young woman, saw his uneasiness and was charmed by it. After the fiasco with Kathos' bodyguard, this pleasant diversion was a godsend. She had to admit she found this stranger very appealing with his extraordinary height, large frame and for a Greek, rare blue eyes. His modest manner was also a quality that immediately endeared him to her. If only he would speak clearly.

"I, I'm sorry. I did not mean to bump into you. It was just that all these people."

Panthea interrupted Dioxippus, "Apologies are not necessary. We both collided with each other."

Dioxippus found himself somewhat surprised at the erudite manner in which this young woman spoke to him. Immediately he chided himself for assuming that because the person in front of him was dressed poorly that she was also educated poorly. Obviously this was not the case.

"I am Panthea. You are..."

"Dioxippus. Some call me Dios."

"I have not seen you here before. Are you a freeman?" asked Panthea.

The boldness of the question was not lost on Dioxippus. Most women would never ask a man if he was a slave or not. In some social circles, Panthea's manner would probably be considered rude. Dioxippus however found it appealing.

"I was made a free man by my master" replied Dioxippus, his stomach knotting with the recollection of his former lord.

"I too am not owned although I do serve another..." continued Panthea. "I have been in Pella for about five years. And since I have been treated well, I have not left."

"What of your husband, children?" asked Dioxippus. His breathing labored as he anticipated the answer.

"Surely I do not look that old, that matronly," laughed Panthea, barely able to control herself. In fact, her laughter acted as a release for all the earlier tension, turning her initial giggling into raucous guffawing.

Dioxippus at first blushed, thinking he had inadvertently insulted his new friend. The almost hysterical reaction convinced him otherwise and unable to help himself joined in the mirth. So hard were they both laughing that the people milling about them turned and moved away. Some even rotated fingers near their heads, indicating that the two young people had gone insane. Dioxippus and Panthea were of course oblivious to it.

"Whh, why are you here?" asked Panthea, choking back further laughter and wiping a tear from her face with the back of her hand.

"I cannot remember the last time I giggled like a child," gasped Dioxippus. He began to choke and cough on the laughter.

"No, no, no. Not again," ordered Panthea, trying to keep from reacting in kind to Dioxippus.

"Oh, come now. We have so few things to laugh about. Me, I've been miserable all morning. When I finally come for water I see a crowd, a man running and...you."

At the mention of the earlier incident, Panthea turned red again. It was with anger not embarrassment or shyness this time. Dioxippus immediately noticed the unease and regretted bringing the subject up.

"That animal thought that because I came for water unescorted that I was no better than a cheap whore. He refused to leave me alone and when some of the other men tried to ask him to go he turned on them like a rabid dog. I was frightened because I did not want to see an innocent servant or slave pay the penalty for this beast's madness. So I implored him to leave, debasing myself for the greater good, so to speak. He refused to let me be and probably saw my begging as a sign of weakness. For men like this, weakness is an aphrodisiac. He began to clutch at me grabbing my robe and making me spill the water I had fetched from the well. That is when I introduced him to my closest friend." And faster than a hummingbird's wing, a tiny, razor sharp blade flew from somewhere in the folds of Panthea's clothing and came to rest on the underside of Dioxippus' chin. "A great equalizer."

Dioxippus had not moved. He was as immobile as granite. He could feel the sharp edge of the blade stretching the tender skin of his throat. He refused to show any emotion of any kind. He stared into the eyes of Panthea, seeing his reflection dance amongst the glittering images contained therein. Strangely, Dioxippus felt himself more relaxed more free than he had been in a long time. This proximity to death liberated him from the constraints of life. He smiled.

Panthea had not meant to put Dioxippus on a life and death defensive. She had been merely trying to demonstrate the effectiveness of a well-handled knife and how she had used it to frighten that pig from earlier on. But now she could not move. The knife lay there, forcing itself on Dioxippus as if it had a purpose of its own. She wanted to retract the weapon; it refused. The whole time her eyes were locked with Dioxippus'. There was no fear or even concern in his eyes. He was either very brave or very simple-minded. His smile remained engaged despite the palatable tenseness charging the air.

Suddenly, Dioxippus glanced away at something behind Panthea. The grip on the bone-handled knife relaxed...barely.

The breath inhaled did not have time to be exhaled. Panthea's wrist was twisted painfully, forcing her to one knee. How she was taken down, when Dioxippus saw the momentary lapse of concentration, she could not answer. Yet, here she now was, on one knee with no knife and her wrist in dire peril of being broken. She looked up, not knowing what she would see.

Dioxippus was still smiling. He released Panthea's wrist from the lock, and with his other hand helped her to her feet. He had used a painful controlling technique but had been careful not to injure Panthea in any way. He would never hurt her.

As Panthea was pulled to her feet, she did not know if she should cry, scream, get angry or just accept what had just occurred. Dioxippus' beaming face, not condescending at all, answered her question. Panthea grinned.

Dioxippus said nothing. It was somehow understood between them. Both could be harbingers of death. Or both could come to care for one another. Dioxippus knew the answer.

He bent over picked up the two-handled hydria full of water by the one handle while Panthea, following his lead grasped the other handle. Together they turned and made their way silently to the home of Panthea's mistress. Not a step was taken on the journey where their eyes separated from each other. The bond had been forged.

Watching them move away from the well area was an old man. Seated, partially obscured by a low wall, this wrinkled raisin of an ancient had been an observer of all the action today. He shook his head as he recalled what he had seen: a man almost skinned, another almost decapitated, a girl almost broken and stranger than all a love affair start. Odd.

Philip espouses on tactics

He was the last person he expected to see in the traders' quarters. After all, only foreigners and those dealers who sold imported goods of questionable legitimacy or targeted for very specific interests ever came to this dilapidated part of town. And none ever came, save a few extremely confident persons such as Piros, without a bodyguard. But there he was, conspicuously alone, examining weaponry from lands so far away that it would take years to make the trip there and back. Who knows, thought Piros, perhaps Philip generated his unusual often innovative military ideas by handling killing instruments foreign to him, discussing their use with their vendors or asking questions about military strategy in other places. No contemporary historian had yet discovered where or how Philip got the idea to lengthen the standard pike to fifteen feet and arrange his soldiers into an almost impenetrable phalanx. This rather simple idea had made the Macedonian infantry the best fighting unit in the known world. And what Piros most liked about Philip's 'invention' was that the casualties in the phalanx were extraordinarily low. Consequently, morale always remained high and the soldiers in those units thought themselves indestructible, furthering their effectiveness even more. Piros considered himself a tactician yet he knew that in Philip there existed a logistical genius. No general utilized his resources, both traditional and non-traditional as competently as the King. Save Alexander.

Philip had not seen Piros. He was completely engrossed with a bow of quite different design than a Greek one. As he hefted it, pulled its string and mentally weighed the arrows, he constantly asked the dark-skinned, black-haired trader how it was used. With great gesticulation, and few Greek words, the trader was able to indicate to Philip how the bow was used by the cavalry when in retreat. Philip was obviously impressed by the narration, and mimicking a turning rider twisted his trunk so he faced rearward and drew the bow right in the direction of the observing Piros.

Piros raised his eyebrows slightly. The querulous expression on his face appeared to amuse the King, as he returned the look with a smile. Piros nodded to his lord. He immediately advanced forward although he did not rush forth like some patronizing commoner or court boot licker. Philip had always wanted his soldiers to be honest and forthwith with him. False airs and other court buffoonery were inevitably rejected by the King. And Piros, one of his most faithful campaigners, had earned the right to a certain familiarity with Philip.

"Piros, have you heard such a thing? In this man's land, Parthia," Philip pointed at the beaming trader, "the cavalry disperses along the flanks of the enemy force, shoots its first barrage and then retreats. While they retreat, the bowmen turn around in their seats and fire their arrows over the hindquarters of their mounts. Incredible use of the cavalry, I must say. Hitting your enemy coming and going. What do you think, Piros?" asked the King.

"I am not sure. How accurate are these mounted archers? And I have yet to see a bow that can be handled in the manner you suggest. I think the Macedonian phalanx would make life very unhappy for these riders."

Philip grinned. There was nothing he enjoyed more than a debate on military strategy, especially with someone knowledgeable in the field of tactics. Philip's grin was not lost on Piros. He too enjoyed the intellectual exercise and was eager to pursue it.

"Imagine for a moment that the infantry is being attacked by this group. With our shields closed tight in our defensive posture, we are as tight as a shell from the shores of the Aegean. The damage to our force would be so minimal as to make the cavalry's maneuver a great waste of time and resources. In fact, if I were their general, I would seek higher ground, fortify the positions, unseat the horsemen, give them armor penetrating bows and arrows and then sit back comfortably and watch the slaughter," concluded a smug Piros.

"Hmmmmm, an interesting strategy, Piros. No wonder you are such a good soldier. However, an attacking force does not limit itself to a strategy of immobility. The Macedonian phalanx is an aggressive machine, one that first confronts the enemy line, then breaks it and finally pursues it until its surrender or destruction is complete. Yet here we are presented with an enemy that is highly mobile, difficult to engage and fights a war of attrition rather than annihilation. I grant you that the damage done to the phalanx might be only minimal--if the discipline to stay within its confines is maintained. But what happens if after repeated attacks, with no casualties taken on the enemy side, your own soldiers decide to pursue this force. Without the protection of those united shields, the infantry exposes itself to a fusillade of arrows from an enemy they cannot reach," concluded Philip.

"You forget my lord, that we too have a cavalry. Your own son commands one of the more effective troops. Are you saying that our elite could not handle these cowards, these horsemen who shoot from afar. Alexander would take Bucephalus and run these men into the ground. I am afraid my lord that you have failed to convince me that any force could outmaneuver or outfight the Macedonians." Piros looked at Philip, assured that he had prevailed.

Philip, looking like a snake about to swallow a bird, replied, "Piros, have you underestimated the enemy. Have you ever questioned my decision to send the cavalry onto the field after the infantry has already engaged the enemy?" Piros shook his head. Philip continued. "The reasoning behind that is as follows. First, the infantry must be broken. This is necessary because the man on foot is still the most vital cog in a military operation. Destroy his discipline, separate him from his unit and sever his line of communication to his commanders and he becomes ineffective. When chaos ultimately results, the cavalry can seek out and eliminate the threat of this soldier with minimal risk. There is no question that a man on a horse is worth a half-dozen on foot but it is also critical that the man on the horse have the room to move unimpeded. When engaging another cavalry, we depend on the horsemanship and martial skills of the rider. So far we possess a superior combination of both. Now Piros, listen to me carefully. These Parthian bowmen may not decimate their enemy in the manner we have come to expect. However, by unleashing a barrage of arrows at our cavalry, they will neutralize it. No horse or man will charge into a hail of missiles relatively unprotected. And the final beauty of these men is that even if we break them, in retreat their effectiveness can be devastating. Our feared phalanx cannot assist to any great extent because it is restricted in its ability to move, particularly if the integrity of the unit is to be maintained." Philip took a breath. "You must learn Piros, that there are different methods employed all over the world when war is fought. It is important not to prejudice yourself against a philosophy, religion, race or anything else different from what you interpret to be normal. I have taught Alexander to adapt his thinking to the situation. I hope that he and other leaders such as yourself remember and apply this."

Piros had nothing to say. Philip's stratagem made sense. Piros bowed his head down in acknowledgement of the well-presented argument. He looked up at Philip but Philip had already turned and was engaged in some rather heated haggling with the seller of the bow. Piros guessed that for now this conversation with Philip was over. Remembering why he had come here, he glanced around, looking for the Persian he knew traded in the herbs and medicines that he would need for Dioxippus. Piros spotted him over in a corner of the alley, arranging dried vegetables and flowers from strings he had suspended from the two walls on either side of him.

Piros noted that the Persian was a large man, with a belly as rotund as one of the barrels he was now pulling his goods from. And like his countrymen, he wore a trouser and shirt made of material unlike anything in Hellas. To Piros, the pants seemed undignified and not befitting a man of position. Then he remembered Philip's admonition concerning prejudices. It was easy, even for an educated man like himself to assume that differences between people indicated weakness or deficiency. He promised himself he would not be sucked into that morass. And with that he signaled the Persian.

The Persian, as large as he was, bowed to Piros with a simple dignity. He had tempered the usual flourish of his countrymen, knowing that many Greeks found the fluid movements unmanly. He presented an image opposite of what the propagandists had branded the Persians serving under Darius III. This was no decrepit, morally bankrupt barbarian. By the way he presented himself it was obvious that the Persian had been schooled in the finer points of conduct. And Piros was impressed.

"I seek a product," stated Piros.

"For one ill, injured or just for maintaining one's health?" asked the Persian already pulling things out of baskets and barrels.

"For one injured. A broken collarbone. I need to deaden the pain so he may compete in two weeks," answered Piros.

"An athlete. What sport is your charge involved in, if I may ask?" continued the Persian.

"The Pankration."

"What! You cannot mean that you want him to compete so soon. How can such an injured man even defend himself much less take part?" The shock in the Persian's voice was obvious.

"With your help my friend," replied Piros. "You know what I seek. All you should concern yourself with is if I have the money to pay for it. If you cannot fulfill this request, I will seek someone else." Piros looked around, emphasizing the point that there were others he could approach and who would be happy to provide the service Piros wanted.

The Persian, not wanting to lose what might be a lucrative sale, blathered, "You Greeks, even you darker ones, have such short tempers. Did I say I would not sell you what you want? Did you hear the words, 'go somewhere else' escape these lips? Why do you talk of seeking other sources when you well know that everything in the traveled world is here in these barrels, bags and other containers. I will help you and your friend. Please forgive me for my rudeness earlier. It is just that the pankration is such a bru...rough sport and I only thought that you might want to spare your friend a more serious injury." The Persian, his demeanor tall, proud, also bore the slight cockiness of the successful entrepreneur. Nevertheless, his words were affected with just a touch of plaintiveness. With Alexander and Philip planning invasions of Asia, it was considered prudent for Persians to limit their trade to the other Arabic nations...and most definitely not to the Greeks. But the Persian considered himself above politics, racism and other prejudices. He was a merchant. What did he care if a black, pink, white, yellow or even green man bought his goods. The business was the important thing. And at this moment he did not want to lose the sale.

"Your opinion is acknowledged. Now what would you prescribe for the injury described?" Piros pointed at his shoulder to emphasize the point. I need something that will dull or eliminate the pain without reducing the mobility of the arm. It cannot be a salve or poultice that requires bandaging. The pankration is too pure to be polluted by clothing, slings or even bandages. Do you have something like this," asked Piros, waving his hand over all the containers surrounding the Persian.

"Hmmmmmmm...let me see," said the Persian. He threw himself into barrels, overturned the baskets and searched through the countless bags stuffed with rotting plants and flowers of so many designations that the watching Piros, himself a man of medicine and used to handling herbs and roots, realized how completely ignorant he was of his own profession.

While the Persian rummaged through the ever-growing mess, Piros felt someone beside him. He did not hear the person. He did not see or even smell him. But Piros, his warrior senses acute, knew the King was standing directly behind his left shoulder.

"Do you trust this Persian? Are you sure he is not concocting a poison rather than an antidote?" asked Philip, his voice not giving any indication by its timbre whether the question was meant seriously.

Piros still had not turned to look at the King. What Philip meant by his comment was unclear. Still, Piros' responsibility lay with Dioxippus and it was him he had to help. Thank the gods that this was not Olympias. She would have been crazed with anger if any of Philip's subjects, rich, poor or otherwise had pretended not to hear her. Philip was different. He was at once every man and the culmination of ambition, ruthlessness and genius. He would not get angry with Piros. In fact, knowing Philip, Piros surmised that the question he had asked had been purely rhetorical and no answer was expected.

"Mix these leaves and herbs with water and vinegar. Allow to sit for a day until it is almost a mud. Mix the ingredients again until all the particles break down to liquid. By now you should have a paste. It will smell slightly. Take the paste and pour it into a small, porous bag or pouch. Then you should take this pack and fasten it to the wounded area. The medicine will leak out the cloth bag slowly, deadening the nerves around the break. Your fighter will retain use of his arm but be warned that this poultice will not heal the broken bone. That requires a sling and rest. However, if your man must fight, this poultice will eliminate the superficial pain associated with the movement of the arm. I strongly suggest that he protect that side of his body as best as he can." So concluded the Persian.

Piros slipped a couple of coins to the trader. By the expression on the Persians face the amount was more than generous particularly considering that no haggling over price had ensued. Even the King was impressed by Piros' generosity. For a moment.

"You have not seen me. You do not know of any pankratiatist who has been injured or has requested medication. Do we understand each other?" demanded Piros, suddenly looking much larger and fiercer than he had mere heartbeats ago.

The Persian nodded assent. He had been generously recompensed. There was no need to let anyone know what had transpired here today. Piros' implied threat was not necessary but it was noted. The Persian bowed gracefully and began to resort his wares.

Piros turned to the King. Philip smiled knowingly. After all, there was no need to make the rest of the athletic world aware of the severity of Dioxippus' injury. Both men understood this most basic of military strategies.

They began to make their way out of the alley Philip carrying his newly purchased bow and arrows, Piros his herbs and leaves. Philip was expounding on the virtues of having geographers analyze potential battlefields as he and Piros turned into the main street and began making their way back to the palace. Their voices trailed off into the distance.

Across the street, barely out of sight, were three dark figures wedged tightly in the recesses of the facing building. All three caressed the sharpened blades they had hidden under their coats. All three cursed vehemently the arrival of Piros. His unexpected presence had ruined their plan. Philip's rendezvous with *thanatos* would have to be postponed until another day.

Phylia

Anybody else would have cried. She had run circles around the palace, looking in every imaginable area for the despot of Macedonia. All those she asked shrugged their shoulders. The King was nowhere to be found. No one was alarmed as this was a common occurrence with Philip. Knowing the King was probably healthy did not alleviate Phylia's stress. Olympias would be furious with her if she returned without the Queen's husband. And even though Phylia was beyond caring what happened to her physical person, nevertheless she did not want to have to listen to Olympias' hysterical haranguing if she did not have to. It looked now that she would have to return to Olympias' quarters with her mission unfulfilled. Phylia sighed once, shrugged her shoulders to rid herself of the last bit of nervous tension and started back. She would not prepare excuses or make up a story to mask what Olympias would deem her ineptitude. Phylia did not fear punishment. She had heard Piros tell Dioxippus that every man was accountable for his own actions. Phylia believed that also applied to her. She would accept whatever the Queen decided to mete out.

With her mind flooded with these thoughts of actions and consequences, Phylia's normal senses became dulled. She was completely unaware that a shadow surreptitiously paralleled her movements and had in fact been following her for quite some time. The specter was clever. It stayed far back and blended in with the court life extremely well. It would have been impossible for anyone to observe the wraith's actions and know that Phylia or any other person was being followed. For the young girl, the person haunting her steps really was nothing more than a shadow. So as she approached the Queen's chambers, she did not even cast a cursory glance over her shoulder. She unlatched the doors.

Without warning a great force shoved her through the opening. The shock forced a scream but it only echoed through her head, an immovable claw had clamped her mouth shut. So powerful was the grip that Phylia's head was unable to budge from its held position. Phylia's heart hammered and with the severe restriction on her breathing the strain on her body sapped her strength as well as if she had run a marathon. She could not see her attacker, as any turning of the neck was negligible. Her eyes however, slightly bugged from the lack of oxygen, flew side to side, desperately trying to identify the attacker to no avail. Phylia felt herself weakening rapidly. Her arms began to thrash as her nervous system fought to survive. But the strength of the stalker was too great. Phylia knew she was about to die. The thought that her torment would finally end made her feel at peace.

Patroclus could feel the young girl slipping. He had not meant to choke her to death. He had only wanted to put a little extra pressure on the carotid artery just enough to make Phylia black out. Now it looked as if he might have killed her. Patroclus was now the frightened one. First he was not a child or woman killer. Secondly, if his mistress, the true queen, found out that he had killed Phylia, he would be the one to face the executioner. These thoughts careened through his head. He let the young woman go.

Phylia slumped to the ground unconscious. Patroclus leaned over the prone body, consternation furrowing his forehead. Ever so gently he picked Phylia up and placed her upon the long chairs in the suite. With his forefinger, he massaged the area behind the ear. It seemed like eons before Phylia's eyes fluttered open.

"Is this the afterlife?" asked a disoriented Phylia. "Where is my sister? Please, please let me see her!"

Even though the voice was faint, the sadness was all consuming. Patroclus knew nothing about the girl other than what Cleopatra had told him: she was the personal servant of Olympias and had probably been abused in some manner. There was a strong possibility that she could be recruited by Philip's youngest wife to spy on the mother of Alexander. That was why Patroclus had been sent to follow Phylia. Further orders pertained to turning Phylia against Olympias. As for who the sister was, or the allusions to an afterlife, Patroclus could not guess. He did see however, that this girl or woman was extraordinarily beautiful. Her features had matured into a type of handsomeness rather than prettiness. It gave the girl a patrician look, one that would last her a lifetime. Patroclus was strangely attracted to this person. He bit his lip in anger. Eunuchs did not love women. They were not capable.

When she heard no answer, Phylia decided to risk looking about the chamber. She then realized that she had not died. She was in her room with a strange man sitting beside and over her. Phylia had heard of women being sexually attacked even within the confines of the palace. More than likely, this was one of Olympias' perverted confederates. If he wanted her so badly he could have her but he would never leave the room alive. The light from the window was at his back, leaving his face cloaked in shadow. Phylia would not even see the man she would kill.

"You have not died. And I promise not to hurt you. Please, speak to me. I implore you, do not be frightened," said Patroclus, his voice strangely throttled, as if he had been the one almost strangled into oblivion. The emotion in the voice was real. Phylia was still not sure of what had transpired and what would transpire. But she was no longer frightened of the man beside her. She nodded affirmatively, making sure that her eyes locked with his.

Patroclus slowly removed his hand from her mouth, the motion similar to the drawing of a bowstring, ready to instantly spring back to its original position. Except for a muted sucking in of badly needed air, no other sound could be heard from the young woman. Patroclus noted that she was completely immobile. Whether she was paralyzed with fear or extremely cautious, there was no perceptible movement of any part of her body. Even her eyes, reflecting his image like a finely burnished bronze shield, refused to blink or flicker. Patroclus had to admit to himself that this woman-child had fantastic control over her emotions, her fears and her body. Patroclus swallowed, trying to diminish the lump in his throat. This admiration, this being smitten by the enemy, was causing chaos within his brain. And he had only been with her for these few moments. Gods in heaven, what was happening to him?

Phylia of course could not read his mind, and Patroclus, like most court eunuchs possessed a tremendous ability to constrain his feelings and emotions. To the young woman, he appeared to be a cold, calculating transgressor who could kill her as easily as stepping on one of the myriad of black beetles that scurried around the palace. Why her attacker did not did not really concern her. She was still alive. Strange how she was not overly pleased about it.

"I will not hurt you," whispered Patroclus, the volume of his whisper adding a harsh-sounding undertone to his words. "The queen, the real one, her majesty Cleopatra, begs a favor. Some risk exists but probably no more than if you were to stay with Olympias for any extended period. I cannot force you to accept anything. If you are uninterested, I will leave only to return if you make mention of what is discussed here today. Then I will return as your executioner," said Patroclus, his tone low, steady. He wanted Phylia to understand the importance of his request and to know that her life might depend on the next few moments because if she answered the wrong way, Patroclus, regardless of the almost unnatural attraction for his prisoner, would kill her, quickly and with little remorse. He purposely avoided telling Phylia that as to not be threatening. Her participation in the game had to be of her own free will, otherwise the queen Olympias would rip through her charade. Patroclus waited.

Phylia did not want to be a spy. She did not want to be a part of any assassination attempt. And she was most definitely not interested in the court politicking of Olympias, and her nemesis, the young queen, Cleopatra. Her head pounded. What a quandary she found herself in. She knew that somehow she would end up the loser in all of this. Olympias had not really mistreated her, and had never involved her in any of the games that Olympias herself was so fond of staging and participating in. Phylia would admit without hesitation that her life in the court had so far been rather sheltered. Why...she could not even venture a guess. Maybe Piros had said something to Olympias when he had first left her there: maybe she was too ugly or ungainly. Whatever the reasons she owed Olympias her well-being. However, there was no denying that as of late, the lust-crazed perverts that shadowed Olympias' every move, were becoming more forceful in their requests that the young woman join their twisted sex contests. And on more than one occasion, Olympias had vacillated in her refusal to allow Phylia to be 'pleasured' by one of her lovers. The situation was further complicated by the amorous advances of Olympias' female paramours. Phylia feared them even more than the men. These women performed violent, often, macabre acts while fornicating. Phylia had witnessed and been sickened by the brutality of these feats passing for love. These factors, when scrutinized, pointed to a bleak future for Phylia. And after what had happened to her sister, she vowed never to let a man (or woman) touch her that way again. She started to give Patroclus' request some consideration.

Patroclus tried hard to maintain his composure. Olympias could be back at any moment and he would have a very difficult time explaining his presence. The girl would have to make up her mind right now or else.

153

Phylia noticed Patroclus lower his right hand. He made it look as if he were adjusting the belt of his chiton. The many creases in the fabric made it difficult to see if anything were hidden there unless you were looking. Phylia was. The knife's handle could not help but protrude slightly, altering the fold of one of the creases. Phylia was not overtly alarmed. Yet, there was only one answer to give now.

"If I cooperate with you, will I be protected?"

Patroclus nodded.

"The queen does not usually allow me to run free through the palace. How will I contact you and how long must I spy on her, if that is what you really want?" queried Phylia, her voice devoid of any passion.

Patroclus could feel his shoulders slump and his stomach muscles relax. It appeared that Phylia would do as he bid. Without even noticing it, his right hand rose from his beltline.

"I cannot guarantee your safety. Obviously, some measure of watchfulness and precaution will be necessary on your part. I do want to assure you that there will always be somebody near and his sole purpose will be to anticipate and if necessary intervene when problems that you are unable to deal with arise. To give him a message, pass a tiny scrap of material, no bigger than this." Patroclus held up his thumb and forefinger to illustrate the size he wanted. When your 'friend' on the other side sees this he will consider it a signal to come to the door so you can pass him an oral message. Do not ever write anything down or risk going out or even to the door when the queen is in her chambers. On those occasions when you are allowed out, walk to the marketplace near the palace grounds and there someone will meet you. Listen for this password..."

Patroclus leaned forward and whispered something to Phylia. The only indication she gave that she heard it was a slight tilting of the head in the direction of his voice. Her face remained expressionless.

Patroclus rose. It was not hard for Phylia to see that he possessed a certain stateliness. Somewhere deep within her, a spark long thought dead, flickered.   As Patroclus exited the apartments, Phylia smiled.

Philip amongst his people

The last few words were swallowed up by the crescendo of voices emanating from the vast wall of humanity bustling about on the outer grounds of the palace. Every person was completely ensconced within their own needs, wants and desires. So odd, thought Piros, how every man or woman regardless of position, felt critical to the well-being of the society they lived in. But what was man? Piros thought of his role in this world. Had his presence had any effect on the society as a whole or was his function limited to interfering in the lives of just a few none of which would affect the community in any significant manner. Was he really as insignificant as an insect, a bug, concerned with nothing more than the survival of the nest, the hive? Piros considered himself a scholar but these philosophical musings were best left to those who dedicated their lives to it. Glancing over to his right, he looked at Philip. The king, as jocular with his subjects as with his friends, was greeting many merchants, slaves, officers, soldiers, by name. Jokes, anecdotes and other insignificant verbal tidbits flew from his lips, yet to the people these words reaffirmed the faith in the man, a man who could ask them to go to the ends of the earth. To be known by, or be spoken to by Philip, a personage far more related to the gods of their religion than to themselves, his good words were as anticipated and relished as if they were a manna from the heights of Olympus. This rare ability to empathize with the masses was what made Philip a hero in his homeland. Finally, his refusal to be deified, a normal occurrence in other lands, endeared him even more to his people. Piros was forced to concede that maybe Philip was more than the allegorical hero.

"Leonidas! Myromos! Anything good to eat today? What? I cannot hear you. Yes, yes I will. What? No, no, no...I will get too fat and then who will collect your taxes!" roared Philip to a couple of farmers manning a small cart loaded with precooked foodstuffs. Much of the conversation between the parties was lost in the din of the market. Philip's laughter, and warm manner shone like a beacon in the middle of an ocean. His grin, somewhat marred by the scarring and the one missing eye nevertheless did more to solidify his relationship with the people than any number of forced edicts or false promises.

Piros also noticed that Philip was not afraid to wade in amongst the throngs, thrusting out his hand to be shaken, his robes touched his back patted. Although by now the bodyguards had begun to make their way to their leader, there was no conceivable way for them to protect their king from an assassin. Piros knew that Philip never entertained the idea of any disloyalty from the citizens of Macedonia. As far as Philip was concerned, he was invincible in the arms of his subjects.

Olympias

"My...such good manners." The words were civil, the tone biting as Olympias, normally quick to anger, maintained her composure.

"You are not speaking to a slave or to one of your lackeys," continued Cleopatra, emboldened by what she interpreted to be a non-threatening response from Olympias. "Look around you, these are a queen's quarters." Cleopatra whirled around graciously, the sleeves of her loose-fitting chiton billowing as they puffed up with air. And with the grace of a trained dancer, her pirouette ended at exactly the same spot it had started. Her triumphant grin illustrated quite clearly her revilement in the insult to Olympias. Dancer, lover, queen--she was all of them and more.

Piros fields a hard question

"Have you then decided?" asked Philip suddenly. Only his head turned as his hands and arms were being constantly grasped, held, shaken and kissed by well-wishers.

"Decided what?" yelled Piros back.

"I want you to enlist Dioxippus. I must have him near me in battle. He would make a glorious King's Companion. With you to guide him, he will achieve glory...maybe even approximating yours my friend," answered Philip. He turned his head away for a few seconds to greet some of the many people clamoring to him.

Piros was not surprised by what Philip had just said. Top athletes were always being recruited by military leaders looking for men with outstanding skills or gifts. To assume that Dioxippus probably the best young pankratiatist in Hellas would be ignored would have been presumptuous at best. Ordinarily, Piros would have been ecstatic to have the ruler of the civilized world eager to recruit a charge personally trained by him. But Piros had matured with the years and no longer felt it necessary that a man distinguish himself by his ability to slaughter. Dioxippus' potential was not limited to the fighting ring; on many occasions he had demonstrated to Piros the ability to discuss politics and philosophy with insight and knowledge. This was quite impressive considering that Dioxippus' formal education had been severely restricted when he had been Dionys' slave. Now Piros wanted Dioxippus to pursue an intellectual course. But to refuse the king would be construed as almost treasonous. Complicating matters further was Alexander who had made the same request earlier. Piros and Dioxippus had discussed it then and had not been able to make a decision. Of course, Alexander or Philip could just press him or anyone else into service but the value to morale that having Dioxippus volunteer would provide was too great to have to force an athlete of Dioxippus' caliber to do something he did not want. So Alexander had never been answered. Now Piros found himself in a predicament where if he could convince Dioxippus to assent to the king he would offend the prince. And as much as Piros was loyal to Philip, there was little doubt that Alexander would one day take over his father's position and it could bode ill for anyone who had crossed or given the appearance of crossing, Alexander. Piros needed to think. He had to get away from this tidal wave of humanity. Piros signaled the king, who by now had become separated from Piros. It was also obvious that the bodyguards, chosen from the elite King's companions, had by now surrounded Philip and were gently yet forcefully clearing a path for him to escape the potential danger presented in this crowd. This was good for Piros as it allowed some time to ponder the request he would have to make of Dioxippus.

Piros turned on a tangent to the direction Philip had taken. He could see Philip, still surrounded, bobbing amongst the sea of heads, his own head nothing more than a fisherman's float. Piros turned away, seeking a quieter route along the periphery of the 'agora'. Eventually the maelstrom of the late day's market was only a memory. The quiet enveloped him, a comforting blanket shielding him from the world he had just left. Piros could feel the tension from the back of his neck dissipate, the stiffness flowing away. His head became light, his mind cleared of worries. For the first time in the last few days, he felt truly cleansed.

From nowhere, a body crashed into his. The impact, completely unexpected upset his balance. Piros stumbled backward, waving his arms, maddeningly trying to grasp at something for support but failing miserably. With little dignity but great force, his posterior slammed into the earth. So straight had the trajectory of his rear end been that he ended up in a sitting position, legs splayed open, his eyes open wide and his mind completely dumbfounded. The perpetrator of his present state had not fared much better. He lay sprawled against the wall that he had so hurriedly come around just moments ago. A hand was raised to his temple, possibly in response to an injury there. The upraised arm obscured the face.

Except for the indignity of his present position, Piros was unscathed. However, the indefensibility of his position coupled with the omnipresent threat of assassination made Piros only too aware that his personal safety might be compromised. He leapt to his feet, the adrenalin charge electrifying his motor reflexes. The bag of herbs and leaves, still clasped in his left fist, was thrown aside as he charged forward, determined to eliminate this would-be executioner before he could draw a weapon or summon accomplices.

Just then, as if anticipating Piros' movement, the man leaning against the wall pulled his arm away, positioned his feet wide and braced himself for the attack.

It never came. Piros pulled up short in front of a disheveled Dioxippus. He began to laugh, deep, emotional laughter--a sound so rich, so contagious that anyone near it would be unable to keep from being drawn into it. Like so many others, Dioxippus joined his friend, his mentor, in that most joyous of emotional expressions.

There they were, two large men, warriors, laughing at their paranoia, a condition that had them jumping from or at shadows. The relief, combined with the ludicrous situation, almost choked the two guffawing friends. Between the tears and the constant coughing they ridiculed each other with rare epithets and timely insults.

From a distance of a few buildings, the encounter between Dioxippus and Piros sounded violent. To Panthea, who had just left Dioxippus a few moments ago, it sounded like a death struggle. She dropped the hydria full of water, withdrew her knife from her chiton and ran back in the direction she had come from, trying desperately to locate the voices she had heard.

Taking a wrong turn, she heard the voices fading away. Panicked, she called out to Dioxippus. Hearing nothing, she began to sob. Suddenly, she heard the voices again, this time much clearer. She also heard coughing, intermittent yet forceful. Dioxippus must be hurt, she thought. That assessment made her even more resolute in her search. The tears gave way to angry expletives a she sprinted round the corner, her knife brandished her fury unabated.

The first thing she saw was a bent-over Dioxippus leaning against the building wall for support. Opposite him was a black man, also stooped although it was difficult to tell if he also was injured. Something about the black man was familiar. Regardless, he obviously was trying to hurt Dioxippus. With her knife in an up-raised position she charged Piros.

Enjoying the comical situation to its fullest, Piros was not as attentive as he normally would have been. He was not aware of Panthea's presence until he felt the knife slash across his shoulder. The metal bit into his skin, splitting it, the pain sharp, burning. Reflexes saved Piros from the follow-up, a downward stab aimed at his heart, by throwing his body into a backward roll. The crimson streak formed by the tumbling Piros, its brilliance muted by the dust and dirt of the street, pointed at the now standing Piros like some evil arrow. The blood cascaded down his arm, its flow forceful, the result of the knife severing one of the tendons and its surrounding veins in the deltoid muscle of his shoulder. The wounded arm was almost useless but Piros, always the warrior, refused to clutch it or even attempt to stem the bleeding. Instead, he stood in the guarded position of the pankratiatist, both legs slightly apart, hands open and raised in front of him.

So quick had the attack been, Piros had not even seen the assailant. His autonomic nervous system had reacted immediately, saving his life. Yet, now that his mind had caught up to his body, he was even more confused. Facing him was a woman, probably no older than Dioxippus, her face contorted with rage, wielding a knife in which she was an obvious expert in the use of. Piros had seen assassins, some of whom were women, but never had he seen one so intense, so committed to the demise of her intended target. Her emotional state, rather than the detached professionalism of most hired killers, was more reminiscent of a lioness protecting her cubs. Except for the obvious threat to his life, nothing about the last, frenzied moments were logical.

Piros' yelp of pain was the first sign that something had gone horribly awry. By the time Dioxippus looked up, miniscule by any standard, he had seen his beloved mentor viciously assaulted. From the back it appeared to be a woman. Piros, trying desperately to evade the deadly blade had moved away. The murderess had followed, effectively putting both her and Piros out of Dioxippus' immediate range. He did the only thing that he could think of--he yelled. It was a battle cry, specifically created and mastered only by a few, to freeze or disorient the assailant in any battle. It pierced the air, a spear of sound, rupturing the confidence, the concentration of the enemy.

Panthea, emboldened by her aroused protective instincts, stepped forward to finish off this man who had tried so arduously to take yet another person whom she cared for from her life. She stopped. A sound or was it some force unknown froze her body as it smashed into her head, disrupting her thought processes, diverting the messages from her brain to her extremities, effectively if only momentarily paralyzing her.

With the speed of a pouncing leopard, Dioxippis leaped at Panthea, his mass so great in comparison to Panthea's that his shadow enveloped her before he even touched her. Her momentary lapse of concentration had been enough though. Dioxippus slapped the back of her hand at precisely the point where the tendons and nerves were most sensitive. Panthea's fingers jerked outward releasing the knife. Without hesitating, Dioxippus encircled the young woman's waist and held her. He called to Piros, the anguish and concern in his voice obvious.

Piros looked over at the oddly combined pair. He could see that Dioxippus had managed to restrain what appeared to be a murderess. He turned his head down and looked at the blood still streaming from the wound in his shoulder. Piros grimaced. This would have to be taken care of quickly. Yet, he felt inexplicably drawn to that young woman. What was it about her that made him want to talk to her rather than twist her head off like he would a rabid weasel? A drop of blood fell on the top of his bare foot, again breaking his sequence of thought. He had to take care of this arm.

"Piros! Are you hurt badly?" asked an agitated Dioxippus.

"I am not sure. My arm does not have much movement left. Control the girl while I make a tourniquet. Find out why she attacked me," replied Piros, by now already tearing strips off the bottom of his robe.

Somewhat relieved, Dioxippus turned Panthea around to face him. As soon as her eyes met his, she began to cry. Then she sank her face into his chest, put her arms around his waist and began to sob. Dioxippus was shocked. Here he was, trying to placate an apparently inconsolable person met within the last while who had obviously cast a spell on him of some sort, while his best friend, a friend closer than almost any parent, sat across the alley trying to control a wound caused by this woman entangled in his embrace. This was insane. Dioxippus' emotions felt as if they had been systematically stripped with an awl.

Panthea was also devastated. She had thought that Dioxippus' life had been endangered and had reacted accordingly. From the concern Dioxippus had expressed for her victim, she had made a tragic mistake. She lifted her head, ever so slightly, and cast a quick look over at the man she attacked. He did not see her watching him as he was engrossed in tending his injury. What was it about that man that tugged at her emotions so? Panthea had seen very few people of his hue in her life. She was sure she would have remembered a man so black, so imposing. Yet, her brain refused to connect the visual input to her memory. It was as if the gods had purposely robbed her of that experience. Panthea choked back a sob, and rested her head again on the chest of the now thoroughly confused Dioxippus.

The young pankratiatist tried to move toward his friend. The young woman however, clutched him so tight that any attempt at real progress would be met with a tumble to the dirt. Dioxippus took a deep breath, inflating his chest like the pig's bladder he used to play kick ball with, and slid his arms in between Panthea's and his torso. Slowly, he forced her away from him until he could look right into her face without any undue effort. When he had her attention, he spoke.

"Why did you attack Piros? You do not even know him. If, you have been sent to assassinate him, pray to your gods now because you will be meeting them soon," said Dioxippus, his tone so forceful it surprised even him.

"I...I was only trying to..to..." Panthea could not finish her reply.

"You have used me. I felt...something between us at the well," said Dioxippus. "Now you stand here, with no answers and the blood of my best friend on your hands. Tell me...now...why I should spare you the same fate you planned for Piros."

These last few words sparked something in Panthea. Although emotionally spent, she had in good conscience tried to save Dioxippus from what she thought had been certain doom. Now he was accusing her of treachery and threatening her with death. Could this man, albeit a young one, be so stupid, so unfeeling that he would assume her guilty of something so vile without even questioning her about it? Panthea's sorrow was quickly transforming itself into rage.

"As of when have you been an all seeing god? You dare accuse, sentence and execute me without the benefit of defense, explanation or trust. What am I to you? Did you think that I would first bed you, then thank you and go on my way? You obviously did not feel the attraction to my spirit that I felt for yours. How could I be so ignorant as to trust a man thick with muscles including his brain? Do not look at me with such surprise. I stabbed your friend. You cannot even comprehend how shamed I feel. I thought that you were being attacked. I admit I over-reacted. But if you had seen your mother, father, brothers and sister hunted down and killed as if they were vermin you would not be so sanctimonious. When I saw you, stooped as if from injury, and a stranger, exotic even in Macedonia, coming toward you I assumed the worst. But why should I explain anything to you." The fury in Panthea's voice attracted the attention of Piros. Dioxippus withstood this tirade as if it had been a physical attack. Panthea was not finished.

"When I was a girl, my family was abused, set upon and attacked so often, that my father, even though he was nothing more than a Helot farmer, stole away from his Spartan masters, taking not only his own family but that of a neighbor. By hiding effectively, covering our trail and working in unison we escaped the tyranny of our masters in Sparta. It was not until we had reached the great and forgiving state of Thebes that we saw what true evil was." Panthea took a breath. At the mention of Thebes, her face twisted into a mask of revulsion. Whatever the association with the Thebans, its end result had been one of hate and bitterness.

"We were pursued as if we were the vilest creatures on earth. We ran then we tried to hide. Still, they found us." Panthea bit her lip vainly trying to force the now emerging tears back into their ducts. She continued.

"My father, my uncle, my brothers, and my neighbors were hacked to death. Not one had a real weapon with which to fight back. Even sheep do not have as ignoble a death. I will never forget, ever, the sight of my father bent over my little sister's body as he tried to shield her from the swords. The soldiers used their weapons like cleavers...and the whole time they laughed." The last few words were barely audible.

Piros was mesmerized. He had been listening intently to the conversation taking place just a few steps away. His own memories were being awakened. Between what the girl was saying and his recognition of her, the floodgates to the past were opened. And the first thing to come through them were the events of that horrible day long ago in Thebes.

Piros remembers...

The march back to the city took only a day. For Piros it was an agonizing eternity. The other soldiers shunned him; his commander treated him like a leper. Only yesterday, Piros had been the center of the barracks' social life. With his martial skills, quick wit and imposing intellect, no gathering no party was complete without him. Now, he trudged along the road, last in a spread-out line. To further aggravate the shame, the body of the dead Yemestos was being carried by four of his comrades directly in front of Piros. Every time Piros looked up from the road, he would see the grimacing face, its tongue lolling, staring back at him, begging him to restore the life, the soul to the physical shell that had previously housed it. Piros averted his eyes as much as he could. Still, the bloody corpse called to him and then Piros, would, despite his reasoning mind's exhortations, invariably look up again. Then the guilt, the anger, the frustration would tear through him with the icy chill of a winter wind. His many years training for the pankration allowed him to maintain almost phenomenal control over his body so none of the other soldiers was aware of his inner turmoil. But coursing through his veins and arteries to every extremity, every skin receptacle, even every hair, was the fearsome bite of the monster, shame.

His nostrils flared. A scent. So faint that it might have been nothing more than an errant puff of air. He caught it again. Piros knew what it was. At this early stage, it was tantalizingly sweet but he knew that as the day progressed and the temperature rose that almost sweet scent that was now perfuming the atmosphere would evolve into a horrifying stench that would attack his nose and throat like a burning brand. Thus the unavenged Yemestos would use his putrefying body to exact one last emotional tribute from Piros.

Was it a day, week or an eternity? Piros' logical mind told him that Thebes lay within a day's march of the camp they had attacked the day before. Yet the onslaught on his finer senses from the suppurating flesh that was once Yemestos, disoriented him to such an extent that he had lost all track of the length of the journey. His eyes struggled to stay open. His breathing labored as he tried to inhale only enough of the polluted oxygen to keep himself alive. He tried to erect a barrier within his mind. Although he could not remove himself completely from the situation he was now in, so effectively had he shut down his sensory receptacles, that he was not aware that he and his small troop had reached the city gates until the shadow of the protecting walls had cast a cool shadow on him. The sensation on his skin, so pleasant after so many hours in the heat jarred him out of his cocoon. The awakening was further accelerated by the rising noise level of the city itself as they drew closer.

As the gates were pulled open, a mass of people surged out to greet the returning war party. Many calls of recognition, promptly followed by cries of adulation greeted the soldiers. Farmers, merchants, soldiers, women and children all milled about the troop. Interspersed with the Thebans were many slaves, many of whom offered to carry the bundles, weapons and loot of the scouts. At first, many came to Piros, praising, then congratulating him. If Piros could have shrugged off the hands touching him he would have. But as he made his way into the city he noticed that fewer and fewer well-wishers came to him and those that did were quickly admonished by the standers-by. Soon it became quite clear that his actions had been made public. Fortunately, no one verbally or physically attacked him. The Thebans' disappointment in him however was almost palatable. Piros wanted to hide.

"Piros!"

The pankratiatist looked around. Who had called him? friend or enemy?

"My hero. Ooohhhhh...you big dark stud."

Now he was really confused. The voice sounded somewhat feminine. Piros looked around. And then he saw...

Panthea

"Blood...you cannot imagine how hard it was to rid my clothes and my skin of it. Every nightmare I had after that day was bathed in it," said Panthea.

Dioxippus shifted on the seat. Panthea's tale had been one of terror and tragedy. He had had no idea how much she had suffered when she began her story. Even Piros had listened attentively although Dioxippus noticed that his mentor's eyes had glazed over, much like they used to in Athens when he used to go into his "thoughts", as Fotis used to refer to the trance-like state. Dioxippus looked down at Panthea. He had not noticed that he was still holding her hand from when he had led her to where they were now sitting, a covered stoop in what appeared to be an abandoned building.

"I know you."

Panthea and Dioxippus looked over to the now upright Piros. They would not have been able to explain why but they rose quickly .

"You have reason to hate me."

Piros' words had no emotion, no life. It was as if a spiritual being was channeling a message through the medium that was Piros.

Panthea stepped closer. She was unsure as to what she heard. She tilted her head in Piros' direction. She felt something press ever so lightly into her body. Dioxippus had also moved forward.

"I am the one who killed the two escaping women that night."

Panthea gasped. The memory, long suppressed, now tore into her mind with the voraciousness of a carnivore. She grabbed her temples with both hands bent at the waist and moaned with a pain more real than if she had been wounded. Tears did not come however. The agony of the experience superceded the emotional response so Panthea found herself unable to cry.

Dioxippus was once again shocked. His first action was to hold the writhing Panthea. Then he looked up at Piros who was standing there immobile. Dioxippus' eyes pleaded with Piros to somehow make this right, to maybe deny what he had just said. Dioxippus worshipped Piros. To find out that he had killed two women, two women who obviously were an integral part of Panthea's life, was shattering to the image he had built, then cultivated of his mentor. His eyes, no longer reflectors of mere images, but transmitters from his soul, begged Piros for answers, reasons, anything that would justify the heinous act he had just heard detailed.

Thus the three stood; three players in a tragedy.

Philip meets with Alexander

"He comes."

Philip did not appear to be listening.

Patroclus gently cleared his throat. He repeated the statement.

Philip turned his head in the direction of Patroclus. The movement was exaggerated as Philip had to half-turn out of his seat in order for his one good eye to see the servant.

Patroclus nodded, turned and left. The movement was a much abbreviated bow in comparison to what Olympias expected. Philip did not like or tolerate the typical genuflecting of the court.

Barely had the door closed behind Patroclus when it opened. Striding in, the light from the hallway bathing them in a surreal halo, were Alexander and Hephaestion. The combination of power, beauty and youth was almost overpowering. Gods had blessed these two.

Philip could feel his heart beat faster. Excitement or apprehension? He could not guess which affected him more at this moment. What he did know was that he loved Alexander with a fierceness and intensity which was at times all-consuming. He also knew that for most of his life Alexander had reciprocated those feelings. Philip had always had a spiritual bond with his son, from his days as an infant to his young adulthood, Alexander had been his father's shadow, first following then sharing the journey Philip had chosen to take. How the Fates had punished him. Now Philip never knew what to expect from his son. Olympias, even more consumed with her son's future than he was, had cracked his sphere of influence and he was not sure he could effect the repairs that would restore his son to him. To help rebuild the relationship they had had, Philip was planning on an expedition with his son. By sharing their ambitions and desires far from the corrupting influences of Pella, Philip knew that father and son could be one again.

"Father."

Philip looked up. Alexander stood there, arms crossed, legs braced slightly apart. His lightly tanned skin, long blonde hair, clean-shaven face and blue eyes all combined to give him the look of a young teenager. To some, Alexander may have even appeared feminine as his appearance was so opposite the Macedonian standard. Philip knew better than to underestimate his son's manhood. The scars riddling the taut, muscular body attested to Alexander's courage. Even his bearing, so confident that probably no indecisive thought had ever crossed his mind, bespoke the power of one chosen by the gods. And now, standing before the conqueror of Hellas, the King of Macedonia and most importantly, his father, Alexander displayed a cool indifference. This attitude that might have been construed as flippant or discordant by others was interpreted by Philip as self-confidence. There was no question Alexander was his son.

"Hellas grows too small for us. It is time that we flexed our muscles. I say we look over the eastern horizon and see what is there." Philip rose out of his seat and started moving toward Alexander.

A spark lit up Alexander's eyes. Otherwise no other emotion escaped the confines of his superb self-control. Nevertheless, Philip noted it and was pleased.

"Are you planning to catch a few fish or the shark itself?" queried Alexander, his eyes narrowing slightly.

"I am too old to cast my line in hopes of catching a minnow. I want Darius himself. And of course all he has," replied Philip.

"Persia." The word flowed out of Alexander's mouth. His austere lifestyle, modeled on that of a Spartan had provided him with the skill to inwardly focus all his feelings, hopes and emotions. Thus he was able to maintain control over every aspect of his life. But now, the thought of conquering Persia was too much for the exuberance of his youth. He smiled, and without noticing, uncrossed his arms and relaxed his posture.

"It can be ours. I have called the cartographers, and with your help, we can formulate a plan of attack that will push Darius so far into the desert that even a camel would be afraid to go looking for him," said a now ebullient Philip.

Alexander did not reply. And the stillness of his body did not belie the whirlpool of thoughts spinning in his brain. Compounding his mental state was a hunger that he could not identify, gnawing at him, alternately begging then threatening him; so painful that an ache manifested itself deep in the recesses of his abdomen. What did he want? What need could there exist that even his physical body craved it to the point of pain?

"Darius has wealth unimaginable to mountain goats such as ourselves," laughed Philip. "He controls lands that extend to the end of the world. He is lord over a hundred different peoples, each one with a culture so different, so unique...so rich, that it would be a mockery of the Hellenistic spirit to allow such a barbarian to continue to be master.

You say nothing. Would it that I could be privy to what you envision." Philip continued. "This is an adventure decreed by the Gods for you and me. Alexander, let your imagination fly with the knowledge, the curiosity that Aristotle has instilled in you. Continue to be an ascetic in the way you live not in the way you think. Unknown worlds await us. Glory and ambition call our names. Make the commitment. I will not set out without my son."

Alexander was impressed not only with the words but with the manner Philip spoke. It would have been obvious to even one of the idiots begging for sustenance on the streets that Philip truly spoke from the heart. The excitement, the conviction in his voice could not be faked. For the first time in too great a time, Alexander felt the almost dead embers of his love for Philip begin to glow.

"You still do not answer," said Philip, trying desperately to keep his anger in check. He could not understand why Alexander was taking so long in giving him an answer. For Philip, going to war against Darius was not only a glorious opportunity to reacquaint himself with the son he loved but to also achieve immortality as the greatest conqueror the civilized world had ever seen. He fervently hoped that Alexander, strangely pensive was not stalling him because of a hidden agenda of his own.

"The idea intrigues me...father."

Philip beamed, took two steps toward his son and with unabashed tears, took his son and hugged him At this instant, his joy was boundless. Alexander had agreed to investigate the proposal. For Philip, it had been enough. And the ultimate had been Alexander's last word, said gently and with love.

Hephaestion and the returned Patroclus had been silent observers of this drama. Inadvertently, they looked at each other. As politely as they could, they turned their heads away, not wanting to share the embarrassment of being intruders during this personal moment between father and son. Both assumed a guarded stance once again.

A voice caught the attention of Philip and Alexander. They separated and watched as Patroclus went to the door. He identified the person on the other side and let him in; an aged man, now stooped with arthritis yet carrying more maps than a man half his age probably could, shuffled in. Patroclus reached over to relieve the old man of part of his load. His arms had barely started to rise when the aged cartographer snapped at him and with almost comical flourish, turned away from the young slave. Patroclus looked quizzically at Philip. The king, his face displaying an open grin, just nodded. Patroclus interpreted this to mean that he was to leave their new guest alone. He stepped back and away.

Alexander moved to the table. Philip joined him on the same side.   Patroclus and Hephaestion moved in behind their respective masters. The cartographer placed the cylindrical bundles on the table and began.

"The first thing we must consider is the topography of the route we will take. If we use Pella as the starting point we have one of two choices," said the cartographer, Strabo.

"We should march east, following the coast of Thrace until we come to the Hellespont.

"Far too slow," interrupted Alexander.

"You have not let me describe the alternative. Nor have I told you about the logistics of moving a large force through a sparsely populated and a supply-poor area. Perhaps if you look at this map again I can show you a much safer route to follow."

Alexander looked at Strabo as if he were a child. He signaled Hephaestion. His friend and bodyguard stepped forward and from within his robe produced his own small cylinder. He handed it to Alexander and stepped back.

A bemused Philip watched Alexander unroll his map. Inwardly, Philip was laughing. Here he had wanted to convince his son to undergo a potentially doomed military expedition and all the while Alexander had been researching and planning for just such a challenge. Between Alexander's obvious preparedness, his leadership and the skill of the Macedonian army, nothing would stop them--not even the Persian god-king Darius.

Alexander was bent over the maps, discussing the enormous detail involved with moving troops numbering up to twenty or thirty thousand with Strabo. The cartographer had known that Alexander was intelligent but to meet such a young man whose knowledge of the technical aspects of geography rivaled his own was disconcerting. Furthering the uneasiness he felt in the presence of this, this...he could not think of a word to describe the prince, was the embarrassment of having this neophyte explain troop movement, supply and transportation better than he could. Strabo looked at Philip imploringly. But the king merely smiled with the satisfaction of knowing his son had come back to him.

Pausanius

A shiver went through his body. He felt the momentary tension in his neck and shoulders. It was hot yet he felt cold. He stopped walking. He listened. Nothing. He cocked his head in the opposite direction. Nothing again. His scalp tingled. He could not be sure: was he being followed?

Pausanius cursed himself. The soldier of old would have been able to confirm whether or not he was being shadowed. And that soldier of old would never have shivered in fear. Pausanius choked back a sob, pride and terror making strange allies against this dark specter squeezing the manhood out of him.

There it was...a sound. Pausanius felt for his knife. "Idiot!" he thought to himself. He remembered now that he had put it aside before he left his apartment. Unarmed, alone and in the dark he knew that whoever his stalker was, he had the decided advantage. Pausanius' arm brushed against his side. Frowning, he felt the paunch that had supplanted the chiseled abdominals he had had for most of his life.

"I am fat and weak. All I'm good for is loving women, and even that has lost all pleasure as of late. Now somebody follows and I don't even feel confident enough to protect myself," thought Pausanius. Imploringly he looked up at the sky hoping, praying that the gods might restore him to his former self. His prayers went unanswered.

A kicked pebble, a glimpse of a shadow. Startled, Pausanius quickened his pace. He walked along the walls of the buildings, using them as a shield from at least one direction. At the same time his eyes scanned the street looking for a sign of when the attack would come.

A few more steps and he would be...

Light exploded. Then it went dark. His body did not respond to his commands. His head felt so heavy that he had to rest it on, on...

Kathos grinned. The small war club studded with bronze nails had proven its efficiency once again. He stared down at the body of Pausanius crumpled up into a shapeless heap. Blood trickled from the base of Pausanius' skull. Kathos frowned. He better not have killed him. He whistled once, twice. Three of his cronies stepped out from the alcove in the building across the alley. All three were cast from the same mold, dark, squat figures with indeterminate features perfect for their chosen profession. They knelt down beside the prone Pausanius, grasped his limp arms and legs firmly and picked him up. They looked to Kathos for further instructions.

Kathos looked about nervously, his senses honed by years of subterfuge and crime. His nostrils flared, smelling the air for even the slightest scent that did not belong. Twice he jerked his head around sharply, looking for someone or something that he felt was there. He saw nothing. After a few moments he signaled his compatriots to follow him.

As the criminals moved down the alley with their quarry, a pair of eyes, occasionally glinting with reflected light from the odd lamp, followed them.

Piros

"Why did you never tell me?" implored Dioxippus. "It has been a long time since I was a child. Have I not earned your trust? Have I not proven myself in the ring...the battlefield? Why must the man I love as a parent keep this evil from me?" The last words came hoarsely out of the mouth of the emotionally spent Dioxippus.

Piros did not look directly at his young friend. The shame of that memory long ago was consuming him. Right now he felt old and weak and he just wanted to leave.

"Piros, I think I love this girl. I should be happy...but I am not. Every time something comes into my life that would provide me with a little of the happiness that ordinary citizens get almost by birthright, it is usurped by some unforeseen evil. I am cursed Piros. No matter what I achieve I will never be granted the pleasure of raising a family and then growing old. I have never been to the oracles at Delphi but I know what they would tell me..."

Piros could not help but be saddened by Dioxippus' rather cryptic view of his future. He knew he should reassure the young man. He would not though. Piros did not think Dioxippus would grow old either. Whether it was a feeling or a divine revelation, Piros knew in his heart that Dioxippus was a man whose destiny had already been chosen by his Fates. Tears welled up in his eyes.

"Can't you answer me? Thakria I see. Are they for me or you?" asked Dioxippus.

"They are for both of us," replied Piros. "It is time that you were told a little more of my past...and yours."

Surprised, Dioxippus just nodded in assent. He moved and awaited the story to begin.

Piros told him of his parents, the African, Tsaka and the Hebrew, Delia He told him of their slavery, their marriage and his birth. He also told him of the mines that killed his father and the grief that drove his mother to insanity.

Dioxippus sat without once interjecting a comment or question. This was a part of Piros never before exposed to him and it completely caught him unprepared.

Piros related all, minimizing nothing. His role in the slaughter at Panthea's camp was told with a brutal frankness. He did not try to justify his actions in any way.

As Piros told his story, he found himself slipping further and further into the nether world of his subconscious. Soon all he could hear was this echoing noise ringing in his ears. He felt his mouth moving but he did not know why.

Piros remembers...

That mocking voice refused to let him be. Piros looked around again searching for his tormentor.

"OOOOOhhh, Piros. Over here."

The feminine voice was identified. It was Philip, the young prince from Macedon and one of Piros' few friends in Thebes. Whilst the rest of the populace had abandoned him for what they perceived as a desertion of the popular Yemestos, Philip still played games with him. Piros saw him standing on a retaining wall, legs apart, head tilted back in laughter. For someone who was really nothing more than a hostage of the Thebans, and was friends with the now very unpopular son of slaves, Piros, the prince was extremely happy.

"Piros, my friend. You return a more miserable bastard than when you left," called out the still laughing Philip as he jumped down from the wall and came sauntering over to Piros. He extended his arms to embrace his friend.

Normally, Piros would have moved forward to clasp his friend around the shoulders also. He could not bring himself to, this time. The shame, the ridicule and worst of all the almost immediate ostrasization of his adopted city made him feel undesirable of companionship.

Philip did not know or care about Piros' inner turmoil. He was just so glad to see the one person he could call his confidant, that all he could think of was to greet him. Putting his thick, hairy arms around Piros' waist, he lifted him right off the ground.

Piros' first thoughts were not of Philip's gregariousness or loyalty. Nor were they of his now sad lot in this city. Surprisingly, his first thought, being a physical person, was, "How strong this Macedonian is, to pick me up as he would a young girl half my weight."

Philip let Piros down and throwing one arm around his shoulder and picking up the dropped shield with his other hand, guided Piros to the barracks they shared. Piros exhausted from the march and the mental turmoil, let himself be led by the loquacious Philip.

As they walked, Piros recounted the story to the Macedonian. Occasionally, Philip would nod his head or alternately shake it. He did not interrupt until Piros finished his tale.

Philip pulled up short of the barracks, turned and faced Piros and started.

"Understand one thing my friend. Be it one, two or a thousand, all battles are wars. In war, some become victims whose only crime was their innocence. These Thebans unfortunately are vultures. They are so brazen, so confident of their skills that they elevate themselves to a level where Zeus would start to get uncomfortable. Do not feel you are a traitor just because you allowed Yemestos' murderess to escape. Who cares? He was a cretin whose time had come. And personally, I am glad that somebody decided to use his testicles for a dissection." This last comment struck Philip as funny and he started to laugh at his own joke. After a few guffaws, he noticed that Piros was not sharing his good humour so he continued.

"This is what I want you to consider. You are not a Theban. You owe no loyalty to these bastards. With your colour, you will have a hard time convincing other Greeks that you are as much a citizen as they are. Join me in Macedonia. I have been given the word that an exchange of hostages is to occur and that I will be returning to my homeland. Come with me. There you will be the hero that I know you are. Your education, your athletic prowess, even your military skills can be honed to a standard that will make these Thebans look like the overfed, pampered sissies that they are. Say yes."

Piros was taken aback by Philip's request. Much of what the Macedonian had said was true. His parents had had their freedom here but freedom had cost his father his life, and his mother her sanity. Thebans had raised and trained him. He owed them that. Yet he had never been welcomed as an equal. He did not mean that he was deprived of any rights afforded a normal citizen, nor did he mean that they had erected barriers between themselves and him. On the contrary, he had access to all things granted natives. What was missing however, was true affection, love and respect. The Thebans fulfilled their societal obligations by looking after him after his parents died but nothing more. No family adopted him. No teacher, in spite of his obviously great intellect, took a special interest in him. Even his trainers in the pankration, when it was apparent that he was the dominant force in the training camp spent no extra time with him. To Piros, the indifference of this city-state to him was the worst transgression of all.

"I will go with you to Macedonia," said Piros.

Philip jumped as a child would. "We will be subjects of many histories my friend" said a joyous Philip. He pulled Piros close to him, whispered something in his ear and pinched his rear.

Piros laughed then pushed the prince away.

Piros confers with Dioxippus

"I do not see what the joke is," said Dioxippus.

"Uuuhhh. What joke?" asked Piros.

"The one that has pasted a smile on your face."

"I guess I was thinking further ahead than what I was telling you. What was the last thing you heard?"

"You were saying that Philip asked you to go to Macedonia with him. Obviously you did. I still do not understand what is so funny about that. But I do understand what happened at that camp and maybe even why it happened. I will explain to Panthea."

With that, Dioxippus raised himself off the couch. He looked at Piros and turned to leave.

"Dios, one more thing."

Dioxippus looked back surprised. Piros rarely referred to him by his pet name.

"One of Philip's eunuchs has found out that you have a living relative. A sister, living in Athens we think."

Dioxippus opened his mouth slightly. Nothing came out. He stood in shock.

"I was only told the day before yesterday and I wanted to try and confirm it before I told you. Apparently it is true."

"How...how di...did you discover her?" stammered Dioxippus.

Piros cast his eyes downward.

"Piros!" snapped Dioxippus.

"She is engaged to be married."

"What...that should be wonderful news. Why has gloom arrested your face?"

Piros raised his eyes until they locked with Dioxippus'. He took a breath.

"She marries the son of Dionys." The statement spoken with an even modulation nevertheless cracked the air like a whip.

Dioxippus reeled back, the torrent of previous memories assaulting him. The news of a sister, so joyous was rent asunder by the choice she had made. For unlike Piros, Dioxippus remembered very little of his childhood other than he had been the slave of Dionys for what seemed forever. To be told that his sibling was to marry into the family of the animal who had tortured and killed Iyea, was paramount to justifying the abuse that monster had put the children of his household through.

Piros respected the sanctity of a man's grief. He made no move to console Dioxippus. The young man would come to him when he wanted to. Still, Piros truly sympathized with his friend. Nothing had ever come easy to Dioxippus, happiness was always just out of reach. Now, when most would have been down on their knees thanking the gods for their generosity, he stood bereft of emotion. In one day, Piros had seen Dioxippus scale an emotional peak only to plummet to depths so low that even agony would have been a relief of sorts for the body.

This brought to mind some of his mother's teachings. Unlike most civilized persons, Piros' mother, Delia, subscribed to a religion that worshipped but one god. She would often take Piros in her arms and regale him with stories of spiritual attainment in the face of great adversity. Piros became familiar with the journeys of Moses, the trials of Abraham, the exploits of David, the wisdom of Solomon. Delia also told him of persecution, of the nomadic way of life her people had adopted as a means of survival. And throughout every tale, Delia emphasized how the nameless God constantly tested mankind by casting obstacles, temptation and evil in the way of even the best of men. Looking at Dioxippus, Piros could see how stringent the test could be even though he could not understand why such a good-hearted youth would be subjected to so many ordeals.

"We cannot make judgments on situations that we are not informed about or are beyond our influence. Be happy that you have discovered a part of you that you did not know even existed. After the games are over, we will go to Athens. Until then, I will send word to her that she has a brother and that he will be meeting her soon."

Dioxippus sighed. Piros was right. He should see the good in everything that occurred and progress from there.

"I will go see Panthea. Shall we meet at the gymnasium tomorrow?" asked Dioxippus.

"Yes, yes...I will see you then. I may have a surprise for you," replied Piros.

"A good one, I hope," said Dioxippus, a sardonic smile forming on his lips.

"I assure you, a good one."

Cleopatra confronts Olympias

Silently, she counted the days one more time. There was no question she was carrying Philip's child. Cleopatra grinned. It would be her child that would assume the throne one day, not that witch's. Nervously she glanced around. She was alone. Traitorous thoughts like these had to be kept secret. She would have to watch herself.

Within moments the apprehension dissipated and she was once more euphoric with the knowledge of impending motherhood. Cleopatra found herself smiling and even though she tried she could not suppress the joy that wanted to leap out of her body. She could barely wait for Philip's return.

The creak of an opening door shocked her back to reality. Cleopatra whirled around, sensing rather than knowing, that the opening door was the one mounted behind the wall mosaic. She held her breath, took three steps to her morning table and picked up a long, slim dagger. With surprising dexterity she turned the knife with one hand, the handle still grasped firmly but with the blade now facing inward, concealed by the wrist. Cleopatra waited.

The figure coming through the break in the wall was stooped as he bent almost double to get through a hole better suited to a midget. By his rather feeble attempt to be quiet, it appeared that he was not here to commit a crime.

"I do not think assassins need worry about a threat to their business from you," said Cleopatra, the gentle mocking barely disguising the relief in her voice.

"If being an assassin entails sneaking around in tunnels barely bigger than badgers' dens, I forego the opportunity," replied Patroclus, straightening up slowly, stretching out the kinks from his cramped lower back.

"You have been gone too long. I began to worry. Did you talk with the slave girl? What did she say?" Cleopatra's tone showed her anxiety.

"My sincerest apologies for the time gone. The girl needed some convincing. By the time I left, most of Olympias' security was returning so I had to take a route that would circumvent anybody who might be suspicious. However, the most important thing is that I believe the girl, her name is Phylia, will do as we ask. I think she knows that she is at far greater risk staying with that lunatic queen than she is with us. But I am still not sure what help she could be. What could she offer us? I am sure that Olympias does not confide to her. And I am certain that if she is planning something, she will not tell a slave girl."

Cleopatra smiled. As intelligent as Patroclus was he did not really understand the machinations of the court. Nor did he have the necessary ruthlessness to survive the plots and counterplots being constantly formulated. Even at her delicate age, Cleopatra knew what was needed to survive the intrigues of royalty.

"I agree the slave girl will probably not be privy to Olympias' plots. However, it is almost impossible to live with another and not be in tune, for better or worse, with their feelings, their desires. Olympias could no better keep a secret from that girl than I could from Philip." Cleopatra smiled at her analogy, knowing that Philip was so engrossed with managing and expanding his empire that he was almost oblivious to the events in her life. But Patroclus did not need to know that.

"I do not wish to end the life of the girl unnecessarily," said Patroclus.

"She will be safe...as long as she uses her wits and does not betray us," replied Cleopatra, her eyes narrowing. "And why should you be so concerned with a slave?" The last few words hissed out.

Patroclus was taken aback by Cleopatra's question. And for an agonizingly long few seconds, she seemed to transform herself into Olympias. Now Patroclus could see what he had always been blind to: both queens were mirror images of each other, the only difference being age.

"Cleopatra, my only concern is a humanitarian one. You know that eunuchs are much more sensitive than whole men. I only expressed an incidental interest in the girl."

This seemed to satisfy the queen. She could not explain why she had angered so quickly upon hearing Patroclus' concern about the slave girl. But his explanation made sense. Everyone knew that eunuchs were oftentimes more effeminate than women. Patroclus did not appear to be an exception.

Patroclus had barely finished talking when a loud pounding at the door jolted his attention away from Cleopatra to the direction of the sound. The young queen too turned to face the portal.

The massive timbers comprising the barrier between the queen's chambers and the rest of the palace squealed horrifically as they were gently pushed into the room. When a space scarce wider than a child's body was created, a young boy, perhaps ten years old, squeezed into the room. His laboured breath, his apparent agitation and his obviously sweating body all indicated that he had some great purpose in Cleopatra's suite.

"The quee...Olympias comes! My cousin who is the personal attendant for her steward told me that she is on her way. And... and I think that she comes angry. I knew that my queen would want to know immediately...so I ran as quickly as I could. I hope this pleases you," concluded the lad, still gulping air as he tried to replenish his lungs.

Cleopatra stepped forward and from within her robes magically produced a coin. With great and probably uncalled for civility, she presented the child with his reward. Almost snatching it, the boy beamed with pleasure as he deftly manipulated the coin through his fingers. He bowed to the queen in gratitude, and as quickly as he had come in, he disappeared.

"Stay. She would not come without good reason. I want you here...I do not trust her," said Cleopatra.

The last thing Patroclus wished to hear was that he would have to stay to face that harpy from hell. But he also knew that to make enemies of two queens would be the surest way to a probably very painful death. For now, he was safer to side with the king's favourite.

"I had no intention of leaving, my queen. It might be best however if I stand to the side so as not to intimidate or anger Olympias unnecessarily. It will be to your advantage if you can control the situation."

Cleopatra forced a wan smile. Patroclus was right. She had to maintain control over at least her private chambers. After all, she was the real queen now.

They both heard the rap. Patroclus stepped back, not out of sight but enough removed from Cleopatra that he would not draw Olympias' attention easily. A nervous sigh escaped him.

"Enter," said Cleopatra.

The door screeched as it was rudely thrust open. A dark, squat man, armed with a short, bronze sword moved back from the entrance and let Olympias precede him into the room. The queen, regal in dress, emotionally poised, charged the room with an almost tangible energy. Diminutive though she was, her stature was magnified by her self-confidence and dangerous unpredictability. She glanced around, her eyes sweeping the room, analyzing, processing the information gleaned in a fraction of a heartbeat. Patroclus did not go unnoticed. A feline smile slowly altered the stoic face that she presented upon entry. The play that was about to be acted out was going to amuse her.

"Welcome to my suite, Olympias," offered Cleopatra, playing at the gracious hostess.

Olympias stared hard at the speaker. It appeared that she might not have heard Cleopatra until the light filtering in through the window reflected off her eyes. The ensuing glare, reminiscent of a mirror casting back the rays of the sun, almost blinded Cleopatra. Those eyes. It was as if Olympias had harnessed the power of the sun god and had used them to create a weapon.

"I see that the eunuch is still in your employ," dripped Olympias acidly. She had ignored Cleopatra's greeting and was now staring disdainfully at a visibly nervous Patroclus.

"I assume that your coming here is something more than an inspection of my staff," replied Cleopatra in a tone simultaneously formal and sarcastic.

Olympias remained calm although someone looking into her eyes may have thought they saw them flare. Olympias then parted her lips, as if to say something, yet no words came out. A gleam of moisture, dancing on the tip of her tongue distracted Patroclus. He had watched these opening maneuvers with interest. Now he found himself staring at the full, crimson lips of this extraordinarily beautiful woman. He had never noticed it before. How blind could he be? It was apparent why men threw themselves at Olympias. The allurement was not limited to her physical accouterments either. Raw sensuality, almost bestial threatened to engulf him and he was supposed to be immune to those base needs. He shifted his position. Again he sneaked a look at Olympias, careful not to draw her attention away from Cleopatra.

A space of only a couple of body lengths separated him from Olympias, yet he felt himself a voyeur, somehow violating the privacy of her being. He could not resist. His fascination with Olympias was as a candle to an insect; he knew he would suffer...still, the pain of trying to negate his mind and body threatened to be overwhelming. What was he supposed to do? Eunuchs were not supposed to be sexually attracted to anyone. To feel these stirrings now, so close to a person who could systematically destroy him as easily as he could spit on a bug, was insanity. That had to be it. Olympias had him so frightened, Cleopatra had him so confused and that slave girl Phylia had him, dare he say it, so in love that when combined with the various court intrigues he found himself involved in, perhaps he was better off being insane.

Olympias had noticed that Patroclus was nervous. That was an incidental fact she would have to remember later. This impudent child-queen was another matter.

"You move graciously. I see that the harlots have learned new dances with which to please their customers. Does Philip pay you an appropriate amount? I hope so. I would be extremely displeased to learn that my husband has become a tightwad over the years. After all, if he is to conquer Asia, he must keep his harem girls in Pella happy." Olympias flashed her teeth, her mouth upturned but not in a way that might be mistaken for a smile.

Cleopatra blushed. The heat in her cheeks made her skin prickly and the tiny beads of sweat forming on her forehead begged to be wiped away. She did not move. The insult had struck deeply. She could not afford to display any weakness to Philip's first wife.

"You may be right. I must remind myself to practice. It is unfortunate that one's physical attractiveness deteriorates so rapidly. It must be very difficult for you. Are there no creams or salves that would restore your skin? I admit that I admire your fortitude. Getting dressed in beautiful clothes every day, dieting so you will not gain weight, combing your hair until it almost falls out...tsk, tsk, and all for a man who will not even bed you. I know that I would be devastated." Cleopatra's return volley had been couched in gentle, caring tones that almost hid the malicious intent.

Only a twitch in Olympias' left eye betrayed her fury. "Age is an evil we all learn to live with. Some like Philip assuage their insecurities by rutting themselves on young, nubile bodies. They see the lack of practical knowledge in these girls as something attractive. I could not begin to answer why. Philip faces so many challenges during the day that he is not able to satisfy both himself and a real woman. Rather than masturbating, he has found himself an object that will stimulate him quickly, present no challenges to his manhood and will thank him incessantly for his attention. You are still so young. For you, that is love or a reasonable facsimile of."

Patroclus could not believe what he was hearing. The catty viciousness of the queens' attacks on each other was scathing. He would rather face a swordsman than have to be the recipient of such abuse.

Olympias continued, noting with satisfaction, the discomfort of Cleopatra. "Please do not misconstrue what I am saying. I am sure, that in your own, cute little way, you are somewhat pleasing to the old cripple. And you are still so young...it is quite possible that the king may not live much longer and then you will be left alone although a fairly attractive girl like yourself should be able to find another husband. When Alexander becomes king, I will speak to him about it."

Cleopatra seethed. Her skin turned a mottled red as her emotions threatened to rip from her body. She knew however that she could not allow any advantage to Olympias. The reason for her presence, other than to insult her, had not been made clear. Before she reached over and tore the hair out of that old bitch, she would have to find out why she was here. Yes, she thought. She would wait. Until then, she would add a little fire of her own.

"Alexander...king? Are you not being premature? I can tell you, Philip is the most vital, alive man I have ever known. Even with his injuries, I doubt that there is any threat to his health from his own body. He should live another forty years...unless someone plots against his life. You of course would know nothing about that...would you? And if I may be permitted to offer advice to such a sage and wise woman as yourself...perhaps it would be prudent to refrain from keeping company with a known murderer and his cohorts. A man like Kathos really has no legitimate business in Pella. You might be surprised as to how the citizens of our beloved Macedonia might object, rather strenuously I may add, to a queen consorting with gutter scum."

Patroclus noticed how Olympias flinched. The spies hired by Cleopatra had been right. Philip's first wife was planning something. To entertain Kathos for so long she must be devising a plot to assassinate someone. Who? Even Olympias would not risk the murder of a King. Alexander's anger would be unstoppable. Patroclus' brow furrowed as he concentrated. Then, just out of the corner of his eye, he saw Olympias' bodyguard slip out the main door. I wonder where he is going, thought Patroclus.

Breathing evenly, maintaining her composure, Olympias replied to the stinging insults and veiled accusations of Cleopatra. "It appears that you are well-informed. But do you consider it proper that the wives of the man who has conquered all of Hellas and will soon conquer Asia, are reduced to tracing each other's movements, spying in their bedrooms?"

Cleopatra ignored the statement. She knew that Olympias would just as soon cut her heart out. "Let us end the charade. You are here for a reason. State your purpose." Cleopatra surprised herself with the firmness of her voice. It was almost as if the life stirring inside of her had manifested itself in her spirit. The future king was speaking through her. A warm flush of pride suffused her face.

Patroclus noted how confident the young queen was. He was amazed that she had been able to face Olympias and trade verbal blow for blow with her. It was not something tangible, but it appeared to Patroclus that Cleopatra was standing straighter, her head was tilted higher and her eyes flashed brighter. Patroclus felt his own unease melt away as he assured himself that he had made the right alliance. A small sigh escaped him. He did not relax long. Olympias' bodyguard had returned with the most exquisitely tied bundle. Could it be a gift? A peace offering?

Olympias did not appear to notice the return of her bodyguard. She said, "I want us to make sure that we have the mutual respect between us that the king would want. You have presented yourself quite...well. I feel it is important that you now pay me the respect that I have earned, as queen of Macedonia. This is for you." Olympias did not signal her bodyguard but he immediately stepped forward with the cloth-wrapped bundle.

Cleopatra was wary. What could Olympias possibly give her? And why? She looked at the package. It had been wrapped with the brightest, most beautiful fabrics she had ever seen. They shimmered and changed colors as they trapped then released the sunlight filtering in through the windows. Even though she was a queen, she had only seen a few samples of this magical cloth rumored to come from somewhere in Asia. To have her most hated enemy present her with a gift wrapped in this treasure was especially annoying. Jealousy, which had so far been well contained, roused itself and Cleopatra could feel herself getting angrier and angrier. How did Olympias do it? How dare she not only find something that Cleopatra desired but also have the effrontery to hand it over as if it were nothing more important than a rough piece of burlap? To add to the insult, Cleopatra had to accept what appeared to be a peace overture. Good sense told her not to...yet...

"If maintaining a peaceful accord with each other alleviates the tension our relationship puts on Philip, I will accept your gift...with thanks," said Cleopatra, taking a step forward and extending her arms to pick up the parcel.

Patroclus may not have been attuned to how complex the various court intrigues could get. But watching Cleopatra now, ready to take the offering from Olympias, sparked a warning signal. Patroclus leaned forward, gently took both Cleopatra's hands and pulled them back from the gift.

"If you would do us the honour?" Patroclus looked right at Olympias. He could feel Cleopatra's hands trembling in his own.

"For a slave with no manhood, you take great liberties. Either you are far more courageous than I give you credit for, or when they cut off your testicles they took a part of your brain too. Nevertheless, as you so desperately want me to open this," said Olympias, picking up the bundle, "...I will."

With a few deft twirls of the fabric, Olympias had it unwrapped.

Cleopatra screamed. And screamed.

Patroclus choked. The vomit fought to escape the confines of his stomach. Only his battle-hardened constitution prevented him from defiling the marble floor. He did not want to look. He swallowed hard and raised his eyes.

Olympias stood defiant. Clutched in one hand and held out in front of her, a trophy of the most macabre kind, was the head of a young woman. The blood had congealed, and the skin had turned a ghastly white so it was difficult to ascertain the identity of the victim.

"It is a shame that one so young, so beautiful..." Olympias brought the dismembered head close to her, and grasping it with both hands, kissed it full on the mouth. And with what appeared to be one long uninterrupted motion, she then threw the blood-matted remnant of a human being across the room where it bounced sickeningly into a corner. "Ssspy," hissed Olympias. "Never again be so foolish as to send someone to inform on me. I am the queen. I am the power that will give you nightmares. Try this again...and even Philip will not save your worthless skin." Olympias was roused to an almost sexual frenzy. Her heart beat rapidly, her skin was flushed and the most pleasurable sensation of all began to slowly manifest itself in the areas concealed by her gown. The power she had...

Cleopatra stood immobile, still in shock. Patroclus shook his head repeatedly. Neither one could have guessed the ruthlessness of the queen. To combat one such as Olympias was obviously the most futile of efforts. They felt defeated, ravished. To even look up at Olympias was impossible.

Olympias stood erect, triumphant. These petty meddlers had been taught that real power was dependant upon how far one was willing to violate every known societal norm. To Olympias, the conventions of her society were to be used or abused; whatever was necessary to further hers and her son's ambitions. Disposing of a naive, simple-minded chambermaid was simple. In fact, watching Kathos and his companions enjoy the brainless twit had in itself been entertaining. It paled however to the entertainment that Cleopatra and Patroclus had provided her moments ago. Standing here now, she felt omnipotent.

No one had moved. It was a tableau from one of the tragedies enacted every night at the Dionyssian theatre. There, almost as if mounted on a pedestal was Olympias, fire-breathing witch-goddess. Beside her, a wraith from the underworld, unmoving yet menacing. A few steps away, a child, in the guise of a woman lay sobbing on the shoulder of a vanquished warrior. Homer, as brilliant as he was, never envisioned such humiliation, such terror.

Olympias smirked. She took one last look, wheeled and without another word, left the chambers of Cleopatra. Her bodyguard noiselessly followed. Patroclus saw her depart. Gently, but with a little more force than planned, he eased the sobbing Cleopatra away from him. Her head hung dejectedly. Now he saw her for the child she was. She had held her own with Olympias but ultimately it had been for naught. As sorry as he felt for the young bride of Philip, there was something he had to do.

Patroclus slowly took a step. Then another. And another. To walk to where the truncated head lay was a journey through Hell. The steps were agonizing. He went on. Now he could see the object of Olympias' ultimate revenge. It lay there a bloody, lifeless, putrefying obscenity. Patroclus swallowed. It hurt his throat. He had moved beside it now. He closed his eyes, took a deep breath and with his foot, nudged the object on the floor. He heard rather than saw it turn over. Ohh, gods of Olympus, please let it not be Phylia. He opened his eyes.

Dioxippus

What a foul smell, he thought. Then thinking aloud, "Not even my mother would come near me." He looked down at the poultice nestling along his injured collarbone. A thin line of fluid carved its way from the warm, sticky mass, through the hair on his chest, until its path was interrupted by the bottom part of his chiton. The meandering trickle went unnoticed as it slowly dampened the cloth gathered around his waist; he was concentrating hard trying to channel his thoughts into the path of the Empty Mind, a plane of meditation beyond prayer, beyond invocation. Dioxippus knew of cultures where the mind's potential for internal healing had been reached by holy men, spiritualists and even warriors. Slowly clenching then unclenching his fists he forced himself to relax. He was aware of the blood pumping to the injured area of his body as he willed himself to heal even though he could feel no physical sensation; his body had been reduced to the shell it was. Pain, pleasure, joy, sorrow, had become intertwined and rendered impotent by the vacuum, growing, expanding in the consciousness of his being. Soon he would leave this place.

Ensconced in this cocoon of spiritual disgorgement, Dioxippus was oblivious to the stimuli being transmitted from his nervous system to his brain. His whole existence had been reduced to a small black circle that had erected itself as a barrier between his physical body and his mind. Not the noises in the street, not the smells of the cooking fires, not the sunlight moving slowly across the floor, could filter through to the meditating Dioxippus. Not even the rush of cool air that flooded in through the opening door roused Dioxippus from the mind-state he had achieved.

"What in Zeus' name are you doing?" challenged Barba Fotis. The little man, as irascible as the day Dioxippus met him, stared at the recumbent Dioxippus with an expression of fierce wonder. And when he did not receive an answer, his temper, frayed by age, circumstance and life, erupted quickly.

"Get up you ungrateful, ill-mannered, muscle-bound simpleton! I am talking to you," said a now thoroughly aroused Fotis. To him it appeared that the young man, sitting cross-legged with his eyes closed and a beatific smile on his face was purposely ignoring him. Did Dioxippus not know that he, Fotis, was already living on some other soul's time? Any day, any moment, he would be crossing the river of the dead into Hades. He did not have time to spare with Dioxippus. "Wake up!" Fotis, always the curmudgeon, kicked the foot of the meditating Dioxippus.

At first all he could sense was a vibration. Then he noticed that the ever-expanding void his mind was being sucked into had ceased to grow and in fact was receding. From deep within the Void came a sound; a screeching, vile noise bent upon the destruction of the spiritual peace he had attained. Dioxippus tried to refocus, to somehow purge the intruder. But the noise grew louder, fiercer. As if it had a life of its own, it fought his attempts to squelch it.

"You call these manners? Get up before I take your lazy ass and kick it from here to Persia." Fotis was working himself up to what soon would be a tantrum. At his age, patience was a memory.

Suddenly, the Void collapsed upon itself. The resulting reverberations forced Dioxippus' eyes open. The first thing he saw was a little man, gray and wrinkled, cocking his right foot back as he readied himself to kick the sitting Dioxippus. More by reflex than by some innate awareness the pankratiatist rolled out of the way just as the foot shot forth from its chambered position. Fotis missed, hyper-extended his knee ligaments and screamed in pain. Dioxippus, now standing, looked at Fotis, his concern apparent.

"Of all the fornicating morons in the world, I had to latch on to the dumbest, stupidest, ugliest, most worthless..."

"I need not hear any more. I am sorry..." interrupted Dioxippus, trying to end the diatribe from Fotis. His sincerity could be questioned as he laughed while saying this.

"Ohhh...the idiot grins. It must be very satisfying to trick and ridicule an old man. Should I bow down to you great warrior?" With that, Fotis curtsied in a most unfeminine manner.

Dioxippus could not control himself. He laughed hysterically. A few times he tried to say a few words but they were caught up in the torrent of guffawing. He laughed even harder when he felt Fotis slap him across the back of his bent-over head.

Fotis still cursed him even though his anger had dissipated. This easy relationship he had with Dioxippus allowed him to vent some frustration without fear of penalty. It was one of the reasons he and Dios got along so well. A few more choice epithets and he was finished.

"Gods of Olympus, you smell like the back end of a mangy goat. Phewwww...what did Piros put on your shoulder?" asked Fotis, his voice nasally as he squeezed his nostrils with his thumb and first finger.

"It deadens the pain from the bone," replied Dioxippus as he slowly removed the putrid mess from his injury.

"Well, if the smell means anything, it is working," said Fotis. He released his nose and took a step toward Dioxippus. He extended his hand and then ran his fingers along the collarbone. "Hmmmm...I cannot even feel the break. It went back together splendidly. Piros is a sorcerer. Now let me see. Can you raise your arm over your head?"

Smiling, Dioxippus lunged forward, swooped low and in one easy motion picked up the little man, lifted him over his head and held him there suspended.

Fotis had time to barely breathe much less start screaming. Nevertheless, as soon as Dioxippus put him down, he started anew; this time the insults included every ancestor human or inhuman in Dioxippus' family.

Dioxippus just stood. His smile illuminated his face. At this moment his joy was boundless. He had recovered.

"Do you want an even more evil-smelling concoction on your body?"

Dioxippus looked behind for the voice. He did not turn his whole body, just his head. But what he saw made him wheel around. Standing there, with grins the size of half melons, were Piros and a tall, lanky, dark-haired youth. As the rising sun was behind them, it was impossible to discern faces. Yet without any hesitation, Dioxippus knew that Piros' companion was his childhood friend and sparring partner, Euphraeus.

Both youths leaped toward each other, hugging, kissing and roughhousing. They had not seen each other since Athens fell to the Macedonians and their pleasure at being reunited overrode any rules of decorum made up by more restrained adults. Neither one could hear the other over their own animated voices. Yet it did not appear to make any difference as they alternately poked, punched and held each other.

Piros and Fotis stood to one side. They were careful not to intrude on the reunion being enacted in front of them. Although neither would admit it, each felt a small pain of bittersweet memory as they recalled the joys of a youth lost forever.

"This...this is the surprise you told me to expect a few days ago? This is more than a surprise--it is a gift! Where...how did you find him?" asked an over-excited Dioxippus, his arm firmly around the shoulders of his returned friend.

Euphraeus looked toward Piros, unsure if he should answer. Piros however responded immediately. "Euphraeus has just returned from Delphi, where he has been preparing for the games. He has decided this year to enter the Olympics as a boxer. As he is still lighter than most of his adversaries, he sought a sparring partner who was heavier, yet still quick, and who could really test him without attempting to kill him. His trainer told another who told another who told another until it came to me. And I thought, what better way to test Dioxippus than with his old sparring partner, Euphraeus. For you Euphraeus I present an opportunity to spar with someone who knows your style is almost as quick and will challenge you well. Add the bonus of having your best friend close by you on the eve of the most important week of your life and what more can I say?"

Dioxippus and Euphraeus looked at each other, the animated expressions on their faces indicative of the joy each felt in the other's company. Arms about each other's shoulders they walked over to the low-slung bench, and began to prepare themselves to train. They would discuss the missing years later.

Barba Fotis did not need to be signaled. He followed the two young men to the bench where he pulled forth from under the bench a plain, undecorated clay container full of oil. Reaching under again, he retrieved a small, woven bag which he put on top of the bench beside the now sitting Dioxippus. With the fastidiousness of a nursing mother, he laid out his instruments, lotions, oils and equipment in front of him, making sure (more out of superstition than practicality) that nothing touched the other. With a grunt, Fotis then signaled the two young men to disrobe. As soon as they stood naked, he poured some of the scented olive oil into his hands, and slowly, methodically spread the slippery substance all over the body of first Dioxippus then Euphraeus. Both stood as still as the columns ringing the workout area.

Piros was pleased with what he had seen the last few moments. Dioxippus, although reckless, had healed well since he had injured himself. The medicine Piros had purchased from the Persian had done its job well. As for the reunion with Euphraeus, what a good choice he had made in offering the Athenian youth the opportunity to not only be with his friend but to also be trained by he, Piros, one of the best in Greece, (he admitted to himself quite sheepishly). Fortunately, this had proven to be enough incentive for Euphraeus to leave the training grounds at Delphi. With their hand skills so well matched both fighters would reap tremendous rewards.

As the two youths stretched and performed warm-up exercises, Fotis pulled several scraps of tanned leather from his sack. Piros, who had by now moved over to the bench, picked one up and quizzically looked at the old trainer.

"It is something I have been thinking about for a long time," said Fotis, nodding in the direction of Piros' upraised hand. "I thought...that maybe I could help reduce injuries during training. Here, let me show you." Fotis picked up a scrap of leather from the bench. Extending his left arm, and with his fingers spread wide, he slid his hand into the glove-like shape. Holding his hand up so Piros could see, he clenched and unclenched the now sheathed hand.

"Hmmmm...let me see." Piros rose to take a closer look at the hand-covering Fotis had invented. He noted that the leather was soft, supple and almost immediately formed to the shape of the hand wrapped in it. Piros then extended his own hand and like a giant claw, clamped it over the gloved fist of Fotis. He was surprised to feel how rigid, how solid the fist still was. His brows furrowed as he thought hard about this development.

Fotis had been with Piros so long he could sense what thoughts were emanating from his master. "The leather is not meant to cushion the blow only to prevent unnecessary cuts and injuries to the hand. I thought that for the sparring exercises it would serve well. After all, I see no reason why Dioxippus should risk injuring or being injured." He looked at Piros apprehensively. Too many times his ideas had been laughed at or dismissed. Although Piros never had been derisive Fotis could not be sure how his ingenuity would be interpreted.

While Fotis spoke, Piros slipped the other pieces of leather over his hands. There were strings to fasten them or to adjust the tightness of the fit; Piros still had to look over to Fotis' hand in order to figure out how to fit the glove properly. When the fit was satisfactory, Piros alternately closed his hands into fists and punched one into the other repeatedly. As every punch got harder, Piros' smile got bigger. Finally, after countless slaps of leather against leather he looked at Fotis and nodded his approval.

The old Helot was overjoyed. He tried to maintain a certain dignity but was unable to contain himself; he jumped from one foot to the other, his feet barely alighting on the ground. By now, even Dioxippus and Euphraeus noticed that something momentous had occurred. Ceasing their conversation, and getting up from the sitting position from which they had been stretching hamstrings and groin muscles, they came over to the bench, their curiosity begging to be satiated.

"Slip these on," suggested Piros to the two young men. "Here, I will help you."

"Are we supposed to fight with these things on?" asked a very sarcastic Euphraeus. "What in the Apollo's name are these supposed to do?"

Dioxippus looked at Piros, his eyes signaling his mentor to not respond to the affront to Fotis. The aged trainer caught the look and was pleased by Dioxippus' consideration.

"Just put them on," said Dioxippus to Euphraeus. "I think it is time that you learned your lesson for today."

"Ohhhh...I shake with fear. You are a little bigger, maybe a little more accomplished but you are still the skinny slave I used to slap at will." Euphraeus smiled at his friend. His words, taunting, were tempered by such good will that it was obvious no insult was intended.

"Well then braggart, let us see how all that training at Delphi has helped." Dioxippus immediately fired off two left jabs. The unmistakable whack of the leather against the bare skin of Euphraeus' cheek snapped the air. Neither blow was thrown hard enough to cause real injury but the speed and accuracy of the punches drew gasps from even Piros and Fotis, who had between them seen thousands such techniques.

Euphraeus stepped back, unhurt but embarassed. He glowered at Dioxippus. Suddenly, he slid forward, the movement in his feet barely perceptible. The only warning of a distance closed was Euphraeus' just released punch whistling toward Dioxippus' cheek. Again the smack of leather against skin popped the air. And in a reversal of the first attack, Dioxippus stepped back, his cheek a mottled red from the impact.

"Break!" said Piros curtly. Both pankratiatists turned to look at their trainer. Piros stepped forward until he was in between them. "I concede both of you your speed with the jab. However, you make the most common mistake of the young. You are so impressed with your technique that you ignore the follow-up or even the counter. Dioxippus, I would venture to say that at this moment there is no one in Hellas with better skills in the pankration than you. Yet, you were almost killed by an inferior fighter because you spent valuable moments during the bout admiring your form. Dioxippus, and this applies to you also, Euphraeus, the pankration or the boxing, is not like the running or the discus events. While we compare, it is not even in the same category as the wrestling. Your sports are nothing more than glorified hand-to-hand combat. If you ignore, or dismiss the potentially fatal results of these contests, you will not only lose the olive wreath but you may also lose your life. Your opponent is your enemy. Given the chance he will crush you like a gnat. You must be so focused, so aware and so aggressive, that the opportunity for him to do you harm is reduced or even obliterated. You will not win in the Olympic games if you lose your concentration and desire."

Neither Dioxippus nor Euphraeus looked at Piros' face. Piros was right. They spent so much time trying to look accomplished and smooth that they neglected to pursue advantages. Euphraeus had been denied the wreath at the youth games because he had spent an inordinate amount of time during the bout sniping instead of creating combinations that would have defeated the more plodding, methodical opponent. Dioxippus of course knew firsthand what could happen if an adversary was allowed to dictate the pace and rhythm of the match. His last foe made it impossible for him to set the pace of the fight. Unable to adapt to the illegal techniques, Dioxippus found himself crippled by the ruthless pankratiatist. Only fortune, a deadly new kick and ruthlessness salvaged victory. Yes, Piros was right.

"This time, put combinations together. Remember, body to head," continued Piros, his hands and arms moving as he tried to show his students what he wanted them to do. Dioxippus nodded, Euphraeus too. As they began to move off, Piros called, "Stop. Before you start again let me see those horsehide straps that Fotis made." Piros took Dioxippus' gloved hands, turned them so he could see the knuckles and peeled back the leather. Other than being slightly moistened, the hand seemed comfortably enclosed. Piros reached up, and with a touch as soft as a lover's caress, felt the cheek of his young charge. Even though it had only been hit twice, a small bruise had already formed. Piros did note that the skin had not been split. Except for the slight discolouring from the bruise, it was impossible to tell that Dioxippus had been hit at all much less hard enough to form a lump. These wraps of Fotis looked like they worked.

"Barba Fotis, I think these creations of yours might have some merit. I want you to work on making ones that provide a little more padding. Be careful. I do not want pankratiatists babied with pillows on their hands. Just put enough material in them so that these two good friends do not do serious injury to each other."

The old man beamed. The greatest pankratiatist of his time thought his idea worked.

"Now what are you two doing? God! The young! Hurry up, do something," snapped Piros to the two youths who had been standing around.

Within seconds the dust swirled as the two future Olympians began their exercises.

Kathos

"I think he is waking up," commented Pythogras. He turned his one good eye toward Kathos. "What do you want us to do with him?"

Kathos smirked. "Right now nothing. Ummmm...blindfold him. The queen was firm on that."

Pythogras tore a strip of darkened material in half. With a few deft turns, he had covered Pausanius' eyes. Without asking Kathos, he tore the rest of the fabric into even thinner strips and with scarcely any movement bound his prisoner's hands and feet. He guessed that Kathos would probably ridicule him but he was not going to take any chances with a King's Companion, no matter how decrepit he had become.

"Feel safer now," drawled Kathos sarcastically.

Pythogras just glared at him. Unlike the other riffraff that hung around Kathos, he was not afraid of his master. Nor was he bothered by his insults. He knew Kathos for what he was; a sexual deviate with an insatiable bloodlust. This combination made him extremely dangerous. However, Pythogras also knew that the feared Kathos was an interminable coward. All the bravado and posturizing was nothing more that a false front. Pythogras did have to admit though, that many important people (who perhaps should have known better) paid Kathos (and his cohorts), a large amount of money to carry out their nefarious deeds. For this reason alone, Pythogras stayed with the degenerate.

Kathos was of course oblivious to Pythogras' thoughts. All he would concern himself with at this moment was the order that Olympias had given him. He sneered at the prone Pausanius, now almost awake. This King's Companion, he thought vehemently, was going to provide him with the best entertainment he had had in a very long while.

"Sit him up!" he barked.

Two of his cronies immediately grabbed the trussed Pausanius and sat him up.

"Sooo...King's Companion, you awake. Forgive our zeal. We only wanted to make you comfortable quickly. I suspect my goodnight kiss was a little forceful. My apologies. Are the ropes a little tight? It seems my compatriot Pythogras fears those legendary skills of the King's Companions. But looking at you, I see those fears are misplaced."

Under the blindfold Pausanius blinked. Otherwise there was no sign of response.

Kathos bent over, pushing his face up as close as he could to Pausanius. It looked as if he was trying to see through the fabric hiding his prisoner's eyes. He stayed in that position, not moving, not saying anything. To his subordinates it appeared that Kathos was trying to communicate with his captive through some sort of telepathic language. But when Kathos leaned away from Pausanius, a sickening smirk twisted his face into an evil leer. There was no higher level of intercourse occurring here: only a subtle psychological assault upon a helpless victim.

"You say nothing. Is this what Greeks call courage?" The hand swung before the words were even finished. Pausanius' head cracked with the impact of Kathos' open palm. He started to fall back but Kathos grabbed him by his hair and with a motion as graceful as a dancer's, he slapped him again with his other hand. "How does this feel? Soldier! Warrior!" screamed Kathos, his open hand swinging after almost every word, the force of his blows splitting skin, bruising bone. Yet no sound escaped the lips of the battered Pausanius.

Pythogras watched with the detachment of the professional criminal. There was no question that this Pausanius was very tough. He had taken an incredible number of blows from Kathos, still, no sound, not even a grunt, forced itself through his tightly closed lips. Pythogras noticed that Kathos was tiring and as if perfectly rehearsed, the other two members of Kathos' little gang started battering the secured captive. The monotonous thud, its brutal rhythm punctuated by the odd whack, proceeded unabated. The only other sound heard were the short exhalations of the torturers as their energy expended rapidly. From Pausanius, cut, swollen, bruised...nothing.

"Is it necessary that we waste half a day beating a man to death? If the queen wants him..."

Pythogras' words choked on blood and broken teeth as Kathos' fist smashed into his mouth. Reflexively, he lifted his hands to the bloody mess now gagging him. Shock, pain, both disoriented him as he reeled backward, his sixth sense somehow guiding him to a bench which he fell onto gratefully. His coolly analytical brain was now a muddled cacophony of sounds and spinning lights. What had happened?

Kathos stared hard at the man he had just struck. The queen had been explicit. No reference was to be made to her. That fool almost gave away the plan. Kathos turned to look at Pausanius. He had been reduced to a crumpled collection of bones and skin, so badly had he been beaten. The blindfold still hid the eyes, but the swelling and bruising could be seen quite easily as the lumps distorted the smooth fabric surrounding the head. Pausanius' beard, normally black, was discoloured to a brown red, as the blood, drool and sweat matted the facial hair. Kathos grunted to himself. This Macedonian would die before he begged: the queen did not want that to happen. Turning to his confederates, who had taken a rest from the assault on Pausanius, he indicated to them that they attend Pythogras. As if to clarify his order, he tossed the shorter of the two men, a clean rag. "Clean him up," he said.

The murky stupor clouding his brain protected him from the more acute pain. The only reality for Pausanius at this point was the darkness. He heard sounds, or, did he feel them. He was not sure. His senses were useless. Nothing was being transmitted to his brain. Where was he? Why was it dark? Was he alone? Nobody could answer the question for him.

Kathos conferred with his men. He whispered something to them, and for emphasis pointed them in the direction of the still bleeding Pythogras. They nodded their assent and took their positions on either side of Pausanius.

"Pausanius, or should I refer to you as traitor? I see the pain does not bother you. I commend you. You present a stalwart defence. Philip was probably very proud of you at one time. It is a shame that your loyalties are now so divided. You think that we are unaware of your betrayal of our king? Do you think that we are not privy to your plot to belittle and denigrate the throne? You are a dangerous man. You should not be allowed to live. However, the man who hired us insists that we spare your life. And do you want to know what he wishes in return...nothing!" concluded a suddenly complacent Kathos.

Pausanius could feel his head pounding. Every pump of his heart, every expanding and contracting vein and artery, he could now feel. Never had he been so in tune with the machinations of his body. He could feel the subtle shifts in the air on his skin. He could taste the combination of bile, saliva and blood on his tongue. He could smell the putrefying stench of his own soiled clothes. Only the darkness remained, preventing a full awakening of his body's other life functions. That and the voice that he could barely hear.

"Strip him," ordered Kathos. A deft twist, a tearing of fabric and Pausanius was naked. "Spread him."

The pummeled body of Pausanius was as malleable as an artist's clay. Kathos' confederates each grabbed an arm and a leg and pulled the soldier's limbs away from his torso. No resistance.

Pausanius was not yet recovered from the multiple blows he had just endured. The control over his body was minimal and his brain was just now starting to reorganize itself. On the basest level he could feel a chill on his trunk, particularly on his genitals. He was incapable of explaining why, but he was newly alarmed and in response, tensed his muscles sharply. The sudden movement caught the two men holding him unaware, and for an instant it appeared that Pausanius would gain back his warrior's vigor. But the grips were tight. He would not be free.

"Excellent. He awakes. I want him to feel this. Over and over until he breathes no more," snarled Kathos. "Hold him!"

Kathos released the cord holding his own chiton. It billowed out and then fell to the dusty red tile composing the aged floor. As naked as the prostate Pausanius lying face down in front of him, Kathos slid his hand down his stomach and across his groin until it seized his own hardening penis. At his touch, the blood rushed to the organ, now erect with anticipation. Kathos dropped to his knees. He leaned over Pausanius and with an almost tender tone said, "You should feel honoured Companion. The lord Attalus does not often pay this much for the pleasure of a traitor. He wants you to remember him every time you think of this moment. I know you will enjoy it."

A sword striking flesh. Burning. Pausanius howled, the shock, the biting pain of the entry catching him unaware. Kathos grunted as he plunged deeper and deeper, faster and faster. Pausanius screamed again, the shame greater than the agony. But this time there was no blessed loss of consciousness. With every violation, Pausanius regained more and more of his dulled senses. And with every thrust, the total feeling of helplessness nauseated him. He would have fought...if he could. Now he only wanted to die.

Expending himself, Kathos raised himself from the prone Pausanius. A short nod of the head was the signal his men needed. Immediately, they started kicking the stomach, the ribs and the genitals of their prisoner. It was their last perverse pleasure.

"Let him go," ordered Kathos. "He is of no threat now." He refastened his chiton about him as he spoke. "Can you hear me Companion? Signal me if you cannot talk, or I will be forced to start our relationship all over."

Pausanius was almost beyond hearing much less comprehending what had been asked of him. But a survival instinct, buried deep within his mind, fought fiercely to regain some control over the pummeled body and defeated spirit. And although he could barely discern what his captor was saying, he managed to bang the floor twice with his hand.

"Good. Very Good!" beamed a triumphant Kathos. He bent down on one knee, leaned forward so he was close to Pausanius and said, "Listen, then understand. You are a traitor to the throne. You have been spared death...today. But know that all who go against Philip and his family will be punished. The man who paid us wants you to know that he is the one who discovered your plans. He saves your worthless hide as a gift to a king you once served faithfully. Otherwise the buzzards would be picking your bones now. I would strongly suggest that you leave Pella, before Attalus has us finish the job we barely started. Take this advice Companion, it is the only thing I give you that will benefit you." Kathos turned his head up. "Throw him in the street with the other garbage."

The two men who had held Pausanius most of the morning once again grabbed him, this time under the armpits. Clumsily they walked and dragged him to the door, and in the most casual manner, tossed what had once been one of Philip's bravest warriors, naked into the street.

And as he lay there, the pain of his wounds rising and falling in interminable waves, the fire in his rectum blazing the shame of the rape into his brain, he could only think of one thing: Attalus, Attalus, ATTALUS!

Philip ponders the future

The arrow turned in lazy circles as it was gently maneuvered through the fingers. Philip was not even aware of the action as his hand mechanically manipulated the slender, feathered shaft. This old exercise had been taught to him by a mercenary in his father's army in a year so long ago that if he had been asked to recollect the moment when he was first shown this activity designed to improve the dexterity of his digits, nothing more than a hazy image would have been forthcoming. Yet, when pondering a problem, or decision, he invariably found himself twirling that piece of wood. And oddly enough, the more concentrated his thought processes, the faster the arrow traveled the space between his fingers. The barbed stick was now spinning.

Darius. Persia. Riches greater than those of the mighty Lydian king, Croesus. Philip was enthralled with the idea of marching into Asia and gaining that which the obscenely wealthy Croesus had been unable to do two hundred years earlier. With his son beside him, he would be unstoppable. And he, Philip, would usher in the noblest civilization yet known. He smiled. It would happen.

The logistics of the operation did bother him though. To move a force of thirty thousand soldiers, several thousand animals and a still undetermined number of support personnel and mere hangers-on demanded precise timing and impeccable organization. So far, his son, unquestionably brilliant, disagreed strongly with his far more experienced chief geographer, Strabo. Philip found himself in a predicament. Did he acquiesce to Alexander in order to maintain the new found peace between them? Or did he trust the word of the always right, always faithful geographer? The consequences of overriding his son's wish could permanently drive Alexander away from him, most likely back to that witch Olympias. That was the last thing he wanted to result from this expedition. However, as king and commander in chief of the army, he had to consider the risks not only to himself and Alexander but to his forces. No soldier was dispensable, particularly for the vanity of his leader. All those men, from the generals to the infantry, depended upon him and him alone to guide them, to protect them and to ultimately bring them home again. That responsibility was not negotiable. He would have to sit down with Alexander again.

Thus Philip sat at his throne, absorbed in thought. Except for the rhythmic, barely perceptible breathing of his two bodyguards, the room was eerily quiet for this time of day. Consequently, when loud knocking was heard at the door, all three occupants started. Philip looked at the two King's Companions, noted how quickly they had drawn their swords and pleased, sent one of them to the portal to allow entry to the knocker.

Philip recognized him immediately. It was the young infantryman he had assigned to watch Pausanius. As he had not heard a report from the soldier for a long while, he had assumed that nothing unusual had been noted and that the young spy had made his report to his commander and the matter had been dismissed. Looking at the flushed, eager face, Philip could see that he had been wrong.

"We are not in Asia. Do not grovel or bow. Make your report as you would to your commander in the field," ordered Philip to the somewhat overwhelmed youth.

Auelias stiffened. He caught himself just before he bent at the waist. He kept forgetting that Philip wanted to be treated as a mere man, not an artificial god. Surreptitiously taking a deep breath, he calmed himself and started.

"I followed the King's Companion as ordered. For the first few days, I noted that other than the taverna in the Agora, he stayed within his apartment."

Philip nodded. He was aware of the deteriorating state of his former bodyguard. It saddened him that a soldier of Pausanius' caliber spent his spare time besotted with wine. An inadvertent sigh escaped.

"But yesterday two things happened. In the morning he had an audience with the Queen Olympias..."

Philip gritted his teeth. Any mention of Olympias always made him tense.

"...but later, after he had gone to the taverna again, I noticed four men watching him. They were dirty, mean-looking and I was sure they meant him harm. However, after awhile, they left so I dismissed them. When it got dark, Pausanius got up from his drink and started back to his apartment. I followed him, from a safe distance of course. Even though he was drunk, he is still a King's Companion, making him much more aware of his surroundings than a normal man. So I kept back. That is when it happened.

Out of one of the alleys stepped a large, dark man. He clubbed Pausanius with something, knocking him unconscious. Two, maybe three others jumped out of the shadows, picked up Pausanius and were gone as quickly as they came. I searched for them, but was unable to find them. I am truly sorry," concluded Auelias.

Philip did not reply. He was unsure of his emotions. At one time, he had loved Pausanius. Never had he seen a braver, more loyal warrior. Yet, that soldier had become a shell of his former self. Confounding matters more was the fact that Pausanius had been duped by Olympias, who knew how to prey on moral weakness the same way that sharks devoured sailors unlucky enough to fall in the waters of Poseidon's seas.

What could he do? Pausanius was almost a traitor. It was hard to sympathize with a man who would betray his master for mere sexual gratification. Philip shook his head. Pausanius had saved his life. He still owed him that debt.

"Find him."

Auelias nodded in assent and exited hurriedly. He had thought that he might be punished for losing sight of his charge. Philip did not blame him but he did not want to tempt fate by remaining in the company of the king. He would go back to the alley and find Pausanius...or what was left of him.

Philip watched the youth leave. He turned to his bodyguards and said, "Olympias is planning something. From now on, I want to know the status of every single person in the royal family. I want to know where they have been, where they are going, what they have done, what they plan to do. I want them observed every hour of every day by my most loyal King's Companions. Everything must be done in the strictest secrecy. Any man leaking this action, be it on purpose or by accident, will face immediate execution. I leave it to the both of you to organize. And remember, the ultimate responsibility for the effective administration of this plan lies with you." The emphasis on the last word was pronounced.

The bodyguards looked at Philip, nodded and then left to recruit the demanded spies. They could not help thinking as they left that their beloved king was slowly letting his paranoia eat away at him. How this court had degenerated!

Philip reached up with his right hand, and grasping both temples with his thumb and middle finger, massaged the throbbing veins. The relief was at best fleeting. Philip, like most true warriors, put far more trust and faith in his own earthly powers than in the supernatural ones. But he could not help feeling that the throbbing in his head was indicative of some sort of drain on his lifeforce. Why did he have this feeling that his time was limited.

"Stop thinking like a small child!" Philip looked around, embarrassed at the inadvertent blurting out. I must be going crazy, he thought. He raised himself from his throne and for the first time in a long while, felt old.

Alexander speaks with his mother

"Mother?"

Olympias hesitated, ever so slightly, as she entered the room. Alexander's tone was coolly inquisitive. This indifference contrasted sharply with the youth who had in the past, unabashedly displayed his pleasure whenever he saw her. Now, one word, and Olympias knew instantly that something had changed in their relationship forever.

"Dearest," gushed Olympias as she moved forward to embrace her son.

Alexander rose yet made no step in the direction of his mother. When she put her arms around him, he felt himself hold back. Why...he did not really know.

Olympias felt him stiffening. Curse that dung-eating tyrant who sired Alexander. Somehow Philip had managed to once again turn her beloved offspring against her. How dare he come between a mother and child? She would make Philip pay even if she were dragged down the river Styx with him.

"Mother." Alexander slowly, gently unwrapped himself from Olympias' arms. "I am pleased to see you." He looked at his mother and smiled.

Olympias, as hard-hearted as any man or woman walking amongst mortals, almost cried when Alexander smiled. He radiated a beauty, an inner essence that she knew she had never had nor ever would have. Her son was a god.

"Mother...mother..." repeated Alexander completely unaware of the effect he had on even the woman who bore him.

Olympias finally snapped out of her daze. "Yyyyesss..." she stammered, unsure of the question.

"I am overjoyed that you have taken the time to visit but as you can see, we are occupied with something of a very demanding nature and as much as I would be honoured, I cannot spare the time to grace your presence with the deference necessary for an esteemed parent. So, unless it is of a critical nature I most humbly request that..."

"I see that Hephaestion is here," interrupted Olympias.

"My queen," said the rising Hephaestion, bowing with a flourish that might have been construed as feminine coming from any less of a man than Alexander's fiercest bodyguard and closest friend.

Olympias returned Hephaestion's obeisance with her own curtsy. Although her relationship with Alexander's constant companion was cordial, something about the unnaturally handsome youth made her uncomfortable. She would of course never mention it to another person but she was jealous of Hephaestion, for he had developed an intellectual intimacy with Alexander that Olympias knew she would never be able to intrude on.

"Hephaestion." Her acknowledgement was a reflex as her mind continued to measure her role in Alexander's life to Hephaestion's.

"Please mother. Unless there is something critical..."

"Can a mother not see her son? Is it not bad enough that I am shunned by your father? You are leaving soon. I can see that. Are you planning on leaving in the middle of the night so as to avoid me? Have I suddenly become repulsive to you?" Olympias' voice rose higher and higher as her questions rapidly accelerated into plaintive wails. How much of this emotion was feigned even she could not answer as she realized that Alexander might be leaving her, both physically and emotionally, forever.

"The hysterics are not necessary, mother. I apologize if my behaviour has been less than considerate. We...I am preoccupied with the organization of the expedition to Asia. I did not mean to slight you." Alexander was gentle, caring with his words. He knew that his mother possessed acting skills that could shame the classically trained thespians performing every night at the Dionyssian theatre but there was no point in accusing her of trying to manipulate him. She would not degrade herself like this unless she was concerned about his impending departure. As evil as she could be, and he had seen examples of it many times, she was his mother; she loved him and he loved her.

Olympias hugged Alexander again, burying her face into his chest. This time she was not gently pushed away. Olympias choked back a real sob.

As he held his mother, Alexander looked over at Hephaestion. He noted that his confidant was busy examining the maps and making notes on the blank scroll in front of him. Hephaestion seemed oblivious to the domestic situation unfolding mere steps away from him. That is probably why I love him, thought Alexander. Hephaestion never involved himself in the machinations of the court or family. And unless Alexander broached the subject, he would never comment on anything he saw or heard. He returned Alexander's love unconditionally.

"When are you going?" sniffed Olympias, not sure whether her role as grieving mother had become real or not.

"We will stay for the games and for my half-sister Cleopatra's wedding. I know my father wishes to wait a while longer also." Alexander did not specify why his father wanted to wait. Philip had told him that that his newest wife, Cleopatra, was expecting fairly soon. Philip had also asked his son not to tell Olympias because he feared for his unborn child's life. And as close as Alexander was to his mother, on this he had to agree with his father. There was no predicting what his mother was capable of if she perceived any threat to Alexander's future as a world leader.

"Good. I do not want my child to go so quickly. Have you decided on a route or how you will deploy your troops once you have crossed the Hellespont?" asked a now curious Olympias.

The professional soldier in Alexander held back his response. Nothing had been finalized. Consequently, any release of information would be premature and possibly displeasing to the Gods. And, if he were to be honest with himself, he did not trust his mother.

"We are still in the early stages mother. When I myself have a better idea as to how this operation will be put into effect, then I will come to your quarters and explain it in detail."

Olympias smiled. Her son knew damn well what his plans were. He simply was not telling her. Olympias smiled again. She would find out what was on that table that Hephaestion was still bent over.

"I know you will," replied Olympias finally. "Can I ask you one more question?" She waited for Alexander's nod. "Is Attalus returned from his trip to Asia? He was expected a week ago."

Alexander shifted his feet. He was still embarrassed at his and his father's behaviour the last time they had supped with Attalus. Sending Attalus to Asia had relieved the tension between Alexander and Philip. Keeping him there had been Alexander's idea.

"No mother, we have decided to maintain a garrison on the Persian border and we need Attalus to stay there for a short while longer. He will come. Is there a reason for your interest?"

"None," replied Olympias. "Just curiousity"

"Then...mother."

"Yes, Alexander. I will go." Olympias reached up and kissed her son on the cheek. She looked over at Hephaestion, unsure whether or not to bid him good-bye. He was still immersed in his maps however, saving her the always uncomfortable feeling she was subject to when she had to speak to him. With one more pat on the cheek of her son she departed.

Alexander turned to Hephaestion and in an exaggerated movement, arched his brows. His friend grinned and resumed his work on the map laid out in front of him. Alexander walked over, sat down, and began to compare the charts to his data.

Suddenly, bedlam erupted on the other side of the oak door, the volume as great in the apartment as if the planks constructing the closed door were made of the delicate Egyptian papyrus. Grabbing daggers, both Alexander and Hephaestion charged through the opening, the latter using his greater bulk to squeeze in front of his friend and master, thus placing himself in the dangerous situation first.

Nothing could have surprised them more as standing there, nose to nose, screaming with abandon at each other, were Alexander's parents, Philip and Olympias. Bad luck, a prankster God or the fates had caused them to meet at a time when both were angrier at each other than usual.

"You plan a major campaign to the Gods know where without consulting me, taking my son and leaving Hellas without any real leadership. What is wrong with you? Has your organ replaced your brain? Is it a Persian delicacy that craves your love, as puny as it is?" yelled Olympias, the sarcasm in her voice as cutting as a hoplite's dagger.

"Who are you woman? How dare you ask me my plans? Were you made a general while I was away fighting with the Thebans or the Athenians? A woman's role is to be submissive to her man, to not question his intentions, to obey without compromise." Philip assumed a more authoritative stance, his voice reflecting one whose every wish is obeyed.

Olympias however would not be so easily cowed. "Where do you give birth to these moronic assumptions? I was not aware that the art of killing men somehow added character to oneself. Nor was I told that a wife, the king's chosen one, would have to defer to or accept the inane ramblings of a man who has probably lived too long and now only seeks one more, probably unattainable triumph. Philip you are an old man. Stay here. Take care of your kingdom. Leave my son alone!"

Philip could not overlook Olympias' tirade. More than any person he had ever met, even more than his overbearing, exacting father, she could rouse him to a fury within the blink of an eyelash. His hatred of her, just as the love for her he once had, was unrestrained by artificial emotional boundaries. She fanned such white-hot passion in him; he was capable of killing her with his bare-hands. Her haranguing now was just another in the growing list of malicious attacks upon him. If not for Alexander, he would have had her "removed" years ago; probably by the same murderous leech she had been entertaining for the last few months.

"You have nothing to say, King Philip?" Olympias' voice slithered.

Alexander took advantage of the momentary lull and jumped in between his glaring parents. He rested his palm on his father's chest and with the other took a gentle hold of his mother's fingers.

"Stop it." Alexander's voice was low yet powerful. "This is not necessary."

Philip continued his silence, his one good eye transfixed on the woman he so hated, and when he dared admit it to himself, feared.

Olympias turned to her son, pecked him on the cheek, and twirled to go. Half-turning as she walked away, she tossed an aside to Philip, "Wherever you go, my spirit will be beside you. If anything happens to my son because of your ineptitude, you will achieve that gods' status you secretly crave far sooner than you believe."

"Gods on Olympus, I hate her," said Philip.

"Father. Just once, could you act civilly to each other. I am the son of both of you. It should not be necessary that I have to mediate every meeting you too ever have--even the accidental ones."

Embarassed, Philip nodded a couple of times. As usual, Alexander was right. He did not say a word but with his head indicated that the three enter Alexander's chambers.

Alexander and Hephaestion assented and all three walked to the table. Immediately Philip was struck by the charts and maps spread out before him. He noticed the detailed notes, meticulously neat and well ordered, written on sheets of papyrus or in some cases directly on the maps. Alexander's attention to detail was one of his strengths as a leader. Philip, ever the judge of men, knew that somehow, someday, Alexander would rule the world. That revelation, or admission, made him light-headed for an instant as the realization that his own mortality would be only a stepping-stone for his son's immortality, came crashing in upon him

"You see father, if we follow the route suggested by Strabo, we will be forced to winter along the river Arda because the mountains and the weather will prevent the successful transport of a force as large as ours. I agree with Strabo that a march closer to the coast and a crossing at the Hellespontus puts us at greater risk of attack. However, by diverting north, then cutting across through Thracia and then crossing into Asia over the Thracicus puts us too far north which in turn will give Darius too much time to prepare as he awaits us. Better to lose men fighting than have them freeze, starve or die of excessive heat. Armies we can fight. The Gods of nature we cannot." Alexander took a deep breath, the words having flown out of his mouth like a cascading waterfall.

Philip nodded. He bent low over the maps, examining every mountain, every valley, every river on the route that Alexander proposed. He noted with satisfaction the various names written on the map denoting both friendly and unfriendly city-states. Upon closer examination, Philip noted that even tribal alliances were marked off, particularly in the mountain areas, where Philip's army would be the most vulnerable to a small, annoying force. The research impressed him. Alexander had sought and gotten the critical data needed for this operation. It was also obvious that he had analyzed the mechanics of the expedition extensively. All that remained was for Philip to give his final approval.

"Father..." queried Alexander, trying hard not to show his eagerness.

"When would you propose leaving?" asked Philip.

Barely able to contain his excitement, Alexander replied."I thought it best to start immediately after my sister's wedding. I think it best that you were here for the ceremony. With the relations you have had with mother for the last while, it would not be prudent to offend her brother. Epirus may not be the power it once was, but nevertheless, my uncle is king and soon he will be your son-in-law. It has also proven in the past that troops who depart right after a festival maintain their spirit better during a long march."

Alexander waited. Philip did not look up. He would be putting a lot of faith in a youth of only twenty years. Philip's most trusted geographer thought an alternate route to Alexander's the safer one. And Strabo had been with him for many years without once making a mistake. Yet, Philip could not help but be impressed with his son's effort. Greatness cannot always take the safer route, he thought to himself.

"Begin the mobilization of the troops. Soon we cross the Hellespont into Asia." Philip looked up at Alexander, the faintest hint of a smile cracking the battle-scarred face, then turned and left.

Alexander turned to Hephaestion, his closest friend and his only confidant, and cried with joy.

Pausanius is found

He lifted his face to the sky. The drops of rain, cool, vitalizing, caressed his skin with a touch softer than a woman. His nostrils flared. The scent of growing fruit, tinged with the salty freshness of a nearby ocean, massaged his olfactory nerves. The heaven that was Creta beckoned, no...begged, him to remain. But deep in the shadow clouding his brain, a fierce, animalistic terror said no. Not until...

"He is waking up," said Panthea to a distressed Piros. No reply was forthcoming so she turned to the man standing behind the black warrior-philosopher. "Moisten this rag again and hold it to his forehead," she ordered Dioxippus. "Now!" The youth jumped up and went to the urn containing the water.

Pausanius opened his eyes slowly, the light of the afternoon sun burning them. He tried to look around but all he could see were hazy images, the largest being particularly dark and frighteningly close. Pausanius panicked momentarily and tried to lift himself up. Immediately, sharp, searing pain tore through his head and he collapsed down onto his back again. The unceasing ache in his head disoriented him and for a few terrifying moments he did not know whether he was alive or dead. Voices called out to him. None were recognizable.

"Pausanius. Pausanius. Wake my old friend," begged a distraught Piros. He laid his hand on the prone Pausanius' bruised forehead, touching him ever so gently, vainly trying to comfort the battered body and defeated spirit of his comrade. "It is me, Piros."

"He is delirious," said Panthea, squeezing out a few more drops of water onto the face of the now tossing Pausanius. She beckoned Dioxippus to hand her the fresh rag that he had just dampened. This time she gently wiped away the dirt, sweat and dried blood from the fallen warrior's scalp.

"You must get your medicine bag, Piros. I am sure he has broken bones and there are probably more serious injuries that we cannot see. Whoever did this to him knew when to stop...just. Still, if his spirit has admitted defeat, he may still die. Tell me where to look and I will go retrieve what you need," said Dioxippus, trying hard to contain his emotions as to not upset Piros any more.

"You are right. I am acting the fool. In my villa, under the couch in the front room," said Piros, his voice firm, conviction strong. Dioxippus left with scarcely a glance. His friend Euphraeus stayed behind, ready to offer any assistance he was capable of.

"We must clean and examine him or we will not know the extent of his injuries."

Panthea nodded in agreement and slowly lifted the sheet away from the naked Pausanius. A shocked gasp betrayed the composure shown earlier. The man before her should not be alive. Large welts and rising bruises had completely discoloured his torso. Where the ribs should have made a symmetrical pattern, there was now tremendous swelling and unnaturally shaped protrusions. The legs had been cut and scraped as if dragged through gravel but they were only a macabre background to the blood-blackened genitals. Veins had obviously been ruptured and the internal bleeding had discoloured and made useless the penis and testicles of this once vital man. Panthea turned away, nauseated.

"Turn him over," said Piros. Euphraeus moved to help him. Even the strength of these athletes was tested as they grunted with the exertion of rotating the dead weight that was Pausanius.

Panthea and Euphraeus gagged. Piros bit his lower lip in white-hot anger. None could avert their eyes from the grisly testament to one man's perversion. Amidst the myriad of cuts, scrapes and bruises vying for space on Pausanius' back, was a thin trickle of blood, not much more than a putrid discharge, emanating from the rent skin and tissue that had once been the rectum.

"Wha...who, who could have done this?" begged a shocked Euphraeus, the words choking on a sob.

"A dead man."

Panthea forced her eyes away from the battered Pausanius to look at Piros. Even though his ferocity was almost legendary, she had never even seen him frown. But those eyes were coal-black now, the dense musculature in his shoulders and back expanding with the rush of blood and adrenalin and she saw now that the roles Piros played, athlete, trainer, scholar were only facades. He would kill whoever had done this to Pausanius--and he would enjoy it. The simplicity of the concept shocked Panthea.

So absorbed were the three that they did not notice Dioxippus' return. He stood there, looking. Unlike, Euphraeus and Panthea, he was not shocked. Nor did he become consumed with fury like his mentor. But he promised himself that whoever could debase themselves on another human being as they had on Pausanius (and on his beloved Iyea, in what seemed eons ago) necessitated squashing like one would a persistent cockroach. He would not deprive Piros of his vengeance but he would be there.

"Hand me the bag, Dios," asked Piros, suddenly noticing Dioxippus.

As Piros mixed leaves and herbs, Panthea gently wiped down the prostrate Pausanius. Dioxippus and Euphraeus watched attentively, every so often bringing a clean rag or some fresh water for Panthea's use. Nobody spoke.

Eventually Piros had his pastes and poultice ready. Pausanius was still unconscious. He did not feel the natural medicines cleaning, disinfecting his wounds. His labored breathing was the only sign he was still alive. Piros noted it and continued his methodical task, only stopping to change a dressing when necessary.

"How did you find him?"

Piros' voice made Panthea jump. They had been laboring in an almost enforced silence and the question had caught her completely unaware. She had sent for Piros immediately upon finding the beaten heap that was Pausanius rolled up against one of the alley walls on her way to get produce from the market. Only a low groaning attracted her attention, otherwise she would have walked right by the dust-covered body that blended in so well with the loose garbage that littered this part of the street. It was even more surprising to her that none of the dogs that roamed the streets had found him first otherwise they might be dressing a corpse now. She had recognized Pausanius from her early days in Pella when she had worked as a personal servant to one of Philip's foreign wives. As marriage to these women was a diplomatic necessity rather than a passionate one, they rarely came into contact with Philip's court. Consequently, their personal servants, such as Panthea, ran all their errands, answered all their messages and did whatever was necessary to maintain their voluntary cloistering. That was how Panthea had met Pausanius, who at that time was a war-hero, unfailingly handsome and desired by most women who saw him. She had also seen Piros with him on many occasions and knew that there was a bond between them. When she had recognized Pausanius in the alley, which in itself was difficult considering not only his state but the decrepit condition he had allowed himself to sink to, she sent a young boy loitering around the corner to fetch Piros. He had arrived with Dioxippus and Euphraeus and between the three of them had managed to carry him back to her apartment, a small room on the edge of her mistress' compound. In the confusion and panic, she had not told Piros the details of her discovery. She proceeded to do so.

The three men listened carefully. None doubted that Pausanius had been the victim of a plot. Yet, doubts as to who might want to punish him in such a brutal manner negated immediate identification. However, through palace scuttlebutt and other gossip, Piros was aware of the rather lengthy stay of the infamous Kathos. And although no direct link could be found to Pausanius, Piros had been involved in enough palace intrigues to know that someone like Kathos did not rest in any one place for long. For him to have remained in Pella over two seasons was out of the ordinary; he had to have had a nefarious purpose in mind to risk being found by one or more of his many enemies. Piros did not know why, but in his mind, Kathos had his hand in this atrocity perpetrated on Pausanius. Being just, Piros would wait until some physical evidence could be produced proving Kathos' or anyone else's guilt in this matter before he settled the matter.

"Ppp...Piros."

The harsh whisper was barely audible.

226

Olympias

Phylia had already seen the sun rise over the eastern hills by the time her mistress, Queen Olympia, began to stir awake. The servant-girl had prepared the bath, brought towels and a fresh chiton for the queen. Phylia had also arranged combs and assorted jewelry on the table so Olympias would have her pick of accessories to complement her attire. Now all that remained was for the queen to actually get out of her bed.

Olympias yawned and slowly uncurled herself. She was so tired. Putting one arm under her head, she turned and looked at her companion from the night before. Hmmmm...not bad, she thought. This trader from the island of Kerkira had proved inventive. He had lent their base lust a dangerous edge which Olympias found exhilirating even addictive. He had told her that the island of Sicilia a region he often travelled to by ship was inhabited by a mixture of Greeks and locals who reveled in hardship and danger. Raids, invasions, natural disasters, all contributed to lives teetering on a delicate balance. Life and death were intertwined and this manifested itself in the Sicilian's day to day existence. Violence, vendetta, feuds were normal occurrences. This fierceness even extended itself to copulation.

It was here, the trader told Olympias, that he had learned how to take a knife or dagger, preferably razor-sharp, and use it to heighten stimulation. And he had demonstrated this skill gloriously to Olympias. He had bound her naked body, hands pulled over the head and tied to the top of the bed's frame, legs spread and each held by a leather thong fastened to opposite corners of the bed. Then he had taken a long, thin shiv, and with just enough force to crease the skin had run the blade along the most sensitive and vulnerable parts of Olympias' anatomy. She tingled with the remembrance of the cool, somehow comforting metal, being drawn down from behind her ear, tracing the path of major arteries across her throat on its way to the taut, tender derma of her exposed underarms. Here the trader, stopped. Shifting the blade in his hands so that the downward pressure manifested itself closer to the point, he danced across the delicate skin of her conspicuously palpitating breasts, slowing to circle the engorging nipples, the razor-sharp blade now scratching the skin although not hard enough to draw blood. Olympias twitched, then squirmed her lower body, the excitement, the need for satisfaction threatening to drive her to an uncontrollable sexual hysteria but the proximity of the killing weapon demanded complete subservience.

Not once had the trader touched Olympias with his hand. He simply twirled the deadly instrument, meandering across her torso, stopping only to turn the blade to its opposite side, sometimes raising the hilt so only the sharp point made contact with the frenzied woman's skin. The closer the trader approached her womanhood, the more tense, the more excited became Olympias, who by now wanted to buck her hips forward and up and take in the bastard who was punishing (or was it pleasuring) her so. But the trader, barely able to breathe himself, continued his journey. He lifted the shiv off of her lower belly and shifted its position to her right ankle. Again he drew the knife up, following a curvaceous path up the back of her leg until it came to the gently curled pubic hairs of her vagina. Olympias had stopped breathing, fearing that the intake of breath would make her explode into wild, tossing abandonment. The danger of that wicked metal so close to her most cherished, most valued pleasure, forced what seemed cruel now, restriction on motion. Then, the trader turned the knife again, this time the flat of the blade making contact with her skin. With just enough force for Olympias to feel it but not cause injury, he parted the petal-soft lips of her labia, exposing the moistened clitoris letting it feel the hard, unforgiving agent of terror. Olympias gasped, her mind, her body begging for relief, begging for penetration, begging, begging...

"If you are ready my queen, the bath is ready."

Olympias blinked. She glanced in Phylia's direction, unsure of where she was. The sheet covering her breasts had slipped away. She ignored her nakedness. She also noted that Phylia barely gave her a glance. Olympias sat up and turned to look at the still sleeping trader beside her. Yes, he had tantalized her to the point of torture but he too got far more than he bargained for. Olympias had ravaged him, forcing herself on him (after he released her) time and time again, until he himself was begging--for her to desist, not continue. She looked at him. He had provided some amusement, and he had taught her something new...time to be rid of him. Olympias caught Phylia's eye, nodded in the direction of the sleeping trader then eased herself out of bed and walked to the drawn drape, on the other side of which was a smaller replica of the public baths near the agora. Slowly,

Olympias eased herself in, reveling in the heat and the fragrance of the warm, scented water. She leaned back, began humming softly to herself and closed her eyes.

Phylia drew the curtain on her bathing mistress. She walked quietly to the door, opened it and whispered something to the bodyguard standing there. Like a well-practiced dance, the soldier came in, gathered the clothes of the queen's guest in one arm and then with the other grabbed the thinning hair locks of the dormant trader and yanked.

"Owwwww, ooooh! Help! Help! Wh...who are you?" screamed the now thoroughly frightened man. He was simultaneously trying to raise himself to a sitting position and trying to preserve some modesty but the iron-like grip on his hair kept him seriously off-balance.

"Time to go." The tone of the bodyguard had no inflection, no emotion. The grip on the hair did not relax.

"I...I,I am the qu...queen's guest." The trader was terrified. Ohhhh, gods in heaven, I am going to urinate myself, he thought.

But before any such humiliation could occur, he found himself outside the queen's suite, naked, bruised and scared. And alive! The soldier threw his clothes at him and resumed his stoic watch over the entrance to the apartment. The trader warily picked up his clothes, then turned and ran down the hallway, joy and relief adding Hermes' wings to his feet.

So fast did he run that he did not notice the dark, ferret-like little man pass him in the hallway. Nor would he have noticed how the bodyguard deferred to this character as if he were a high-ranking soldier or politician. Regardless, this new player in the court gained access to the queen's apartment immediately.

Phylia glanced up as the door opened. She did not recognize this person but the odor of treachery and death was about him so strongly that it approached a stench. The queen knew and consorted with many low-life criminals, of which Kathos had been the basest and most cruel. But an unexplainable feeling, cold and biting, told her--no, warned her--that this man was to Kathos what a viper was to a rat. As quickly and as unobtrusively as possible, Phylia drew the curtain to the queen's bath and whispered to her mistress. Olympias nodded, asked to be dried and stepped out of the bath. She saw Kinovas standing there, watching her.

In many respects, Kinovas presented an odd figure. Shorter than most men, without much bulk, he resembled a forest sprite. His thinness was deceiving. Kinovas redefined the word, wiry. Muscles and tendons were stretched tighter than the skin on a drum. The blood tearing through his veins with what appeared to be a constant fury was almost visible to the naked eye. Kinovas was a man who never relaxed, tension being his elixir. Even sleep, the great rejuvenator, was sporadic and never enjoyed. Kinovas had no wife, children or lover. He existed only to serve Olympias. Without her, he was nothing.

Olympias remembered the day she met this man. He had been one of the very few survivors of the seige at Thebes. His critically injured body had been brought back to Pella on a whim of Philip's. Nobody expected the little man with the grievous wounds to survive for long. And he would have died had not Olympias, who at that time still got along with Philip, not been privy to a conversation between her husband and son. They were talking about how this little man, stood back to back with his mate in the legendary Sacred Band and fought with such ferocity that Alexander's own bodyguard was unable to break through his part of the line. It was not until the warrior fighting beside him was felled by a thrown spear that Kinovas, distracted by the death of his comrade, was overrun by the Macedonians. In the resulting chaos and orgy of violence, the small Kinovas was lost among the bodies, blood and gore. Much later, when the corpses were being gathered and burned was he discovered. Alexander, who had fought hand to hand with the Theban elite, recalled him, told Philip, who being impressed and magnanimous in victory, spared him. Olympias found herself intrigued and calling the most-skilled physicians in her court to her, ordered them to save Kinovas. Knowledge, possibly coupled with fear, achieved the impossible, and today Kinovas stood before her, very much alive.

"Well..." queried the queen.

"It has been done," said Kinovas.

"He is still alive?" The queen's question was hopeful.

"Yes. But barely."

"Who has him now?"

"Piros."

Olympias' eyes flared. This was better than she had hoped. She lifted her arms slightly to allow Phylia to finish toweling her down.

"And Kathos?" asked Olympias.

"He has been paid and is preparing to leave. No one knows of his role in this."

"Kill him...and his cronies." Olympias' tone was cool, businesslike. It was time to rid herself of that sewer scum. Kathos was a lowlight who had outlived her need for him. Too bad she could not tell anyone of her order. Many would kiss her feet out of gratitude.

"Anything else?"

"Make sure the bastard knows who did this to him. And if it is at all possible...take your time."

Kinovas bowed graciously and turned to leave.

"One moment more. I want Piros to find out about Kathos...after you have killed him."

Kinovas bent his head in acknowledgement and exited the room.

Olympias stood staring at the door Kinovas had just gone through. He would do what she said most effectively. Loyalty like his was invaluable. Even though Philip disapproved, and Alexander had his reservations, she was beginning to think that maybe the Thebans had been right to form a company of warriors who were more than just comrades. Pairing male lovers, training them to a point of martial superiority and then putting them in a unit that up to the final battle with Philip had been considered the elite of the elite, was an idea born of genius. Warrior-lovers would and did fight with a phenomenal savagery. Had not Philip told the whole Greek world how the Sacred Band had been the toughest of all his opponents? Had it not taken Alexander to personally lead his own elite against these Thebans? And Kinovas, would he have been taken if his own lover had not fallen to the pikes of the Macedonians? The queen did not tarry with these thoughts. It was enough that the loyalty Kinovas had almost been bred with was now transferred to her.

"Phylia. Dress me."

The servant girl quickly gathered up some clothing and began to dress her mistress. She tried to be as unobtrusive as possible, not wanting Olympias to pay her any undue attention. Phylia also thought of something else. How was she going to get a message to Piros? Should Patroclus also know what was transpiring? For that matter, did she?

Dioxippus refines his technique

Sitting cross-legged in the dirt, his shoulders stooped, and head hanging, he appeared to be mourning. But Dioxippus did not grieve. He was immersed in a brutally cutting introspection. His goals, his desires, his dreams, did not seem to make any sense to him anymore. Within a few short weeks, he would partake in the most important festival and contest in the civilized world, the Olympics. He was considered a favourite yet he himself could not understand why. Piros spoke to him of the spiritual beauty of the event honouring and sanctioned by the Gods. Yet Dioxippus saw many competitors, in his and the other events, accept bribes and gifts. Many spoke of the immortality of the victor's names, yet Dioxippus was hearing more and more criticism of the athletes from the masses. Some said that a victory at the Olympiad would guarantee success in the future yet Dioxippus only saw a future in the elite military wing of Alexander's or Philip's bodyguard. Defeat would bring anonymity. Victory...misery? He just was not sure.

Dioxippus raised his head and looked up over his shoulder at the compound behind him. A scream cracked the silence. Dioxippus shivered. Pausanius' body was on fire and the resulting delirium threatened to strip what little was left of his sanity bare. Dioxippus could not hear the words but his ears or a sixth sense could detect Piros' gentle, placating voice. It appeared to have no effect because within moments, another scream knifed its way through the compound. Dioxippus half-raised his hands to cover his ears then thought better of it and dropped them. He was a man.

But was he? His body, maybe. His mind and soul...he could not be sure. He understood loyalty, responsibility. He maintained, even raised the ideals of friendship. He worshipped well and willingly served his king. Few could fault the path his life had taken. Still, Dioxippus was unhappy. And he knew why. History, particularly if he won the Pankration in the Olympiad, would paint him not as an athlete, an innovator, a winner. He would be shown for what he had become, a crippler and murderer of men. And what frightened Dioxippus the most was that he would not be able to deviate from this course. Death and violence were as much as part of him as any limb from his body. He would never escape it.

Another scream. Dioxippus winced. What had happened to Pausanius was brutal. No human being should be subjected to that type of violence. He shook his head. Reality dictated otherwise. Pausanius had made the mistake of becoming involved in the various court intrigues. Bad mistake. He was lucky that he had a friend like Piros. Otherwise he would be dead. And who would feel for him. He had no family, few friends. Even his comrades would barely note his passing. After all, had Pausanius not chosen his life? Had he not been warned? Sometimes vanity and stupidity brought another's wrath down on one. Pausanius in effect should have expected the attack and been better prepared for it.

"Have you lost what little is left of your mind? Do you so easily justify the evils of man?"

Dioxippus realized that the voice berating him was coming from within. His cheeks flushed scarlet. How could he try to justify what happened to Pausanius? Was this the man he had become? At this instant, Piros was tending a man disgraced, humiliated and most certainly out of favour. The repercussions for this humanitarian act could be disastrous for Piros. Yet he stayed by the side of his friend, administering medicine, cleaning his wounds and most important, comforting his fellow. Piros was a man. A true man.

Dioxippus opened then closed his hand. He stared at the fist. The knuckles were surprisingly free of scars. I can kill with these hands...thought Dioxippus. He sighed. This melancholy and self-criticism was serving no purpose. His fate had been chosen for him at birth. The gods had blessed him (or cursed him--stop it!) with the ability to use his body to fight. The way he was built, the way his mind broke down and dissected facts, the way he observed the great torrent that was life, all these served the lord that was combat. It was as if all his experience was compressed and spun wildly into a whirlpool from whose vortex emerged something feral. It was this Dioxippus that reveled in the killing of Dionys. It was this Dioxippus who shunned weapons on the battlefields of Charoenea. It was this Dioxippus who systematically destroyed his opponents in the pankration. It would be this Dioxippus who would win the Olympiad. Or die.

"Boy, what do you do there?"

Dioxippus shot up to his feet.

"Well, your reflexes still work...somewhat," said Barba Fotis, a tinge of playful sarcasm in his voice.

Dioxippus walked to the trainer, every step shutting the door on his melancholy tighter and tighter. By the time he reached the old man, a smile, still a little sad, had managed to crack the set grimness of his contemplation.

"I have been looking for you and Piros. Why are you here? And where is my master?"

"A friend of Piros' suffers. He attends to him now. I decided to stay here for awhile," answered Dioxippus.

"Mmmmm..." Fotis was not convinced but thought it better not to pursue this subject. There was something different with Dioxippus. He could not identify it yet. For now it was best to start the training again. "Are you ready to practice?" he asked.

Dioxippus shrugged his shoulders. "Why not?" With that he began to limber up his body, rotating first his neck, then his arms and finally his trunk. While he engaged himself in this, Fotis took out what looked like a small sack made of a dark, shimmering material. He held it up to his mouth and began blowing into a small hole that must have been hidden by the murky colour. Slowly, the material began to expand and in a few moments, the empty pig's bladder had inflated until it resembled a ball, much like the ones the young children kicked around the street.

"Anytime you are ready," said Fotis.

Dioxippus slid up to the bag. He knew the drill. But an idea had come to him in the night. An involuntary grimace flashed across his face. All his ideas, some of which were brilliant, according to Piros, centered on ways to expedite his opponents. To Hades with it, he thought. I am here to fight. With that reflection, he snapped out a flurry of left-right combinations at the bag Fotis was holding. The old man stumbled back, being caught by surprise at the rage exploding through those hammer-like fists.

"Easy...easy, Dios!"

Dioxippus stopped. He mumbled something barely discernible. He let out a deep breath and raised his hands to the ready position beside his face again.

Fotis was not convinced that his young charge would slacken his attack so he braced himself and gripped the target a little tighter.

The fists tore out of their chambered positions again. Although one preceded the other so great was their speed that the whack-whack of the two impacting fists could barely be separated as the reverberations blended into one sound. This time Dioxippus stopped after a couple of combinations to allow Fotis to recover himself. The old man slapped the inflated bladder with his left hand and indicated to Dioxippus to continue. Dioxippus slid a half a step forward and in one fluid motion raised his knee almost to his chest, pivoted his supporting leg and with a sharp turn of the hip, released the lower part of the leg and with a combination of strength, speed, technique and centrifugal force, catapulted a vicious kick off the front leg. It tore through the inflated bladder so hard that the bag exploded as it was ripped through the hands of the completely shocked Fotis.

The old man stood mouth agape. He looked down at the piece of animal skin still left in his hand. Then he looked across the yard at the remnant of what had just moments before been a valuable piece of training equipment. He shook his head. Dumbfounded. That was the only word to explain his feelings.

"What do you think?" queried a grinning Dioxippus.

"I think that you are a conceited, insolent show-off who ought to learn to have respect for those who are of a gentler age," snapped Fotis. "However, if you are asking me if that aberration of a kick has a chance for success...I might be tempted to say yes."

Dioxippus reached over and with one quick motion rubbed the top of the balding Fotis' head. The crusty trainer muttered something about the ancestry of Dioxippus then waved him back to the middle of the makeshift ring.

"Well...you obviously have been thinking about new techniques or combinations. And with your apparent lack of control, I had better stand back and have you show me. Not that I will be interested but it is best to allow you to burn off the excess energy that your poor training as of late has failed to do."

The corners of Dioxippus' mouth turned slightly upward. He had been thinking about these techniques that he was about to demonstrate to Fotis for quite awhile. Dioxippus no longer even considered whether or not these new kicks, these radical combinations, these untested theories, even worked. He knew they did as surely as he knew his name. God blessed or cursed, he had been given a gift that one day he would give to the world.

The sun was not yet overhead. Shadows were still being cast. Dioxippus positioned himself so that he could use his shadow as a mirror image. Then, taking a deep breath, shrugging his shoulders once, he started.

A foot arced through the air, its parabolic path a mere blur. Two fists, left then right followed, popped the same space just vacated by Dioxippus' left foot. Barely had he retracted his hands before his right knee came flying upward, so high it almost bounced off his chest. But the knee merely carried the leg and just before it reached its apex, it hinged outward, lifting the foot straight up, toes pointing at the open sky and the ball of the foot, now exposed, struck the imaginary opponent. Dioxippus did not stop. He chased the fleeing shadow, moving ever forward. The right foot had barely touched ground before the left hook whistled through to the exact spot where all the other techniques had landed. This time Dioxippus did not retract his punch but let the momentum carry him through so his left side now lay fully exposed. But before any part of his body could possibly be targeted he had raised his left knee and with a strong thrusting action extended his leg in a linear trajectory up, his heel now rushing to impact. This technique too popped the air where all its predecessors had gone. Suddenly, Dioxippus put the left foot down and just like that, his demonstration was over.

Five...or was it six...or even seven. Fotis was unsure. How many techniques had he seen? All were done within a blinking of the eye. The speed, the accuracy were phenomenal. And the height! Every attack struck what would have been head height on a real adversary. This was unheard of. All pankratiatists, as far back as recorded history had always focused their energies on the lower part of the body, the legs, the thighs and particularly the trunk, the center of one's being, the source of one's physical and spiritual strength. Even the mighty Piros always attacked the base of his opponents, chopping at them as one would a tree before he moved in for the grappling which would finish the fight. But Dioxippus had changed that. His method depended upon utilizing distance, opening and closing space as need demanded it. His style of fighting avoided the clinch. The rough often deadly ground-combat was supplanted by long-range sniping followed by multiple barrages. Gods of Olympus! It was possible for Dioxippus to win a contest without once entangling himself with his foe. This was too much. Dioxippus had taken the pankration and in a few short years undone five hundred years of history. For all intents and purposes, Dioxippus had forever changed the sport. Even if he lost, which secretly Fotis did not think likely, Dioxippus would be imitated. Had they all not seen what an impact his new kicking style had already had on other pankratiatists who even now mimicked what Dioxippus called the front kick? Did Fotis, almost every day on his way to train Dioxippus see children, who only weeks ago were wrestling in the dusty, dirty streets, practicing kicks on the walls, trees or even on each other? Dioxippus probably did not know what he was creating nor did he probably know what an influence he was on the other practitioners of the pankration but Fotis had lived long enough to recognize what some might construe as a revolution. And like it or not, one was brewing in the pankration.

"Well, what do you think?" asked the growing impatient Dioxippus.

"Not too bad. Some of what you did has...possibilities. The rest...best to talk to Piros about it. I do not want to be the one to depress you. For now, let us concentrate on the drills that you were supposed to be doing." Fotis very calmly walked over, picked up the tattered and deflated bladder from the ground and signaled Dioxippus to follow him.

Dioxippus was mildly disappointed. He had not expected Fotis to jump up and down, but he thought that his demonstration had been somewhat impressive. Maybe he was wrong. He sighed, then crouched low and began stretching his legs.

Fotis stared down at Dioxippus. This boy, he thought, will change a sport forever. Long after they have all died, somebody, somewhere, will be performing these kicks, these punches in a way that will differ from everybody else. That will be Dioxippus' legacy. And, damn it he is just a boy, he thought.

Alexander and Hephaestion

"So, he plans on joining my father's bodyguard," said Alexander.

"No commitment has been made but his loyalty to Piros is almost fanatical. I doubt that he will forego the opportunity to serve alongside his mentor." Hephaestion took another olive in his mouth.

Alexander's eyes narrowed. He absent-mindedly reached and took an olive from the plate and casually tossed it into his mouth. So Dioxippus did not want to serve him. Idiot! Who did he think would run this empire shortly?

Hephaestion surreptitiously watched his friend. Best not to say anything, he thought. Alexander did not outwardly display his anger but the chewing of the olive had taken on a fury totally inappropriate for the activity.

"Is it his skill at the Pankration that makes him so bold?" asked an increasingly angry Alexander. It was obvious now that Alexander's pride had been hurt by the rumoured defection of Dioxippus to the King's Companions.

"We are Greeks. A man makes the choices he wants. You do not mean to force Dioxippus to enlist in the Companions," said Hephaestion, trying to reason with the hot-tempered, easily offended Alexander.

"I will be king. I will decide what choices he or anybody else makes!" roared Alexander, the emotion so strong he half-rose from his chair.

Hephaestion said nothing. He had seen this type of behaviour too often to count. It was the only part of his personality that Hephaestion did not care for. Alexander was notorious for losing his temper at even the most insignificant slight. Insults, sometimes violence resulted. And invariably it was left to Hephaestion to soothe emotions on all sides.

"What are you looking at!" screamed Alexander at his closest friend.

"You...you moronic son of a ..."

"Watch what you say about my mother," interrupted Alexander, the anger now dissipating as quickly as moments before it had come.

"What you need is a good slap!" said a now smiling Hephaestion. "If you plan on becoming king you had better learn to control your temper although I am probably wasting breath talking to you about it. And what in the gods' names is so important about having Dioxippus in your bodyguard as opposed to your father's. Both are part of the Macedonian army and ultimately under your command."

Alexander shrugged his shoulders. "I want him fighting with my unit. Maybe I am not being reasonable. But think about it Hephaestion, he is probably the best pankratiatist in Hellas today. His last match with Dimitrius is becoming legend, even though few saw it. He not only does things with his hands and feet that are new to the pankration but also displays an inner toughness that no training in the world can give you. Men like him are almost impossible to find. When you do, you must grab them like a starving man grabs a bowl of food. And, do you know what a man like him does to the morale of the troop? He imparts fearlessness to those who share his air. His fighting ability is worth five men--his ability to turn men into fighters is worth fifty men. That is why I want him after these games are over."

"You cannot threaten him. Cajoling or bribing him will probably not work either. He must come to you because he wants to; otherwise he is of no use to you," interrupted Hephaestion.

"I know. And that drives me to insanity. How do I make him want to come to me?"

"You cannot."

"That is not a sufficient answer."

"It may not be but that is how the situation exists now. If you are truly committed to enlisting him, wait until after the games. Convince Piros. He is the key. Befriend him. Talk to him. Do not attempt to enlist him. He is fiercely loyal to your father and may resent the invitation or worse interpret it as a test of his allegiance to Philip. You must control your temper. To men like Piros, emotion is perceived as weakness and he will use it to his advantage. Be the leader he expects," concluded Hephaestion.

Alexander did not appear to be listening. He had risen and was now staring out the window. That was another habit that annoyed Hephaestion; Alexander's mind could shift from topic to topic within a heartbeat. Hephaestion did admit though, that Alexander, even when it looked like he was not paying any attention to the conversation, always knew what was said, the context in which it was said and the emotion which made one say it.

"Have you heard of the fighter, Yiorgakas?" asked Alexander.

Alexander had not even turned around to address Hephaestion. Hephaestion knew however, that Alexander rarely if ever asked a rhetorical question.

"Yes. Is he not that half-wit who killed that boxer...uhhh...I cannot remember his name, at the Lydian Games last year or the year before?"

"That is him. Several of my lieutenants watched that and some of his other matches when we were in Asia last year. Their reports, unexaggerated, detailed what transpired in all his contests. And they tell an interesting story. Yiorgakas appears to be either more than human or less--depending upon your perspective. Regardless, his ferocity in and out of the ring is becoming legend in Lydia. In fact, his reputation extends beyond the borders of his homeland. It has even been rumored that if he were to enter the Olympiad, he would win by *akiniti*, a walkover. Imagine, no one has ever won the pankration crown without having to face an opponent in a final."

"So I am impressed. There is obviously a reason why you are narrating the autobiography of this Yiorgakas," interrupted Hephaestion.

"I want him to fight Dioxippus."

"Why!" gulped a surprised Hephaestion.

"I think Dioxippus is a threat to us."

"How...where did you get an idea like that."

"Think about it. The premier athlete in Hellas does not want to be commissioned into the most prestigious military force in the world. What does this say about the Companions? What does it say about its leaders? What does it say about me!"

Hephaestion arched his eyebrows. Alexander might be right, he thought.

"You mean to kill him then?" queried Hephaestion.

"No. I do not think Yiorgakas can kill him either. What is important is that he be perceived as a mere man--subject to the same laws as his audience. If he is defeated or if he is killed, this worship will end. And you know Hephaestion the odd thing is that I do not even think he is aware of his popularity. After all, he is barely more than a child. That is why he has to be controlled or eliminated. Yiorgakas will do one or the other."

"But if he is still in Lydia, he may not get your message in time to be here for the Games."

"Surprisingly, he was assigned to the garrisson at Amphipolis in Chalcidice. He can be here in a few days."

Hephaestion realized that Alexander had planned for all contingencies. For whatever reason, real or imagined, Alexander considered Dioxippus' growing fame and steadfast refusal to join the Companions a threat.

"You have nothing to say." It was more of a statement than a question.

"You are probably right. But I suggest that Yiorgakas stay in Amphipolis until just before the games start. You may also want to think about how far you want Yiorgakas to take Dioxippus," said Hephaestion.

"I will. Are we in agreement then?" asked Alexander, the timbre of his voice gentle for the first time today.

"Did I ever have a choice?"

"Always." Alexander jumped up, threw an arm around his friend and began to laugh.

Hephaestion joined in the laughter. But in the back of his mind he could not help thinking that maybe Alexander was allowing himself to become a victim of the Macedonian court's paranoia.

Piros goes to Philip

"I must speak to him."

"Why? There is nothing he can do now. We have no witnesses. No motive. What can you possibly say to him?" Dioxippus was trying to reason with Piros but was not having much success.

Piros was adamant. "Philip should know that one of his most loyal soldiers has been violated. He should be the one responsible for hunting down these cowardly savages. I know Philip. I have fought beside him. He will discover who is responsible for the attack on Pausanius."

"Why are you so sure that Philip will feel the same way about Pausanius that you do? Pausanius is not the same man he was a few months ago. You saw him. Even though he was beaten, it is obvious that he has become a decrepit wreck. That is not the comrade-in-arms who saved you at Chaeronea. Nor is that the Pausanius who beat the Thebans off of Philip during the siege of Thebes. This man we rescued is nothing more than the queen's bootlicker."

Piros glared at Dioxippus. The sudden rush of anger made him unconciously open then close his fist. His breath came out in short, shallow gasps. Even the tendons in his neck knotted through his ebony skin.

Dioxippus did not let Piros' fearsome transformation frighten him. He continued to try and convince Piros not to go to Philip.

"How do you know Philip is not part of the plot against Pausanius? You have heard the rumour. Gods on Olympus, you heard Pausanius himself say that his attackers let slip that Attalus was behind this plot. Attalus is the king's new in-law. Why would Philip jeopardize his relationship with not only a family member but also one of his ablest generals? And do not forget, Attalus has been in Asia for half a year. It makes no sense, logistically or otherwise, for Attalus to be implicated in this supposed conspiracy. You risk your standing, your rank, when you speak to Philip because no matter how diplomatic, you are in effect accusing him of the vilest form of treachery. When you do that, all the history between the two of you will mean nothing."

Piros had not said anything for awhile. The anger had abated slightly. Piros knew that some, maybe all of what Dioxippus had said, might be true. But he could not believe that Philip would turn on his own bodyguard. Pausanius had been one of the best of the best. His reputation for fearless devotion was almost legendary. Philip could not ignore that. If restitution to Pausanius was to be made, Philip was the key. Dioxippus presented his argument well but he was simply not as well-versed in life. Piros decided--he would see Philip.

"You mean well. Still, I must speak to the king."

"Have I then been arguing for nothing? Please, think about what you are doing Piros. You are siding with someone many think of as useless, or worse, a traitor. Pausanius is your friend. If you really love him, cure him and then get him out of Macedonia. That is the only reasonable way to deal with this crime. We will eventually find out who is responsible. When that time comes, I promise you, I will personally destroy the bastards who did that to Pausanius. Until that time, stay quiet; do not make accusations that you cannot substantiate. Piros, I beg you. We need you. Do not sacrifice yourself." Dioxippus was almost pleading now.

"Over two years ago I made a decision that made me an exile in the city I loved," answered Piros.

Dioxippus could not reply. Piros had sacrificed everything for him. It was not Dioxippus' place to criticize Piros' efforts to help his long-time friend, Pausanius. Breathing a sigh of defeat, Dioxippus nodded to his mentor.

"I cannot say how long I will be. Wait for me." And with that, Piros left the room.

Dioxippus and Panthea

Dioxippus never heard the door open.

"He is hurt."

Dioxippus looked up. Standing there was Panthea. When or how she had slipped into the room, Dioxippus did not know. This girl has many skills of which I only know a few, he thought.

"I have missed you," she said.

"And I you." Dioxippus moved toward Panthea, smoothly gathered her in his arms, and so tenderly that it was almost nothing more than the flitting of a bird, kissed her on the lips. Panthea's arms glided in unison until they crossed each other behind Dioxippus' head. With unresisted force, she pulled her beloved down toward her. Her lips, so full, so sensuous, caressed gently as they traveled over Dios' cheek, eyes and finally his mouth. At the last juncture, Panthea parted her lips slightly and with an almost ravenous passion, used her tongue, her teeth, her body, to demonstrate the lust she now felt for her man. Dioxippus, caught somewhat unaware, could only react. But his love for Panthea, so far tempered by restraint and circumstance, now unleashed itself. Twisting, turning, touching the two young lovers seemed out of control. Dioxippus slipped his right hand down, seeking then finding bare skin beneath the folds of Panthea's robe. The writhing body teased, tantalized while the soft, delicate skin burned the sensitive tips of his fingers. Both gasped, the shock of the naked touch almost too overwhelming. But Dioxippus would not be satisfied. Trailing his hand along Panthea's hip and over the heaving contours of her ribcage, he laid the palm of his hand gently over her rounded breast. She let out a small cry, her desire heightened beyond any normal sensibilities. Dioxippus continued, alternately squeezing then stroking the swollen, furiously erect nipples. Panthea's body was now thrown against his, so intensely that it felt that she was trying to fuse the two together. He too came against her, trying beyond reason to touch as much of her as was possible with one human body.

"Say it!" begged Panthea, gulping air.

Dioxippus lifted his head up from the hollow of Panthea's neck. Squeezing her even tighter to him, he said, "You torture me. I want you. I need you."

Panthea threw her mouth onto her lover's. For a few moments, her lips practically melded onto Dioxippus. Suddenly, without warning, she bit at the corner of his mouth.

The sharp pain snapped his head back. Dioxippus frowned, gave Panthea a look of mock anger and then leaning over her, whispered in her ear, "You are a harpy, worse than the sirens of Odyssey's voyage...but I love you more than life itself."

The joy of hearing those few words was apparent as Panthea attacked with renewed vigor her lover's body. She slid her hands down his back, marveling at the many valleys and mountains formed by his musculature. Her nails grazed baby-soft skin stretched tight over a rock-hard frame. The heat between them had caused him to perspire; the tiny droplets imparted a silky sheen over his back, so smooth her hand glided down to his hip. She felt him tremble to her touch. And it took no seer to figure out that the growing pressure against the most sensitive erogenous parts of her lower body came from the almost out-of-control manhood of Dioxippus. She could feel her own moisture as her body and mind responded to the carnal lust manifesting itself between her and Dioxippus. Panthea wanted him in the basest, most primal way.

Dioxippus too had succumbed to this passion gone mad as his body desperately tried to bond with Panthea's. His breath, mere puffs occasionally disrupted by gasps, vainly attempted to fuel his lungs with enough air. He could not think; all he wanted to do was enter this ravenous creature eliciting so much emotion, so much desire, so much lust from him. To that end, he somehow maneuvered both of them to the bed.

They fell onto the bed in unison, still entangled but now barely covered by their remaining clothes. Dioxippus inhaled sharply, mesmerized by the physical perfection of Panthea. Her breasts, now exposed, heaved with their earlier exertions. Dioxippus stared, not knowing whether to touch or look at the perfectly curved bosom. The nipples, normally pink, flamed red as did the surrounding aureole. They almost glowed, godlike spheres begging to be devoured. His eyes reluctantly tore themselves away as they traveled downward over the flat stomach and curve of the lower abdomen. They stopped. The swollen mound of tender skin, framed by gently curled hair, beckoned him, teasing him with the promise of ravaging desire fulfilled. Suddenly, he could not move.

Panthea had no such difficulty. She was as enraptured by his semi-nude form as he was by her's the only difference being that she was not hesitant in her desires. Slowly, carefully and not with a little trepidation, she reached under the robe that was now barely concealing Dioxippus' erection and gently grasped it. Dioxippus groaned, almost painfully. Panthea squeezed the marble-hard member, pulling slightly upward at the same time. Dioxippus twisted as if to get away but they both knew that that was the last thing either wanted. Panthea continued exerting pressure on Dioxippus, opening then closing her hand. She found herself mesmerized by this raw sexual thing. She was no longer even aware that she was breathing. With her free hand, she touched her own womanhood. The damp stickiness caught her unaware and she pulled back involuntarily. But Dioxippus noticed the movement and with his own hand reached over and began to massage the swollen labia of Panthea. It was her turn to gasp then moan as Dioxippus' fingers touched things she had no concept of prior to this moment. She pushed her pelvis forward, taking deep the probing digits of Dioxippus. Panthea needed more. With a movement as graceful as a dancer, she threw her leg over the prone Dioxippus, straddling him. Her right hand guided his engorged penis toward her and with almost no effort slipped it into her aching vagina.

Both shuddered, the quaking in their bodies greater than any natural geological force. Dioxippus thrust his hips up, harder and harder as he tried to insert his whole being into the woman he loved. And every time he could bear to open his eyes, he saw Panthea's breasts, swinging like perfect, god-shaped pendulums, mere breaths away from his open mouth. He extended his arms, his claw-like fingers grabbing at the bosom of the woman astride him. He lifted his head up and with the hunger of a starving dog closed his mouth over the nearest breast. Panthea leaned forward, grasped Dioxippus by the head and rubbed her chest even harder into his face. The result was manic. Dioxippus shot his hips up, faster and faster. Panthea bucked harder and harder. Their groans became screams. Screams became cries. Faster and faster they moved. They shrieked. The tandem became one.

Outside, sitting cross-legged on the ground underneath one of the shade trees, was Fotis. He could hear the animal-like noises emanating from the small cottage and he was not so old he could not imagine the gyrations taking place therein. Normally, he would have left: he did not like feeling like a voyeur. But he had walked far and he was tired. There was no energy left in his aged form to walk around until the two young lovers were finished. So he sat. And to occupy himself, he grumbled.

After a while it became quiet. Fotis listened carefully. No sound. They must be finished, he thought. An image of the two lying together flashed across his mind. Before he could savor it or castigate himself for thinking it, a vision appeared before him. It was a woman. He could not see her clearly but he knew that she was small, frail and his wife. The apparition did not move. Fotis rubbed his eyes, a vain effort to see better but the ghostly entity had dissolved. Fotis looked around him. Nothing. I am like Orpheus, he thought; forever doomed to look back at my fading Eurydice as she slips back to Hades.

The melancholy distracted him. Fotis did not realize someone was standing beside him until he felt the hand on his shoulder. Startled, he leaned back sharply, lost his balance and fell over onto his back. Immediately, the little man began to swear furiously.

"You have not changed," laughed Phylia. She had not seen Fotis for at least a couple of months. His tirade did not offend her; it was the reaction she expected. "It is good to see that time has not mellowed you Barba Fotis."

"Hmmmph. Precocious little..."

"Stop. I am sure I can guess what you want to say next," said Phylia, still laughing.

"Then give an old man a hug," came the reply.

The two embraced. Fotis felt a tear on his cheek. He did not know if it was his or Phylia's. What he did know was that he had missed this child. But a premonition honed by age and experience told him that Phylia was not here to reminisce. He held on a little tighter a little longer.

Phylia too knew that this reunion possessed an artificiality to it. Yes, she was glad to see the old man. And yes, she was eager to see her beloved Dios. She would even be glad to see Piros, who although he had always been kind, caring and gentle, nevertheless frightened her. During the escape from Athens they had had to traverse a territory ravaged by war. Piros and Dioxippus had been forced to take extraordinary measures to protect the little band. Phylia had seen what those measures sometimes entailed. She trembled at the memory.

Fotis relaxed his grip about Phylia's shoulders. "Come, sit with me," he said.

Phylia eased back from Fotis. She quickly glanced around her and spotting no stool or bench, shrugged her shoulders and squatted down onto the patch of earth where Fotis had just been sitting. The few tufts of grass and weeds secured the soil so dust was minimal. The shadow cast by the olive tree a few steps away added a much needed bit of coolness. The combination made their position relatively comfortable.

"Well..." queried Fotis, eager to get whatever subject Phylia wished to discuss started.

"Where is Dios? And Piros?" asked Phylia.

Fotis furrowed his brow. How would he explain what his young charge was up to? Would Phylia be jealous? It was no secret that she loved the young man. How would she react when she found out that he was passionate about a woman ten years her senior? Fotis decided that Dioxippus could deal with it.

"Dioxippus is in the house. Sleeping. Piros has gone to speak to Philip. A close friend of his was..." Fotis caught himself. He saw no reason to disclose the particulars of Pausanius' rape and beating to a child who had suffered so much as a victim of just those crimes. "...attacked by criminals and Piros feels the king may know who might have been involved."

"I do not know why this might be important to Piros but knowing Olympias, anything she takes a direct hand in must mean something to someone," said Phylia.

"Anything that witch gets her hands on becomes sullied," interrupted Fotis, the edge in his voice apparent.

"That is why I have come. She has ordered that Kanavos to Kathos' quarters. Why? I do not know. Perhaps it has something to do with the disappearance of the slave girl Tamina. What I cannot understand is that she sent one man against hyenas--a small one who is barely larger than I am. Kathos is not tall either yet compared to the man in the queen's chambers this morning he is a giant. Kathos also has help. There are at least three others with him and even though I have seen them only a few times, they look as savage as rabid dogs. I cannot understand why the queen did as she did. It makes no sense. Olympias never does anything without considering every part of the problem. I thought Piros might be interested in this information."

"I am sure he will be."

Both Fotis and Phylia turned to the direction of the voice. Standing there, flushed with the exertion of his earlier passion-filled endeavors stood Dioxippus. Half a pace to the right and slightly behind him was Panthea. To the seated Fotis and Phylia, they were as demigods; so beautiful, so vibrant they defied description.

Phylia leapt up and threw her arms around the neck of Dioxippus. He embraced her gently, enjoying the warmth and affection of the child he always thought of as his little sister.

Panthea knew of Phylia and her history. Dioxippus had told her much. However, the wide-eyed child he described was not the blossoming woman with the alabaster skin and raven-colored hair throwing herself on the unsuspecting Dioxippus. A twinge of momentary jealousy curled a corner of Panthea's upper lip. This child that Dioxippus had always talked about might have been only thirteen years old but she was as much woman as she was. And in Hellas, thirteen was a common marrying age. In fact, she, Panthea, was the anomaly. Here she was, twenty-three years old, in love with an eighteen year old. To complicate the situation further, she had been a virgin until she gave herself to Dioxippus. Soon she would be beyond her childbearing years. This child was probably better suited to Dioxippus than she was. I should be jealous, she thought.

Philip and Piros

"Let him in," sighed Philip. He did not need to hear what Piros had to say; his spies had already briefed him. Philip lowered his head until the hair in his beard scratched the soft skin just below his neck. He scanned the floor, the tiled pattern amusing him with its order as he compared it to the disorder of his court. He sighed as the melancholy effectively immobilized him. When Piros came in, Philip was barely discernible from any of the other inanimate objects placed about his room.

Piros felt a torrent of emotions; all of them compounded by anger and frustration. He felt himself tighten, his breathing slow. Once someone had compared him to a compact siege machine. At this instant Piros felt like a machine: all wound up, ready to fire missiles at this man, this king sitting so laconically in front of him. This was the man, now mere steps away from him, who had orchestrated or knew who had, the vilest abomination on his best friend Pausanius. Now Piros would demand the answers from Philip that no one else in the court would provide. Piros had been forced to seek an audience with Philip. And even though they had been close friends in the past, events in the last year or so had strained that relationship. This would not make it any easier to get the information he wanted.

Philip seemed unaware of the black man standing in front of him. His mind was preoccupied with Persia, Alexander, Olympias, Cleopatra, his kingdom, the Greeks and so forth. Incessant voices pounded his brain and all Philip wanted to do was to leave, to seek a place removed from the chaos his court had fallen in. Yes, he thought. I should take Cleopatra and my future child and sail to an island, far away and inaccessible. My mind will then know peace.

Piros had been born with an innate sensitivity to people's emotions. He sensed that Philip was troubled. But his friend had chosen not to confide in him. Regardless, he was here for Pausanius. And upset or not, the king would have to answer some hard questions for Piros.

Philip's eyes were still locked on the swirling colours of the tile inlays at the base of the two stairs located in front of him. It might have been moments, it might have been a day, Philip did not know.

The scratchy sound of shifting feet snapped a chord in his brain. He looked up.

"Philip."

The king winced. There was a time when his closest confidantes could use his given name with impunity, Piros more than anyone. Now it grated on him. By all the gods on Olympus he had already conquered a good third of the world. That merited some respect. History would show him to be one of the world's greatest kings. The way the Macedonians revered him one would think him a god. In fact, there was a growing movement afoot that wished to deify him. He had turned them down repeatedly, knowing that his soldiers might not be amenable to the idea. After all, it was his accessibility that endeared him to the man slogging in the infantry. He was one of them. He had just been born with certain advantages. Yet, Philip could not help but be intrigued with the idea of being worshipped. Had not lesser kings and emperors been lionized. Who were they in comparison to him? Who was Piros? What gave him the right to address him as one would an equal? Philip felt himself begin to anger.

"State what you want." Philip was terse.

"You know why I am here," replied Piros, surprised at Philip's tone yet nevertheless unafraid.

"Hmmmmmph..." Philip grunted. "I suppose it has something to do with that boot-licking lapdog of my wife's, Pausanius. Well, what would the indignant Piros request of this humble king?"

The bitter sarcasm was not lost on Piros. It did not appear likely that Philip would be overly sympathetic to his former bodyguard. Nevertheless, Piros was obligated to seek some sort of redress for the atrocity that Pausanius had been subjected to. He thought for a moment. Then he half-smiled. Phlip was not going to get the fight he wanted. He began.

"Strange how one man's sufferance can so affect his family, his friends...or his subordinates." Piros paused. The king leaned back slightly, confused but curious of the direction this conversation had now taken. Piros continued. "There was a time when rank, birthright and political office meant nothing to you. You were a soldier. And like the rest of us, your first loyalty was to the man next to you. Now that you campaign against empires, that loyalty may not seem as important as it once was. But I remember when it was the only thing that mattered to you. Was it so long ago; did seven years pass so quickly?" Piros looked at Philip searchingly. Philip's curiousity was piqued but the blank expression on his face showed no hint of recalling what Piros was so obviously intimating at. Whatever happened, happened seven years earlier.

Piros' eyes narrowed. For a moment he looked like a snake that had slithered unexpectedly up to a rat. "Surely you can remember...the mountain tribe blocking a pass from the north to Olympus? We were not able to take a large force with us because of the limited room to maneuver. So you chose one hundred of us."

An involuntary smile flitted across the face of Philip. Yes, he was starting to remember that conflict. It was hardly a fly landing on an elephant in terms of the Macedonian empire. But the fly turned into a hornet, he thought.

"You chose the surliest, meanest and most undisciplined men in your bodyguard. It made no sense to me at the time. These Companions would have just as soon killed each other for the warm spot by the fire as they would have the enemy. This motley crew was so bad that you personally had to lead us."

This time Philip was unable to contain his smile. The memory of that troop complaining, cursing and fighting from the first light to the last still amused him. A dirtier, nastier group would have been hard to find. But a unit as effective at this type of hit and run warfare would have been impossible for anyone but Philip to hold together.

"Many in the court advised you against going up into the mountains. You scoffed at their concern. We admired that.

But once we were up there...there was nothing to laugh at. They ambushed us on the one day that an early blizzard hit. It was chaos. Everything was out of control. The men did not know who to fight or what to aim for. Commands could not be communicated because of the snow. And all the while, these half-man half-animal savages shot arrows (some tipped with poison), threw rocks the size of a man's head and cast spears with barbed points. When they ran out of weapons they threw anything else that they could launch at us from the safety of their perches."

Philip's face turned grim. How could he have forgotten? In a hundred battles, most of the time against far larger, better armed forces never had he been so afraid as that time in that nameless mountain pass. Not even the adrenalin rush that cascaded through his body during combat, which made it an insatiable thrill, could counter the panic he felt in that surreal hell.

"Some of us were trying desperately to fight back and still protect you. But the snow, by now a whirling dervish, made it impossible to see further than a few meters. I remember crying in anguish because I could not see you. I called and called but it was impossible. I managed to gather a few men together. Somehow we were able to move as a unit; not quite a phalanx but at least a body that could protect itself."

Even though Philip knew the story he found himself mesmerized by Piros' retelling of it.

"Those of us in front were using the butts of our pikes to feel for bodies buried in the snow. Whenever we came across one we prayed that it was not you. Our progress was slow because the savages were still hailing down on us. Eventually we made it across the open space to the shelter of some trees. To a man we felt disgusted because we had lost you. Our anger and our grief knew no bounds so when we saw, just beyond the little grove we had just come in, some fifteen to twenty fur-clad barbarians screaming and jumping and waving weapons we went crazy. The blizzard had eased somewhat so we were able to see relatively clearly. We charged them like ravenous beasts; our hunger for vengeance tearing at our guts. Yet even in those few steps it was obvious that our attackers had surrounded someone and whoever it was had managed to instill a fearsome respect in them."

This part was a forced blank in his memory. The ravaged space where one of his eyes used to be began to throb.

"We tore into them like the bears in the animal pits. Even though these warriors were exceedingly strong and insanely fearless, in hand–to-hand combat with the fiercest of the King's Companions, they were slaughtered with the ease of a butcher cutting up a side of beef. Not one was left alive. And as the snowfall began to abate, the others, seeing the carnage, left as noiselessly as they had come. The survivors of our troop began to call out and as some were wounded I sent men out to attend to or retrieve them. I myself was going to lead the search for you. But first I had to see who had managed to hold off so many of the enemy by himself."

Philip shifted in his seat. He was very uncomfortable now.

"Sitting there, in the snow, his face a mask of blood was Pausanius. A spear had pierced the upper part of his thigh, his hip had been chopped open with an axe and two arrows, their feathers still quivering, protruded from his left shoulder. Only his armor and the thick fur coat he had on saved his life. In his right hand he still clutched his sword; waving it feebly at us, the pain making him so delirious he did not know the enemy had been defeated. But your highness..."

Philip winced at the title. He blushed with embarrassment at his earlier thoughts. Vanity...

"...half-buried in the snow, stuck full of arrows was this body that was so bloody it was almost unrecognizable. Pausanius had thrown himself over top of this person to protect him. No one helped Pausanius. By himself he had held off the savages until help arrived. You know of course, that the body was yours Philip. You are here now, not by the grace of the gods, but by the courage of your most loyal bodyguard, Pausanius. Now it is he who is the beaten body. We did not save him from his attackers so that he could become the victim of some unnamed plot. His sacrifice for you should at least be rewarded with some compassion for him. We cannot undo what has transpired. Let us at least avenge the vile transgression against him."

Philip swallowed. His anger had abated as the story was being told. Everything Piros had said was true. Pausanius had willingly used his body to shield him. He had shown tremendous courage and resolve to keep the savages away from his king. Now he lay beaten, the victim of some sick plot. Philip clenched his teeth as

258

he exhaled fiercely through his nostrils. The bastards who did that to Pausanius deserved the worst punishment the sickest of minds could come up with. The only trouble was that Philip did not know who was responsible. His spies suspected that sewer scum Kathos but there were no witnesses and no evidence. Philip's spies had also told them that a rumour was circulating that Attalus had hired the criminals. Philip knew that was not true. His new in-law and ablest general was so far in the Persian desert that the necessary means to formulate and execute a plot like this were impossible to get access to. No, whoever had done this had an agenda.

"If I were to tell you that I do not know who is responsible for what happened to Pausanius, would you believe me?" asked Philip.

"At one time, if you had told me it was raining while the noonday sun burnt my body, I would have believed you. But circumstances have changed. The man Pausanius himself believes is responsible is your father-in-law. How can you turn against a family member?"

"I have ruled forcefully. Those that are guilty of crimes are punished regardless of alliances. If Attalus were involved I would slit his throat myself. But think Piros, use your intellect. How could Attalus order such a thing? He is in the desert, two thousand miles away. And why would he do that to Pausanius? He barely knows him. If anyone has a grievance, it is me. I am the cuckolded husband. More than anyone, I have the right to punish Pausanius. Yet, you do not accuse me. Or do you?" Philip looked directly into Piros' eyes.

Piros bowed his head slightly. Logic would dictate that the king was right. Attalus may have been a decoy, thought Piros. It was not likely that Philip would employ such clandestine means to eliminate an enemy. Somebody was using Pausanius as a pawn in a game--but what game?

"Do you have to think about it?" asked the waiting Philip.

"No," answered Piros.

"Then what would you have me do?"

"Let me find the guilty parties. And when I do ignore what results." Piros' tone had a steely edge to it. It took no imagination to guess what Piros would do when he caught up to Pauasanius' assailants.

"Done," replied Philip. "However, Pausanius is still guilty of indiscretions with my wife. You know me well, Piros. He can have the bitch if he wants her." Philip leaned forward, his eyes meeting Piros. "I grieve for what he has suffered. It is true I owe him my life, probably a few times over. Yet I cannot and will not have any further contact with him. Engaging a king's wife, even an unfavoured one, in adultery, negates any rights or obligations. I hope too to find his attackers. We will exact vengeance. But do not let Pausanius contact me; reinstatement can be examined later. For now this discussion is over." Philip's head dropped to his chest, weariness having sucked all the energy out of him.

Piros knew nothing more would be gained. Declining his head forward slightly, he said, "Philip," turned on his heels and left.

Phylia

Tapping.

The sound, normally barely discernible amongst the profusion of noises invading her world, now assaulted her ears. Phylia looked over at the source of the sound: the offender to her solitude and peace.

Olympias was unaware of Phylia's rancor. She sat, on a low, elaborately carved stone bench, looking out through the window. Her eyes were transfixed, as if they were examining something in great detail. But Olympias' eyes saw nothing. Colours and images flitted across her pupils, refusing to hold still long enough to have their message relayed by the retina to the brain. The visual stimuli was to Olympias as it would be to a blind person, nothing to nothing. Still she sat. Trancelike. Waiting. Waiting. And tapping her long, exquisitely coloured fingernails on the windowsill beside her.

Phylia was bored, tired and desperate to leave the suite of her mistress. She chanced another look at Olympias. The queen was still staring out the window, looking but not seeing, rolling her fingers, the nails tapping that incessant beat. Phylia sighed, careful to muffle the action. She's waiting for someone, she thought. Phylia surreptitiously cast a glance over at Olympias again. Whoever the queen was waiting for had managed to capture and hold still the fierce beast that took refuge in the beautiful Olympias' body. Lover or enemy? Phylia could not decide whom Olympias waited for. She had never seen Olympias in this coma-like state and although Phylia could not care less about Olympias she felt herself obligated to watch over the obviously distracted monarch.

A faint rustling of material snapped both women's heads up in the direction of the far wall. A wraith-like spirit stood there, seemingly materialized from nothing. Phylia took a sharp breath, the sudden intake of air an instinctive response to the sudden appearance of Kinovas. Olympias too could feel her heart take a couple of extra beats but her self-control quickly assuaged her body's defensive mechanisms. After all, she chastised herself, what made Kinovas so valuable was his innate ability to move as furtively as a ghost, to appear when unexpected. To be frightened of him served no purpose.

To use him did. And the fact that he had come now indicated to Olympias that some news was forthcoming.

"Well..." The inflection in Olympias' voice evidenced a mutual understanding of objectives.

"It is done."

Olympias beamed. Then her smile turned into a hard line. She turned to Phylia. "Out...now!"

Without a word, Phylia gathered her cloak and exited the queen's apartment. She did not dare look back. The queen's vicious temper was not one to be challenged--particularly when some sort of plot was being discussed with one of the most dangerous men in Macedonia. I need to tell Patroclus, thought Phylia. A smile danced across her face and her eyes sparkled momentarily. Patroclus.

Kinovas

"Check the doors...and the walls," ordered Olympias. This unusual concern over security weakened the normally haughty demure of the queen.

Kinovas immediately drew a long, silver-handled dagger from a compartment in his outer robe. The knife was double-edged, and so slim it looked almost like a woman's ornament. But the glint of metal as the weapon was flicked into a reverse position belied its brutal purpose. Grasping the handle firmly, the razor-sharp blade lying gently along the inside of the wrist, Kinovas prowled through every aperture and opening in the room. His low cat-like stance added further to the feral impression he imparted to Olympias. And like a cat or panther, when he found nothing he slowly stretched erect until he faced Olympias.

"Well..." drawled the queen, barely able to contain her excitement.

"He lies secured. I killed the others."

Kinovas' unadorned, flat-toned statement of fact nevertheless exuded a deathly chill even the hard-hearted Olympias could feel. Kathos' band of anonymous butchers was no more. Her loyal servant had eliminated them with about as much compunction as stepping on a bug. Still, he had not killed Kathos...yet. And that was reason enough to savour Kinovas' accomplishment and to look forward to, with salacious hunger, the moment she had envisioned months ago-- the moment when she would direct the destinies of her husband and his cronies. After today, she thought to herself, we see how long you and that bitch remain in power.

Kinovas stood immobile. Nothing about the queen's ruminations, barely disguised by her demeanor, interested him. Whatever she wanted him to do, now and forever, he would do: no questions asked.

Olympias blinked. The haze over her eyes disappeared. Quickly, almost furtively, she glanced around the room. Then she picked up her cloak and whirling it around to her back, threw it over her shoulders. She looked at Kinovas. Without a visible response, he turned and made for the door, Olympias not more than a half step behind. Neither turned to look at the apartment they had just left.

Outside in the corridor various groups of people milled about, the usual chaos no different today than any other. Those who inadvertently crossed in front of the queen and her escort immediately bowed their heads and moved out of her way. Nobody wished to risk the wrath of this all-powerful monarch. Olympias was so caught up with thoughts of Kathos that she did not even notice much less enjoy the consternation her mere presence evoked amongst her husband's subjects.

Kinovas led Olympias down the corridor, through the main square and out through the palace gates. Removed from the security of the thick stone and mud walls, Olympias felt wary. At the best of times it was not a good idea for a personage such as her to travel beyond the palace walls without an armed escort. Revolutionaries, anarchists, murderers and thieves patrolled these streets like rabid dogs. For one of them to come upon a hated queen would be like a dream come true. They would chop her into so many pieces that not even the gods of Olympus would be able to reassemble her. Few if any things frightened Olympias. Few if any men had her courage, her fierce will. Yet like many rulers, she would admit to herself that the masses, her subjects, frightened her. To be so openly exposed...it was too much. She glanced at Kinovas. He walked slightly ahead, protecting as much as leading her. His self-confidence and utter fearlessness radiated from his body like some god-like essence. Olympias became enveloped in the force emanating from the little man walking ahead of her. Even Philip's elite bodyguard did not make her feel this safe. Thank the gods he belongs to me, thought Olympias.

Strangely, few people were about. This did not bother Olympias but she wondered where she might be. She had long ago lost her sense of direction as Kinovas weaved through the maze of streets and alleys. Olympias was further confounded by Kinovas' elaborate precautions to avoid being followed. He was constantly doubling-back, circling, stopping. All this added time and distance to the walk and Olympias began to feel herself tire. The faintest moisture at the collar of her robe made her aware of how strenuous her exertion thus far, even in the cool shade of the surrounding buildings, had been. Just as she was about to ask Kinovas, how much longer, he signaled her to stop.

They stood in front of a small, irregularly shaped building. It was not quite a rectangle, the rear wall being somewhat elongated in comparison to its parallel. This front facia was so inconspicuous it was as if whoever had built this home had wanted to conceal as much of it from the street as possible. Its nondescript, muddy yellow walls combined with the small wooden windows, barely covered by the rotten grass shutters contributed even further to its anonymity. Olympias had to admit, if one needed to hide or to hide something, this was the perfect place.

"In there?" Olympias cast a querulous look at Kinovas.

"Yes."

Kinovas moved to the door. Slowly, carefully, he opened it just enough to slide his hand through. Olympias could not see what he was doing, but it appeared that he was lifting something if the motion of his right arm was any indication. Within moments Kinovas finished. He turned and motioned to Olympias to follow him. Casting one more look around her, Olympias moved forward and through the door.

Immediately, Olympias scrunched up her nose. The reek inside this house was almost unbearable. Odours from stale grasses, rotted food, human and animal excrement and of putrefying flesh all competed with each other in offensiveness. The sunlight, fighting its way through the covered window, provided scant illumination. Although Olympias' eyes quickly adjusted to the haze, she found the impairment to her vision uncomfortable and annoying. Kinovas had already moved to the next room so it appeared to the queen that he would not be lighting a lamp or torch to assist her. Grudgingly she followed him. She was careful not to lift her feet too high, just in case she tripped or stumbled over something lying hidden on the debris-strewn floor. So intent was Olympias on watching her steps, she was unprepared for what she saw next.

Auelias

"Worrying so much will not help you or this child," said Cleopatra, gently rubbing her distended belly. She looked up at Philip's back. He was still staring out the window.

Without turning to face his pregnant wife, Philip replied, "As of late, I face too many intrigues, plots and treacheries. Years ago, running this court was a relatively simple affair. Now we are flooded with self-servers, cheats, liars and worst of all the bureaucracy. As much as I try to maintain control, I never really know what is transpiring anymore. I am certain of such few things..."

Cleopatra was dismayed to see her husband in such melancholy. Rumours of revolt and assassination had eaten him up and spit him out. Cleopatra knew that his mental state was not wrought by fear but out of concern for her and her unborn child. Philip never backed down. He truly feared little. But the conflicts within his family, the problems with the settlements in Asia Minor, the upcoming campaign, the Olympics and the impending birth of his son, were for the first time beginning to stress him seriously. Cleopatra knew that the only means at her disposal to console or comfort him was to leave him to his introspection and to always be available to him.

"Soon you will have another son to gloat over. And he will, one day, help Alexander rule over the civilized world. Be thankful. Come sit near me. You have not been as affectionate of late. Do I repulse you?" laughingly asked Cleopatra. Philip's amorous charges had slowed in the past few weeks and to be honest with herself, she was glad. Her size made her uncomfortable and making love was too much of a chore. Of course she would never tell Philip. And in his mind-state, sex was not a priority. Still, to assuage his ego, Cleopatra grabbed at him.

"What...are you in heat woman?" asked Philip, squirming to get away from Cleopatra's groping hands. "Easy...stop it!" yelped Philip, mocking anger.

Cleopatra laughed as she gently and good-naturedly wrestled with her husband. Both squealed like children.

266

"Your highness..."

"King Philip..."

Suddenly, a short cough came from the other side of the room.

Philip turned quickly, half-rising out of his chair as he simultaneously drew a dirk from about his waist. "Who are you?" he demanded sternly. "What do you want? How did you get in here? Where is my bodyguard? Prepare to die..." Philip's sharp-edged tone had been heard outside the door because suddenly it burst open as both bodyguards charged through.

Auelias immediately backed up toward the wall, his arms outstretched with his hands open. His fright was obvious and he blubbered out, "Philip, it is me Auelias. You told me to watch Kathos. Please. Don't you recognize me? The guard let me in. You told me (and them) that I was to be allowed access to you at any time, day or night. I am not an assassin. Please. Listen to me!" The words gushed out at such a rate they were difficult to understand.

Philip stopped his attack. He turned to his bodyguards. Both looked rather sheepish. They had let Auelias in to see Philip because he had told them that he carried important news. Never had they expected this to occur. And both were confused: Philip had given them specific orders, now he was acting like a madman because they had followed them.

Philip too was confused. So engrossed had he been with Cleopatra, that he had not heard the announcement from his guards. When Philip looked up and saw Auelias standing there, he had failed to recognize him. Fearing assassination he had attacked. The resulting foolishness had frightened his wife not to mention Auelias and had embarrassed him and his bodyguards. I have to get control over this fear, Philip thought to himself. He took a deep breath, and smiled. But in the pit of his stomach he felt dread.

Seeing his king relax, Auelias sighed, relieved that the situation had not escalated. A shudder, like the aftershock of an earthquake, rippled through him as he tried to regain his composure.

267

"I...I..." he stuttered. Now angry with himself he swallowed, grit his teeth and began again.

"I followed Kathos and his henchmen...just as you ordered."

Philip felt his face flush. Ordered. He could not remember any more what he had ordered.

Getting no visible response, Auelias continued. "For awhile after Pausanius was found, Kathos hung around a tavern not too far from the wastes." The wastes Auelias referred to were the areas the city dumped its garbage. "Most of the time, he and his cohorts just drank. Sometimes they fought with each other...sometimes with others. No one unusual talked to them. I was about to report to you that this mission was accomplishing nothing until two days ago. A man, a little man, approached Kathos while he was having dinner. He looked so odd beside Kathos that I decided that I would not leave until this had played itself out. I was too far away to hear what was being discussed but whatever it was it pleased Kathos. Soon after, Kathos called the rest of his men to him. They laughed and clapped each other on the back. Then they left. The little man too." Auelias had tried to modulate the earlier panic in his voice. He hoped that the softer, even tone reflected the officious nature of his report.

By now Philip had sat down beside his wife on the couch. He listened with interest to the young soldier's story. I picked a good one for this job, he thought. Philip leaned toward his wife who whispered into his ear. Philip nodded in agreement.

"This little man you saw...was he a dwarf?" asked Philip.

"No. He was shorter than most men; maybe half a head less than Alexander. And his face was dark. Not like the famous Piros. But darker than most Greeks."

"Anything else?" Philip was curious to know who this new player was. The memory he had of Kinovas had long faded.

Auelias shifted slightly. There been something; something that made no sense, an intangible that he could not prove. Philip was looking at him, expecting an answer. Auelias stiffened his back and continued.

"Yes." Auelias took a breath. "He knew."

"Knew what?" asked Philip.

"He knew that I was watching him. I don't know how but he knew that I was following Kathos. Even more confusing, I am fairly confident that he didn't tell Kathos."

"Why would you think that?"

"He made it easy to trail them without being obvious. There was no way that Kathos could have known I was dogging him. The little man doubled back, took Kathos on dead ends, and even moved through houses and other buildings. Yet none of these evasive actions was enough to lose me. And I am no braggart. He wanted me to follow them but he didn't want Kathos to know..."

"So he did just enough to put Kathos at ease," interjected Philip. This was getting interesting. Even Cleopatra was fascinated by this report. Philip could tell by how hard she was squeezing his hand as she listened to Auelias.

"I followed them to a small, abandoned house. I watched it for a while. No one came or left. Eventually I heard laughing. It appeared to be a party. I moved in closer to hear..."

"...what? What did you hear?" interrupted Philip again.

"I heard Kathos say, 'I wish that Companion was younger. He was a little flabby for my taste'. I'm not sure but I think he was referring to Pausanius," said Auelias.

"Give me the directions to the house. Then go and find Piros. Tell him what you told me and bring him there." Philip barked out the command like the leader he was. "You, Buros and Archeos, come with me. And bring my sword." By now Philip was on his feet and moving to the door. Fury had cloaked his face in shadow. Cleopatra saw and was frightened.

Auelias quickly drew a diagram on a scrap piece of parchment. Philip waited for Auelias to finish then he grabbed the scrap, signaled his bodyguards and charged down the halls, not once looking back. Auelias too took off as he went to fetch Piros. Cleopatra, suddenly left alone, trembled once then closed and bolted the door.

As soon as Philip and his guards left the palace grounds, they settled into an easy lope, the kind of running that consumed miles without excessively tiring the runners although Philip's gait was more of a hop and skip due to his lameness. All three men moved in silence, only the occasional clanging of a sword against a shield or belt interrupting the forced silence. They passed many Macedonian citizens but as Philip's presence among them was common, few looked up from their labours to see the king. Others however, yelled greetings to Philip but neither Philip nor his bodyguards paid them attention. All three were consumed by the need to find Kathos and extract some measure of retribution for the atrocity perpetrated on Pausanius. Philip also suspected a plot and wanted answers.

As they approached the dilapidated dwelling, Philip signaled his escort to slow their pace. The king had seen too many traps to allow a charge headlong into a potential ambush. He stopped across from the little house. With his bodyguards, he silently surveyed the street, looking for anything that did not belong in this environment. The street, nothing much more than an alley, was littered with the flotsam of a growing city. Old clothes, broken pottery, rotted food, human waste all combined to give this area the most forbidding appearance. Even a soldier like Philip realized that on this, the decaying underbelly of a growing metropolis, life had only as much worth as the living could contribute. Philip sniffed. The stench came not from the myriad objects strewn about the street but from fear and despair. Hopelessness was a tangible entity in this dirty little corner of Pella. No marches, no wars, no victories could improve the condition of this ghetto. Philip was stunned by the ferocity of this air. The wind, less even than the breeze that had gently fanned Philip at his castle, carried a searing odor, a scent strong enough to order Philip away from this little house.

All three men huddled against the wall. Except for their eyes darting back and forth, none of them moved. Even when a rat, foraging for food, inadvertently bumped into Philip's foot, no one so much as twitched. The control Philip's mind exerted over his body precluded any reaction to external stimuli, even to something as revolting as a rat.

Philip and his guards had not been there long when they heard the sound of approaching footsteps. Within moments, Auelias, Piros and Dioxippus turned the corner of the house next to the one Philip was standing beside. Auelias spotted Philip, and signaling Piros and his companion, joined the king and his bodyguards. Now the group was up to six, but so well did they blend into the shadows along the wall, the six were all but invisible from across the street. Nobody spoke. The only sound to be heard was the slightly laboured breathing of the new arrivals.

Piros caught the eye of the king. Both men looked deep into each other's eyes and read there the tenets of friendship. To Piros, Philip was vindicated. Not only had he found the criminals who had attacked Pausanius he had himself come to exact retribution. Piros did not need to hear Philip. In his eyes he could see that whatever Philip had become, or was becoming, he would always remain the loquacious youth who used to so annoy his Theban "hosts" with his various pranks and profligate mouth that when it came time for him to be returned to Macedonia, they all but threw him out of the city. At that time, Piros had chosen to follow the young prince. There had been few times since then that he had regretted his decision. Now standing here, waiting for the word to destroy Kathos and his twisted henchmen, Piros was glad that Philip appeared to once again be the man he served, admired and even loved.

"Auelias. Is there a back exit?" whispered Philip.

"No, your highness. Only through the front door or side windows can you gain entry. I doubt they suspect anything. Only one person concerns me. The little man. He can smell us. And I don't know if he is with Kathos at this moment," replied Auelias.

"He is one man. On my signal, Piros, Dioxippus and I will break down the front door. You three watch the windows. If no one tries to escape that way, follow us into the house." Philip's instructions came out in a harsh whisper, but all understood. "Draw your swords. On my count, charge them."

Low scraping sounds scratched the night still as the swords were drawn from their leather scabbards. Only Dioxippus was silent, having refused to carry a weapon. Philip looked around once more then using a hand signal to alert the group, charged across the narrow street.

Kinovas shows what he has done

"Ohhhh...Gods of Olympus...what have you done?!" screeched Olympias.

"What you asked," came the quiet reply. Kinovas watched his queen's hysterics impassively.

Olympias forced herself to look. Even someone as hard-hearted, as merciless as her, was not prepared for the destruction before her. Strewn haphazardly around the dirty, dingy room were the savagely violated corpses of Kathos' henchmen. All the violence, the criminal actions, the disregard for human life or dignity that Kathos' men had made a crucial part of their existence appeared to have imploded, leaving their bodies nothing more than bloody husks. Great gaping wounds about their necks and torsos left little mystery as to what finally snuffed out life's spark. But these were as nothing compared to the mayhem that had been ravaged on them before they mercifully died. Kinovas had somehow managed to bind the hands and feet of the members of this gang. Then he had made them pay for every atrocity they had ever perpetrated on another human being. With the delicate hand of a surgeon, Kinovas had first amputated whatever extremities had caught his attention. Fingers, toes, an arm on one, the tongue of another had been as neatly severed as a string under a knife. Blood, skin and shards of bone, mixed carelessly with bits and pieces of body parts, polluted the floor, the walls, the very being of this tiny hovel. And from the evidence that was so sickeningly apparent, not one of the victims had been allowed to die until he had witnessed the systematic insanity exercised on his comrades. The terror was palpable. The fear that Kinovas had managed to extract from what had been men still resonated against the walls. And perhaps the greatest abomination of all, at least to the now sickened Olympias, was that Kinovas now stood before her, unperturbed.

"Was this...necessary?" asked Olympias, her voice quavering.

"You asked that I make them suffer. They suffered." Kinovas still showed no emotion.

Olympias forced herself to look down at the carnage. Although of a tougher mettle than most people, she could feel herself inadvertently swallowing as she willed herself to calm. She looked at the bodies closer. The poor light, fighting its way into the dankness of the back room cast a murky haze over everything so it was difficult for Olympias to identify what were now nothing more than faceless cadavers.

"Which one is Kathos?" she asked.

"He's not there," answered Kinovas.

"What! You wasted your time with this garbage and you let the ringleader get away? Have you lost your mind? It is Kathos I want...not these degenerates. Find him...idiot!" Olympias was unaware that she was yelling, so angry was she. It was beyond comprehension that Kinovas could subdue three men, torture and kill them, and still be incapable of apprehending the leader of the group. Her anger had squelched her disgust; she began to move around the room, kicking corpses, stepping on body parts and ranting at Kinovas.

For the first time since he had gone to get Olympias, Kinovas displayed a faint hint of emotion. But rather than anger or frustration at being the recipient of the queen's vitriol, the Theban looked hurt. The verbal assault hurt him more than the physical assault he had taken when he subdued Kathos and his cohorts. He could not understand why she was furious. He had done what she asked.

"Why are you still standing there?" snapped Olympias.

"Your Highness. Kathos is here."

Olympias stopped. Her head whipped around as she scanned the room. "Where..."

"Here." Kinovas kicked what appeared to be a pile of rags. A few pieces of cloth fluttered across the floor. Where they had been, lay Kathos, bound, gagged and terrified. Although his face showed evidence of a severe beating, it was the blood-soaked rag wrapped around his genital area that drew Olympias' eyes. It took little imagination to guess what Kinovas had done to Kathos.

"Will he live...for long?" asked Olympias.

"As long as a rapist deserves."

Olympias nodded. She was aware that Kinovas' timeline for Kathos was very short. It was unfortunate that she could not have been here while Kinovas was emasculating Kathos. That she would have enjoyed.

Suddenly, Kinovas wheeled around to face the front entrance. "Somebody comes..."

"Kill him," ordered the queen.

Kinovas drew his dagger. In one fluid motion he had stepped over to the prostate Kathos, lifted his head by the hair and slit his throat. Except for faint gurgling, the operation was silent.

Just as his blade was completing its diagonal trek, the front door exploded with the impact of Philip and Piros' bodies. Sunlight flooded the two-room hovel, removing the muting shadows. Every detail of the earlier carnage blazed forth. Piros, Philip and the slightly trailing Dioxippus stopped: the shock momentarily immobilizing them. But within a few heartbeats, they resumed their advance. Yet, they moved cautiously, not ever suspecting that only one man was responsible for this slaughter. When they saw Kinovas, a small, almost frail-looking man, standing beside Olympias, they were speechless.

Olympias decided to break this verbal impasse. "Well...as usual, you are too late to do anything. This scum..." Olympias swept her arm in a low, semi-circle, indicating the dead bodies, "...wanted to kidnap, maybe even murder me. If not for Kinovas, I would have probably been in their place. By your late arrival, I assume that you did not particularly care what happened to me. Your lackeys sure proved to be of no value, other than to destroy a rotten door. And...where are your other morons? You don't usually go out without them."

Almost on cue, Buros and Archeos, the king's personal bodyguards, entered the building, crowding it even further.

"Your highness must have been truly terrified to have feared a man trussed, beaten and castrated." Dioxippus' sarcasm was not lost on the Queen.

"You speak...puppet? I never thought you capable of an intelligent utterance. It appears that Piros has taught his pit dog well. What next? Should I throw a stick?" Olympias' haughty return silenced the young pankratiatist.

"Please forgive Dioxippus. He has not yet learned to phrase his questions in a manner that bears no insult," said Piros to Olympias. His carefully measured tone was intended to mollify the queen. It didn't.

"Shut-up Piros. Do not attempt to kiss my ass with your whiny supplications. I am not Philip. I don't need to be liked or admired. I don't need to be flattered. I know what I am, what I want and how I will get it. If something stands in my way I eliminate it. Like Kathos and his..." Olympias did not finish before her delicately sandaled foot arched back, then shot forward in a vicious kicking motion toward the head of the dead Kathos. The impact, muted by the bare foot hitting skin and hair, nevertheless reverberated through the tiny enclosure.

Up to this point, Philip had remained silent. He had watched and listened to the exchanges between Olympias, Dioxippus and Piros as unobtrusively as possible. This story of attempted kidnapping was farcical. This witch had Kathos killed. That was certain. She had also made him pay in pain; for whatever Kathos had done to incur her displeasure had been returned with almost unparalleled savagery. And this little man...where did he fit in this equation?

"Well. What are you staring at? Are you going to allow these trained apes to question me? I am still the queen. Call off these baboons now!" snorted Olympias, her glare scorching the objects of her vitriol.

"I serve the king. I have no need to listen to the maniacal ramblings of the court's supreme..."

"Silence," Piros whispered harshly to the offended Dioxippus. "Now is not the time for your remarks."

"It will never be, Piros. Your plaything there has his days numbered. I don't care what he does in the Olympiad or the battlefield. His disrespect will be punished. No mortal talks to a queen in his manner. And...little one," the words slithering out of her serpentine mouth, "...Philip will not be around forever. Sooner or later...you will be mine."

Suddenly, Philip stepped forward, cocked his arm then released it in a vicious sweep that flew until the back of his hand cracked against Olympias' cheek. The blow, coming from a large, battle-hardened warrior, knocked the tiny woman halfway across the room, whereupon she stumbled over one of the corpses causing her to fall to the blood-soaked floor. Kinovas was already leaping to her side and almost caught her before she made contact with the putrid mess under their feet but it was too late to keep her from soiling the beautiful and probably very expensive chiton she was wearing. Olympias reached for Kinovas' arms and pulled herself up. She straightened herself as well as she could, pausing almost reflexively to pat a few loose tresses of hair. Then, like a bolt from a catapult, she flew across the room and with just as much anger, if not ferocity, she slapped her husband. Immediately, large red welts appeared on his cheek where the long, elegant nails had strafed the sensitive skin barely showing above his beard. This time Philip's hand rose to his face, sensing, then feeling the tiny droplets of blood.

Fearless, the queen stood before him, challenging him with flashing, triumphant eyes. Olympias reveled in this type of confrontation and her absolute disrespect of Philip made a psychological victory over her husband a given. Although no words came out of her mouth, her whole physical demeanor dared the king to try again.

Philip was furious. With little prodding he would have joyfully beat Olympias to death. But her inner strength transcended mere mortal limitations. Her aura, vehemently sexual leaped out of the confines of her body, crackling obscenely in the charged air of that little room. Philip could feel it, even taste it. But his own vitality was as nothing compared to Olympias'. He did not move toward her.

It was Kinovas, who gently but forcefully, cradled the queen's arm in his, and moved her away, breaking the impasse between the couple. Olympias could not resist one last glare even as she moved from her spot.

"Get her out of here!" snapped Philip at Kinovas. "Now...or I'll kill the both of you." He leaned slightly forward, jutted his jaw out and said, "I know that somehow you two are involved in this, this..." Philip motioned with his arms, indicating the carnage violating the sanctity of what had become a sacrosanct temple of death.

"I would not be so quick with my words...as stupid as they are," snapped Olympias, the edge in her voice indicating that she was ready for another fight even a physical one. "And while you are standing there like the moron you are, think of this. Kathos was the one who raped your precious Pausanius. And as he lay dying he confessed that he had been hired to 'service' Pausanius by someone in the King's court. Could it be loving husband, that you hired Kathos in a jealous rage over my coupling with Pausanius. Are you jealous, love of my life?" Olympias' acerbic wit angered the king again and he would have lunged forward save for the powerful hands of Piros gripping him like a vise. "Let him go Piros," whispered Olympias. She was almost gasping with anticipation, the thrill of the moment exciting her, wetting her in the innermost parts of her body. She longed to feel the sexual frenzy that always came whenever she was combating power such as that represented by the most powerful regent in the civilized world. It was this struggle to fulfill her childhood desire to be the ultimate authority that forced Philip away from her. She knew this. He may have been a brilliant strategist and utterly maniacal in battle but with her he was as a child. Olympias exploited this flaw while cursing the gods who had made her a woman and therefore unlikely to ever hold absolute power over these simpletons Philip called subjects. Olympias took one more look at her husband. Absent-mindedly her tongue darted between her teeth to moisten her slightly parted, full red lips. Her almost coquettish expression belied the intense hatred she now felt for the man she had at one time loved enough to conceive a child with.

"We will leave." Kinovas' voice distracted Olympias. Unhurriedly, she looked away from Philip to Kinovas, nodded assent and with barely a glance, walked between the parting warriors barring the exit, and out the door.

Piros, Dioxippus and the other bodyguards stood shell-shocked. This whole confrontation had taken only a few moments yet all four felt as if they had been bested in some type of martial arts contest. Philip on the other hand was angrier more than he was flabbergasted. Somehow, that puny bitch had once again managed to humiliate him. He felt like the idiot in some macabre tragedy she was directing. He would probably never best her as long as Alexander was alive to protect her. Philip felt a momentary pang of envy as he realized that Alexander would always favour his mother over him. This irked him; it bothered him even more to recognize this jealousy as a weakness in himself. Gods almighty he cried to himself, rid me of her...I cannot even avenge my loyal servant Pausanius because she, with what appears to be no more help than a man barely taller than a child, has beaten me to it and in the process shamed me. Philip looked around at his men, who were by now silently watching him, their expressionless faces still failing to disguise their confusion.

"Pausanius has been avenged. We will go back." Without so much as a glance at the men in his party, Philip walked out the door. Like loyal hunting dogs, Archeos and Buros fell in behind him.

"Philip," called out Piros.

But the king did not respond.

Dioxippus laid his hand on Piros' shoulder. "It's over," he said. "We too should return."

Piros shook his head defiantly. His fists clenched and unclenched while the tendons in his neck bulged with unreleased tension. The earlier adrenalin rush had keyed up his body for an action that never came and he was finding it difficult to subdue the torrent raging through his veins. If only there were some release...

Piros remembers...

It had been his first Olympics. And as a participant in the pankration he had garnered an inordinate amount of attention for a young rookie. His close alliance to the new Macedonian king, Philip, along with his Theban upbringing made him an object of mystery. His exotic colour also did nothing to alleviate the intense curiosity of the spectators that year. Although Piros was neither intimidated nor flattered by the unwanted notice of the masses he was aware of it and strove to minimize his profile by only appearing in public when it was his turn to compete. So far this had proven to be a successful method for maintaining his composure. Until today.

It was his quarterfinal match today. As other events were being run concurrently, most of the officials projected relatively small crowds--even for an event as popular as the pankration. But Piros, on his walk to the venue, could sense a static electricity charging the air. As he came to the open amphitheatre, he heard the clamor of thousands of moving, shuffling bodies gradually unite into a rising roar of anticipation. Piros was spotted almost immediately and the crowd erupted in a raucous medley of applause, jeers, compliments, insults and everything in between. To the young Piros, this almost fanatical horde of spectators was as fearsome an enemy as the opponent he would be facing momentarily. He was tempted to stare at this throbbing, pulsating organism composed of thousands of human cells. And although he feared a weakening of resolve in the face of this external pressure, he was more afraid of allowing himself to believe that he might gain some psychological advantage from all his well-wishers of which there were many. The debate within his brain would have probably continued if he had not been distracted from his meditation by the sudden storm of voices as the crowd stood on their seats, straining to catch an early glimpse of their favorite, Piros' opponent, Archimides. Unable to resist, Piros turned to see.

A massive, moving monolith lumbered across the sand-packed floor of the combat ring. With nary a glance at the whooping crowd, Archimedes focused his baleful gaze upon a suddenly unsure Piros. Piros tried to keep from gawking by averting his eyes but like a bird to a snake, he could not control himself. Even at this distance, Piros could not help but notice the heavy brow, accentuated by the scar tissue of myriad battles, pulling the sloping forehead of his soon to be enemy, down even further, giving the faintest impression of retardation. Coupled with a demeanor that bespoke tiredness and resignation, some might have been fooled enough to assume that Archimedes was beyond his prime but Piros was not. He could see that the hulking shoulders, stooped by too many years in the ring, failed to conceal the ferocious power lying there. Further examination revealed a trunk, albeit layered by fat, as thick and hard as a wine barrel. Supporting this structure were legs shaped like bowed posts, as though the weight they bolstered was so great that it warped the very bones within them. Consequently, Piros did not need to second-guess the power lurking in that body. An experienced pankratiatist acknowledged size; there was always somebody bigger. That Piros could handle, as he had on innumerable other occasions. What caught Piros' attention even more than the sheer physicality of his adversary was the practiced ease and grace of movement with which Archimedes spread the traditional oil over his now naked body. This too was an indicator to Piros that the bout making ready to start would be a hard--if not fatal--one.

As Piros took his turn slowly spreading the thick, lightly scented oil over his body, he concentrated on relaxing his muscles and freeing his mind. Still, he was barely aware of the oil, or the deep massaging action of his short, powerful fingers. He was too consumed with strategy after strategy springing forth in his brain, only to dissipate seconds later. In response to the chaotic ricocheting of ideas in his head, his body began to twitch with nervous apprehension. Mumbling curses at his lack of mental control, Piros looked up and across the ring at his opponent.

Archimedes waited. Smiling. Confident. Ready.

Piros averted his eyes. Again he swore to himself, his anger vying to wrest control away from his fear. Suddenly he trembled, frustrating himself even further. And making his discomfort, his confusion worse, was the happily grinning Archimedes who through some telepathic sense knew that Piros had already suffered defeat.

"Are the combatants ready?"

Piros' head snapped to the right. The referee, clothed in a long, cream-colored chiton pulled up and secured between his knees, exposing the lower part of his legs, stood ready, his switch (used for *enforcing the rules) clasped tightly in his left hand. He looked at Piros expectantly.*

"Yes. We're both ready!" boomed Archimedes' voice from across the ring.

Again Piros found his will wanting. He could only nod affirmatively at the referee.

"Then begin."

Piros had barely taken two steps into the ring before Archimedes crashed into him. Knocked backwards, Piros stumbled, falling onto his backside. Archimedes leaped after him, a predatory cat about to slay its crippled prey. But Piros, instantaneously comprehending that he would be as defenseless as a turtle if turned onto his back, curled his spine, raised his knees and in one blurring instant rolled backwards, somersaulting onto his feet and safely out of the range of the diving Archimedes. Then, by reflex more than plan, Piros lunged back at Archimedes who was desperately trying to get to his feet before the counter-attack. He saw Piros and raised his huge, roughly calloused hands to fend off the assault. Piros launched two whistling blows to the unprotected face of his opponent. Archimedes reacted by turning his cheek away from the first and raising his arm to deflect the second. But Piros' punches were fakes. His catapulted limbs were scarcely pulled back before he suddenly dropped himself to one knee, thrust his whole torso forward and within the same movement, wrapped his prodigious biceps around the upper thighs of his adversary. Before Archimedes could fall or attempt to pull away, Piros stood erect and with the added leverage, lifted Archimedes high into the air, turned him and threw him onto his stomach. Piros maintained his grip on the legs with his right arm and used his left to help him keep his balance on Archimedes' back. But fumbling about on the oil-slick skin thwarted Piros' attempt to get a submission hold on Archimedes' arm.

Archimedes, aware that his opponent was losing control, twisted violently, the centrifugal force not only propelling him to his feet but also sending Piros flying. Piros scrambled to regain himself but the leviathan he had only momentarily downed descended upon him like some earthquake driven force. Piros dove to escape a clinch. Archimedes, too far away to grab the much smaller, much faster Piros instead lashed out with a kick to Piros' midsection. Piros crossed his forearms in front of him, intercepting the kick. Unfortunately for Piros, Archimedes' foot and shin tore right through the defense, pushing Piros out of the drawn circle. Archimedes pursued him, scenting blood. He had barely taken two steps toward Piros before a whistling sound followed by the snap of wood against skin stopped him cold. Glowering he turned to the referee and mouthed an epithet, the muffled words barely concealing his fury. The referee, significantly smaller than the man-mountain he was controlling with his puny switch, nevertheless stepped between Archimedes and the prone Piros, and waved the bigger man back.

Elis, Pella, Olympia, Aegea, 336 B.C.

Dioxippus

The light, languorously crawling over the dawn horizon, barely illuminated the modest hovel serving as a barracks for the pankratiatists. Exhaustion from the previous day's training clamped their eyelids tight--so tight that the torpid rays of an early summer sun were unable to stimulate them to wakefulness. Except for one.

Dioxippus lay with his arms crossed behind his head, his eyes flitting about as they searched for patterns, marks and other oddities impressed upon the ceiling. The satiny, yellow-red softness of the growing light, cast muted shadows about the room as it draped the still sleeping athletes. Peace, pure and natural, gently settled over Dioxippus--for no reasons that he could probably pinpoint. For the first time since he had come to Elis to prepare for the Olympics, he felt relaxed.

He turned onto his left side. Before him, laid out on what used to be a tile floor, were two rows of four, blissfully snoring pankratiatists. Dioxippus smiled. In two days, the Olympics would start. On the fourth day of the games, he would have to fight for the olive wreath against some of these men. But for now, it was enough just to enjoy the closeness, the unity in purpose--the comradeship. Dioxippus fit in this group comfortably. He regretted that he would have to engage in combat with the athletes who over the last two weeks had become his friends.

He turned onto his back again. Closing his eyes slightly, he began to muse over the controversy that he had somehow managed to generate once again. It was less than a month ago, just after Petros had injured him in the qualifying match. He and Piros had been trying to placate an enraged Pausanius. The former King's Companion had just been told that his assaulters had been terminated before they could be made to confess. And even though Philip had shown great character and loyalty to the discredited Pausanius by pursuing Kathos and his henchmen, Pausanius still refused to accept that Philip was somehow not involved with the personal violation he had been subjected to. He believed, with god-inspired passion, that Attalus, in revenge for his effrontery in fornicating with Olympias, had planned and had executed this attack on him. Pausanius' enkindled rage blinded and deafened him to the pleas of his friends, Piros and Dioxippus. All he could rant about was revenge against

Attalus. It took Piros awhile to calm him and to convince him to seek reinstatement in the bodyguard. Pausanius grudgingly agreed.

Dioxippus, more loyal than practical, publicly supported Pausanius. Unlike Piros, he felt that he did not owe the king anything more than a normal subject would. And even though Philip's eager willingness to rectify the wrong done to Pausanius was admirable, it had just been too convenient to find Kathos and his band already dead when they came upon them. Dioxippus did not, like Pausanius, believe that Philip had orchestrated the attack. He did however suspect Attalus, who was protected by the king. This viewpoint had made it uncomfortable to stay in Pella, so Dioxippus waived the special exemption that Philip had arranged for him and came to Elis to join the other Olympians, most of whom had been there for ten months already. Of course, that meant he had forsaken the opportunity to meet Yiorgakas, Alexander's champion, in the arranged preliminary. This had angered the young prince, whose delicate ego frustrated easily. Even Piros had felt slighted, as Dioxippus' action was interpreted by some as cowardly which obviously reflected on his trainer.

Having offended both friend and enemy, Dioxippus had arrived in Elis, burdened with doubt and interminably lonely for his friends, particularly Panthea, with whom he had fallen in love. But the rules were strict. No visitors, friends or lovers. Yet being alone somehow focused him in a way he had been unable to before. It was as if all his problems could be controlled by the action within the ring. Dioxippus had come to the realization that when engaged in combat his worldly problems subsided. The struggle to survive then win shunted aside the petty and the serious concerns storming his mind. The more he fought, the more relaxed he became. That was when he was his most dangerous.

While training, Dioxippus continued to introduce new, untried innovations into his style of fighting. His reliance on long-range punching and kicking had already made him famous. By forcing his opponents to contend with his extensive array of striking techniques, he had elevated the pankration to a new level. The days of rolling around in the dirt, clutching and grabbing in some poor imitation of wrestling were coming to an end. Across Hellas, young boys were throwing high, fast kicks closely followed by perfectly executed boxing combinations. Brutality was giving way to speed and finesse and even veterans as acknowledged as Piros were recognizing the effectiveness of this new "way". Dioxippus was only marginally aware of his influence. He was far more concerned with the evolvement of the art as he saw it. And now, lying here on his mat, mentally secluded from his fellows, he reviewed yet another discovery.

It had happened shortly after he had been so traumatically injured by the unconstrained Petros. Piros, eager to find Dioxippus an easy opponent, chanced upon the unknown Agemmemnon. And in most respects, it was a good choice Piros made. Dioxippus' challenger possessed enough skill to test the young champion without presenting an undue threat. It also allowed Dioxippus to employ his whole arsenal with confidence. Coupled with the fact that his battered shoulder had held up, Dioxippus had counted this session a great success. Except for one fleeting moment.

While kicking relentlessly at various targets on his opponent's body, Dioxippus slipped in the sand. The momentary imbalance left his foot and leg hanging a second too long. Agemmemnon grabbed the extremity and pulled hard to his right, desperately trying to throw Dioxippus to the ground. Dioxippus, bigger and stronger, managed to yank his foot free but not until he had been turned so hard that his back now faced his opponent. Instinct, honed by years of practice, warned him that Agemmemnon was about to leap on his back. Unable to roll, with not enough time to spin away, Dioxippus was defenseless. Whether inspired, lucky, or by reflex, Dioxippus thrust out his other leg in a rearward direction. Instantly, he felt the flat of his foot impact something hard. Turning his head over his shoulder, Dioxippus saw Agemmemnon stagger back, his hands clutching at a spot on his hip. The surprise counter had not really injured Agemmemnon but there was no question from his reaction that it had surprised maybe even frightened him. No less astonished was Dioxippus. This was something completely new. His prior modifications to the system had been revelatory only in the sense that the established means of combat contained incredible potential that had never been realized until Dioxippus systematically recast the way a kick was delivered, a punch thrown, a man grappled. But this spinning, then delivering a technique from an apparently defenseless position was divinely inspired. The possibilities were endless. Attack was no longer limited to a frontal assault. Dioxippus could perceive how the pankration could ascend to an even higher level, as feint and parry could now be complemented by fakery and trickery. The science of the art would gain mastery over the brutality.

Dioxippus sat up, startled. Someone or something had bumped into the empty water containers left outside. Suddenly, Dioxippus heard a cat screech and a blur of fur flash past the open window. Relieved, Dioxippus lay back down but not before he glanced around him to see that not one of the other sleeping pankratiatists had so much as even shifted. He made a sardonic mental note that if these athletes ever became soldiers to transfer to another unit.

As Dioxippus slipped back into that shadowy netherworld that existed between conscious thought and unconscious sleep, a world where thoughts and ideas could unfold slowly and where nothing was limited by the constraints of actuality, he summoned back the images that had impressed themselves upon him over the last few days. The contests, the people, the foods, the tiredness, the exaltation, the pain, the rapture, the tension, all these fell upon his mind's eye like a torrential downpour. But one image, standing solid amongst the fleeting wisps was again, Dioxippus on his hands and knees looking at Agemmemnon staggering back with the ludicrous expression on his face. Again and again the body was spun, and again and again the leg flashed out of its chambered position in a rearward direction.

As good as the lingering image was, Dioxippus' intellect pushed through the dreamworld to disseminate the frivolous throng of voices, faces, events. Logic charged Dioxippus' brain with the task to analyze then adapt what had been a fluke of circumstance and physics to a strategically sound counter-offensive. From the complacent state of his almost-sleep Dioxippus was roused to a hard analytical assessment of his discovery. His eyes flashed open in response.

Still, no one else had awakened. Dioxippus raised himself up to a seating position. He would not be able to sleep any longer. He reached forward, gathered up his chiton and in one practiced motion, pulled and secured it about him. Then cautiously, so as not to disturb anyone, he got to his feet and surreptitiously let himself out the door. Outside, the rising sun hurled long thin shadows over the hard-packed ground. A few birds scratched about the dirt, looking for worms attracted to the surface by the residual moisture of the morning dew. The bright yellow-white of the midday sun had not manifested itself yet. Rather, a soft, almost pink incandescence flowed over the landscape, lending an ephemeral gentleness to this sacred place.

The serenity of the scene was not lost on Dioxippus. However, this ideal time, eroding rapidly, needed to be used for purposes other than meditation.

Just beyond the dilapidated courtyard was a solitary olive tree. Little vegetation surrounded it and the ground was relatively clear of bumps, roots or other obstacles. Perfect, thought Dioxippus. Stepping into the area shaded by the knurled old tree, Dioxippus removed his chiton. The dawn sun had not yet warmed the air and the young pankratiatist trembled slightly when the still crisp air hit his naked body. The slight discomfort was ignored as Dioxippus slowly stretched then did some warm-up calisthenics. When he had exercised enough to warm his body again, he took the combat stance and faced the tree. His feet were positioned almost parallel to each other, the left one ahead of the right by about the width of a shoulder. The hands were raised, the left slightly lower and ahead of the right also. To most observers, Dioxippus resembled more a boxer than a pankratiatist, and that would have been a fairly accurate assessment as Dioxippus always favored the boxer's offensive position to the wrestler's defensive one. Dioxippus did however differ from his boxing brethren--his legs were drawn up a little closer to each other so that when kicks were utilized, travel-time and balance were maintained. Dioxippus looked at the tree-trunk in front of him. Mentally-imaging a target, Dioxippus quickly pivoted his front foot, turning it in. Instantaneously, his head and neck turned in the same direction but in a half circle, to be closely followed by the spinning trunk, hip and legs. When the revolution was almost complete, the right leg, drawn up tight during the rotation, ripped out of its cocoon. Dirt and pieces of bark exploded as the hard calloused heel slammed into the brittle bark of the ancient olive tree. Dioxippus grinned.

Dioxippus did not let his pleasure become euphoria. Although the spinning kick, as he would refer to it from now on, had the potential to be a maliciously painful counter-attack the efficacy of the technique was questionable. There were in fact, inherent problems with it that Dioxippus, now a seasoned veteran of the ring, recognized. The spinning action necessitated turning his back, albeit momentarily, to his opponent: his balance was maintained on one foot while his body was being simultaneously subjected to a whirling centrifugal force. These factors exposed him to counters that would not only negate the spinning kick but also handicap the rest of his arsenal.

Surprise, thought Dioxippus. The strength of the spinning kick lay in surprise. Its effectiveness was dependent upon Dioxippus' ability to first choose the moment then disguise its utilization. And it would probably be a one-shot, desperation-driven stab at victory. That thought sobered Dioxippus.

From the antiquated abode across the dusty yard, sleepy, disgruntled voices arose. The rest of the pankratiatists were beginning to rise.

Smiling evilly, Dioxippus ran back to the dwelling, screaming, yelling...and laughing. His friends would all wake up now.

Alexander is counseled by Hephaestion

"We have come a long way. Now you want to go back?"

"I have a campaign to plan. I cannot waste time watching adults play children's games."

Hephaestion shook his head. Alexander's answer to his question was almost blasphemous. The Olympics were far more than a series of physical contests. It was a homage to gods who idealized the human form and reveled in the celebration of it. Alexander's pique notwithstanding, these Olympics were also of critical importance to the political stability of Philip's Greek Empire. Alexander's attitude would do nothing to help his father maintain control over the Hellenes.

"The games start the day after tomorrow. Your father and his retinue are here. Most of your generals are here. Thousands of Greeks from all over Hellas are here. Many foreigners have also come. And you stand there moping about a campaign that is still a year away. Your responsibility is here. You are the heir apparent and it is your duty to help your father oversee the games. This is the first time in many decades that relative peace has existed. It is also your father's first Olympics as the head of government. Even more importantly, it is your first Olympics. And one day, you will be the leader of the Hellenistic world and I believe it would not be a good choice you would be making in leaving Elis to go back to Pella, just two days before the festival starts." Hephaestion took a deep breath. "You must stay!"

Alexander glared at his friend and bodyguard. He hated to be corrected. And he really hated it when the person correcting him was right.

"Hmmmpphh...by the way you tell me what to do, I wonder which one of us would be king," said Alexander sarcastically. "We will stay...for appearances."

Hephaestion bent his head in a slight bow. Alexander had acquiesced but prudence suggested that the issue be dropped. The volatile temper of the young prince could be sparked by the slightest of provocations and Hephaestion had been with him far too long to lord a victory, no matter how small or inconsequential over Alexander. Obviously, Alexander felt slighted by the actions of Dioxippus yet this imagined offense was nothing compared to his feelings of jealousy toward his father, Philip. And nowhere were these feelings accentuated more than at Elis where physical perfection, excellence and divinity fostered fanatical worship, where a king could be made a god and a prince, even one such as Alexander was regulated to the ignoble task of being a mere observer. For a man accustomed to the limelight, not being the center of attention at an event as wildly popular as the Olympics was tantamount to being ignored. Alexander refused to be ignored even if it meant that it might conflict with his father's plans. Hephaestion had realized this, had foreseen the problems that Alexander might face and had endeavored to mitigate the circumstances that could lead to a confrontation. Having Alexander agree to stay had been a significant compromise.

"What of Yiorgakas?" asked Alexander, already on a different subject.

"Well...we are still experiencing problems with the Hellanodikai, the game officials. They have refused to grant Yiorgakas a place in the pankration until they have reviewed our application with the king. Apparently, they feel that any athlete who has not resided in Elis for at least ten months prior to the games is unclean. Already they are upset with the exception they made for Philip's favourite, Dioxippus."

Alexander winced. Dioxippus' refusal to side with him still exasperated him. Bringing Yiorgakas from Asia to combat the Greek champion had been a good plan until Dioxippus had decided to go to Elis earlier than planned. Philip had interceded with the Hellanodikai in order to get Dioxippus reinstated. Now the officials felt that yet another ruler (or worse, the child of one) was trying to denigrate the purity of the games by bringing in a professional fighter. Although no rules actually prohibited Yiorgakas from competing--he was Greek--it reflected poorly on the organizing committee of the Olympics. And as this was about to be one of the greatest Olympics ever, the Hellanodikai were reluctant to accommodate Alexander's request. Alexander had been furious. The destroyed suite of his lodging was evidence of that. But Hephaestion, after letting the prince demolish the apartment, convinced Alexander that the best plan was to use diplomacy and tact. So far this method could be deemed a success because the Hellanodikai were still debating about Yiorgakas. However, they had left themselves a way out by telling Alexander that Philip would make the final decision. Alexander did not think that Philip would vote against him but the humiliation of having one's father giving allowances to strangers but not him was very offensive.

"May I make a further suggestion?" queried Hephaestion.

"Will I be able to stop you?" answered Alexander.

Hephaestion smiled in response. He could see that the tension that had been creasing Alexander's face earlier had eased and the normal good nature of the handsome young prince was emerging. Hephaestion did not want to upset Alexander any further so he decided not to pursue the earlier subject.

"We should go to the hippodrome. Apparently one of the merchants from Asia Minor has brought a team of horses from Ephesus. Rumour has it that these horses are bred from a desert stock kept by nomads who live in the lands east of Daruis'. All who have seen these horses say they are the most handsome animals on earth and must have been stolen from the gods themselves. They are also I have been told, as fleet as birds on a wing...and even more beautiful." Hephaestion took a breath. No greater horse-lover existed in the world than Alexander and he would never miss an opportunity to see these animals that were almost mythologized by all who saw them. Hephaestion also hoped that Alexander would take his mind off the various intrigues, real or imagined, that seemed to occupy him so much as of late.

"Yes. That is a good idea. In fact, it is the first good idea either one of us has had today. Let's go."

Hephaestion tilted his head in response and turned to gather up a couple of cloaks.

"Then we can go watch the pankratiatists."

Hephaestion snapped his head around. Alexander stood grinning, his brows slightly arched and his arms crossed in front of his chest. Hephaestion had not fooled him. He knows everything I think, said Hepaestion to himself. Alexander's prescience was unsettling, even for a confidante as close to the prince as Hephaestion.

"Well...are we going?" asked Alexander.

"Yes...yes. Now is a good time. It's still morning and they should just be starting their exercises...at both venues," said Hephaestion, now standing by the doorway.

"Then let us leave." Alexander motioned to Hephaestion. The dark, young Greek preceded Alexander as they began to make their way to the racetrack.

Unlike Pella, with its endless streets and proliferate alleys, Elis consisted of one main thoroughfare bordered on each side by comparatively small, less permanent buildings. This was a town that came alive every four years: the time in-between was rarely used for anything commercially-productive, consequently, the few true residents, mostly farmers, servants and slaves did not have the energy or desire to expend themselves unnecessarily when it would not profit them. Elis thus remained a small town notable only for its proximity to Olympia.

Alexander could not care less about what Elis was or was not. He had seen hundreds of such villages and if they did not present some sort of tactical advantage before a battle, he was not interested in them. To Alexander, Elis was nothing more than a holding pen for the athletes so why should he ascribe it any more importance than that.

Hephaestion thought differently. He could feel the history, the sacredness of this place that served as a place of spiritual cleansing for the athletes that would participate in the holiest of games, the Olympics. Hephaestion looked about. The Gods had chosen Elis, not man. He glanced at Alexander. Alexander was striding ahead, his attention focused on the horses he would soon see, not the street he was currently walking on. Hephaestion was so finely tuned to Alexander's feelings and emotions, that quite often he could anticipate Alexander's thoughts and actions. But it did not take any great gift of insight to know that Alexander's attitude to this town, the upcoming festival and the Olympic games was insolent and rude.

Hephaestion feared no man but he feared what insulted gods might wreak upon a contemptuous Alexander.

"There...ahead."

Hephaestion turned to see what Alexander had called his attention to. The heat had formed a rippling haze and it took some concerted effort to peer through it. Hephaestion assumed that Alexander had spotted the stables so he didn't panic because he was unable to discern clearly what Alexander was pointing to. Within moments, the acrid yet sweet smell of the stables flooded his olfactory nerves. Hephaestion smiled; he was definitely near horses.

By now Alexander's pace had increased, leaving Hephaestion several yards behind. Hephaestion, casting a quick look about, trotted to catch-up to his friend. But Alexander, overwhelmed by his curiosity concerning these strange new beasts, hurried even more, forcing Hephaestion to run.

As he caught up to the rapidly moving Alexander, Hephaestion found himself stunned. Just a few yards away, standing docilely, were the most beautiful animals he had ever seen.

Alexander had already moved to the side of the nearest, an alabaster-white stallion whose inviolate form looked like it had been chiseled from one, unblemished block of marble. Slowly, with the practiced hand of the expert equestrian, Alexander caressed the muscular neck, the thick mane. Not once did the horse's shapely head move or the compact body flinch as the young prince examined the eerily calm animal.

Hephaestion tried to observe as unobtrusively as possible but it was impossible to witness this strange symbiosis and not be moved. Alexander may have had the innate ability to command men but his control over animals, particularly equine was something divinely determined and Hephaestion was awed.

One of the trainers had noticed Alexander and Hephaestion and had wandered over. With an elegantly casual grace, he bowed to Alexander, more in the manner of an Asian than a Greek.

Alexander acknowledged him with a nod and then turned back to the horse. He continued running his hands over the animal's body, soothing it with his gentle touch and soft voice. After a few moments, without turning his head, he spoke.

"From where did this breed originate? I have never seen a horse that looks like this one."

"My lord, he, his father and his ancestors all come from the desert," replied Magios, the trainer.

"Hephaestion, look at this," said Alexander, pointing. "This horse has such a beautiful form. See...look right here. Do you notice how the head is small but shapely while its broad forehead cradles this small star. And those eyes. They burn as bright as fire. Surely this horse must be of greater intelligence than those woeful, undersized creatures that we use. Look...he understands the compliment." It appeared so as the horse nuzzled Alexander's neck. "Notice how he carries his tail...upright, proud. This horse is a king amongst his peers. I must have one," concluded Alexander fiercely, his hands still caressing the creature of his affections.

Hephaestion tilted his head slightly, agreeing with the young prince. There was no question, that this horse (and its companions just now emerging from the stable) was unquestionably beautiful. But Hephaestion also knew that aesthetics were not always indicative of practicality. This animal might be beautiful to look at but would it be able to withstand the travails of war, particularly the hard-charging style of the Macedonians. Looking at the horse again, Hephaestion noted how pronounced its musculature was, how well developed the withers and how deep the chest were. Power emanated from this beast and Hephaestion found himself doubting whether there was any arena that this horse could not only survive in but excel in.

"This one is known as Haj--the chieftain. He leads the team."

Alexander nodded at Magios' comment. "After the games, how much do you want for him?" asked Alexander, not even turning to face Magios.

"My Lord, how can I sell such a one. He is part of my family, more valued than even my two worthless sons. I cannot part with him. Could you...could you part with the magnificent Bucephalus?"

Alexander turned to look at Magios. The trainer was small, as short as Alexander but frail of body. His dark skin, black hair and elaborate beard were accentuated by the shimmering, sun-coloured fabric of his chiton. The only adornment was a leather belt cinched about his waist. In all, a non-threatening personage who appeared, on first impression anyway, to be quite earnest in his insistence to Alexander that he could not sell the horse. Alexander's impression of Magios rose significantly because of that. Smiling, he said, "Never. Bucephalus is no more a horse than a pig is. He is a spirit...perhaps part of mine, perhaps one of the many that inhabit our world. Bucephalus is linked to me by power, ambition and Gods. I do not exist without him: he does not exist without me. If or when one of us falls, the other will follow...I understand your bond to this animal. May you spend many years together." With that, Alexander petted the desert horse one more time, signaled to Hephaestion and began walking toward the gymnasia.

Hephaestion was caught slightly unaware and stumbled in an attempt to catch Alexander. The resulting misstep brushed him up against the still motionless steed. Immediately, the horse reared back, snorting in anger, its sharp, unshod hooves flailing through the air. A disconcerted Magios leapt to the side of the angered horse, calming it with his voice and hands. Hephaestion had himself jumped out of the way and other than some dirt on his clothing was unharmed. His heart however, beat faster than a hummingbird's wings as the unexpected fright coursed adrenaline throughout his body.

Up ahead, Alexander continued walking, seemingly oblivious to what had just transpired a few steps behing him. Yet, creeping slowly across his face, a secret little smile began to form.

Philip's security

"The precautions are not enough."

"What would you have me do, go back to Pella?" snorted Philip derisively. The overzealousness of his commander of the Bodyguard was beginning to grate on him. "What am I supposed to fear...assassination?"

Gemellos flinched. As the officer in charge of Philip's personal security his was one of the most difficult commands in Macedon. Philip's fearlessness, albeit a noble characteristic on the battlefield, bordered on foolhardiness off it. With every major king, political leader and tribal chieftain in Hellas expected to attend the first unified Olympic games in close to a millennium, the king's safety could not be guaranteed. Rumours of violence and regicide were always making their way to the palace and most were ignored as nothing more than discordant rumbling. Yet, Gemellos could not help but be concerned about the latest comments he had heard. It was as if those criticizing and wanting harm to the king had become particularly vitriolic. Gemellos had no real evidence but he would have gambled his life on it; Philip, more than at any other time was in real danger of assassination. And to confound things even more, Gemellos knew that Philip was aware of this malevolent force ready to destroy him. But a belief in his own strength, perhaps even in his immortality, superceded his concerns about his safety and this was making Gemellos crazy.

"How do you expect me to protect your person if you insist on walking about with few even no soldiers to protect you? This is not a campaign where death is imminent and you prepare yourself and your forces for it. No assassin will call you out to a duel nor will that assassin charge upon you in full view of both you and your soldiers. The assassin could be anyone, a friend, a servant, a woman even a child. To walk about unprotected, even at the Olympics is inviting disaster. Do not forget, Philip, Hellas may be one now, but only because you conquered her. To most Greeks, you are a tyrant. The Greek ideals of citizenship and government demand that all tyrants be put to death. Killing you will be considered akin to stepping on a scorpion--unpleasant but necessary."

Philip leaned back in his chair. This Gemellos spoke his mind: a nice change from the whispered conspiracies that were beginning to dominate his court. Perhaps Gemellos was right, there were probably fewer friends out there now and as the Gods well-knew, the list of enemies had grown at an accelerated pace. Philip looked at the commander standing in front of him.

"Do what you have to do. Keep from making it obvious. I have to show these Greeks and anybody else who shows up that I am more than a king. In fact, if I can convince even a few that I am a God, we will reduce and eliminate any rebellions that may be brewing before they get a chance to become a cancer to the Macedonian Empire."

"And which God is it that you claim to be related to?"

Philip wheeled at the snickered question. "So...now you insult me? Will I never get the respect I deserve from you, Theban?"

Piros grinned at the insult Philip had countered his query with. It had been many months since Piros had felt comfortable with his close friend, Philip. The relationship had regained its strength, as far as Piros was concerned, the day they had found Kathos' mutilated body. Even though they were never able to avenge Pausanius' assault and rape satisfactorily, Piros was impressed with how earnest the king had been in finding and punishing the criminal deviate who had violated one of his most dependable soldiers. And revenge would have been theirs had not Olympias, as usual, beaten them to the scene and exacted her own accounting from Kathos and his henchmen. Philip and Piros had questioned her--to no avail. Her demeanor was imperturbable: no amount of cajoling or threats could get her to reveal why she had Kinovas execute Kathos so brutally. Piros still found it implausible that Olympias' frail-looking companion, Kinovas, had not only been able to protect Olympias from such a ruthless gang of villains but had also managed to bind, then systematically dissect them with apparently no outside help. The man-killing skills of the Queen's confidante impressed Piros, who perhaps more than most men, understood the difficulty of ending a life that did not wish it.

"Piros, if your feeble little mind continues to wander, not enough will be left to even show you how to piss, much less have an intelligent conversation with me," joked Philip.

"Given a choice between wandering and engaging in an exchange of feeble witticisms with you, I am sure my mind would just as soon remain in the netherworld," replied Piros, barely containing his laughter.

"If you've spent as much time training Dioxippus to fight as you have in preparing your comic skills, he will walk away with the olive wreath with a minimum of effort," replied Philip. "Don't work yourself to a lather. I bear the boy I mean young man, no ill will for leaving Pella. He's young, impetuous and fanatically devoted to what he thinks is right. His character is similar to Alexander's and with proper nurturing he could be a great leader of men too. So let him compete. Let him enjoy his day."

Piros was astounded. He had convinced himself that Philip resented Dioxippus for having the audacity to waive his exemption (granted with the influence of the King) and come to Elis earlier than either Philip or Piros had planned. The magnanimity of Philip's statement clearly indicated that Philip was less concerned over his ego than he was with Dioxippus' desire to win the Olympiad. Again Piros was impressed.

"Except for your sarcastic rejoinders, you are strangely mute my friend," said Philip.

"My apologies. I am pleased that you do not begrudge Dios. He is young, sometimes foolish but a better, more loyal person you would be hard-pressed to find and he will make a welcome addition to your bodyguard after the Games. I am somewhat concerned that Alexander nurtures resentment toward Dios. Even that lumbering behemoth, Yiorgakas, appeared in Pella a few days after Dios left. My sources tell me that he was sponsored by one of the lieutenants in Alexander's personal guard. With no disrespect meant toward the prince, I do suspect his influence." Piros couched the last statement in cautious, non-offensive tones, knowing how easily Philip could anger when anyone criticized his son.

"No offense taken. My spies tell me that Alexander did in fact arrange Yiorgaka's return. Don't concern yourself with it. Alexander is the ultimate competitor. He himself won't compete--believes it is beneath royalty. But he sees the pankration as a contest where the competitors can be bought or sold like the horses he trades in. So for him, bringing in a brute like this Yiorgakas, is his way of entering the games and with a little bit of luck, showing up his father, who is of course backing his own fighter. A little father/son rivalry, Piros. I have not worried about it--neither should you. But assure me of one thing."

"Name it."

"Dioxippus has gained much fame for his innovations and unquestionably is one of the finest pankratiatists I've seen, save you of course." Piros bowed his head as Philip continued. "What I question is his emotion? He always appears calm, never flustered or angry. I cannot help but wonder how this might affect him in the ring, especially against an animal like Yiorgakas. I see you ready to object Piros...patience. I do not want Dioxippus to lose against Yiorgakas or anyone else for that matter and I want you to understand how critical it is to Macedonian rule that a champion supported by the new ruler of Hellas wins, ideally in a convincing manner. I am rambling, I know. Reassure me that Dioxippus is as tough as he is talented."

"Philip, concern yourself with your kingdom. Dioxippus is unbeatable. His technique is so far advanced that it will take generations for the rest of the pankratiatists to learn what he knows. And, I am flattered by your compliment yet it is inaccurate. My skills pale next to the boy's. In fact, his height, coupled with his size and speed, has made him too dangerous for me to train with. I leave it to younger, dumber sparring partners now. Dioxippus will not lose, of that I am confident. I still see doubt. Remember Philip, I trained this boy when he was a child, an orphan taken as a slave by a man so evil that Athens to this day refuses to acknowledge that such a one could live within their city. Dioxippus broke free of this monster with almost no help from me: he then fought at Chaeronea in your army, with only a club, no shield or armor. He has been involved in some of the most brutal matches in the ring that I have ever witnessed and always, often while injured, triumphed. Dios is not tough...his spirit is indomitable, that is why he cannot lose."

Philip slowly eased himself off the sofa he had been lying on as Piros came to the end of his oration. "You have convinced me."

"Then may I make another suggestion? Let us go down to the gymnasia and watch this morning's training session. Watching Dios should prove comforting to the both of us."

"Excellent idea," replied Philip. He looked over to see Gemellos still standing there, all this time as immobile as one of the pillars supporting the roof. "I suppose you're going to want to bring a legion along. Hmmmmppphhh...I think it was better when I wasn't a king, then I could go anywhere. And the places we went, eh Piros? No woman in Thebes was safe when we were around." Philip, then Piros laughed at the bawdy reminder of their youth. "Hurry up, Gemellos. Bring your guard, Piros and I are going to the gymnasia."

Dioxippus trains

There were fifteen pankratiatists lined up along the line crookedly drawn in the dirt. Facing them was their trainer, a grim-faced, barrel-chested brute whose only purpose in life was to bring misery to the sorry excuses standing in front of him. He surveyed the line with the piercing gaze of the hunting falcon. These men were his prey and he would chew them up and spit them out. Hopefully, what he spit out would be better for the mastication.

"I said, twenty pushups not two, you miserable little pukes! Again. Do them again before I have to disassemble each one of you! Are you deaf, twenty?"

"Claudius must not have gotten it last night," gasped Herodites to Dioxippus. He dropped his body down so he could begin his next pushup. "Speaking of which, did you see the women the Illyrian brought? For a few drachmas..."

"Hey you...over there. What in Hades do you think you're doing, you moron? If you can still talk, you puissant little bug maybe you're having too easy a time. Let's make this interesting. All you...Greeks...your friend here, the one up front with the pecker smaller than a thimble...yeah, this one. Well, he seems to think that all of you 'girls' need to exercise harder. So in his honour, you can all start again. You, Herodites, obviously you can talk, why don't you count instead."

Herodites groaned out another pushup. His arms, his shoulders and his upper abdominals were on fire and the strain in his deltoid muscles was beginning to feel like someone was tearing them apart. His body begged him to stop but the presence of this trainer from Hell precluded any relief soon. And now he had to count...

"One...two...three...four..."

Herodites turned his head to the voice. Dioxippus, smiling widely had started the count and by the number four, the whole group of pankratiatists had joined him. Dioxippus' voice, almost lyrical as it picked up the cadence of the exercise stood out strongly amongst the chorus. Claudius was impressed with Dioxippus' leadership. Granted he was not so moved that he halted the calisthenics.

"...eighteen...nineteen...twenty..." A staccato of dull thuds reverberated through the gymnasia as fifteen exhausted bodies collapsed. Gasps and whimpers from everyone but Dioxippus filled the air. He lay calmly on his belly, his torso half-raised and supported by his elbows and forearms.

"So mule-kicker, you feel like a little run?" Claudius asked Dioxippus, using a disparagement that was currently popular amongst those who did not like or did not bet on Dioxippus.

"Will you lead us, great emperor of Italia?"

"You mock me, goat-fucker?" Claudius snapped back. He knew that this last epithet always ignited Macedonian passions particularly amongst those who still recalled the almost primitive agrarian lifestyle of the Macedonians before Alexander the First transformed the sheepherders of the mountains into a fighting force that by Philip's reign would be considered one of the finest on earth.

Dioxippus was dismissive of the trainer's comments. Claudius was paid to advise, guide, oversee and agitate the pankratiatists. His knowledge of the human body, coupled with his ability to identify and correct weaknesses in technique made him invaluable to the combatants preparing for the Olympics. Although every pankratiatist there utilized the services of a personal trainer, during the preparatory month before the games Claudius supervised the practice and conditioning sessions. Dioxippus had met Claudius on the periodos (the Circuit); the Olympic, the Pythian, the Nemean and the Isthmiun Games. Dioxippus had competed and won as an adult at all but the Olympiad. Claudius, whose presence at these and other contests in Hellas was as expected as the sun, had come to know Dioxippus through his close friend and former charge, Piros. And even though many considered his gruff, unforgiving manner as indicative of a closed, restricted mind, in actuality he was quite progressive in his conceptualization of the sport. Claudius had been among the first to see that Dioxippus' innovations would change the sport and he had embraced the opportunity to work with him at Nemea. He had learned much from the Greek, enough to return to his birthplace in Syracuse and open his own gymnasia. With luck and hard work, one day one of his fighters would be competing for the olive wreath. But today, these men before him would work harder than the pack mules at the Lydian mines.

"You...yes you...don't pretend you're deaf or I'll come over there and hit you so hard, your ears will ring until you wish you were deaf. Gather up your boyfriends, and run over to the hippodrome--the horses aren't training yet--and complete at least twenty laps of the track. The two who come in last must stay behind and sweep the dirt so that it's smooth for the horses. Do we understand each other?" yelled Claudius at Dioxippus who was still lying down in front of him.

Dioxippus slowly got to his feet. "I hear you oh wise one. And may I thank you for rewarding us so graciously." The sweet sarcasm dripped off of Dioxippus' lips. "Come my friends, this Syracusan does not believe that we Greeks are the finest athletes in the world. Let us show him how twenty laps of the hippodrome are nothing more than a little sprint." Dioxippus waved the troupe on and began to run.

"He's become quite the man, hasn't he?"

Startled, Claudius looked behind him.

Standing there, almost shoulder to shoulder, were Piros and the Macedonian king, Philip. And right behind them, arrayed in a protective semi-circle, were ten of Philip's private bodyguard.

"You are allowed to talk to an old friend," continued Piros,

Claudius started to turn toward Piros before he caught himself. He turned to Philip and said, "Sire, you do me honour with your presence." Then Claudius shifted his attention to Piros. "I see that you still retain that black hide of yours. By now I thought that your supple skin would be hanging from a peg in some admiring lady's kitchen. Alas, you appear as slippery outside of the ring as you once were in. I still remember your first real fight."

So do I, thought Piros. So do I.

Piros remembers...

Fear. Not fear of death but the fear of defeat. Second place meant nothing. Being a finalist meant nothing. Even dying meant nothing if you lost. And to lose by submission was even worse. But at this moment, with his arm impossibly locked by the gargantuan Archimides, the young Piros could feel imminent defeat and he was terrified. Reflexively he squirmed and twisted, doing anything to relieve the pressure on his arm but the hold was too strong. The only relief that Piros felt as he scrambled crablike in the dirt was that Archimedes who would have normally struck Piros to render him unconcious was having so much difficulty merely holding on to his greasy, naked opponent that the opportunity did not present itself. So Piros kept moving, hoping, praying that an idea would come to him. Again and again he spun, his feet and one free hand churning up the dust but little else.

The crowd was on its feet now, cheering for Archimedes, clapping derisively for the apparently defeated Piros. Through the sweat, the blood and the pain, Piros could feel the heat of shame beginning to burn his cheeks. If he did not surrender, Archimedes would cripple him.

Suddenly, a memory flashed in Piros' mind. The story told to him by Prince Philip. Yes, that was it, the legend of Arrachion, the champion pankratiatist who while being throttled in a match, managed to break his opponent's toe and gain a win by submission even as he expired. That desperate measure was all that was left for Piros.

He spun away again, forcing Archimedes to move with him. This time however, he turned into his opponent, bent low and grabbed Archimedes' fourth and fifth toes. Unhesitatingly, Piros wrenched hard, twisting the toes in the opposite direction of their normal position. Piros heard several pops as the small bones snapped. A stifled scream, then a furious grunting bellow were the next things Piros heard. Archimedes was in a fury but Piros' arm was free.

Claudius

"I thought you were a dead man," continued Claudius.

"Almost, my friend, almost." Piros was still grimacing from the recollection.

"What of Dioxippus? How does he look to you? Is the injury he suffered healed sufficiently?"

"Your questions are honest and insightful Sire, and if you allow me a few moments, I will answer them." Claudius could see the king was excited by his favourite and was eager to gain Claudius' opinion on the fitness of Dioxippus. It took little, considering Claudius' sources, to find out that the champion of Asia, Yiorgakas, was coming to the Olympiad at the behest of Prince Alexander. Claudius also knew that Yiorgakas had fought in both Greek and Persian sanctioned events and he was equally adept at fighting under the marginal rules of the Hellenistic pankration or the free-for-all pit combat of the Persians. Although Dioxippus had fought against the best and the most brutal in Hellas, he had not faced anyone with the skills and unbridled savagery of the war-dog, Yiorgakas. Claudius was positive that Dioxippus possessed a higher degree of technique but he could not be sure that the young Greek had the inner toughness needed to outlast Yiorgakas. Dioxippus, a winner at the Nemean and Pythian games, as well as a score of others, nevertheless had fought fewer matches in his adult career than Yiorgakas normally fought over a six-month period. In short, it would be very, very difficult for Dioxippus to hurt Yiorgakas.

"You do not inspire me with confidence, trainer." Philip was displeased with the expressions flitting across Claudius' face. He did not want to be told that his champion would lose.

"I don't believe that Claudius thinks that Dios will lose," interjected Piros. "But there is no question, Yiorgakas is the strongest challenge that Dioxippus has faced to date in the ring. And we must prepare him for that challenge. And let me reiterate my friend, that Dioxippus has never been defeated in spite of the fact that he has at times suffered serious injury. To combat Alexander's favorite he needs to do but one thing..."

"And what is that?" asked Philip.

"Be ready to die."

"That is somewhat cryptic, is it not?" queried Philip.

"Not so. Dioxippus is by nature a kind, compassionate person. The ugliness he grew up around failed to warp his soul. Even during the war, he refused to participate in the looting that followed the defeat of our enemies. In a sense, Dios is a pure, divine-inspired warrior. He has a purity of purpose that few in Macedon can claim. He will fight, fearlessly...and give no quarter. But the question which will only be answered on the day of the match is, will Dioxippus risk his own death for nothing much more significant than a physical contest and the pride of two competing royals. Ultimately, that is all these contests are," concluded Piros, again realizing that he was pushing the boundaries of Philip's pride.

Philip did not reply. It was crucial to prove to the Hellenes that he was their sole despot and backing a popular fighter whose reputation to date was beyond reproach would do much to add to the idea that he was infallible. To run a nation of Greeks, he needed them to believe that he possessed powers beyond the normal man; again it had been suggested to him by his sages and advisors that he deify himself in much the same manner as the Great King, Darius. The thought was tempting but he would have to tread warily with it unless he wanted his Macedonian elite, who made no secret of their hatred for ordinary men acting like demigods, hacking him into tiny pieces. For now he considered it best to continue to support Dioxippus, and if the young man won then he could lord his prescience over the Hellenes.

"If Dioxippus requires anything..."

"Yes, Sire...I will not hesitate to seek your services," answered a suddenly nervous Claudius. Although Philip was a king with what many believed was the commoner's touch, Claudius had been around too many regents in too many areas to be completely trustful of the king. He had seen power corrupt even the most moral of men and Philip was anything but. Claudius could not help but feel that if Dioxippus lost so would he.

"Will you be that generous to the rest of your charges?"

Philip, Piros and Claudius turned simultaneously. Positioned behind them were Alexander and Hephaestion, resplendent in ankle-length chitons, the first dyed an iridescent blue, the second a wine burgundy. Philip blushed at the recollection of his earlier thoughts. Before him stood a god, his son.

Claudius' reaction was much different. His bluster, buoyed by his sizeable girth and ferocious manner, dissipated as quickly as a drop of water on a summer day. Claudius had been around violence all his life; he could sense dangerous men. And Alexander was the most dangerous of them all. Terror struck at Claudius as he contemplated what Alexander might have done to him in response to the almost traitorous words that had just spewed out of his mouth.

"All athletes must be on an equal footing. My offer to Dioxippus only addresses those needs he may not have been able to avail himself of because of his late arrival in Elis," said Philip, trying to control his nervousness at being found out.

"Can I then assume that the loyal Yiorgakas, should he be allowed to participate, may expect the same attention?" asked Alexander, suddenly looking, despite his smaller stature, twice as big as his father.

"Of course...if the Hellanodikai approve his application."

"And why would they not, Father?" pressed Alexander.

"Well...I...I see no reason why not." Philip could see a way out of this embarrassment. "I will speak to them, after all, if they did it once, they can do it twice."

The snake has just swallowed the bird, thought Piros as he noted how well Alexander had just manipulated his father into granting his fighter the same exemption that Philip had wangled for Dioxippus. Now his beloved Dios, who was just now appearing at the far end of the gymnasia, would face the greatest challenge of his young life.

Clytemnestra

"He should not have gone."

"Mother, is this necessary. You have not stopped criticizing since you arrived. Please...let me enjoy my new son. His father will return soon. The Olympics only last five days."

"Cleopatra, listen to me. I don't like this place. I worry for you. Your husband Philip is in Olympia, your uncle Attalus is in Asia and you are here...without a friend. Olympias makes no secret of her hatred for you, especially now that you have given birth to a male heir. That little boy in your arms is a great threat to Alexander. She knows it and will do anything to prevent his ascension to the throne. Come with me. Your father can protect you and my grandson."

Cleopatra sympathized with her mother's sentiments. Since she had given birth, every day was spent in fear. Even when Philip had been in Pella, the threat of assassination never abated. Olympias' courtiers, brazenly hostile, had created a palatable tension at the palace which had driven Philip to distraction and Cleopatra to terror so real, she rarely ventured out of her apartment. The only thing which prevented her leaving Pella was the fact that she was not only the favored wife of the King but the mother to the only Macedonian heir and it would not behoove her position to run away.

"You know I cannot go with you," said Cleopatra, her voice barely above a whisper.

Clytemnestra stopped her pacing and sat down on a stool opposite her daughter. Tears welled up in her eyes but she kept them back by forcing herself to take a deep breath. A seer had foretold the premature death of a son of the king. Clytemnestra could not be sure if that prediction referred to Philip's half-wit and illegitimate son Arrhidaeus or to the older, god-blessed son of Olympias, Alexander. Most terrifying of all, the seer may have condemned Clytemnestra's newborn grandson to a premature death. Given the opportunity, Olympias would see the last prediction realized.

The baby, wrapped in swaddling, began to squirm as he tried to let out a small burp. Both Cleopatra and Clytemnestra looked at the infant then each other. They began to cry.

Patroclus

Patroclus twitched nervously. He kept looking down the corridor. People streamed about but apparently nobody Patroclus was interested in came by. He cursed softly to himself. Unconsciously, he fondled the long, slim dagger concealed within his robe. Where was she, he asked himself.

The soft touch on his shoulder made him wheel around to face his attacker. The Sicilian blade was drawn in a blur of speed but before it could impale its victim, Patroclus pulled back.

"Did I surprise you?" asked Phylia, looking surprisingly composed, in spite of Patroclus' paranoia-driven assault.

"Yes. Could you not make at least a little noise before you come up on somebody? You scared me half to death. And Gods forbid, what would I have done if I had killed you?" Patroclus, so tense this last while, was visibly upset.

Phylia had thought it almost cute how Patroclus had jumped when she snuck up on him. But obviously that had been a mistake. Court politics and intrigue had shattered Patroclus' nerves and Phylia could see that he was a man ready to snap. Phylia sympathized with the paranoid Patroclus but otherwise could not identify with him. After her recent past and to survive the present, Phylia had adopted a fatalistic outlook. Events beyond her control she did not worry about. Plots and counter-plots did not faze her; she took precautions, thought before she opened her mouth and made sure her enemies were few and far between. Unlike Patroclus, she had developed a mental toughness that enabled her to survive the court and in many cases anticipate changing alliances. Although Phylia was not happy, she was also not on the verge of a mental collapse as was Patroclus. Knowing this she tried to alleviate the pressure on the young guard by smiling and joking but Patroclus was beyond being consoled by quips.

"If you had killed me, I would have come back for you," replied Phylia, smiling beatifically. It was no secret to either of them that a strong, romantic attachment had evolved over these last few months between them. His being a eunuch did nothing to dampen Phylia's desire for him. If anything, her own aversion to the sexual act made it easier for her to love Patroclus. He possessed qualities she had thought unattainable for most men: kindness, sympathy, understanding and courage. Phylia was enamored of this soldier.

Patroclus managed a cautious smile in response to Phylia's statement. He too was in love with her and even though he cursed the loss of his manhood, indescribable feelings, some of them physical, rampaged through him every time he was with her. He prayed nightly for the opportunity to spirit Phylia away. But the reality of the court negated even the remotest possibility for escape. He was as involved in the twisted machinations of Cleopatra and Olympias as the principals. More than anything else, the knowledge that he would die in this palace depressed him greatly. And making it worse still, it was likely that Phylia too would die in what was fast becoming a hellhole. Regardless, he was here for information.

"Olympias has had visitors."

"Who?" asked Patroclus eagerly. Anything that he could report to Cleopatra that would rid Pella of that sadistic bitch Olympias was extremely valuable.

"Three brothers, the sons of Aeropus."

"Aeorpus from Lyncestis?" Patroclus' question was rhetorical because he knew very well who Phylia was talking about. "Do you know which brothers?" he continued.

"Alexander, Heromenes and Arrhibaeus."

"Alexander. Mmmmm...is he not the son-in-law of Antipater, one of the King's most trusted officers? I wonder...is he involved in something with Olympias?" Patroclus was talking to himself, trying to figure out how one of the oldest, most trusted families in Macedonia, could find itself sneaking around with the estranged wife of the King. This reeks, thought Patroclus. But Cleopatra would be glad to hear it.

"Whatever they are discussing, it is secret. She had all her servants removed from her apartment until she personally retrieved them. I have seen many things in her quarters, some of them odd, some different, many disgusting but never have I seen her so fanatical about her security. Only Kinovas has free access to her. The rest of us have been shut out." Phylia took a breath. "One more thing. It seems kind of odd but I have noticed that Pausanius has been keeping company with the queen, especially when the Lyncestians are there. I know they are planning something but..." Phylia shrugged her shoulders.

"You've done splendidly." Patroclus reached over and kissed Phylia gently on the lips. "I have to go to Cleopatra. If I can, I will try to see you later. Come to the market at dusk if you can get away. I don't think that it is a good idea for me to be near Olympias' lodging. She hates me and looks for any excuse to be rid of me."

Phylia nodded in agreement. "Look for me," she whispered and then as quickly as she had come she left.

Patroclus watched her weave her way through the crowded corridor until he had lost sight of her. Then he made his way back to Cleopatra.

Pausanius voices his anger to Olympias

"That bastard." Pausanius spit out the words with such vehemence that even Olympias shied back. They were the only two in the room now, the Lyncestians having left along with Kinovas. "He calls himself King but rules over nothing but his concubines. Conqueror...hah. That one-eyed billy goat doesn't deserve the throne of Macedonia. Better to give it to one of the noble families. Let them command the Hellenes. At least they will do it with honour and respect. Not like the rutting pig, Philip."

A feral smile slowly wended its way across Olympias' face.

"As always, your are right, my sweet. For what Philip has done to Hellas and for what he had done to you, he should die."

A few weeks ago, Pausanius would have recoiled in horror at the queen's traitorous words. But much had transpired since then.

"I could kill the pig myself."

"And you would be a hero." Olympias replied. She opened her arms and beckoned Pausanius to come to her. When he was within her reach, she threw her arms around his neck, pulled his face close to her's and kissed him with an almost maniacal fury. Their heads twisted and turned as they attempted to devour each other. Pausanius, consumed with lust, pulled at the flimsy, chemise-like fabric of Olympias' summer chiton, ripping it slightly. The tear vented Olympias' rising body heat, almost scalding Pausanius as he forced his hands between the folds of Olympias' robe. At Pausanius' touch, Olympias jerked herself hard against the man clutching her, wanting him, begging him to take her. Pausanius responded to the body squeezed against him by salaciously grabbing the bodice supporting Olympias' breasts, tearing it away and burying his open mouth on the exposed, now rigid nipples. Olympias gasped, then pressed her stithos into Pausanius even more, urging him to bite and suck even harder. Taking further control, she grabbed him by the hair and yanked his head from one breast to the other, directing his lust while barely controlling her own.

Pausanius, maddened beyond comprehension, lifted Olympias off her feet, pulled then tore away the last vestiges of her garment and in one desperate push tried to penetrate her. Olympias willingly threw open her legs in anticipation exposing her sweat and fluid-soaked womanhood to Pausanius' rutting thrusts. She then reached down between the two heaving bodies, seized Pausanius' erect member and in one motion guided it into her. The fiery union was too much for Pausanius and in his eagerness to bore into Olympias he carried her halfway across the room and slammed her into the wall. She cried out at the new pain but the increased pressure made her delirious with joy. She arched her back, seized his shoulders and as much as she could from the position she was in, lifted then twisted her hips, grinding down hard on the appendage that was pleasuring her so. Abandoning any hope of prolonging this crazed union, Pausanius accelerated his thrusts. Faster and faster Olympias' body bumped against the wall, creating a pernicious tempo broken only by the increasing grunts, groans and screams of the two lust-crazed fornicators.

Kinovas stood motionless. Pausanius and Olympias were so involved in their sexual frenzy that neither noticed the dark little man watching them mere paces away. Kinovas, always vigilant for the safety of his queen, had re-entered her apartment from the secret passageway hidden in her bath. The sexual bedlam whirling in front of him was a surprise but not unexpected considering Olympias' appetites. Nevertheless he was far more concerned with Olympias' well-being than by the eroticism of the deviant gymnastics before him so he decided to stay. He had, unlike most men and contrary to how it appeared, no voyeuristic tendencies--just a fanatic loyalty to the queen and nothing could distract him from his duty. He stood as unobtrusively as possible, seeing nothing, hearing nothing, saying nothing. Even the slapping of Olympias' taut skin against her profusely perspiring paramour, interspersed with wild cries of sexual abandon, did not elicit any response from the stoic Kinovas. Physical love held no interest for him: particularly the animal-like coupling taking place before him now. This type of base lust could not compare to the beauty of the love he held for his beloved Nearchos. The two in heat before him had no concept what it was like to lose a part of your soul. Nearchos had been his life. Losing him at the fall of Thebes had ended it.

Olympias shrieked, her orgasm sending spasms of trembling pleasure throughout her body. Pausanius thrust once more, then he too climaxed, the rush of searing ejaculatory fluid feeling like a torrent of burning lava. Relieved, exhausted, his muscles relaxed, forcing him to lean against the still entwined Olympias, who having the wall behind her managed to hold them both up. Neither moved to disentangle themselves from the embrace until Kinovas coughed.

Immediately, Pausanius turned to face Kinovas but the entwined Olympias prevented him from moving as smoothly or as quickly as he would have liked. The resulting whirlwind of legs, arms and bodies resembled one of those slapstick comedies most often seen in the streets just outside of the Dionyssian Theatre in Athens. Even Kinovas' stoic face began to unravel as a grin fought its way across the normally tense mouth.

But Kinovas was the only one smiling. Olympias screamed obscenities at him as she gathered up her clothes. Pausanius did not even bother to dress himself. The initial fright at this invasion of privacy had turned into fury and he began to advance upon Kinovas, determined to beat the little snit into a pulp. Olympias made a motion to hold him back but Pausanius was too full of anger, past and present, to let even the queen prevent him from tearing apart Kinovas.

Kinovas did not move even though the Pausanius advancing upon him was not the round-bellied, out of shape drunkard of a few months ago. This Pausanius was the warrior who had distinguished himself well in many of Philip's campaigns and he was a very dangerous adversary. Kinovas' mind blasted this information to him. He still did not move.

Pausanius had not taken more than two steps before he rushed his adversary. Kinovas instantly recognized Pausanius' sudden movement for what it was: an attempt to smother the smaller man under a greater mass. And it might have worked.

Kinovas took a half step to his right, almost but not quite out of Pausanius' trajectory. Then just as Pausanius came upon him, Kinovas thrust his hip back into his opponent's path. The surprised Pausanius had too much momentum to stop and with almost dancer-like grace was catapulted over Kinovas' hip into the far wall where he lay crumpled. Kinovas, slowly, unhurriedly walked over to the prone Pausanius. But just as he was about to speak, Pausanius, obviously feigning injury, leaped up and swung a long, arcing hook punch at Kinovas' head. Again, as if anticipating the attack, Kinovas moved just a hair-breadths out of the way and without interrupting the fluidity of his movement, snapped the inside ridge of his right hand across and into the throat of Pausanius. Down went Pausanius, gasping, coughing. Kinovas took a step back.

"My apologies. I did not mean to hit you so hard...bend your head forward and try to control your breathing. The damage is not permanent so do not be frightened. Control. That is the key." Kinovas was now kneeling in front of the hoarsely breathing Pausanius. "Relax. I will get your robe." Kinovas stood then went to retrieve Pausanius' chiton. Kinovas had noticed that Pausanius was shaking with shock and cold and felt somewhat guilty that he was the cause of it.

"What did you do to him?" asked Olympias, sounding concerned but more wary than anything else.

"Nothing that he will not recover from. He was somewhat overzealous in his concern for you. I will not hurt him again and I ask, sincerely, for your forgiveness. My actions were inexcusable," said Kinovas, his manner almost sheepish.

Olympias never failed to be impressed by Kinovas. He had said more to her in these last few moments than he had said in the last few weeks and in the process demonstrated that he was obviously more intelligent than she had given him credit for. He had also shown her that the fighting ability of Thebes' Sacred Band was phenomenally superior to most of the Hellenes. The work of the late, great Theban general Epaminondas lived on in the superbly trained Kinovas. Who would have guessed, she thought, that a military unit made up of homosexual lovers would become one of the most effective units in military history? It was a wonder or a testament to his ferocity, that Alexander had defeated the Sacred Band. It was sad that all that was left of Epaminondas' legacy was the almost demure little man standing in front of the sputtering Pausanius. And how lucky I am to have him, concluded Olympias.

"Here...let me help." Kinovas stooped to help Pausanius who was still sitting on the marble floor, holding his throat. The fallen warrior still could not talk as he hacked up bloodied spittle. Kinovas noted the injury and tried to placate the hurt and somewhat frightened Pausanius by reassuring him in quiet, mellow tones. He had once had his throat partially cut in a battle and if not for the quick action of Nearchos would have perished. Even now he could remember with vivid clarity the terror at not being able to breathe as he choked on his own blood. For that and other reasons he was sympathetic to Pausanius.

Slowly Pausanius rose, still somewhat dazed but relatively fine. He looked sheepishly over at Olympias, too embarrassed to say anything. Normally Olympias would have verbally lashed Pausanius. But she had other plans for him and did not want to jeopardize them by tearing down the ego of the one who would bring those plans to fruition. She held out her arms and beckoned him and like a lost puppy he went to her. And even though he towered over the petite woman, Pausanius put his head on her shoulder, just as a child to his mother. Olympia caressed the back of his head and cooed soft words of reassurance.

Kinovas observed this little drama and said nothing. His eyes did narrow slightly and even though he made it his business to not know what the queen was up to, he concluded that one would have to be deaf, dumb and blind not to see that Olympias was playing Pausanius as delicately as she would a lute.

These few moments of peace might have continued if not for the sudden knock at the chamber door. Kinovas drew his blade as he moved to the portal. Holding his face close but to the side (in case the door was kicked open) he asked, "Who goes there?"

"Friends of Macedonia," came the muffled reply.

"Let them in," ordered Olympias.

Kinovas eased the door open, bracing his leg in case those on the other side tried to rush it. But the two men slipped through without incident and Kinovas closed the door behind them.

"Alexander, what a pleasure to see you again," said Olympias as she moved forward to buss him on the cheek.

Pausanius noted how effortlessly Olympias could charm. When she smiled, the radiance filled the room. Only one other person could control a room like her, and her son Alexander was far away in

Elis, waiting for the games. In sharp contrast, the Alexander before them now was not much more than a Lyncestian sheep farmer whose only claim to honor was a marriage to the daughter of the great general Antipater. Pausanius sniffed in derision as he asked himself why the queen would so warmly greet this insignificant shit-gatherer. It was beyond his comprehension. And nothing from their earlier meetings surfaced to change his opinion of Alexander and his brother Heromenes. They always whined about the same things: Philip was ignoring Macedonia in his mad quest to conquer Hellas and Asia; Philip's multiple marriages affronted the Macedonian aristocracy; and finally, Philip's adoption of Greek dress, language and customs seriously undermined the cultural integrity of Macedonia. They had not discussed treason yet but there was no question that they wanted something done and that something somehow fit into Olympias' plans. Pausanius did not really care what these Lyncestians wanted. Their criticisms of Philip were minor compared to his and Olympias'. The old cripple had betrayed him and if he did not orchestrate the monstrosity perpetrated on him, was just as guilty as those who had. And the queen. How many times had she told him that Philip was jealous of Alexander? How many plots had Olympias told him she had discovered against her beloved son? Philip was out of control and all these Lyncestians could gripe about was a perceived loss of cultural identity. Pausanius surreptitiously snorted in disgust. Macedonia was as Greek as Athens but if these farmers wanted to differentiate themselves from the glory of Hellas and align themselves with the primitive tribesmen of the north, let them.

"May I offer you wine?"

Pausanius' eyebrows arched in surprise. He had never heard Olympias offer anything to anybody.

"Your hospitality is appreciated but we must decline," answered Heromenes, bowing slightly to show his good manners.

"Then let us continue the discussion we started a few days ago," said Olympias as she sat down on the chair near her bed. All the men in the room remained standing.

"I believe that we are all in agreement that Philip is not the leader he once was. He has dreams of grandeur that go beyond the wildest aspirations of the greatest Greek heroes. In fact, it has been reported to me that at the wedding of our daughter, Cleopatra, he is planning to reveal a commissioned set of statues representing all thirteen gods."

"Forgive the correction, your highness, but there are only..."

"...twelve," interrupted Olympias. "Philip seeks to deify himself. He feels that he is a god."

"What! Is he insane? Even Achilles dared not believe he was a god!" Pausanius shouted.

"Your highness, if this is true what will become of Macedonia? Is this megalomaniac to be in charge of our destinies?" asked Alexander, his voice quaking with indignity and rage.

"Not if we do not allow him," replied Olympias, her voice low, her tone mellow.

"But who...who would risk themselves in such a venture?" asked Heromenes.

"Perhaps if we could provide an escape and then protection from prosecution, a patriot might take the chance," answered Alexander, looking directly at Pausanius.

"Perhaps..." whispered Pausanius as he gazed into the eyes of Olympias.

"Perhaps..." replied the queen, moistening her full red lips with the tip of her tongue. "Perhaps..."

Piros and Philip

"Come now, you must admit, those desert horses put ours to shame," said Piros, taking another draught of his wine cup.

"Piros, what do you know of good horses? You're an African. Elephants maybe, but not horses," replied an obviously inebriated Philip.

"My Lord, I could have been raised by goats and I could still see that the winners of the chariot race were so far ahead they could have dried and fed their team before the others even knew they were done," answered Piros. He took another swallow. Although he was drinking less than the king, he was beginning to feel somewhat light-headed himself and why not. These last four days had seen some of the best competition in years. From the gloriously opulent opening ceremonies to the thrilling chariot races, the first days of the Olympiad had surpassed Philip's wildest expectations. For the new regent of Hellas, these games announced his arrival in grand fashion. Competitors from all over the Hellenistic world had come, lending the games a truly international flavour. Spectators, Greek and foreign were still arriving swelling the numbers of Olympia well over the forty to fifty thousand capacity. Vendors and traders had set up their own tent city just outside of the venue and the plethora of colour and activity gave the event a life of its own. Philip was overjoyed with how things had proceeded. Not since he had himself won the chariot races a few years ago had he been so thrilled. Even having a marginally Greek trader like Demetrius win the chariot race with a team of horses unlike anything ever seen in Hellas, had not dampened his enthusiasm. In fact, the exotic origins of the winning team had only made the race more memorable. Piros was pleased for Philip. The Greeks still did not look kindly on their conqueror and the jeers on the opening day were not appreciated by any of the Macedonian luminaries. But Philip had accepted it nobly and had made a point of enjoying the festival. And even though the races and track events had been entertaining, the opening chariot race had taken all their breaths away. Since then Philip had been as pleased as a teenage girl with her first love. Piros looked at the smiling Philip and noted how relaxed he was. For the first time in years, Philip looked delighted with the course of events. Piros grinned and took another sip.

"They will sing about this Olympiad for years to come, my friend," Philip said, his last words cut short by a deep belch. "Did you see my son? Did you see how excited he was?"

Piros nodded affirmatively. Philip's joy paled beside his son's. Piros had not seen Alexander so thrilled since the prince was a child. Immediately after the race, Alexander had raced down to the paddocks to see the victors. The Arabian stallions, unapproachable to all who ventured near, came willingly to the golden-haired young man. And it was clear, even to the most jaded of observers, that Alexander was blessed once again with powers beyond all others. Piros had glanced at the king. Philip's pride in his son was blatantly obvious but more astonishing to Piros was how the battle-scarred veteran of a hundred conflicts, the backwoods king who had brought the greatest city-states in Hellas to their knees and the mortal who would destroy the great God-King Darius, stood slightly aback from the stable, choking with emotion while his Alexander played with the horses.

Philip turned to the trader, Demetrius, and said, "Whatever the cost, you will deliver these animals to my son's stables in Pella." The horses' owner began to stammer but Philip cut him off. "I will not entertain a refusal. The only question I will answer is 'how much are you willing to pay'. And my answer is whatever is necessary to gain Alexander possession of those horses. He already owns the finest beast in Hellas, if not the world. But Bucephalus is one. It is time that he starts a line with the finest breed we have ever seen. No...do not wave at me. You will honor my request. Alexander will rule the world one day. It is only fitting that he possesses these most noble creatures. Give us a price and..."

"...make sure delivery is made within the moon. My sister is being married and my father's procession must be led by these god-blessed steeds," interrupted Alexander.

Philip immediately grabbed Alexander around the shoulders, hugged him tight and then in a moment of absolute tenderness, kissed him gently on the forehead, much as he had when Alexander had been a mischievous toddler. He then placed his hands on either side of Alexander's face, and looking into his son's eyes whispered, "We shall conquer the world, you and I. The gods look with favour upon us.

Now go to your horses. And be careful how you break the news to Bucephalus."

Alexander smiled then laughed. It was well known throughout the cavalry how fierce and protective Bucephalus was of his master. Any other horses vying for his attention would be sure to set off a jealous rage in the war-horse. But a chance to own and breed these exquisite equines was worth the risk.

"Do not worry father, this line will carry us to the end of the earth, maybe even to the great ocean."

"Then it is done. Trader, you will be paid in gold. See my quartermaster." And with that Philip and Piros left Alexander in the paddock. That had been two days ago.

Now as they sat here sipping the last dregs of a definitely inferior wine, Piros and Philip could look at the events of the last week with a warm glow of satisfaction. That first day with Alexander had set the tone for the Games. A general feeling of kindness and cooperation permeated the air and there were few if any problems with the athletes or the referees. Even the spectators behaved, noteworthy considering the poor water supply, the non-existent sewage system, the lack of proper shelter and the diversity of the spectators themselves. This goodwill could be attributed to a combination of factors, not the least of which was Philip himself. After that day with Alexander, Piros noticed that the gregarious, free-spirited Philip of his youth had returned and had managed through wit and charm to win the loyalty and admiration of his new subjects. So convincingly did Philip win over the crowd that Greeks from every known corner of Hellenic culture flocked to greet him every time he ventured from his encampment. Piros knew that Philip would use this adulation like other statesmen would use a sword. His personal charisma manipulated the masses as adroitly as the feared Macedonian phalanx. And this Olympiad was his latest victory.

Tomorrow would bring foot races in the morning and the highlight of the Olympiad, the martial contests in the afternoon. The tens of thousands who had gathered at Olympia were so eager to view the boxing, wrestling and pankration matches that the hellanodikai, the officials of the Olympiad, had decided that they would move the martial sports from the area around the temple of Zeus to the stadium.

This was sure to raise some controversy amongst the religious zealots but the officials felt that crowding tens of thousands of people into a small space like the temple grounds would cause extensive damage to the area, possibly to the temple itself. Philip had approved the move. Although changing the venue for these events was the best idea logistically Piros also knew Philip well enough to know that it was yet another means of drawing attention to what he was billing as the greatest games ever.

Piros yawned then took another sip. Philip had already fallen asleep. Piros yawned again. It had been an action filled, emotionally challenging four days and now the combination of liquor and exhaustion was rushing him off to sleep. Piros closed his eyes. Tomorrow would be the longest day.

Dioxippus readies

"Owww...that hurts!"

"After all these years with you so-called fighters, I still cannot believe that a thing as simple as a massage can drive you to tears. Is there some special rule that says that all pankratiatists must be wimps? Tell me, oh great champion Dios."

Dioxippus looked over his shoulder at the gnarled old man supposedly massaging his upper back. Fotis had not changed; the bombastic sarcasm still cannoned from his mouth. But Dioxippus did not care. After a couple of weeks with the Italian, having his own trainer back with him was a blessing. Even though Dioxippus had a tremendous amount of confidence in his own skills, on this day, the day of competition, he was more than glad to have the veteran trainer beside him. It was unlikely that Piros would get the opportunity to be his second considering how pre-occupied he was with Philip's personal security. He had promised however to come down to the warm-up area as soon as the races ended. And from the roar that came cascading through the walls of the gymnasia, it appeared that the races were almost over.

"You had better hurry old man," said Dioxippus. "It won't be long before the procession begins."

"Don't you worry, pretty boy. The oil is ready. If your highness stands up, I'll be able to apply it. With all that beef you are carrying, I'm going to need an extra container," snorted Fotis, simulating disgust yet secretly pleased at how well Dioxippus had developed himself. From the tall, gangly boy that he had first met to the chiseled physique before him, Dios had become as fearsome-looking as the biggest and meanest pankratiatists.

"Easy with the oil. I want to be slicked, not cooked."

"Shut up you ignorant punching bag. I've known how much oil to put on a body since you were too small to take a piss by yourself. Hold still, you're making me spill this and..."

"...it would be considered not only sinful but bad luck also."

"Piros!" exclaimed Dioxippus as he whipped around at the sound of his mentor's voice.

"Dios." Piros went to hug Dioxippus but pulled short laughing. "Unless I want to join you in the arena, I will save my affections for later."

Dioxippus smiled as looked down at his oil-streaked torso. "Well then, will you be able to second me?" he asked.

Piros' smile faded. "I do not think so. My sources tell me that there is a plot to assassinate the king. I have no further details but as I am in charge of his well being it is best that I stay near him. Coming here now was a challenge even though he insisted. I had to leave ten of his Companions with him, just so I could relax."

Dioxippus took a step closer to Piros and laid his hand on his shoulder. "Do not worry. You have a greater responsibility. The old man here will suffice," said Dioxippus, nodding in the direction of Fotis.

"Why you precocious pup? Do you think a few muscles and a couple of years make you superior? Why if were not for the fact that you'll be competing shortly, and I have invested too much time to not let you compete, I would take you out and beat that swollen head of yours to a pulp!" retorted Fotis.

Piros broke into laughter. "Well, well, well...Barba Fotis is certainly riled. If you can muster half his emotion, you will do well today."

"Half...a quarter! Losing doesn't frighten me. Losing and coming back to face this reject from Hades--that frightens me."

"You mock me, child. Let me tell you..."

"Enough my old friend. Dios knows that with you as his second he cannot lose. Promise me, Fotis that you will look after my young charge. I love him like a son."

Fotis glanced up at Piros' suddenly sombre face. He did not know how to reply but he nodded affirmatively.

"Now listen," said Piros, directing his attention to Dioxippus. "The pankratiatists here present little threat as you have beaten almost all of them on the circuit. Just don't be careless. Otherwise no matter what the draw is, I do not foresee any significant problems. However, two opponents managed exemptions and you have not faced either." Dioxippus was about to interrupt but Piros signaled to be quiet. "Yes, I know that only one was to be exempted but the second was allowed in at the request of the king of Sicilia. Regardless, the first, Alexander's champion, Yiorgakas, is well known on the Asian circuit. He has also fought in the Persian pits where the winner is declared only after the opponent dies. Expect no quarter from him. There is no doubt in my mind that he will try to kill you, rules be damned. Be aware of that. I do not want you to win by disqualification because he has killed you. That would give us both little satisfaction."

"I have heard of him. What of the other?"

"The other is one of my father's countrymen. He comes from a Greek trading post just east of the Phoenician capital, Carthage. Despite the colour of his skin, his lineage is as Greek as Philip's. Apparently, this Aristides has ancestors who fought at Troy. His parents are wealthy merchants and they provided their son with a good education and the best trainers available. Aristides has been fighting all over North Africa and Italia. The Sicilians have championed him and like Yiorgakas he has faced a tremendous variety of styles and situations. He has even fought Celts, and they are supposed to be mad. As you progress through the rounds, you will meet one or both of these men. Promise me, you will look to your survival first."

"You worry too much..."

"Promise me!"

"Consider it done. I choose not to die today." Dioxippus smiled.

"Good. Now listen. Yiorgakas is a brute. He will savage you like a dog if he gets in close. Keep him at a distance. I don't have much information on Aristides but one of my men has a relative in Egypt who once saw him fight. He is very unorthodox and tends to crouch low and go for the legs. I suggest that you watch your high-kicking with this one."

"Noted," replied Dioxippus.

"Good luck, may your gods guide you." Piros clasped Dioxippus' shoulder once then left.

"He has much confidence in you. Just show a little extra care. Now sit still. I have to finish oiling you and I can see one of the procession Marshals coming." Fotis bent down and began slathering the scented oil on Dioxippus' arms and legs. Although hurrying he still took care to grease every muscle and every fold of skin.

"Prepare yourselves. The procession starts shortly and I want all the pankratiatists together. The wrestlers and boxers are in formation already," snapped the Marshall.

"We are coming," replied Fotis, picking up his bag as he signaled Dioxippus to follow. "We are coming."

Mistophanes

"You are not breaking any rules. You merely do a favor for Queen Olympias. Alexander himself would have made the request but thought it imprudent to be around judges the day of competition. One small moment of your time and you will be rewarded handsomely."

Mistophanes, one of the ten Hellanodikai, and the one responsible for the draw in the pankration, hesitated to reply. True, what was being asked of him was not illegal, but it begged moral considerations. It seemed that the Queen, at the behest of her son Alexander, wanted Yiorgakas, Aristides and Dioxippus all on the same side of the draw. This would create a hotly contested quarter and semifinal but would leave only one to fight in the final. There was no possible way that the final match would elicit the same response from the spectators as the earlier ones. The fight for the wreath would therefore be anti-climatic and considering how well the games had been going thus far it would be a sad way to finish. But the request came from the royal family; Mistophanes did not want to offend or make enemies of Olympias or her son Alexander. They were also willing to pay a significantly large "gratuity" and that could not be ignored.

"Well..." pressed Olympias' representative, who had conveniently neglected to mention his name.

"Hand me my tablet. It is done," replied Mistophanes somewhat curtly. He was not comfortable with this.

"I will let the Queen know of your cooperation." A bag of silver was dropped into the hand of Mistophanes.

Alexander

"Yes, yes, yes!" screamed out Philip as leaped to his feet. "Alexander did you see that? What a combination! One, two, three...and he was out. What speed! Alexander, did you see that?"

Alexander smiled sweetly, maybe even condescendingly, at his father. Unlike Philip, he found these contests boring. War, the planning and execution of it was thrilling, not these competitions that measured nothing more than who felt good on a particular day and who didn't. The chariot races had been exciting on the opening day and he had received an extra bonus because of them that would mark these days as something special for the rest of his life but these man to man exhibitions bored him. And although he himself had been trained in the martial arts, armed and unarmed, the wrestlers he watched earlier and the boxers he was watching now, depended far more on brute strength than technique. This would have been apparent to even the most moronic observer. The wrestlers were big enough, but the boxers were gargantuan. No ordinary man, much less somebody of smaller stature such as Alexander, could hope to compete against these behemoths. Consequently, the events had an air of artificiality about them that ruined them for Alexander. Alexander did realize though that his father not only enjoyed them on their own 'merits' but that he was depending upon these contests to cement his popularity over the Hellenes. He did not feel right spoiling it for Philip.

"He was fast, very fast, Father."

"Piros, have you seen speed like that? Pop, pop, pop...one, two, three...and he's down. Look at this crowd, they love it too!" Philip waved his right arm at the spectators who were on their feet cheering the Boetian boxer's victory over the Cretan.

"The final should be interesting. Euphraeus has won easily so far. His hand speed is phenomenal. Don't you agree Alexander?" asked Philip, still puffing from excitement.

Grudgingly, Alexander said it was so. Euphraeus did not fit the mold of most boxers. He tended toward slim, was tall, and used the science of the art to beat his opponents. So far, technique had won out over brute force. But in the final, he would be facing Clitomus, a hulking, battle-scarred veteran of a thousand matches whose mastery of the art was rumored to be almost if not as great as Euphraeus'. And because Dioxippus would himself be warming up for the beginning of the pankration, Euphraeus could depend on nobody's help but his own. This situation piqued Alexander's interest because he was the ultimate strategist and he was eager to see what these combatants would utilize to win.

"This I am looking forward to," said Alexander to his father.

"Good. Good. Piros, any wagers?" asked Philip, not even looking at his chief of bodyguards.

"Two talents on Euphraeus," replied Piros.

"Two...that's it?"

"I am afraid you do not pay me more, my liege," answered Piros.

Philip rubbed his beard. "I tell you what. Euphraeus wins, I make you a field captain when Alexander and I take Asia."

"And if I lose?"

"I make you a field captain...but you have to kiss my ass first!" And with that Philip leaned back in his chair, guffawing until he made himself senseless.

Alexander, Piros and Hephaestion (who had just joined them) looked at each other once then began laughing hysterically. They probably would have continued if not for the call by the official for the final match to start. Everyone sobered quickly.

The Boxing Match

Both men entered the dirt circle. The referee, a dark-skinned Persian Greek, bowed slightly and stepped back so that the contestants could acknowledge King Philip. Euphraeus, the taller, more slender of the two bent his waist and with a practiced grace paid homage to the king. His opponent, a Spartan known as Konros, was obviously bearing the ill will of his countrymen even though Sparta had wisely chosen to forego the battle at Chaeronea. His salute to the new king of the Greek city-states emoted no passion greater than a grudging duty. Many spectators moaned and a few even hissed at the bad manners displayed by the Spartan but Philip, showing himself to be the generous host, smiled at Konros, and with a gentle sweep of his hand, motioned the audience to silence. Philip turned to the Hellanodikai, nodded once and sat back. The officials signaled the referee to start the match.

As the two boxers warily circled each other, Piros turned to Philip and said, "That was most admirable, my friend. Other rulers would have had such disrespect torn out of Konros' body by a dozen wild oxen. Yet you sit here as if you are pleased by his attitude. In fact, you look smug. I don't..."

"I have control over his nation," interrupted Philip. "Sparta has been one of the strongest forces in Hellas for over a thousand years. I would be dismayed if the Spartans were any more respectful than they show. I want to control, not extinguish their spirit. If I expect to govern Hellas, then Asia, I must not be so foolhardy as to think that force alone will put then keep these states under my domination." Philip turned to watch the action but added, "Let him be angry. One day I will re-direct that anger to a common enemy. That is when he becomes mine."

Piros did not reply and Philip ended the conversation just as Euphraeus landed his first combination. The resultant roar from the spectators completed the job of distracting the regent. As Euphraeus chased Konros across the ring, Piros chanced a glance at his king. There is no question, Piros thought to himself, that Philip will rise to the two greatest challenges ever undertaken by mortal man-- conquering the civilized world, then administering it. Piros' thoughts were interrupted as a quick counter by Konros brought the crowd, including those surrounding Piros' party to their feet. Piros found himself looking through a forest of legs and lower torsos, his curiousity bettering his assessment of the king who would be a god. Finally, Piros stood so he too could see the battle in the ring.

Across the field, hidden by the gymnasia, Dioxippus and the other contestants were preparing themselves for their upcoming matches. The paddock they were using was filled with pankratiatists, trainers, managers, officials, and a wide assortment of hangers-on and family members. Yet within that confusion, a sedate peace reigned. Many were listening attentively to the noise from the throng watching the boxing, trying to gauge the fortunes of Euphraeus and Konros from the cheers, jeers and moans echoing into the waiting area. Others concentrated on calisthenics, trying to keep their muscles warm and their tendons and ligaments limber. Still others meditated, withdrawing their physical senses from the secular chaos encircling them. Dioxippus, ever the observer, cast his eyes around in a random scan and noted the strange order slowly overpowering the almost psychotic frenzy that invariably manifested itself just before the most important and most popular of all the Olympic contests began.

Suddenly, a great wave of sound crashed down upon the waiting pankratiatists. Dioxippus reflexively stood up, turning his head in the direction of the stadium but the ringing cacophany of voices precluded an accurate assessment of the cause of the din. Dioxippus then attempted to move to the entranceway to get a look at the commotion but the hellanodikai motioned him back. It was considered very bad luck to watch any contest immediately preceding yours and the officials did not want to be accused of bringing a curse upon any of the contestants. So, politely but forcefully, they kept all the pankratiatists back from the entrance.

In the stadium, no such restrictions existed. Philip and his retinue along with thousands of spectators were on their feet, delirious with excitement. Euphraeus had connected with a left jab, right uppercut combination, knocking Konros down. The Spartan had raised himself to one knee but had not yet decided if he would continue. The referee, pushing Euphraeus away with one hand, bent to ask Konros if he was ready to submit. Konros shook his head and said something, but the thousands screaming drowned out his voice. The referee tried again, this time yelling his question. Konros shook his head from side to side, indicating he could not hear the referee.

"What is he doing?" Piros cried out. "The Spartan is stalling so he can recover." Piros turned to the king. "Do you see that? That is blatant cheating. He was knocked out. Now he's getting a rest. This match should be over."

Philip only smiled. Then he replied, raising his voice so Piros could hear him over the crowd, "He is doing only what I would do if I were in the ring with him. To win you must take advantage whenever the opportunity presents itself."

Piros could not really hear Philip at this point but from the expression on his face it was obvious that Philip was pleased with the events in the ring.

Euphraeus too was angry. Konros was feigning deafness in order to buy more time and the referee's attempts to elicit an answer from him merely sparked more nodding. Euphraeus was not helping his cause either as he kept trying to push his way past the referee so he could get at Konros. With the situation in the ring about to degenerate into anarchic confusion, the referee signaled Konros to stand. He snapped out his switch to emphasize the need to hurry. Konros pushed himself to his feet. The crowd roared again as they realized that this most entertaining match was going to continue. Euphraeus had fought too many times to believe that Konros was still hurt. Rather than lunge at him and try to finish him off as some others might try, Euphraeus hung back, patiently waiting for Konros to make a mistake.

The Spartan was also wary. He had expected his opponent to rush him; had in fact hoped he would. Although the rest had revitalized him, the punishment had sapped his inner reservoirs of strength, and at this point he needed to get the match over with quickly if he were to entertain any hope of winning. He had to become the aggressor and this did not fit in with his plan.

The spectators, rabid for action, began to hiss and whistle in derision. They screamed epithets and many began to laugh at the now cautious boxers. In the ring, Konros grew furious with Euphraeus' refusal to close with him. Out of frustration, maybe even fear, Konros rushed his adversary, throwing rapid-fire left jabs at Euphraeus' still unmarked face. The young Greek could only retreat as he attempted to block or avoid the exploding left fist of the desperate Konros. He backpedaled as quickly as he could but the sharp sting of the hazel switch striking him in the back warned him painfully that he was at the edge of the ring. Konros would not abate. He followed up his jabs with right crosses in an effort to open up the defence of Euphraeus. He almost achieved success when a low, partial uppercut tore between his pumping arms to strike him just above the ribcage on his left side. Konros gasped. Once. Clutching his chest with both hands, he slowly collapsed to his knees. His eyes rolled white and with scarcely a whisper, he rolled onto his back.

The referee signaled Euphraeus the winner then hurriedly ran to the fallen Konros. He had seen heart punches kill before and hoped that this was not what was happening now. He bent over the barely breathing Spartan and as gently as he could, massaged the area above the ribcage. This seemed to revive Konros although it was obvious he was not going to move any more than he had to. The crowd, hushed as they awaited Konros' recovery, now broke into rapturous applause as Euphraeus was granted the olive wreath by the chief hellanodikai. The cheers turned into a crashing roar as thousands rose to celebrate Euphraeus' victory.

"I guess now, I'll have to kiss your ass!" yelled out a laughing, cheering Philip to Piros.

Piros only smiled in response as he turned his eyes to the far end of the stadium.

The Pankration

Parading across the field were the pankratiatists. Another wave of sound crashed over the stadium as the games' most popular competitors were recognized. Some of the athletes waved good-naturedly to the crowd but others, consumed with the job ahead barely lifted their heads.

Dioxippus was neither cheery nor miserable. As he walked beside what would soon be his adversaries, he assessed his competition carefully. While warming up he had paid particular attention to Piros' "countryman" the black, Carthaginian-based Greek whose unorthodox style had gained him many victories in North Africa, Italy and Northern Europe. To get to the final, Dioxippus would probably have to fight this Aristides. The strange, almost crablike fighting style, was not going to be easy to master for Dioxippus and he hoped that someone who fought along more traditional lines would get lucky and take the Carthaginian out early on. Dioxippus looked around. Yiorgakas, the Asian champion sponsored by the Prince Alexander, had yet to arrive. Although Dioxippus was not frightened by rumour and innuendo, deep inside he felt relief at the absence of what many were calling a monster.

The spectators were still cheering when the procession of pankratiatists stopped in front of the king. Philip rose to greet the contestants. The stadium hushed.

"My fellow Hellenes..." Philip's voice boomed across the stadium. "We have been blessed by the all-seeing Gods of Olympus. Zeus himself would have found it difficult to provide so much entertainment for so many. The athletes here have run, jumped, thrown and fought as if the Furies themselves were driving them. This standard of excellence may not be repeated in our lifetimes so enjoy it, savor it."

Philip did not need to say more. The stomping, clapping and applause started another crescendo of appreciation. Philip beamed with pleasure, reveling in the plaudits of his subjects. For the briefest of moments, he felt like a god.

Dioxippus too could not help but be inspired by this mass show of goodwill flowing over him like a warm, gentle wave. He felt buoyed, inspired and invincible. He could feel it; today was his day.

At first, no one had noticed him come in. Most of the pankratiatists, including Dioxippus were listening to the king and enjoying the crowd. He made his way surreptitiously to the rear of the group facing Philip, trying his best to appear unobtrusive. But at a head taller with a girth twice that of most of his competitors, Yiorgakas was anything but unobtrusive. As he was recognized, the people in the stands stopped cheering and began to whisper and point until the raucous noise petered out to a few, quickly silenced mumbles. Yiorgakas had caught Philip's eye and although Philip did not wish to draw any more attention to the latecomer than necessary, the surprise caught him unaware and for a few seconds, he had nothing to say. His extra sense, always so useful in battle, also told him that his son Alexander was smiling.

Dioxippus was too young, too curious not to turn around. And what he saw shocked him. Yiorgakas was gargantuan, bigger than anyone he had ever fought: in fact, bigger than anyone he had ever seen. Dioxippus noted the thick, corded forearms, the chest and abdominals expansive, flat, square, as if they were cut out of one piece of granite. The head was huge yet there were no heavy ridges over the eyes or a forehead sloping sharply as one saw in many giants. Yiorgakas was a relatively handsome man, with straw-colored hair streaked even blonder by the ferocious Asian sun. His skin was a burnished bronze color and his nakedness only enhanced his magnificent form. Dioxippus exhaled deeply. Yiorgakas appeared as if a consortium of pankratiatists had met, designed then put together their ideal fighter.

Similar thoughts raced through Piros' mind. In the hundreds of contests he had been involved in, never had he seen a fighter as physically imposing as Yiorgakas. Glancing about, Piros could see that the other pankratiatists, including Dioxippus, were standing with their mouths agape. Piros could only shake his head at the realization that Yiorgakas had already won the psychological battle and unless the other fighters composed themselves quickly, Yiorgakas would dispose of them as easily as a cat swallowing a bird.

Fearing that Alexander's favourite was stealing the crowd from him, Philip raised his arms and called out. "Friends...the pankration promises to be the highlight of this year's games. Let us call on the hellanodikai to commence this competition. We wait no more!"

Thousands cheered in agreement. Many who were joined by many more began to chant. The game officials, urged by the king and harangued by the spectators, saluted Philip and turned to the competitors. Small wax tablets with the names of the competitors and their opponents were produced and with a few quick words between them the various officials broke off to get the matches started. They set up four "rings", each with its own referee. Until the semi-finals, multiple matches would be taking place. Trainers, managers and pankratiatists moved to their assigned areas and awaited the call that would start the competion.

Dioxippus was already standing in the ring. His name had been one of the first drawn and he was grateful as the adrenalin surging through his body was beginning to make him tremble with anticipation. He looked across the ring at his visibly shaken opponent, Perditheus. It was Perditheus' first Olympics and the nerves were getting the better of him. Nevertheless, Dioxippus refused to underestimate his adversary. It was well known that Perditheus had trained for most of his life as a boxer and although he had never reached Olympian levels in that discipline he was probably the best boxer amongst the pankratiatists. Other physical attributes Dioxippus observed were Perditheus' height, equal to his own, and his slightly longer than normal arms which added a potentially deadly extension to his boxer's reach. Dioxippus' training with Euphraeus had prepared him for those pankratiatists like Perditheus: fighters overly dependent upon the exploitation of one specialized skill or strength. But unlike his good friend, Dioxippus was neither cautious nor merciful in the ring. When the referee raised his switch to signal the start of the match, Dioxippus had one plan: he would eliminate his opponent in the shortest possible time.

The referee called to the competitors to face each other. He said a quick prayer then raised the signal. Unhesitating, Dioxippus charged Perditheus. The latter raised the knee of his lead leg to help block the low-diving Dioxippus and quickly fired off a left jab, straight right, left uppercut combination. Dioxippus slipped the first, dodged the second and absorbed the third in his shoulder as he bent low and clamped his massive biceps around Perditheus' upper legs. He was countered by a vicious blow as Perditheus joined his hands together into one large hammerlike fist and smashed down upon Dioxippus' back. The sudden impact on the area near his diaphragm knocked the breath out of him but Dioxippus did not relinquish his hold on Perditheus' legs. He had gambled that his opponent would try to box him so he had done the opposite; he had gone for the grappling technique. And now, in control of Perditheus' lower body he lifted his opponent off the ground, turned him in the air and brutally threw him to the ground. With scarcely a blink, Dioxippus grabbed Perditheus' right arm, twisted it backward and up and locked it. He followed by wrapping his other forearm around his opponent's neck and then using as much force as he could muster he squeezed so hard that the only question remaining was whether the hold was a choke or a bonebreaker. Perditheus was ensnared and unlike the fly in the spider web that might break free, he knew he would be dead before that might happen. He tapped the ground twice.

The official rushed in and pulled Dioxippus away from his opponent. With the weight off him Perditheus slowly raised himself to his hands and knees and although he had not been seriously hurt, the arm and shoulder had been twisted so hard that even the most miniscule physical effort sent splinters of pain across the deltoid and pectoral muscles. Pride however made him stand.

Dioxippus had stepped away from the ring. As a winner in a preliminary match, there was no ceremony for a victory other than the applause of the spectators. Dioxippus felt good and was pleased that he had been able to eliminate his first opponent so quickly. His pleasure at this accomplishment was short-lived. Over in ring three, two hellanodikai and a trainer were carrying the Cretan Thebos out of the fighting area. The Cretan, the practical joker and friend to all during the training period, had drawn Yiorgakas in his first match. And from the bloody face and torn ear, Dioxippus could tell that his friend had been savaged by the Asian Greek. Even more remarkable was the extent of damage done in a match that had taken less time to complete than his own which he thought had gone by with inordinate swiftness. The pure ferocity of Yiorgaka's first match threatened to overwhelm all the pankratiatists. Worse still, Yiorgakas was in the same bracket of the draw as Dioxippus. They would be meeting soon.

As the afternoon wore on the matches became more brutal. Dioxippus had been able to dispose of two more competitors with relatively little difficulty. The first of these two had been another submission; the second had been a knockout. Over in ring three, Yiorgakas had also taken his next two opponents with little difficulty. Both he had knocked down and out, the second so hard that many in the audience believed that he had decapitated him with his bare hands. But the action did not center only in Dioxippus' and Yiorgakas' areas. The Carthaginian Aristides had displayed a ferocity nobody expected and a range of techniques and movements that outshone all his rivals maybe even Dioxippus'. His contests had been dominated by vicious, chopping leg kicks, followed by fearless leaps onto the upper bodies of his opponents. There, gripping tightly with his legs, he rained percussive blows on the major tendons and arteries about the necks and heads. What made his attacks even more unusual were the ways in which he curved his hands so that only the outer edge of his hand impacted on the target. The thin area of contact concentrated so much force on the attacked body part that the recipients of this punishment found the resultant pain unbearable. Dioxippus noted this.

"Dios. It is time again," whispered Fotis to his young charge, trying hard not to disturb Dioxippus' concentration.

Dioxippus smiled at his trainer and turned to the ring. The unexpected surprise failed to cheer him.

Standing there, as immobile as a basilisk carved from black granite, was the dreaded Carthaginian, Aristides. Obviously, the draw had been manipulated for Dioxippus to meet the Carthaginian before the finals. He shrugged his shoulders and advanced to the ring. The few moments it took provided the first and only opportunity for Dioxippus to assess his latest opponent.

Unlike most mainland Greeks, Dioxippus did not find Aristides' ebony skin and long, curly black hair unusual. Superficial characteristics such as skin colour meant nothing to the young Greek. What concerned him more were the overdeveloped quadricep and gluteal muscles, which indicated to Dioxippus great leg strength. Therefore, an attack directed at the lower body, particularly one using a grappling technique, was probably doomed to fail. Dioxippus had already seen the Carthaginian's explosive leaps and he realized as he took his last few steps that an aerial attack would probably be forthcoming. He did not get a chance to analyze his situation any further.

The referee called the two pankratiatists together. He whispered some instructions to them then pointed them to their opposite sides. He looked up to the king, who nodded his assent, and raised his switch. The match began.

Immediately, the Carthaginian leapt up and lashed a kick at Dioxippus' head. Quick reflexes helped Dioxippus dodge the strike but he found himself off balance. Aristides barely hesitated as he landed then jumped again, this time opening his legs wide then scissor-locking them around Dioxippus' upper torso. Dioxippus reacted by trying to bearhug the Carthaginian but the oil-slickened skin precluded getting a good grip. While his opponent struggled, Aristides managed to grab a fistful of Dioxippus' long, blond hair with his left hand. He twisted the golden locks, forcing the head to follow. This left the right shoulder exposed and with scarcely a breath between movements, Aristides struck Dioxippus with the knife-edge of his hand right on the clavicle that had been hurt just a few weeks before. The thin ridge of calloused palm centered the strike on the injured area, allowing absolutely no dissipation of the blow. Dioxippus let out a sharp cry as the nerves around his collarbone exploded into burning shards of agony. Tears welled up, momentarily blinding the young man but worse he was forced to relinquish his hold on Aristedes. The Carthaginian, pressing his advantage, slammed the base of his right palm into the underside of Dioxippus' jaw. The mouth, still open from the exhalation of pain, shut forcefully, breaking a tooth and puncturing the tongue. Blood filled up Dioxippus' mouth as he tried to ward off the rain of blows descending upon his head, neck and shoulders. Somehow, in what seemed hours but was mere seconds, Dioxippus yanked Aristides' hand off his hair and with a violent twist of his trunk and shoulder he threw the unorthodox Carthaginian off.

Aristides barely touched the ground as he rolled to an upright position. Dioxippus, underestimating the recovery speed of his adversary, turned his hip, chambered his leg then fired off a scythe-like kick to the midsection of Aristedes. But the Carthaginian had fought many matches in Africa, many of which featured fighters who relied almost exclusively on their foot techniques. As Dioxippus' kick rushed toward him, instead of blocking it, he threw himself into a

343

backward somersault, jumped up then countered with his own front kick. Dioxippus, unlike most kickers, had supreme control and when his kick missed, he retracted it almost instantaneously. Aristides, committed too much to the counter, suddenly found his foot trapped in an X-block and before he could retract it, felt Dioxippus' hands lock on the heel and the ball of the foot. Aristides could not do anything but bend his leg and leap into his opponent. Dioxippus anticipated that, stepped back and pulled the leg out so it was fully extended again and then with a quick movement of his hands twisted the foot hard. The inhumane torque would have broken the small bones into a hundred pieces but Aristides, using his superlative jumping ability, leapt into the air and with the fluidity of a Cretan acrobat spun his body horizontally. The centrifugal force coupled with the long extension, whipped his free leg around and up towards Dioxippus' unprotected head. Dioxippus ducked but not quite quick enough as Aristedes' heel caught the top part of his head. Even though it was only a glancing blow, it hurt Dioxippus enough for him to lose his concentration momentarily: long enough for Aristedes to free his trapped foot. But it had cost. Dioxippus' lock had been so strong that in freeing the foot, Aristedes had come close to dislocating it. Now the pain of the twisted tendons and sprained muscles had rendered him effectively lame.

Sensing the injury, Dioxippus became the predator. Kick after kick was directed toward the injured extremity. Bravely, Aristides tried to throw counters while hopping out of the way of the axelike swipes Dioxippus was unleashing against him but the scalpel-like precision of the attack was unabating and Aristides' bravery notwithstanding, he was chopped down. Dioxippus dove onto the fallen Aristedes twisted his way onto his back and with as much power as he could muster, reached down, grabbed Aristides by the jaw with his right hand and by the forehead with the left and pulled back hard.

Aristedes' neck muscles, honed by years of physical training, tried to resist the force being exerted on them by the relentless Dioxippus but there was too much power concentrated against that small, naturally fragile area. Aristedes would have struggled further if the increasing pressure on the vertebre had not signalled him through excruciating pain that he would end this fight either a cripple or a corpse. With what little strength he had left, he tapped the ground.

The referee rushed in, pried loose Dioxippus' hands and signaled him the winner. This time the spectators went crazy with delight and the cheering crashed over the pankratiatists like a tidal wave. Dioxippus slowly raised himself up, took a deep breath and with as much grace as his exhaustion and wounded state allowed, bowed to acknowledge the crowd.

While the applause wrapped itself around Dioxippus like a well-made sheepskin cape, trainers rushed in to help the wounded Aristedes. Although not critically injured, the abuse his body had just suffered rendered him temporarily immobile, necessitating the help of his seconds. He was carried out as gently as possible, his limp form hanging between his friends, his body no more than a trophy.

Others watched the drama unfold. Sitting on a low wooden stool, far away from the action that had just taken place, and apparently relaxed, was the mammoth Yiorgakas. His naked form blended harmoniously with the swirling, gold-tinged dust cutting paths between the ivory-coloured, well-worn marble structures surrounding the ring. In contrast, the pankratiatist Levendis, paced nervously on the periphery of the waiting area. He had proceeded to the semi-finals where he had just won his last match. He was assured of a place in the final but the relatively easy journey to get there did nothing to assuage his growing fear of facing either Dioxippus or Yiorgakas. The winner of that match would so outclass him that defeat was a secondary consideration to the possibility of death. And though Levendis was a good technician, he was a professional and professionals fought for more than just fame; they fought to eat. And to be destroyed by the lightning-quick, highly skilled Dioxippus or by the barbarous, desert lion watching the action from afar had no appeal. To Levendis, pride could be bought and sold like any commodity in the market outside of Olympia. He did not need to be a hero. He had a plan. A little smile of self-satisfaction played across his face. Then he looked up.

The mass of spectators, moving as one immense, eerily silent organism, slowly undulated. The resulting mosaic of rippling colour, another dimension of the synergistic spectacle surging to a climax unrivalled in the annals of the Olympiad, created a tension so palatable that it could be felt crackling through the air, surrounding then enclosing every living thing in the stadia in a cocoon of expectation. And the objects of those expectations, Dioxippus and Yiorgakas, sat immobile, ensconced in their thoughts.

Eventually, the hellanodikai managed to get organized. Petros, the Cypriot judge and referee for the match called on its principals to come to the circle. Dioxippus rose from his seat, his just oiled body glistening in the muted glare of the late afternoon sun. Slowly, with the grace and fluidity of a feline, he glided to the ring. His opponent, Yiorgakas, raised himself at the official's signal but with a rumbling, machine-driven power rather than an athlete's symmetry of motion. The sun's rays also refracted of his burnished derma but the sun god did not bless Yiorgakas with gentle eye-pleasing halos but rather with sharp shafts of blinding light. To the breathless, salivatory crowd it was as if Yiorgakas radiated some unnatural force. Sentiment may have been with Dioxippus. The bets, whispered almost reverently, were on Yiorgakas.

As the Cypriot official whispered instructions to the combatants, Dioxippus looked into the eyes of his opponent. Surprisingly, he did not find Yiorgakas glaring at him like the depraved fiend so many had cautioned him about. The eyes that reflected his image back at him were soft, almost gentle. For a moment Dioxippus almost relaxed deceived by the kindness masking the intent. His unwavering stare flickered as his focus slackened for a few heartbeats. The hellanodikai finished his instructions but at the moment when Dioxippus was about to turn away, he caught one fleeting glint of hard-edged appraisal in the eyes of Yiorgakas and realized in a revelatory way, that the Asian Greek, through almost vapid eyes had stripped him of his fighting secrets. Dioxippus now perceived that almost all of Yiorgakas' victories were assured before anybody even swung a fist. An involuntary tremor shook him. Opposite Dioxippus, Yiorgakas, the lion smelling fear, smiled.

All eyes now turned to the standing Philip as the principals awaited the signal to start. Piros too, who had been relatively silent through the previous matches, looked up expectantly at his king. Philip raised his arms into an outstretched position and in a voice befitting a king or maybe a god, he called out. "Begin!"

Dioxippus immediately braced himself for the rush as he anticipated a much heavier Yiorgakas smothering him with his sheer mass. The attack never came. Yiorgakas hung back, his every

346

movement an economy of motion yet positioned to thrust forward or to defend with equal alacrity. Dioxippus had assumed that the match would start off with him in an evasive role. Now it looked like he would have to mount an offense before Yiorgakas formulated his own. Dioxippus slid forward, chambered his left leg tight and in what appeared to be one motion but two snapped out his left lead leg into the side of Yiorgakas' knee then high. The foot sliced the air as it whistled toward Yiorgakas' head. The Asian, distracted by the sharp slap against his leg, dropped his right hand, exposing his ear and right temple. It was enough. Dioxippus' instep cracked against Yiorgakas' head, momentarily stunning him. Dioxippus put his left foot down and with a violent twist arced his rear leg around in a semi-elliptical trajectory and smashed the instep of his right foot through the lowered arms of Yiorgakas into his ribcage. The Asian staggered, stunned, pained and looking for the next attack. Dioxippus followed up with a short, brutal left hook to the side of the neck. But he missed the carotid artery and his opportunity to knock out the giant Yiorgakas. Nevertheless, the blow hurt the Asian and he stepped back. Dioxippus, too scared to let his opponent recover, followed him with a front kick off his right rear leg which connected just above the sternum and with so much force Yiorgakas reeled. The spectators rose as one, cheering rabidly at the unexpected course the fight had taken. Dioxippus was as a man possessed. He unleashed a left jab, right cross and left uppercut combination. Each connected fully with their intended target as Yiorgakas desperately tried to maintain his balance, chancing the exposed position it left him in and paying for it dearly. Dioxippus smelled blood though and with the nimbleness of a court dancer closed the distance between himself and Yiorgakas while simultaneously firing a barrage of left, right, hand combinations. Yiorgakas could only cover his head and within moments had sunk to his knees.

The whole stadia particularly Philip and Piros jumped up and down deliriously, their ecstacy almost orgiastic in its intensity. Only Alexander and his ever-present companion Hephaestion did not join in the elation. Through narrowed eyes they watched for a change in the fortune of their favorite.

Dioxippus was merciless. With Yiorgakas on one knee, he sensed the match was over. Again he kicked out, this time connecting with the upper left shoulder of the Asian. And again Yiorgakas was hurt but this time instead of defending he countered. Using his ground position to his advantage, he shot forward, low and compact. Dioxippus, too committed to the long-range attack was unable to dodge the human missile. Yiorgakas, diving, was able to seize his opponent's rear leg with one hand and the opposite ankle with the other. With hands so strong they could crush small rocks, Yiorgakas easily pulled out Dioxippus' legs and brought him heavily to the ground. Now he was in control as his superior size, strength and grappling skill neutralized the striking speed of the precariously positioned Dioxippus.

The spectators were stunned. Piros was in shock. His young charge had looked like he was going to win this match with relatively little difficulty. Now it had become a ground match and Piros, champion of more matches than he could remember, knew that in the pankration, the superior ground fighter or grappler invariably won. And Dioxippus, innovator that he was, was not a great wrestler nor was he an expert in the locking and choking techniques that ended ground matches so quickly. Piros feared for Dioxippus.

Dioxippus had not yet panicked despite the vise-like grip on his ankle. Dioxippus was still able to squirm, and his oiled body provided little grip. But Yiorgakas was a highly skilled grappler and within moments had put a painful lock on Dioxippus' knee. Dioxippus tried to thrash; to no avail. The pressure on the kneecap made it difficult if not impossible for him to move and in a few heartbeats he would have to surrender. Yiorgakas had given up the ankle and was now focusing all his energy into the leg lock. Dioxippus was trying to pull away but the pain only increased with every tug. Desperate he countered the only way he knew; he moved in the same direction as the force being applied to the leg. This unexpected maneuver loosened Yiorgakas' grip slightly. It was enough. Dioxippus yanked his leg loose and scrambled over Yiorgakas' back to put a leg-scissors lock around his neck and arm. Now Dioxippus had the submission hold on his foe. The surrender never came. Dioxippus had grossly underestimated Yiorgakas' strength and the seemingly unbreakable lock he had on the arm of his foe came loose. In one superhuman effort, Yiorgakas pushed back into Dioxippus and arched his back and neck into a wrestler's bridge. The combination of weight and power forced Dioxippus to relinquish the grip he had maintained and in order to save himself, he rolled away from Yiorgakas and regained his feet.

The Asian also scrambled to his feet. Except for a few welts about his head, Yiorgakas looked unscathed. Sweat drops sparkled like diamonds against the dust and oil-streaked bronze skin but they were the only indication that he had been in combat. Even his chest was not heaving with exertion like most pankratiatists would be at this point. Yiorgakas straightened himself to his full height, showing off his imperious form. The many gasps he heard from the spectators brought a grin to his face.

Dioxippus was not impressed. Nervousness and fear had given way to anger. He had almost snatched defeat from the jaws of victory and he was upset with himself. If he was to end this match he was going to have to minimize Yiorgakas' effectiveness on the ground. Dioxippus was suddenly cognizant of the fact that superior grappling techniques could neutralize his striking attacks, particularly if he closed with his opponent. Although there was no time for a plan, instinctively, Dioxippus knew he would have to finish Yiorgakas before they both ended up rolling around in the dirt.

The referee raised his switch but he did not need to strike. Yiorgakas charged Dioxippus, determined to tackle him to the ground. Most would have stepped back or to the side to escape the thundering giant. Dioxippus did neither. Just as Yiorgakas was about to make contact, Dioxippus took an angular step forward, lashed his right arm up and away from his own body and into the throat of the lunging Yiorgakas. The snap of the ridge hand against the soft cartilage could be heard across the stadia. Yiorgakas' momentum had carried him forward but the pain in his trachea coupled with the rapidly growing inability to breathe threw him to the ground. Dioxippus wasted no time. He clambered onto his opponent's back, forced his arms between Yiorgakas' and began to put pressure on the carotid artery.

Yiorgakas, panicked for the first time in his life as he struggled to get air through the swollen airway in his throat, made one last desperate move; he jerked his massive head back with all the might he had left. The dull thud of skull meeting skull brought a weak smile of safisfaction. But to Dioxippus, the collision between Yiorgakas' rock hard skull and the left side of his face was the culmination of all the torments he had endured so far. Blinding daggers of agony coursed through his face, the worst of it just below the eye socket where the shattered cheekbone set fire to all the nerves surrounding his eye. Effectively blinded, Dioxippus staggered to his feet. Yiorgakas, gasping for breath managed to thrust himself up toward Dioxippus and with one last stabbing motion plunged his rigid fingers deep into the back of his enemy. New, ugly miseries ravaged the severely wounded Dioxippus as he fell away. Yiorgakas, still reeling, made one last desperate charge, determined to finish off Dioxippus. But Dioxippus, out of reflex, perhaps by divine inspiration, sensed the attack and with the very last reserve of strength, spun his body and catapulted his rear leg on a direct 45 degree trajectory into the already ravaged throat area of Yiorgakas. The crackling, breaking sound of fine bone was heard as clearly as a bellow from hell. Yiorgakas fell, his throat crushed, dead. Dioxippus sank to his knees, the excruciating pain and accompanying blindness obliterating any sense of victory.

Aegae, 336 B.C.

Philip becomes a god

"I cannot accept that argument. You decry absolute rule yet you propose something even worse. You are becoming a tyrant and are unrecognizable to me!"

"Do you forget that you are talking to a king?"

Piros winced at Philip's counter but he did not back down. "I thought that his majesty was my friend and that an opinion, no matter how divergent from his own was welcome. Am I to be proved wrong now?"

Philip glowered at his subordinate. Piros had not been the first to question Philip's decision to deify himself, after all, the idea had been discussed for months. Yet, only Piros had been so blatant in his opposition and only their friendship had prevented Philip from removing Piros permanently. Now, on the eve of his daughter's wedding, and only a few short weeks before he and Alexander would start their campaign in Asia, his popularity was at its peak and there would never be a better opportunity to recast himself as a godhead. The political advantages that would be afforded him in this role seemed to Philip to far outweigh the criticisms of those who did not comprehend the enormity of his ambitions. The only flaw he saw with this course was the resentment that might be fostered amongst the men in his army. In spite of his dreams of divinity he realized that the men who did the fighting served him so unfailingly because he was deemed as one of their own. Consequently, in Philip, they saw not a king but a comrade; somebody who had the ability to empathize with their concerns be they in Pella or on the battlefield. A god, however no longer counted himself a part of the group, he was a separate entity. To soldiers, Philip's choice carried no benefits to themselves. The move was seen as self-serving. Philip did not need his spies to tell him of these sentiments. He had served with these men too long to not be privy to their desires. And looking at Piros standing impatiently in front of him made him realize that his friend was speaking for all the soldiers in his command. Yet in spite of Piros' entreaties, Philip refused to change his mind. Darius and his forbearers had conquered most of Asia by making people believe that they were gods. If superstition could be used so effectively in Asia there was no reason the same could not be done in Hellas.

"My plans, in spite of your objections, will proceed as scheduled," said Philip, his tone hushed.

"Listen, my friend. You were my spiritual saviour in Thebes and have been the best partner any man or woman could ever ask for. We have seen many battles together. We are bonded as much in blood as in friendship." Piros took a breath. "I am forced to question the path you are taking, not as a critic but as someone who has treasured your companionship for many years and wishes to treasure them for many more to come. You are not a god. You are a man. A great one but still a man. You presume that the Greeks can be manipulated by their superstitions. I doubt they can be. One of the principles of this society is that all men are equal. Tyranny is seen as a societal abomination that must be eradicated before it has the opportunity to control. You are considered a tyrant to many. And making yourself a god...is the ultimate affront to probably the proudest people on the earth. They will not suffer this insult idly. Dire consequences are a given if you pursue this plan." Piros leaned forward and lowered his voice. "Your safety cannot be guaranteed if you create the circumstances where treachery can take root. Abandon this plan. You will conquer a world; your name will be infamous for ten thousand years. Strike down the statue I have seen the artisans constructing and become the man you were destined to be. Your enemies will dissipate like leaves to a wind and you will have the freedom to truly immortalize yourself."

Philip listened. What Piros said was true. But the same hindrance that had prevented Piros being appointed a general blinded him on this issue. Piros was limited by his inability to risk everything to make a gain. A combination of his upbringing, parents and religion erected a wall within his imagination. And even though Piros was a brilliant fighter and a competent tactician, many times (and this was one of them) he was unable to see the overall plan. Philip had no doubt that Piros was genuinely concerned about his welfare but he could not waste any more time discussing an issue which he had thought about for months and in his own opinion could bring him tremendous rewards.

"That will simply not happen. I am committed to this course of action and I will not be put off by petty fears and frivolous superstitions. You Piros will have to live with the fact that I will be made a god." Philip moved in a little closer and leaned conspiratorially to Piros. "And only you and I will know that the only thing godlike about me is the length of my..."

"Get away," laughed Piros, pushing Philip from him. "You son of a goat-herder, can you take nothing seriously?"

Philip grinned and replied, "No."

Piros could not help himself; he started laughing again. No matter how frustrating or antagonistic Philip was he never failed to wring every bit of humour out of any situation. Piros shook his head, resigned to the fact that Philip was not going to change his mind.

"Are we finished arguing?" asked Philip, almost pensive.

"Do I have a choice? You don't listen, you mock me and you threaten me with your position? I am powerless."

"You never have been nor will you ever will be powerless," replied Philip. "Your strengths are needed. More importantly, I need you. There may be some difficult days ahead. I'm not so stupid as to ignore them. I will need the only man I truly trust. You may not like what I am proposing but I depend on you to safeguard my life and family."

Piros squirmed uncomfortably. Such talk was almost maudlin even though it was true. Trying to change the subject he said, "Then I guess I had better throw up a guard around you."

"There now we agree. Try to make it as inconspicuous as possible, particularly when I walk into the stadium on the wedding day. It is important that I appear fearless to the various kings and political leaders who will be attending. Many of these rulers will be from places we know little about and it is critical that they see me as omnipotent."

"I can arrange that but be wary. The fact that we don't know most of these men will hinder our security efforts. I suggest that in addition to our uniformed bodyguard, we have men in plain clothing interspersed through the crowd. Anybody coming near you will be searched for weapons and as a final caution I will surround you with men taller than yourself. King Darius uses this formation to good advantage and he has more enemies than you have hairs on your head."

"It sounds good. Might it be a bit excessive?" asked Philip.

"It might. But if an assassin wants to get to you, this will be his best opportunity. We have disagreed over much today. Let me take care of your security. Your safety is my primary goal."

"Done."

"Good." Piros was relieved. The king's security was always difficult to maintain so he was pleased to hear Philip agree to his measures.

"Will Dioxippus be part of the guard?"

"No, my lord, he has accepted an offer to join Alexander's bodyguard. Your son made a very generous offer to him and coupled with the youth of the prince and his confidantes, Dioxippus felt he could better serve Alexander."

"Hmmmmm...you're probably right," answered Philip.

Piros nodded, relieved to hear the king"s reply. He had been nervously anticipating another confrontation between father and son but it appeared Philip was willing to acquiesce on this one.

"Piros, a word of caution however. I love my son, more than life itself. But beware. Alexander has a long and sometimes vindictive memory. Dioxippus' victory shamed him. And having Dioxippus win by akiniti was the worst affront to his pride that he has suffered in years. I may say I am god-like but I think that Alexander believes he is. His mother thinks he is. And when somebody who considers himself infallible is proved wrong, as Alexander was in backing Yiorgakas, redress will be sought. Tell Dioxippus to be careful in the friends he chooses and to always watch his back."

Piros tilted his head in assent. What Philip had just said to him he had said to Dioxippus a few days earlier. His young charge had laughed then hugged him as he told Piros not to worry. Dioxippus had just scored one of the greatest victories in Olympic history by defeating the man-mountain Yiorgakas and taking the final by akiniti, or default. Although Dioxippus was a level-headed, very intelligent young man, that victory had swelled his head slightly and he was not too open to suggestions these days. Piros did not push the issue but he made a mental note to keep his spies close to Dioxippus.

"I have nothing but the greatest respect for the prince. He is a brilliant and absolutely fearless warrior and I would gladly die for him. But some who are close to him wish to poison his mind and like you, I fear future reprisal against Dioxippus."

"Then let us make sure it doesn't happen," said Philip.

"I will do my best."

"Good. Now let's go over the routine for the wedding procession."

Piros pulled out a clean parchment. With a few quick strokes of his ink stick, he had drawn a facsimile of the stadium. He turned the paper to Philip.

"Yes. I think this will do. Where do you plan on posting the guards?".

"Here and here," said Piros, pointing with the stick. "When you walk in, I will have you surrounded by..."

A sharp rap at the door interrupted Piros. Both men looked up to see the door open and a bodyguard enter and then stand at attention.

"Well...are you going to say anything?" asked Piros.

"He doesn't have to. I can speak for myself."

Philip sat up sharply. Piros half-rose out of his seat his hand on the pommel of his short sword.

"Tell your war-dog to sit, shut-up and behave!"

Philip flinched as if the tart tongue had physically slapped him. Olympias could always do that to him. And no matter how many times she insulted him or his subordinates he was at a loss as to how to squelch that meddlesome mouth without Alexander finding out.

"Piros, go fetch a bone. Or better yet, go stick that monster into a hole that you can crawl into later." Olympias' sneer possessed a wicked joviality to it as if making ribald insults was the sole source of her good humor.

"I am glad to see that the former queen still has her teeth, considering her age and lifestyle," countered Piros, his eyes narrowing.

"Are you still a king, or do you let your animals speak for you?" asked Olympias, redirecting her question and insults to Philip.

"Piros is my brother. His primary concern is my welfare. What is yours?" replied Philip, the tremor in his voice belying his anger.

"My, my, my...it seems the responsibilities of parenthood have robbed you of what little humor you once possessed?" smiled Olympias. "Come Philip, I wish to talk to you civilly. I promise to behave. Just get rid of him...even for a few moments."

Philip signaled Piros with his eyes. Piros' resulting scowl darkened his black face until he resembled one of Hades' avenging spirits. But Piros had been with Philip for close to twenty years and when Philip wanted him away, there was no room for argument or question. Piros let himself out, and the bodyguard, who had also been signaled by Philip, followed.

Olympias

"Good, now we can talk," said Olympias, seating herself on the bench that Piros had been in moments before.

"Whatever you have to say, make it quick. I am trying to organize too many things in too little time just so I can indulge your petty gripes." Philip leaned back slightly, waiting for the verbal barb Olympias would hurl at him.

"I have no gripes," said Olympias, her voice curiously gentle. She straightened her chiton using long, graceful arcs in her motion, bestowing upon her an almost angelic dignity.

As much as Philip professed to hate his wife, he was still spellbound by her. And even though he knew that she was using this frailty as a means to getting something from him, Philip let her cast her spell.

"I believe that making yourself a god is a good idea," said Olympias.

Immediately, Philip was on his guard. If Olympias supported the idea it could not possibly have any merit. Nevertheless, he asked, "Why?"

"You have conquered those who would never be conquered. Xerxes himself could not bring the Greeks to their knees. But you have. They grovel now. By becoming a god, you will have them on their knees permanently."

Philip was interested in Olympias' statement but still suspicious. "So, why are you so pleased about it?"

"Selfish reasons. If you become a god, will then Alexander, by birth and association, not become the same?"

"Yes."

"You and Alexander will conquer Asia. Eventually, Alexander will become king. It is critical to his future as well as yours to maintain an image of omnipresence. You will be safer, and more importantly, Alexander will be safer. After all, no one can strike down a god!"

Still suspicious, Philip was nevertheless impressed by the almost sincere attempt at cooperation Olympias was making. He knew that she could not care less about his welfare but she was correct in stating that Alexander would benefit greatly by his father's deification. And whatever else she was, Philip knew that Olympias was a fanatically devoted mother to their son. If she saw merit in Philip making himself a god it was because of what it could bring to her son. This argument put a different perspective on the whole issue. It also made him want to hear more.

"Continue."

Olympias squeezed her jaw tight to prevent herself from smiling. She had him.

"You control the most glorious civilization in the world. You must enter the ceremony as if Zeus himself were accompanying you. And who is to say that he is not."

Philip smiled.

"You must not lead the procession. From king to pauper, everyone at the wedding must be ready to burst with anticipation for the spectacle that will be your entrance. You will be last, just after the statues of the thirteen gods, the last one bearing your image, are brought in." Olympias stopped to take a breath and to let the image linger. She continued, "The people will rise as one as you take your first steps into the stadium and upon the first notes of the trumpets, will explode with applause. Rapture will blind every mortal, and the name of Philip, then Alexander will be whispered with fear and reverence from the lips of every man, woman or child in Hellas. You will be god!"

Philip was taken aback. The zealousness of Olympias' statements almost shocked him. He did not for one moment believe that she ever considered him divine but she obviously saw the benefits such a ceremony could bring not only his kingdom but his family. For the first time in a long while, Olympias managed to impress him with something other than her sexual proclivity.

"What I am or am not, is not important to anyone other than those in the royal household. I agree the Greeks need to see me as someone greater that they are or they will spend eternity trying to shake the yoke some say I have thrown on them. When you interrupted a few moments ago, Piros and I were going over the security for just such a procession. I had not planned the entrance but to be truthful, I like your suggestion. I thought it might even be a good idea to have Alexander walk beside me or even as part of the most elite bodyguard ever assembled."

"That is a good plan," said Olympias. "However, I think you should consider a small alteration."

"What is that," asked Philip, suspicious again.

"You should walk in yourself. Alexander's day should be his own just as yours should be yours. You have conquered Hellas. You are the one having your statue dedicated by the priest from Delphi. You should enter alone. You are telling the rabble that you are a god. It is critical that you appear to be one." Olympias' tone had become formal, sounding much like a military commander reporting a position to his superior.

"Yes...I agree...but...Piros has some reservations about security," said Philip.

"What...you take the word of a ..."

"Careful!" snapped Philip.

"...somewhat over-cautious soldier to the advice of your closest advisors. Piros, as much as I dislike him, is an exceptional soldier. But he is not a diplomat. Look how he failed you in Athens before the battle of Chaeronea. And who was his opponent there? An old man whose entire argument against the Macedonians was a personal diatribe against you. Piros not only failed but had to flee the city. Piros can fight but he does not understand government or the responsibilities of the regent."

Philip gritted his teeth. He wanted to spring to Piros' defence but Olympias was right; the only diplomatic mission Philip had sent Piros on had miscarried. Although Philip did not deceive himself with the idea that every citizen loved him, he was beginning to doubt that there was any real threat to his safety.

Olympias noticed Philip's hesitation. She pounced. "Of course, it would be prudent to prepare for all contingencies. But you must impress upon Piros that he not make you look cowardly."

"Not in a thousand years!" bellowed Philip. "I fear no man, living or dead!" The last few words were the roar of a lion.

Olympias was nonplussed. Philip's anger was the reaction she was looking for. She knew that Philip would do anything rather than appear gutless.

"I know that you are not a timid little girl. All of Hellas knows it too. But you don't have to prove it by committing suicide. Let Piros protect you."

"I don't need your concern, Olympias," snapped Philip, still angry. "I'll walk through a crowd of armed Thebans if I must but no one will ever accuse me of being afraid!"

"Well then, nothing I can say will change your mind. Maybe, just maybe, the gods may have chosen you. I must take your leave and go see to our daughter. I'm sure she is nervous." With that, Olympias rose from the chair and moved to the door. She stopped just before she opened it and said, "Philip, on our daughter's wedding day, a light will shine from you like a beacon to storm-tossed sailors. That day, you will be the god that does what no other has ever…take Asia. In spite of our differences, I cannot help but admire you." Olympias opened the door and went through it.

Philip stared after her, not sure of what had just transpired. He sighed once then called out for Piros. The heavy oak door opened once more and Piros came back into the room. Philip called him over and told him to sit down.

Outside the apartment, Olympias pretended to adjust her robes while Philip's bodyguard stood watching. Within moments she was rewarded: two muffled voices, obviously arguing, seeped through the thick, slab door. This time the smile on Olympias' face was that of a feline, just after it has caught the mouse.

Panthea

"Are you sure you have made the right decision?"

"I feel it is the right one. If I'm to be a soldier it might as well be with the future king of Hellas."

Panthea frowned. Dioxippus' reply had a certain resignation to it, not joy. The euphoria of winning the first Olympic pankration by akiniti had subsided and now Dioxippus was beginning to regret some of the decisions he had too hastily made. Panthea had chided Dioxippus for joining Alexander's troops. She had been in Macedonia since childhood and she had heard many tales of Alexander's ferocious temper. She also knew that the Macedonians, particularly the upper classes, lived by the vendetta and she had little doubt that Alexander would one day find a way to punish Dioxippus for past insults, real or imagined. To Panthea, Dioxippus' enlistment in Alexander's Companions was the equivalent of the antelope joining a pride of lions. But she also knew that it was too late for Dioxippus to withdraw.

"I have been promised a commission," said Dioxippus.

Panthea wanted to scream, *"who cares!"* but she knew it was pointless. Instead, she placed her hands on her lower abdomen and said, "Our future lies with this child I am carrying. I do not want him to grow up without a father. Do what Alexander wants. Serve him well. And stay alive."

Dioxippus smiled in response. Panthea's pregnancy had caught them by surprise but the news had been greeted with great joy and pleasure by both. Dioxippus was looking forward to being a father and for the first time in his life, the recurring nightmare depicting an early death for him, had not appeared. It was as if the child not yet born had changed the fates. Therefore in spite of his reservations of serving with Alexander, Dioxippus was the happiest he'd ever been. Only Panthea's oft-expressed concern for his welfare could affect his usual good humour. And he understood and sympathized with her concern.

"Don't you know? I can't be hurt. The gods have blessed me with a woman who will make the greatest wife the world has ever known and who will bless me with the finest sons any father has ever sired. We shouldn't be melancholy. We should be laughing, dancing...maybe making love." With that, Dioxippus lunged playfully at Panthea.

"You idiot!" she laughed, pushing his groping hands away from her bosom. "Leave me alone!"

Dioxippus wrapped his arms around the still giggling Panthea and lifted her until her face was even with his. He bent forward to kiss her when...

"Gods of Olympus, not again!"

Panthea pushed Dioxippus away as she disentangled herself from his arms. Phylia had come upon them so quietly that a few heartbeats later she would have found her two good friends in a very compromising position. As it was, Panthea found herself quite embarrassed.

"Don't you lock doors?" asked Phylia, obviously amused at the discomfiture she was causing.

"And don't you knock?" replied Dioxippus, still breathing hard after his exertions.

"Who was to know that you would attack Panthea in the middle of the day?"

"Very funny," replied Dioxippus, mocking anger.

"Hmmmmmphh! It's not you I want to see anyway," sneered Phylia. "I've come for Panthea. We are going to the market...if parts of your body can spare her."

Dioxippus leaped forward, grabbed Phylia and lifted her off the floor. Then he said, "From someone who hasn't talked much these last few years, you've become someone who never shuts up. That lover of yours must plug his ears with wool every time you two are together."

"Panthea, tell this muscle-bound freak to put me down...before I get mad." Suddenly, Phylia closed the first two knuckles of her right hand on Dioxippus' nose and twisted.

"Owwwww...that really hurt," cried out an indignant Dioxippus as he released Phylia.

"You deserved it," laughed Panthea. "Let's go now, before he thinks of something else." Both women turned and with a flip of their hair, exited the apartment.

Patroclus

Dioxippus was still rubbing his nose when he heard a knock. Thinking it was the women returned, he ran to the door. He swung it open wildly and leaped into the breach screaming.

Patroclus stood in shock then quickly drew his dagger. Dioxippus immediately stepped back and away. Then they both laughed.

"I could have killed you, you moron!"

"I'm too fast for you, my friend," replied Dioxippus.

Feigning a frown, Patroclus pretended he was angry, but it was difficult to stay mad at Dioxippus. "Where's Phylia?" he finally asked, glancing around the apartment.

"She's gone to the market with Panthea."

"Oh, I thought I would catch her here. Well then, how are you? Eager to start your service with the prince?" asked Patroclus. Dioxippus shrugged. Patroclus noticed the apathetic reply. He tried another tack. "How does fatherhood sit with you?"

Dioxippus found it awkward to express his feelings. How did one express the joy of procreation to a eunuch? Dioxippus had grown to care for Patroclus who with his kind, gentle soul loved Phylia passionately. But his love would always be spiritual and never would he know parenthood. Dioxippus knew that to most women, a eunuch was as useful as a corn on the foot but to Phylia, abused as a young girl, the physical component of a relationship had minimal appeal for her. The tender, compassionate man that was Patroclus had made her fall in love and that love had sparked a spiritual reawakening. The dark, brooding girl who had come to Macedonia years ago had become a vivacious, happy young woman in a matter of months. And in spite of all the court intrigues, Patroclus had effected a monumental change in Phylia. To Dioxippus, Patroclus was deserving of the title hero. That was why he found Patroclus' question so hard to answer.

"I know it must be wonderful for both of you," said Patroclus, who having sensed Dioxippus' unease, had decided to relieve his friend of the self-imposed pressure.

"It is...it is," stammered a relieved Dioxippus.

"Excellent. May I wish you all many years of happiness. And by the way, when are you planning to marry this girl?"

"Soon. Very soon. And of course, you will be attending."

"Just try to keep me away," laughed Patroclus.

Dioxippus smiled.

"Well, it is probably good that we are alone," said Patroclus. "I've heard some things that maybe our women should not." Dioxippus' smile began to fade.

"Are you and Piros still close?" asked Patroclus.

"He wasn't overjoyed when I enlisted with Alexander but there has been no criticism or argument. I still think of him as a father."

"Good." Patroclus took a deep breath and continued. "As you know, Cleopatra has retained me to spy on Olympias. So far, Olympias has done nothing more than engage in her Dionyssian rites with her various lovers. However, within the last few days I have noticed a change in her and her retinue. Suddenly, all those deviates have been cast out of the palace. Her slaves, including Phylia, have been replaced by paid servants from her father's estate. Although having Phylia out of her clutches pleases me, I am curious as to why Olympias has brought so many changes in so short a period. It is as if she is surrounding herself with a wall of people who owe their loyalty more to her than to the kingdom. I have also kept track of the Lyncestians who now show up at her door at least once a day. They are plotting something but I don't know what. I relayed my observations to Cleopatra and she in turn to Philip, but apparently he dismissed them. Piros is the only one close enough to Philip to make an impact. Cleopatra asked me to ask you to tell Piros of what I saw and to convince the king to upgrade his security. Dioxippus, you must do this. All our lives depend upon the king living a long, happy life. And I think that we both have too much to lose now."

"I agree. I'll tell Piros. Maybe I should also tell Pausanius. After all, he is the captain of the bodyguard."

"That it might be wise to wait on."

"Why?"

Patroclus looked around, as if somebody was hiding in the room. "I'm not sure but I think I've seen Pausanius leaving the queen's quarters at night."

"They were lovers once. Maybe he still services her occasionally," replied Dioxippus.

"Probably. Can you still mention it to Piros? I don't feel comfortable with having the king's chief protector in bed with his worst enemy."

"Consider it done." Dioxippus moved to a side table. He picked up a small, gracefully curved urn. "A little wine..."

Patroclus grinned. "Yes. And a toast...to us."

Dioxippus handed Patroclus a cup. "To us."

Unto the Gods...

Pausanius leaned forward and whispered something to Piros. The dark-skinned Greek, resplendent in his burnished armor, nodded in assent but did not turn around. Piros' attention was focused on the huge throng of humanity packed onto the palace grounds. His eyes continually scanned the multitude looking for anything or anyone that appeared odd, different or dangerous. He had deployed over a hundred of the King's Companions throughout the crowd yet he did not feel secure. Nobody in their right mind would attempt an assassination at the wedding of the regent's daughter but who was to say that a sane person would be the only one to try it. Piros turned to look at the king. Philip, about twenty paces back of him appeared calm and in a very good humour. The bodyguards Piros had assigned were tightly drawn in a circle around the king. All were taller than Philip and all looked ferocious enough to kill without a second's warning. Piros glanced back at Pausanius. Even though Piros had been warned to not include his friend in the security team, Philip himself had insisted that the captain of the bodyguard remain. Pausanius did seem to be attentive and there was no question of his valor. Still, Piros was uneasy and he pledged to keep Pausanius close to him.

"Hey...Piros!"

Piros immediately stopped when he heard Philip's voice. He trotted back to where the king was waiting.

"Piros, how much longer?"

"They are taking the statues in now. After each has been placed, they will sound the horns and we will make our entrance. And please, no more arguments. There are far more people here than we had planned, and many from foreign lands. It makes me uncomfortable. Please go with our original plan."

Philip smiled. "We'll see. How does my robe look? Godly enough?" Philip then laughed uproariously.

Piros just shook his head. He gave the guards one more order and returned to the entrance of the stadium. There was a short, enclosed passageway that went under the seats to the field and so far the King's Companions had managed to keep it clear. Piros took a mental count of the steps to the center of the arena then counted the number of men he had positioned along the route. Although he wasn't overconfident, Piros thought that they could get the king in and out with little difficulty. The passageway's close confines concerned him but an assassin would have to hack through so many bodies that this problem was not a priority. What was a problem was Philip's propensity to greet his subjects as if they were old friends. Piros was determined that he would not let Philip glad hand his way through an assemblage that included as many enemies as friends.

A commotion behind the group startled everyone and suddenly two dozen swords were drawn. Piros pushed Philip to the side and leaped to the forefront. The quick action proved unnecessary. Philip's son Alexander, and his soon to be son-in-law, Alexander, had arrived with their bodyguards. Some minor jostling had occurred as the two bodies of armed men jockeyed for position in the narrow confines of the passageway but no one was hurt. Philip was overjoyed at the sight of his son and pushing his guards away forcefully, went to Alexander. The prince almost diminutive in comparison to the bodyguards leapt into his father's arms. The king, overcome with emotion, barely kept back the tears. Only the pandemonium from the eager crowd was able to distract him.

"I am glad you came."

"You are my king...and father," replied Alexander.

"A world awaits us."

"Soon. Very soon," said Alexander. He took a look at Piros. "The African has done a good job with security. Listen to him. I'm not as comfortable with this situation as you are. Keep the guards with you at all times." Alexander's joyous expression became dour.

"Hah...you all worry too much," laughed Philip.

"Today that is our prerogative," interrupted Piros. "The last statue, yours, is being carried in now. Soon we will be out in the open. Stay near me." Piros turned to Alexander. "Your highness, I request that you stay back at least four to five paces from your father; it will be easier to protect you also."

Alexander nodded. He was concerned but didn't know why. His mother, Olympias, had begged him to not accompany his father. She had in fact acted quite hysterically and only his agreement to let the Lyncestian nobles accompany him had placated her. This whole situation made him suspicious and even more determined to stay close to his father. But it was obvious that Piros had planned for every contingency.

"Your Highness, we are ready," Piros said.

"Yes...yes, let's get on with it," Philip replied. He gently squeezed Alexander's arm, winked and moved away.

Piros gave some last instructions to the bodyguards then moved to the front of the procession. Pausanius was waiting there patiently. His apparent calm did not belie the anxiety he must have felt as the captain of the bodyguard. Only his eyes, flitting back and forth like hummingbirds as they scanned the crowd displayed any concern.

"Anything?" asked Piros.

"Nothing obvious," came the curt reply.

Piros did not hear Pausanius, the cacophony making any conversation impossible to carry on.

Suddenly, a new swell of sound surged up from the thousands of guests. Piros could not see too well but he knew that the massed throng had just noticed the thirteenth statue, the one of Philip as godhead. The time had come.

Piros turned to go back to Philip when he found his passage blocked by the members of the bodyguard. For a moment, Piros thought they were coming for him. Then he saw that Philip was barking orders and pushing soldiers away from him. His son Alexander was involved in a fierce argument with him but the distance combined with the cascading din from the field prevented Piros from hearing the words flying between father and son. Something was wrong and for the first time, Piros felt a twinge of panic. He pushed his way to the king.

"...and I say that as king, I have the right to decide what I need and don't need. I will not enter with a bodyguard. Only tyrants need that sort of protection and the Greeks know it. I will not give them the opportunity to find reason to rebel. I must be seen as benevolent. I must be seen as fearless. I must be seen as a god!" Philip glared at his son.

"Piros, tell him he is insane!" cried Alexander to Piros.

"Philip, listen. You are the ruler of Hellas. It makes no difference whether a guard accompanies you forty paces or not. There are too many people here we don't know. Let us protect you. You cannot take chances today. A few steps, that's all. No one will notice. Come now, let me call back the bodyguards." Piros spoke loudly but calmly. He did not want to anger the king.

"If it's only a few steps, I don't need the guards. I order you to precede me, with the bodyguard, onto the field. Alexander and my son-in-law will follow me after I have entered. I will not discuss this further. Now hurry, the people are calling me."

Piros bit his lip. He felt stymied by Philip's obtuseness. He had to obey the order even though he questioned it. Shrugging his shoulders, he organized the guards into parade formation. He looked back, hoping to appeal to Philip through his eyes. It was to no avail. The expression on the king's face showed that he was resolute in his decision.

Piros took his position at the head of the parade. He hailed his troop and then moved forward. As he moved forward, he examined the crowd lining the procession route. Most of what he saw was a blur but he noted the faces of Dioxippus, Panthea, Phylia and his ever-faithful servant, Fotis. He saw the king's new wife sitting with her retinue and two children a little further on. Her servant, Patroclus, stood at attention, his right hand squarely on the hilt of his sword. Piros had taken a few more steps before he noticed Olympias. Alexander's mother was sitting on a dais not far from the statues. Oddly enough, Antipater, the Macedonian general from the north was right beside her. Piros did not remember the two being friends. He took a deep breath and continued his march. The troop followed. Unable to help himself, Piros looked back over his shoulder.

Philip presented quite the figure as he stepped forward to join the procession. His robe, an alabaster white, flowed about him like gossamer, lending his solitary form an ethereal, truly god-like appearance. Even his scarred face and blacker than black hair and beard served to accentuate the effect. Philip was aware of all these factors and they made him grin with pleasure as he took the first step onto the field. The roar as the thousands of guests caught their first sight of him rocked him as if it were a physical force. This moment was his.

At least it should have been. Coming toward him was Pausanius. Philip reacted angrily. "I told you and all the guards to stay away from me until I reach the podium. What in Hades do you think you are doing?"

Pausanius smiled and pointed to his ears, indicating that the noise prevented him from hearing. He leaned close to Philip cocking his head slightly.

"Idiot! I said that you were supposed to be with your troop. I'm going to have Piros' ass over this one. Now move!" Philip was still grinning, trying to maintain his composure but he was furious that his orders were ignored. How would it look for a god to have someone walk in with him.

Pausanius saluted, then leaned toward Philip to say one more thing.

"Die you bastard!"

From beneath his cloak, Pausanius pulled a short, oddly shaped sword. In one drawing motion the sword left the confines of Pausanius' person and was driven into Philip's ribcage. Even in the din, the metal plunging through skin, muscle and bone reverberated across the field. The blood and other bodily fluids streamed down the blade and within two heartbeats had stained the virgin white robe of the king.

Philip, his body in shock, could only grab feebly at the hilt of the blade buried in his chest. His mouth gasped and a few flecks of blood spit out. He was still standing but more because of Pausanius' hold on the sword than his own strength. Philip could not feel any pain yet he was having great difficulty breathing. Still, he had one question.

"Is...is...is this the way I die...like a...dog?" The effort was too great and Philip collapsed to the ground.

Pausanius looked down at the fallen regent then spit on the crumpled form. Leaving the murder weapon he took off back through the tunnel, the shocked bodyguard chasing him.

Alexander had not been paying attention and the first inkling he had that something was amiss was when he was pulled away from the center of the passageway and surrounded by the king's bodyguards. He still did not know what had transpired until he saw Piros.

As Pausanius slayed the conqueror of the Hellenic city-states Piros watched helplessly. He was too far away to take the sword himself and he cried from grief and frustration as he fought his way through to the fallen king. The soldiers forming the human barricade encircling Philip parted to let Piros through. He immediately knelt and as gently as if Philip were a newborn, he lifted the badly bleeding monarch into his arms. Piros cradled Philip and with his free hand caressed his forehead while he called to him to live. Philip's eyes opened but it was obvious they were unseeing and all those watching knew that the life was seeping out of the fatally wounded king rapidly and many crowded around to hear what if any words he might have to say.

The circle opened again as Alexander was led to his father. The young prince was overcome with grief and he wailed as if the sword had torn his guts out. He picked up Philip's limp, bloodstained hand and held it to his cheek. The movement sparked something in Philip and his eyes managed to refocus for a moment on his son.

"It...it...it...it was...Ccccc...Cel...tic," hoarsely gasped Philip, the effort costing him more blood.

Both Alexander and Piros looked down on the king, confused by the statement. Then Piros noticed the hilt of the blade still lodged in the chest of the regent. Philip, dying, had still managed to recognize that the weapon that had killed him was Celtic. Piros didn't know whether to smile or cry.

While the dying Philip was being attended to, Pausanius was running across the courtyard, the soldiers of the bodyguard close behind in pursuit. Pausanius felt exhilarated and he had gotten a good enough start to easily outdistance those bent on apprehending him. As his feet pounded the tile lining the open area he was traversing he thought about what he had just done. Pausanius had no regrets and as soon as he escaped he would sail to Sicily, to be there hidden by one of Olympias' paramours. As he turned a corner a pair of horses, prepared and packed with supplies, came into view. Good, thought Pausanius, the Lyncestians had delivered what they had promised. A few more steps and he would be free. He almost whooped with elation.

The joy was short lived. A tree root, forcing its way through a crack had managed to protrude itself. The fleeing Pausanius, oblivious to all but the waiting horses, did not see it and his foot, as if directed by the gods in revenge for the slaying of one of their own, hit the petty obstruction, tripping the assassin. Pausanius stumbled then fell. His outstretched hands managed to lessen the impact but the fall knocked the wind out of him.

Pausanius saw that he could not escape the three soldiers who had just come up. Yet he was not frightened. Leonnatus, Perdiccas and Attalus, the three standing before him now, were part of the plot orchestrated by Olympias. Pausanius smiled.

Leonnatus returned the smile and extended his hand to help Pausanius up. The assassin lifted his but he never got the chance to grasp Leonnatus' hand. Without warning, all three of the pursuers thrust their short javelins into Pausanius. Repeatedly they impaled their co-conspirator until what had been Pausanius, captain of the bodyguard, was nothing more than slaughtered meat. So quick was the execution that the surprised somewhat frightened expression on Pausanius' face remained etched on his corpse. The three Lyncestians nodded to one another, then called out to the others just coming around the corner. Leonnatus, stepping forward to meet his comrades in arms, pointed to the bloody mess at his feet and said, "Philip's murder has been avenged."

Epilogue
Athens, 336 B.C.

Patrida

Piros raised his right hand to his forehead but the miniscule shade it provided did little to cut the harsh glare of the noonday sun. What he could see was distorted by the rising heat waves and he was rapidly growing frustrated. They were supposed to have arrived an hour before and Piros was getting worried. Philip's assassination had thrown all of Hellas into political turmoil, making even a civilized city like Athens a dangerous place to be, particularly for a Macedonian or Macedonian sympathizer. That was why it was imperative that they leave as early as possible.

A few weeks ago no such problems existed. As Philip's close friend, Piros had looked forward to the campaign in Asia. Pausanius' treachery had changed all his plans and in fact had hastened decisions he had been pondering for awhile. Alexander's accession and consequent purging of many of Philip's top aides had laid the foundation for the future persecution of the old regime. Although Piros had not been prosecuted for any crimes, real or imagined, he knew that sooner rather than later, Olympias, who hated him fiercely, would find a means to convince her son to eradicate him. His time to leave had come. And with him he would take Dioxippus, Panthea and Phylia.

A commotion on the dock caught Piros' attention. Two tall men, along with two women carrying bundles, were forcing their way through the milling crowd but the sheer mass of humanity impeded their progress badly. Even so, Piros could not help but notice that the two males easily knocked aside anyone who did not respond to their polite requests to move. Dioxippus and his good friend Euphraeus were cutting a swath through the crowd as effectively as a farmer threshing his wheat in their eagerness to get to the ship. Piros turned to one of the crewmen, barked an order and leaped over the side of the ship onto the dock.

"Dios, what has taken you so long? The ship's master is ready to leave and only by threats have I been able to keep him here," said Piros. His breathing was somewhat labored as he tried to control the tension within him.

"We have been delayed by..."

"Piros, he doesn't want to go! Talk to him!" interrupted Panthea, barely able to contain her hysteria.

Piros could see from Panthea"s puffy, red eyes that she had been crying and now it was obvious why. "Are you insane? What do you mean you are not coming? Hellas is no longer safe for any of us!" snapped Piros at Dioxippus.

"That's the way it has to be," replied Dioxippus. "My wife carries my child. She and the child have to live. I can't guarantee their safety if they stay with me in Pella and I know Alexander will look for me if I desert. My only recourse is to send them with you. You must protect them. You must help raise my child if I am unable to come back. Promise me!"

Piros was too shocked to reply. His plan had not included Dioxippus' change of heart and now he was unsure of exactly what he should do.

"Answer," pleaded Dioxippus. "You must promise me. I am entrusting you with more than my life. Promise me!"

Piros looked first at Panthea then Dioxippus. He nodded affirmatively.

"Nooooooo..." wailed Panthea. Phylia moved to hold her friend.

"Thank you," said Dioxippus softly. He gently took his pregnant wife from Phylia and held the now sobbing Panthea close to him.

Piros looked to Euphraeus but before he could ask him the question, he spoke.

"I will stay with Dios. Where he goes I go."

Piros turned back to Dioxippus. "There must be an alternative. I have friends to the west, toward Sicily. Alexander has no immediate plans to conquer that side of the world. There we will be safe. With a small blessing from God, we can live in peace in a kingdom strong enough to resist Alexander." Piros took a breath.

"Between us we have some fame. Let's use that to seek shelter. Any of the western Greeks would be overjoyed to have amongst them Olympians. We can start a new life, maybe as trainers. A school teaching the pankration as only we can would bring the best from around the world. Even Alexander would respect such an institution. Come with us, Dios...please." Piros rarely rambled but the urgency of the situation coupled with a rapidly growing despair made his thoughts so jumbled he wasn't sure whether he was making any sense.

"Piros, we have decided. I will march with Alexander."

Piros could see that Dioxippus was resolute. The boy he had taught a few years ago was now a man, with a man's responsibilities, and he would not risk his wife and child. Grudgingly, Piros accepted the decision.

Dioxippus carefully lifted Panthea over to the ship. Two crewmen, slaves from Egypt, helped the pregnant woman onto the deck. Euphraeus went to help Phylia but she climbed over herself. Dioxippus lifted over the rest of the luggage then called Piros over to him. Dioxippus took his mentor to the end of the dock and in a voice low enough to not be heard by the crewmen or any of the other dockworkers said, "Piros, sail far away, farther than you had planned. Pella is in complete chaos and all of Philip's former confidantes are being exiled or executed. Alexander is barely in control. Between his mother and the general, Antipater, no one is safe. You of course noticed that Patroclus is not here."

Piros nodded. He had been about to ask but the blank expression on Phylia's face had been enough to tell him that something dreadful had occurred and Piros needed no imagination to figure out that Cleopatra's most trusted eunuch slave had met with a horrible fate.

"Olympias has gone insane. While you were helping prepare Philip's funeral and looking for anyone involved in a possible conspiracy, Olympias had Asian morticians clean and preserve the body of the assassin. The rumour going around the city now is that Olympias threw herself on the body of the murderer and grieved as if he were the one who had been her husband. She also was seen to have draped the body with gold and she called out to the gods to treat Pausanius' soul with the love they would give a hero from the Iliad."

Dioxippus stopped to take a breath and look around. He continued. "The witch has murdered Cleopatra and her children. A friend of mine in the palace said that he saw the queen's servants remove the body of the boy-child. It looked as if it had been chopped up with a butcher's cleaver. And she did this in front of the mother. And again from what I heard, Patroclus tried to intervene on behalf of his mistress but Olympias' guards cut him down on the spot. That is why Phylia is like she is. I fear that with these losses she will kill herself. Only the fact that I have asked her to help look after Panthea while I am gone has given her a purpose to live. You must make sure that she is always needed. I don't want to lose her too."

Piros was speechless. Of the things Dioxippus had told him some he had heard about. That the situation in Macedonia's capital had deteriorated to such an extent he was not aware. Obviously, the empire that Alexander envisaged would not include him or Dioxippus' wife and progeny. They would leave now.

Dioxippus slipped his arm about Piros' shoulder as he walked him back to the waiting ship. As they approached they could see and hear the ship's master yelling orders to his oarsmen while other crewmen loaded the last of the food bales and water onto the deck. Also on the deck a forlorn Panthea and a grim Phylia stood holding each other, the former still sobbing quietly. Their eyes reflected nothing but anguish and Piros himself was on the verge of bawling like a child.

Amidst this confusion, Dioxippus hugged the man who had been like a father to him and said one last thing.

"Someday we will be reunited. We will celebrate our lives, our loves and our children. But most of all we will celebrate the return to our homeland, *i patrida mas.*"